Praise for V. M. Burns an.............er

"A promising debut with a s............usion."

—*Publishers Weekly*

"Cozy mystery readers and historical novel aficionados will adore this warm-hearted, cleverly plotted new series."

—*Kings River Life*

"V. M. Burns is off to a fantastic start."

—*Escape with Dollycas*

"This debut cleverly integrates a historical cozy within a contemporary mystery. In both story lines, the elder characters shine; they are refreshingly witty and robust, with formidable connections and investigative skills."

—*Library Journal* (starred review)

Books by V. M. Burns

Mystery Bookshop Mysteries

THE PLOT IS MURDER

READ HERRING HUNT

THE NOVEL ART OF MURDER

Dog Club Mysteries

IN THE DOG HOUSE

Published by Kensington Publishing Corporation

The Novel Art of Murder

V. M. BURNS

KENSINGTON BOOKS
www.kensingtonbooks.com

KENSINGTON BOOKS are published by

Kensington Publishing Corp.
119 West 40th Street
New York, NY 10018

All Kensington titles, imprints, and distributed lines are available at special quantity discounts for bulk purchases for sales promotion, premiums, fund-raising, and educational or institutional use.

Special book excerpts or customized printings can also be created to fit specific needs. For details, write or phone the office of the Kensington Sales Manager: Kensington Publishing Corp., 119 West 40th Street, New York, NY 10018. Attn. Sales Department. Phone: 1-800-221-2647.

Kensington and the K logo Reg. U.S. Pat. & TM Off.

ISBN-13: 978-1-4967-1185-4
ISBN-10: 1-4967-1185-8
First Kensington Trade Paperback Printing: December 2018

ISBN-13: 978-1-4967-1186-1 (ebook)
ISBN-10: 1-4967-1186-6 (ebook)
First Kensington Electronic Edition: December 2018

10 9 8 7 6 5 4 3 2 1

Printed in the United States of America

Acknowledgments

Thank you to Dawn Dowdle, Blue Ridge Literary Agency, and John Scognamiglio, Michelle Addo, and all of the wonderful people at Kensington.

Thank you to my Seton Hill University family. Thank you to my tribe and to Kaelyn Harding for braving the unedited edition of this book and for providing excellent feedback. I appreciate all of the support I've received from my Whirlpool family. Thank you to Tena, Grace, Jamie, and Deborah—you guys are the best training team. Thank you to Sandy Morrison and my fellow Barnyardians for being so supportive (Lindsey, Jill, Chuck, Stephen, Jamie, and Tim).

Thank you to Dr. Brittain and all of the wonderful, caring people at Community Animal Hospital in Cleveland, Tennessee. Thank you to my friend Debbie Bennett for allowing me to borrow a few personality quirks. I appreciate all that you have done to promote and support me.

As always, I have to say thank you to Jacquelyn, Christopher, and Jillian Rucker and Benjamin Burns. Without your prayers, caring, and support, this dream would never have come to pass. Thank you doesn't even come close to expressing what I owe to Sophia Muckerson and Shelitha Mckee. You two have done so much to help me live my dream and I will be eternally grateful for your brutal honesty and unfailing support.

Chapter 1

"What the blazes do you mean I didn't get the part?" Nana Jo's face turned beet red and she leapt up from her chair.

I had never been so happy for a slow morning crowd at the bookstore as I was at that minute. My grandmother was about to blow a gasket and, while it might prove entertaining, I preferred keeping the drama contained to family and friends.

"Josephine, calm down." Dorothy Clark was one of my grandmother's oldest friends, which was probably why she was nominated to break the bad news to her.

"Don't tell me to calm down. I am calm. I'm always calm." Nana Jo pounded the table with her hand. The mugs shook and splashed coffee on the table. "If I want to kick up a ruckus, I'll kick up a ruckus." She pounded the table again and then marched over to the counter and grabbed a dishcloth to wipe up the mess.

Ruby Mae Stevenson, another of Nana Jo's friends, shook her head and moved her knitting out of the way of the spills. "I told you she wouldn't take it well."

"I've had the lead role in the Shady Acres Senior Follies for the past ten years. That role was created specifically for me.

I don't just play the part of Eudora Hooper, retired school marm dreaming about becoming a famous showgirl. I *am* Eudora Hooper." Nana Jo wiped up the spilled coffee.

"I know, and you've played the role splendidly." Dorothy's face reflected her sincerity.

Dorothy wasn't merely humoring my grandmother. Nana Jo's performance was inspired, and each year she got better and better.

Nana Jo looked at her three closest friends. "Who got the part?"

Ruby Mae put her head down and refused to make eye contact.

Irma Starczewski reached for her mug, but it was empty, so she pulled a flask out of her purse and took a swig.

Nana Jo put her hands on her hips, narrowed her eyes, and stared at Dorothy.

For a large woman, almost six feet tall, Dorothy shrank as she stared at Nana Jo. "Maria Romanov."

I thought Nana Jo was red before, but the beet red coloring from earlier was nothing compared to the purple red that crept up her neck.

"Maria Romanov? That two-bit hack's only acting talent is in her ability to convince people she's a decent human being." Nana Jo pounded the table again, rattling the mugs.

Just as quickly as the anger flared up, it vanished. Nana Jo flopped down in a chair. Nearly as tall as Dorothy, Nana Jo went through a transformation. Instead of the vibrant, active, five-foot-ten, sharpshooting, Aikido-tossing woman I knew and loved, there was a seventy-something, old woman in her place.

She took a few deep breaths. "If that's what Horace wants, then I guess I wasn't as good as I thought I was."

"Bull—"

"Irma!" we shouted.

Irma coughed and clamped her hand over her mouth. Years of heavy smoking, drinking, and hanging out with truckers, if Nana Jo was to be believed, had left her with a deep cough, a salacious sexual appetite, and a colorful vocabulary.

I leaned over and gave Nana Jo a hug. "Your performance was amazing and I'm not just saying that because you're my grandmother."

She absentmindedly patted my arm. "Thank you, Sam, but Horace Evans is a top-notch director. He once directed Ethel Merman."

"He even won a Tony award. I've seen it. He keeps it in his bedroom." Irma smiled and then broke out in a fit of coughing.

The fact that Nana Jo didn't acknowledge Irma's quip about the location of the award was an indication of her state of mind. "We've been fortunate to have someone with his experience and credentials at Shady Acres."

"Really? I didn't know he had a Tony award. They always run something about the Senior Follies in the newspaper, but they've never mentioned it."

"He likes to keep it low-key." Dorothy nodded. "He worked on Broadway for more than twenty years."

"How in the world did he end up in Michigan?" I asked.

"He wanted to be close to his family." Ruby Mae looked up from her knitting. "I think his son was an engineer for one of the car companies."

North Harbor used to have a lot of manufacturing plants that supplied parts for the Detroit automobile industry, but when the economy went south in the seventies, so too did most of the manufacturing jobs.

"I appreciate the kind words, but Horace is an expert. If he thinks Maria Romanov will make a better Eudora Hooper than me, I'll just have to accept his decision."

We tried to cheer Nana Jo up, but nothing we said had any effect. She smiled and continued to shrink. Only once did she perk up and demonstrate the flash of fire which characterized her personality.

The door chimed and a customer entered the bookstore.

Nana Jo rose from her seat. "It's time to face the music. On opening night, I hope you all break a leg." She pushed her chair in and headed to the front of the store. "And I hope Maria Romanov breaks her neck."

Chapter 2

Market Street Mysteries was a small bookstore which, as the name implied, specialized in mysteries. It didn't get a ton of business, not like the big-box bookstores. However, neither North Harbor nor its sister city, South Harbor, had a big-box bookstore. Southwestern Michigan book lovers either traveled forty-five minutes to get their book fix or ordered online. In the months since I retired from teaching English at the local high school, I built up a nice clientele which was enough to keep my dream afloat.

Weekdays weren't especially busy, so Nana Jo was well able to handle things while I took a break. When I left, the girls were still trying to convince her to continue with the Senior Follies, even if she took a lesser role, but I knew my grandmother well enough to know they were fighting a losing battle. Losing the lead role had wounded her pride. I needed time to think how I could help her. My stomach growled, so I decided to grab lunch.

November in North Harbor, Michigan, can be schizophrenic to the uninitiated. One minute it's warm and sunny. The next minute a biting wind rolled off Lake Michigan, which rattled your teeth and made your skin quiver. Today was, thankfully, sunny and bright. The wind was crisp, so I walked quicker and lingered less as I made my way to North Harbor Café.

Even after the noon rush, the restaurant was crowded. I looked for a seat and my eye caught the gaze of the proprietor, Frank Patterson, behind the bar. He smiled and my stomach fluttered.

I hopped on an empty seat at the bar.

Frank finished mixing drinks and handed them to a waitress. Then he grabbed a pitcher of water from a small fridge, along with a few sliced lemons, which he placed in the pitcher. He grabbed a glass and placed them in front of me.

He leaned close. "I'm glad you came. I missed you."

The warmth of his breath brushed my face and I inhaled his scent. He smelled of a strong herbal Irish soap, red wine, coffee, and bacon. He was surprised that a non-wine drinker like me could tell the difference between red and white wines. My late husband used to say I had a nose like a bloodhound, but I called it a gift. Coffee and bacon were two of my favorite things and my pulse raced.

"You smell good."

Frank grinned. "Let me guess, coffee and bacon?"

I nodded.

He joked that he drank so much coffee the aroma seeped through his skin. The bacon was either a figment of my imagination or grease from the kitchen attached to his shoes. Whatever the reason, it was extremely sexy.

Frank Patterson was in his forties. He cut his salt-and-pepper hair in a way that betrayed his military background. He had soft brown eyes and a lovely smile. "As much as I'd like to believe my manly charm brought you in today, I suspect it's my BLT."

I laughed. "What can I say? A man that can make a good BLT is irresistible."

"Whatever it takes to keep you coming back."

Heat rose up my neck. I took a sip of my lemon water to try to hide it.

"One BLT minus the T and a cup of clam chowder?"

I nodded. I loved how he remembered things like that.

"I'll be right back."

I tried to suppress a grin, but it wouldn't be suppressed and I dribbled water down the front of my shirt. Our conversation was lame, but it'd been a long time since I'd flirted. Leon and I had been married for over twenty years when he died. It'd been over a year, but I'd just now opened myself to romance.

Frank returned carrying a tray with a steaming hot bowl of clam chowder, a BLT which was piled high with bacon, and a rose. He placed the food in front of me, got a tall beer glass from behind the bar and filled it with water and placed the rose in it.

"Thank you."

"That looks delicious." A large man next to me glanced at my plate and then picked up his menu. "Is that clam chowder? I didn't see it on the menu."

Head down, I crumbled crackers into my chowder.

"It isn't on the menu. It's something I keep in the back for my . . . *special* friends." He winked at me.

My neighbor took a whiff. "It looks and smells wonderful." He looked at me. "You're a lucky lady."

I smiled and shoved a spoonful of soup into my mouth.

Frank pretended not to notice the heat that came up my neck, but I could tell by the look in his eyes that he had seen the redness. "There may be enough for one more bowl. Would you like to try it?"

He nodded eagerly. "If you have enough, that would be great. I love clam chowder."

Frank headed off to get another bowl of soup.

I didn't have time to practice flirting. The restaurant was busy, and I felt guilty taking up a seat. So, I finished eating, waved goodbye, and left.

The rest of the afternoon was uneventful. Nana Jo got rid of the girls and we worked in relative silence until closing. I'd hoped we could talk but she stayed busy and unapproachable until I locked the front door. When we were done cleaning, she announced she had a date and hurried upstairs to change.

My assistant and tenant, Dawson Alexander, was out of town for an away football game. When Nana Jo left, I was alone in my upstairs loft, except for my two poodles, Snickers and Oreo. It was peaceful. Although I was alone, I didn't feel lonely. At some point, Frank had left a large container of chili in my refrigerator, which I heated up for dinner. There was also a platter with lemon cream cheese bars on my kitchen counter. Besides being a great quarterback for the MISU Tigers, Dawson was an amazing baker. His small studio apartment over my garage didn't have a large stove, so he often baked in my kitchen. I placed two of the lemon bars on a plate and poured a cup of Earl Grey tea. The two men in my life, Frank and Dawson, kept me well fed.

Frank cooked when he wanted to relax, and Dawson baked. I wrote. Opening a mystery bookstore was a dream my husband, Leon, and I had shared. We both loved mysteries, and a bookstore specializing in mysteries seemed ideal. However, my dreams extended beyond selling mysteries to writing them. I kept that dream hidden, out of fear and insecurity, from all but Leon, my sister, Jenna, and my grandmother. After Leon died, I filled the lonely nights by writing a British historic cozy mystery. When Nana Jo sent my manuscript to a literary agent in New York, the dream moved from a hazy wisp of smoke and fairy dust into a solid reality in the form of a contract for representation. I was both thrilled and terrified at the same time. Even though, the thought of people I didn't know reading my book sent a cold chill down my spine. I sat down at my laptop with my lemon bars and tea and realized the thrill was greater than the terror. I started writing.

Chartwell House, Country estate of
Winston Churchill—Drawing Room—November 1938

Lady Elizabeth Marsh sat on the sofa in the comfortable sunlit drawing room. Despite the sunshine streaming through the windows, there was a nip in the air. She was grateful for the warmth from the large fireplace and extended her legs to enjoy more of its heat.

"Elizabeth dear, would you care for a cardigan?" Clementine Churchill rose from her seat.

"No. I'm fine, really. I've thawed out now."

Mrs. Churchill sat back down. "I don't know what Winston was thinking, dragging you out in the cold to show you his brick wall." She tsked.

"He was very proud of his masonry skills." Lady Daphne stroked the large yellow tabby, which jumped on her lap the moment she sat down.

"You'll have cat hair all over your skirt. Tango, get down," Mrs. Churchill ordered.

Tango looked up at the sound of his name but apparently decided the order was an empty threat and ignored it.

"Stubborn cat. Let me take him." Mrs. Churchill rose.

"It's okay, Aunt Clemmie. I rather like him." Daphne smiled. "A little cat hair won't matter. Besides, he gives me courage."

Clementine Churchill was only a distant cousin to the Marshes but had always been "Aunt Clemmie" to Daphne and her sister, Penelope Marsh. She settled back onto her seat and looked fondly at her adopted niece. "You don't need courage. I'm sure Lady Alistair will love you as much as we do."

Lady Elizabeth pulled a ball of yarn from her knitting bag. "What's not to love? You're intelligent and beautiful, and you come from an excellent family."

"I wish I could feel sure. James seems so nervous about me meeting her that it's got me frazzled."

"Your aunt's right. You come from an excellent bloodline and have an impeccable pedigree. She could hardly do better."

Daphne laughed. "You make me sound like a race horse. I hope she doesn't want to examine my teeth and medical history for potential breeding stock."

Daphne intercepted an odd look between Lady Elizabeth and Mrs. Churchill. "Oh, no, you're joking right?"

"I wouldn't put it past her. You know the monarchy still require new brides to submit to . . . tests," Mrs. Churchill said.

"You can't be serious. That's archaic." Daphne stared from one to the other. Her outrage had stayed her hand from stroking Tango, who made his displeasure known by standing up, turning around, and kneading his claws into her lap. "Ouch. Okay. Okay." Daphne resumed her stroking and Tango resumed his position and allowed himself to be stroked.

"I agree the practice is outdated and completely

unfair." Lady Elizabeth was, to her husband's dismay, a strong proponent of women's rights and equality. "I've heard Lady Alistair is a bit . . . old-fashioned and—"

"Pretentious," Mrs. Churchill supplied.

"Yes, but James is only a duke and rather far down on the list for ascension to the throne. I think we're safe in assuming Lady Alistair wouldn't demand anything of the kind," Lady Elizabeth said.

"I'll refuse. That's what," Daphne declared.

Lady Elizabeth knitted. "Of course, dear. You'd be well within your rights to do so."

The elder ladies sat quietly.

"But if I refuse, they'll say it's because I have something to hide. They'll say I've done something to be ashamed of."

Mrs. Churchill sipped her tea in silence.

"Well, I won't do it." Daphne sulked. "It's not fair."

"I agree, dear." Lady Elizabeth knitted.

"I do love him so." Daphne bit her lower lip. "But modern women must take a stand. I won't submit to any tests unless James is required to submit to the same humiliation."

Lady Elizabeth smiled and continued to knit. "Of course, dear. Whatever you think is best."

"When does *her highness* arrive?" Daphne asked.

Clementine Churchill suppressed a smile. "Lady Alistair Browning's train arrives later this afternoon."

"Who else are you expecting?" Lady Elizabeth asked.

Clementine Churchill poured more tea and returned the pot to the tray. "Leopold Amery."

"Leo is one of the nicest men I know." Lady Elizabeth smiled.

Mrs. Churchill nodded. "I suppose he's here to keep Winston in line."

Lady Elizabeth frowned.

"Someone named Guy Burgess with the BBC arrived earlier. He's trying to convince Winston to commit to a talk on the Mediterranean. I suppose Leo is arriving to convince Winston *not* to talk about it." She took a sip of tea before continuing. "Lord William Forbes-Stemphill."

"Oh . . . my." Lady Elizabeth stared at Mrs. Churchill.

"Yes, I know, but he wrote and asked if he could come. He mentioned his mother and I couldn't say no."

"Wasn't there something about him in the news?" Daphne asked.

Mrs. Churchill nodded. "Yes. He's a traitor."

"A traitor?" Daphne gasped.

"He leaked secrets to the Japanese back in the twenties." Lady Elizabeth sipped her tea.

"Why wasn't he arrested? He should have been hung," Daphne said.

Lady Elizabeth and Mrs. Churchill exchanged glances.

After a few seconds, Lady Elizabeth said, "He's a British Peer. No one wanted a scandal that might reflect negatively on the royal family."

Lady Daphne digested this bit of information. "How did they catch him?"

Mrs. Churchill sighed. "Supposedly, he had quite a few gambling debts to some unsavory characters. He needed more money and tried to blackmail his contact."

Daphne stared. "You mean the money he received for betraying his country wasn't enough to pay off his gambling debts, so he tried to blackmail his cohort in crime? What unbelievable gall."

Lady Elizabeth shook her head. "Apparently, the cohort had a sliver of conscience and wanted out."

"He had to know if he gave into blackmail, he'd have to pay forever. So, in exchange for clemency, he gave Stemphill up to the authorities."

Daphne shook her head in disbelief.

After a moment of silence, Mrs. Churchill continued, "Anthony Blunt."

"Anthony Blunt?" Lady Elizabeth stared at the fire. "Where do I know that name?"

"He's an art historian from Trinity College," Clementine added.

"Is he here to look at Winston's paintings?" Lady Elizabeth asked.

"I believe he's here to value something or other." She frowned. "And, I'm sorry to say, Randolph phoned to say he's coming and bringing a young woman he wants us to meet."

Lady Elizabeth squeezed her friend's hand. "I'm sure it'll be alright. Maybe the young lady will be a calming influence on Randolph."

"I doubt it. Some girl he met at a party with John Amery. She's bound to be unsuitable." She sighed. "I just hope he doesn't cause a scene. Winston's been depressed about the way things are going in Parliament. The last thing he needs is Randolph stirring things up."

Lady Elizabeth patted her friend's hand and continued knitting. "Is Diana coming? I'd love to see that adorable grandson of yours. He must be so big now."

Mrs. Churchill smiled. "Julian's two and practically grown. Diana's expecting her second child soon. So, they're staying close to the hospital in London."

"What about Sarah and Mary?" Lady Elizabeth asked tentatively.

Mrs. Churchill's smile faded. "Sarah's in America. The last I heard, she was working on a film with her husband. Mary's in Limpsfield at Manor House School."

"Sounds like you'll have a full house. Penelope and Victor should be down tomorrow."

"The more people, the harder it'll be for Winston to brood. He does have a tendency to brood." Mrs. Churchill turned to Lady Elizabeth. "I'm so thankful to have Thompkins. He'll be a tremendous help. Inches would have tried to muddle through with a broken ankle, but he needs rest. He likes Thompkins and trusts him."

"You're very welcome." Lady Elizabeth smiled.

"How *did* Inches manage to break his ankle?" Lady Daphne asked.

Mrs. Churchill's lips twitched. "Winston climbed atop the garden wall to get a better perspective for a painting. Inches and one of the gardeners was trying to help him down when he stumbled."

"Oh my," Lady Elizabeth said. "Was Winston injured?"

Mrs. Churchill shook her head. "Thankfully, no. I'm afraid Inches broke his fall."

Daphne cringed. "That had to be painful. Uncle Winnie is a considerable amount heavier than Inches."

Mrs. Churchill nodded. "I'm sure it was. Winston doesn't show it, but I know he felt badly, even though he scolded Inches for not moving out of the way quickly enough." She smiled. "Of course, he told the doctor to send us all of the bills."

Lady Elizabeth stared at her friend. Rarely would she consider love for one's husband a fault, but Clementine Churchill's love for her husband blinded her to almost all of his flaws. Winston was Elizabeth's cousin and she was well acquainted with both his virtues and his flaws. He was intelligent, articulate, well-read, and witty, with a large capacity for kindness, when he chose. He was also egotistical, self-centered, self-absorbed, given to excess with food and drink, a gambler, and a poor manager of funds. Elizabeth looked around the drawing room. The large room was awash with light. It was comfortable and cozy, with a large fireplace and a boldly patterned Mahal carpet. This room was part of the addition he'd added to the house. Family gossip reported Winston spent a minor fortune purchasing and renovating it. Winston loved Chartwell House and the vast grounds, and Clementine loved Winston. The house she merely tolerated.

The peaceful setting was interrupted by the arrival of Winston, Lord William, and Rufus, the Churchills' brown miniature poodle.

Winston bound into the room huffing and puffing on a fat, smelly cigar. He left a trail of ashes in his wake. Rufus waited for his master to get settled into his chair and promptly jumped into his lap and laid down.

Mrs. Churchill looked adoringly at her husband, shook her head, and poured him a cup of tea.

"Thank you, dear."

Lord William followed and warmed himself near the fireplace. "You ladies should have joined us. Bracing walk across the property and down to the pond."

Lady Daphne laughed. "Thanks, but I'm perfectly

content right here with a cat, a good book, and a warm fire."

Lord William walked over to his niece and looked at her choice of reading material. *"Burke's Peerage?* Not exactly light reading." Lord William frowned at the large tome, the definitive guide to the genealogy of the titled families of the British Isles.

Lady Daphne blushed. "I thought I should brush up on James's family history before I meet Lady Alistair."

Lord William smiled indulgently at his niece. "Good idea. Good idea. Never hurts to learn about the family skeletons."

Daphne's blush deepened. "Maybe I'll look up the other guests while I'm at it. It'll give me something to talk about with them."

Lady Elizabeth knitted. She turned to her cousin. "How is the great opus coming along?"

Winston sipped his tea. "Slowly."

"Whatever possessed you to write the history of the English-speaking people, Uncle Winnie? It sounds like a daunting task to me."

Winston stared out the window. "I was possessed by the need to complete the swimming pool and create an Orfe pond."

Lord William puffed on his pipe. "But to write the history of the English-speaking people . . . it'll take a hundred men. The British Empire is . . . vast. Where does one even start writing?"

"Where does one end?" Lady Daphne asked.

Winston petted Rufus and puffed on his cigar. "I started at the beginning. I'll end when I no longer have anything to say."

The door to the drawing room was opened by the

Marsh family's stiff and proper butler, Thompkins. "Lady Alistair Browning."

Lady Alistair Browning wasn't expected until later in the afternoon so her sudden arrival more than three hours early caused a slight amount of confusion amongst the ladies. Surprise crossed the face of Mrs. Churchill, while Daphne turned a shade paler. Lady Elizabeth hurried to put away her knitting and dropped a ball of yarn. The yarn rolled across the floor, catching the attention of Tango, who had been reposed on Lady Daphne's lap. Before Lady Elizabeth could retrieve the yarn, Lady Alistair Browning entered.

Helen Browning was a tall, slender woman with piercing blue eyes and unnaturally blond hair, which she wore in a conglomeration of styles from the last two decades, including finger waves, pin curls, and coils. She wore a chocolate-brown suit with a fur collar, matching fur muff, and cloche hat. The hat was festooned with large ostrich feathers which fluttered whenever she moved her head. In her arms, she held a small Chihuahua.

Lady Daphne lifted Tango from her lap, stood, and moved forward to greet Lady Alistair. As she moved forward, Tango got sight of the Chihuahua.

Rufus growled. Tango arched his back, hissed, and lunged forward. The Chihuahua yapped. Daphne reached for Tango but tripped over the ball of yarn and fell onto the table, knocking the teapot and tray off the table. The teapot flew up into the air, spraying hot tea onto Lady Alistair.

Despite his age and stiffness, Thompkins grabbed Tango out of the air, seconds before the cat landed onto the yapping dog.

Clementine Churchill stood openmouthed and frozen.

Lady Elizabeth and Lord William helped Daphne up from the ground. Thompkins retreated with the screeching cat, and Lady Alistair shrieked.

Daphne was red-faced and on the verge of tears.

Only Winston seemed at ease. He puffed his cigar, stood, and bowed curtly to Lady Alistair. "Now, that was a bloody fine entrance, madam."

Chapter 3

Weekends were when I missed my nephews, Christopher and Zaq, and my assistant, Dawson, the most. The twins were juniors at Jesus and Mary University, or JAMU as the folks around River Bend called it. Even though neither of my nephews shared my love of mysteries, the bookstore provided the freedom to try out their natural talents and education in different ways. Christopher was a business major and enjoyed incorporating marketing and sales techniques from his classes in the bookstore. Zaq was my technology wizard and kept my POS and computers humming. They were going to keep the store running while I went to New York with Nana Jo during Thanksgiving break. I was both nervous and excited at the prospect. However, as Nana Jo said, "How much damage could they wreak in a week?"

Dawson Alexander was my former student from North Harbor High School, who had gotten a football scholarship to Michigan Southwestern University. MISU was a small local school, and Dawson was a sophomore and the star quarterback. He'd come to live with me six months ago and discovered a talent for baking. Between the three of them, the store would be fine. Frank promised to check in too.

MISU had an away game, so I had the radio tuned into the game. Hot apple cider and football-shaped sugar cookies decorated with MISU's colors were the treats Dawson left for bookstore patrons, and they were vanishing quickly. We didn't have our restaurant license yet, so we put the baked items out along with a jar for donations. His baking was gaining quite the reputation, especially after the local news interviewed him a few weeks ago. The interview was intended to show him as a local kid trying to rise above his poor beginnings and abusive father. . . . The extra publicity had been good for the bookstore too.

A steady stream of customers kept me busy, and closing time arrived before I knew it. After work, Nana Jo and I were going to the retirement village to pick up the girls for a night on the town. I'd convinced Nana Jo to go into the auditorium later and talk to the Tony award winning producer, Horace Evans. If for no other reason, she still had the costume from last year and could return it. She'd gotten it dry-cleaned and never bothered to return it, since everyone assumed she'd be playing the role again this year.

The drive from my building in downtown North Harbor to Nana Jo's South Harbor retirement village went fairly quick. Nana Jo owned a villa in Shady Acres Retirement Village. It was a private, gated community for active seniors with a variety of housing options. There were detached single family homes the residents called villas, town houses, condos, and apartments.

Each resident had a card that opened the gates and unlocked the main doors. I pulled up to the main entrance and parked. Dry-cleaning bag in hand, we entered the lobby. The security guard at the front desk looked up when we entered. He recognized Nana Jo, waved, and continued watching a football game.

We passed a number of people we knew, but Nana Jo kept walking. The first floor of the building looked like any other apartment complex. There was a comfortable lounge area with sofas, flat screen televisions, and a massive fireplace. On one side was a workout facility. There was a pool and a large auditorium, which was where we headed.

Nana Jo stood outside the auditorium door, took a deep breath, and then opened it and marched in. The room was a large open area that could be reconfigured for whatever activity the residents wanted. Today, there were folding chairs near the rear. In the front of the room, a group practiced leg kicks and choreography on a platform. A man played the main number on a piano. One woman stood at the microphone wearing a tight leotard, which showcased every bulge and ripple, of which there were many. She had the largest chest I'd ever seen and her hair looked orange. I hoped it was a result of the spotlights directed at her. She had a large bow atop her head and was belting out a nasally rendition of the main song.

I halted. "Oh my."

Nana Jo stopped and stared. "*That* is my replacement."

"Oh my." I realized, after a few moments, my mouth was open, and I closed it.

Saying Maria Romanov couldn't sing was akin to saying Lake Michigan was a large body of water. It was obvious and didn't begin to scratch the surface. Maria Romanov was a horrible singer. Not only couldn't she hold a tune, she didn't appear to have any rhythm. She was chunky and out of shape and moved as if she had two left feet.

"Wow." I looked at my grandmother.

"She's got a voice that would curdle milk."

The producer, Horace Evans, was seated in the first row. He hopped up and stopped the music. He sounded as though he was gritting his teeth. "Maria, I believe you've changed keys again." He walked over to the piano. "Can you please give us the chord again, Freddie?"

When Horace went to the piano, I saw the pianist was Nana Jo's boyfriend, Freddie. They'd been dating for close to a year and seemed pretty committed.

"I didn't know Freddie played the piano."

Nana Jo nodded. "He rarely plays now, but our old pianist broke a hip skydiving, so Freddie agreed to help out."

Freddie obliged by playing the chord again.

Maria turned red, flung the sheet music down on the floor, and stamped her feet. "How can you expect me to stay on key when I'm being blinded by that light?"

I failed to see how the light affected her vocal chords, but with one throat-slashing motion, Horace gave a signal which killed the spotlight. "It is a dress rehearsal, so you will need to get accustomed to the lights before the performance."

When the spotlight was turned off, I realized the unnatural orange color of her hair was the result of hair dye and not the lights. I leaned over to Nana Jo. "Are my eyes playing tricks or is her hair tangerine orange?"

Nana Jo nodded. "Looks like she's got a pumpkin on her head, doesn't it?"

"I'm accustomed to performing on larger stages with the latest lighting," Maria boasted with an accent that sounded like a cross between Russian, French, and the Bronx. "I have performed on the grandest stages in the world and with some of the greatest musicians and dancers. This"—she swept her arm to encompass the entire stage—"is beneath me."

"If you'd prefer not to perform—" Horace said with a certain amount of eagerness.

"No! A star must adapt. I would never disappoint my audience." She smiled. "Besides, the show must go on, despite the . . . obstacles." She gave a condescending look to Freddie. "As my Eddie used to say, you cannot deprive the world of your gift."

I could feel the steam emanating from Nana Jo. She huffed and pursed her lips.

I frowned. "Who's Eddie?"

"Supposedly Edward the Eighth."

"Edward the Eighth? King Edward the Eighth who married Wallis Simpson and abdicated the throne of England? That Edward the Eighth?"

Nana Jo nodded.

"But no one called him Eddie . . . ever." I'd just finished writing a book which featured Wallis Simpson. I had tons of books on the abdicated king and his American wife. "His family and friends called him David."

She nodded. "Yep. The dumb twit has no idea." She fumed.

"Why don't we take a short break," Horace said.

Nana Jo's eyes narrowed and she marched to the front of the room. When she got to the stage, she flung the costume at Horace and walked up to Maria. "Now listen here, you no-talent two-bit hack. If you ever insult my friend again, I'll take that microphone and wrap it around your neck."

Freddie hopped up from the piano and hurried to Nana Jo's side. He placed a hand on her arm to calm her, but she shook it off.

Maria's smile looked more like a grimace. "You are jealous. Did you come to see a *real* actress perform?"

Nana Jo snorted. "When you find one, let me know."

The argument got louder and the ladies attracted a crowd. Not only were the performers watching, but several of the employees, including property manager, Denise Bennett, entered the auditorium to watch.

Maria bristled. "I see you've brought my costume. I shall, of course, have to have it altered. You are so tall and masculine, it will not fit." She straightened her back and thrust out her huge chest.

"Right. You'll have to add fabric to cover those watermelons you've got strapped around your neck."

"Why, you . . . you . . . brute. How dare you." She turned away from Nana Jo, took two steps, and then stumbled. She would have fallen if Freddie had not instinctively reached out to steady her. When he did, Maria leaned into him and clutched him as if he were a life preserver.

"I have a very delicate disposition. I'm not accustomed to being treated in this way."

Freddie was holding up Maria while Nana Jo scowled and steamed. He looked panicked.

Maria heaved a heavy sigh and flung her arm around his neck. "You are so kind." She stared lovingly at Freddie. "If you will help me back to my room, please, I must take my medicine."

Her face was mere inches from Freddie's.

"Perhaps you'd prefer to sit down. I can go and retrieve your medicine." He attempted to steer her to a nearby chair, but Maria refused.

"No. No. I moved into a new apartment. Everything is in turmoil. You would not find it. I alone can find the medicine. I knew you were a gentleman." She stared into his face. "You have kind eyes. I know you will not fail to help me."

Freddie turned to Nana Jo.

If she weren't so angry, she would have seen the anguish in his eyes, but Nana Jo was furious. "Freddie, if you go off with that hussy, then you can just stay with her, for all I care."

His eyes pleaded. "Jo, you don't mean that. Look, I'll just help Miss Romanov to her room and I'll be right back. I promise."

Maria gasped and clutched at her chest. "Oh, please, I am unwell."

Freddie helped Maria out of the room. He looked back at the stone-cold wall of Nana Jo's face one last time as they went through the doorway.

"If I had my gun, I'd deflate those weather balloons and turn Freddie from a rooster to a hen in one shot." Nana Jo turned on her heels and marched out.

Chapter 4

I caught up with Nana Jo in the parking lot. "Are you okay?"

She paced. "I'm madder than a wet hen."

Irma, Dorothy, and Ruby Mae hurried out to the parking lot.

"Calm down, Josephine. You'll send your blood pressure through the roof," Dorothy said.

"I think we should go up there and kick her—"

"Irma!"

Irma broke into a coughing fit and then pulled a flask from her bag.

"Gimme that." Nana Jo held out her hand and Irma handed over her flask. Nana Jo took a swig. "New apartment, my big toe. That tramp might as well strap a mattress to her back. It'd be easier." She wiped her mouth and handed the flask back to Irma.

"Josephine, you can't let that pumpkin-haired hussy get to you," Ruby Mae said. "No self-respecting man would have anything to do with her. There's no way Freddie would lower himself."

Nana Jo paced. "According to her, she comes from a long

line of trollops. Her grandmother was a courtesan to King George the Fifth, and she had an affair with Edward the Eighth after he tired of Wallis."

"If you believe that, I've got a bridge I can sell you," Irma spat.

"Pshaw." Ruby Mae snorted. "Edward the Eighth wasn't a rocket scientist, but he had better taste than that."

Dorothy nodded. "Ruby Mae's right. Now, let's get out of here and get a real drink."

Nana Jo stopped. "Look, I know we're supposed to go out tonight and I know you all mean well, but I'm just not up to it."

"We don't have to go out. We can go home," I said.

Nana Jo shook her head. "I'm fine and I appreciate you all, but I need a little time alone. I'll be fine. I promise."

We looked at each other. Ruby Mae shrugged.

Dorothy stood toe-to-toe with Nana Jo and looked her in the eyes. "Josephine, you're my oldest friend and you know I'd do anything for you." She paused. "Are you sure?"

Nana Jo hugged her. "Yes. I'm sure." She straightened up. "Just because I don't feel up to going out on the town doesn't mean you all shouldn't enjoy yourselves. Go out and kick up your heels. Have a good time."

It took a little convincing, but Nana Jo finally convinced Ruby Mae and Dorothy they should go out. Irma didn't take much convincing. She was always ready to have a good time. In fact, she suggested a male stripper might perk Nana Jo up, but once that idea was vetoed, she resigned herself to a night out with the girls instead.

We ended up at the Four Feather's Casino. It was a good one-stop shop. We got food, drinks, and entertainment all in one location. Ruby Mae had a large extended family that always managed to arrange free buffet meals for us, so the evening would be relatively inexpensive, especially considering we weren't hard-core gamblers.

Ruby Mae never gambled much more than twenty or thirty dollars. She spent most of her time knitting by the large fireplace in the lobby and talking. Everywhere we went, she ran into people she knew. People liked her and they talked to her. She had one of those faces people trusted. The old saying, *she never met a stranger* fit her like a glove. It was a trait that meant it took her twice as long to go through the checkout at the grocery store while the clerk shared their life story; however, it came in handy when investigating murder cases.

Irma didn't gamble much either. Instead, she spent her time, as Ruby Mae described it, *chatting up* men at the bar. Dorothy and Nana Jo were the biggest gamblers. As soon as we finished dinner, Dorothy headed for the high-limit room. She played twenty-dollar slots and table games. When I started hanging out with my grandmother and her friends at the casino, I worried. I didn't want them to end up gambling away their pensions. When I broached the subject with Nana Jo, she laughed. That's when I learned Dorothy Clark was a millionaire. Her husband owned a string of dry cleaners, which she sold after he died. She played and probably lost more than the rest of us, but she still stayed within her comfort zone.

Hanging out with an older crowd caused me to notice seniors more than I had previously. A lot of them came to the casino for companionship and cheap entertainment. The retirement village even had a bus that transported seniors on weeknights, as did several other facilities in the area.

I sat at a penny-slot machine with a picture of a wolf on the front and tried not to jump every time the machine howled. It took thirty minutes before I figured out the basics of the game. It was a bit of mindless fun, which allowed me to think without taxing my brain. I was a low-budget gambler and twenty dollars went a long way on penny slots. A few weeks ago, I had a big win at the casino in Michigan City, Indiana.

However, a lifetime of scrimping and saving didn't vanish overnight.

We stayed until midnight and then settled up. The girls had a strategy whereby they always split their winnings at the end of the night. That way if someone had a losing night, it wasn't devastating. Between the five of us, someone usually won. I felt guilty initially, especially since I didn't gamble as much as Dorothy and Nana Jo. However, I felt much better after I won over fifty thousand dollars and could share my windfall.

I dropped the girls at the retirement village and drove home. Tonight Nana Jo stayed in her villa at the retirement village, so it was just my dogs, Snickers and Oreo, and me. After my husband, Leon, died, I sold our home and moved into the space over the bookstore. When a dead body was found in the back courtyard, Nana Jo moved in and stayed with me off and on. With both Dawson and Nana Jo away, the house was very quiet.

Snickers barely rolled over when I turned on the bedroom lights and refused to get up. I carried her downstairs to go potty. I opened the door and she squatted where I placed her, did her business, and looked up as if to say, *now return me to where you found me, wench*. Oreo normally barked at leaves blowing across the yard and sniffed every blade of grass before taking care of business, but apparently he was too tired to bother tonight. They were both slowing down. Their muzzles had a lot more white and, while their hearing had always been selective, I could now open a bag of potato chips without waking them. I had to face facts. My poodles were old. The very thought that I might not have many years left with them made me weepy. Snickers was a good cuddler and endured a tight hug while I carried her back upstairs. She was also fickle and her concern waned quickly. She yawned, licked my nose, and wiggled out of my arms and got in her bed. She turned a few circles and then settled down. Oreo wasn't a cuddler and ran into his crate and waited for me to close the door before he settled in.

I undressed and got in bed. I was tired, but I couldn't stop thinking about Nana Jo. She and Freddie would probably be okay. He was a nice guy and I think they really cared for each other. Normally, she was very self-assured and wouldn't have blinked twice at someone like Maria Romanov flirting with him. Losing the part in the Senior Follies had been a serious blow and had eroded her confidence. I wasn't sure how to help her. Eventually, I got tired of tossing and turning and got up.

⌒‿‿‿

"I can't believe I spilled tea all over your mother." Daphne looked stricken.

James FitzAndrew Browning, the 15th duke of Kingsfordshire, fought to hide the smile that threatened to break out on his face.

"She hates me."

James pulled Daphne into his arms. "She doesn't hate you. She doesn't know you."

Daphne stared into James's face. "Do you really think so?"

"I know so. How can anyone who knows you not love you? Trust me." James bent down to kiss Daphne but was interrupted by a sudden noise.

"Ah, sorry, old boy." Randolph Churchill stumbled into the studio. "I thought his majesty was here."

"Randolph, how are you?" James extended his hand and he and Randolph shook.

Randolph Churchill, the only son of Winston and

Clementine Churchill, was a handsome man in his late twenties. He was tall with movie star good looks. He had light hair and eyes which held a spark of intelligence behind lazy, droopy eyelids.

"Now, who do we have here? Don't tell me this is the delectable Lady Daphne Marsh." Randolph leered. "How about a kiss for your cousin?" He reached for Daphne, but she stepped aside and Randolph stumbled.

"Hello, Randolph. Your mother warned me you'd be here." Daphne crossed her arms in front of her and created a barrier of separation.

Randolph chuckled and stared at Daphne as a starving man looked at a steak dinner.

James's fist clenched by his side and he took a step forward.

Daphne gently touched the duke's sleeve and recalled him to her side.

Randolph noticed the gesture and threw back his head and laughed. "Steady on, old boy."

"She said you were bringing a guest." Daphne said the last word as though it were a disease.

"Yes, well, that's why I'm here. I wanted to introduce Jessica to the great one." Randolph smirked.

Daphne looked scathingly at her cousin. "Uncle Winnie isn't here. I believe he was to meet with that BBC producer. Perhaps you should try his study."

Randolph gave Daphne one last lecherous look, smiled, bowed to the duke, and walked out.

Daphne shuddered. "What an odious man. I pity the woman willing to put up with him."

James put his arm around her. "If he bothers you, I'll wring his neck."

Daphne smiled. "I can handle Randolph. He's a

tiresome boor who's been indulged and pampered his entire life. Uncle Winnie raised him as though he were the *dauphin*."

James frowned. "Heir apparent to what? He isn't a peer. His uncle inherited the title."

Daphne sighed. "Chartwell, The House of Commons, England. Randolph told me once he has two goals. He wants to be rich and he wants to be prime minister."

James stared in disbelief. "Well, I suppose anything's possible, but . . ."

"Randolph's a fool. He's a drunkard and he's rude."

"I'd heard he inherited his father's gift for oration."

"Oh, he's smart enough, but that just makes it worse. He's intelligent and he knows it. He looks down on people. I've never liked him."

James smiled.

"What's so funny?"

"I was just thinking. If Randolph continues the way he's going, my mother will have someone else to focus on. He's bound to deflect some of her ire away from you."

"I just hope he doesn't pick a fight with his father. That will make both of them cross. Uncle Winnie will get in a funk and Aunt Clemmie will worry and fuss, and then she'll get angry with Randolph. It'll be a horrible mess."

James kissed Daphne. "Well, come on, old girl, we'd better get back to the house and see what trouble is brewing."

I was startled out of my 1938 reverie by my cell phone. In the early hours of the morning, the sound reverberated off the walls and echoed. I looked at the clock. It was three in the morning. I picked up my phone and saw my grandmother's picture.

"Nana Jo, do you know what time—"

"Sam, get over here quick."

The sound of my grandmother's voice acted like a freezing glass of water to wake me.

"What's wrong? What's happened?"

"Maria Romanov's dead. She's been shot and that twerp, Detective Stinky Pitt, thinks I killed her."

Chapter 5

I was so frazzled by Nana Jo's call, I didn't remember getting dressed. I should've been suspicious when I saw smirks on the faces of the policeman who tried to prevent my entry into the retirement village. However, I was focused. Eventually, I was admitted and walked to the security desk.

"I'm looking for my grandmother, Josephine Thomas."

He stared for a second. The sides of his mouth twitched but he quickly contained them. "Down the hall and to the right, but—"

I was halfway down the hall and never caught the end of his sentence. When I got to the room, I looked through the window. Nana Jo and Detective Stinky Pitt were inside. I opened the door and went in without knocking.

"Nana Jo are you alright?" I hugged her. "I've been trying to call Jenna, but I keep getting sent to voice mail. Did you call her?"

"Mrs. Washington—"

"You better have a darned good reason for holding my grandmother, Detective Pitt. This is ridiculous. My grandmother wouldn't kill anyone. Just because she threatened to

kill her and is an excellent shot doesn't mean she actually did."
I was rambling and pacing in the small office.

"Sam!" Nana Jo held my shoulders and looked me in the
eyes. "Stop. You're going to get me hung if you keep talking."
She hugged me. "By the way, what's that in your hair?"

"My hair?" I instinctively reached up and felt my hair and
landed on a comb tangled in a bird's nest of frizz. It took a bit
of manipulation, but I got it out and stood holding a large-
toothed blue comb. It must have gotten stuck when I was
dressing. In my nervous state and haste, I'd apparently forgotten about it.

Nana Jo reached in her purse and pulled out a handkerchief, licked the corner, and then wiped under my eyes.
"You'd better start removing your makeup before you go to
bed, or you'll regret it when you're my age."

Under normal conditions, having my grandmother spit
clean me like a mother cat cleaned a kitten would have embarrassed me beyond belief. Whether as a result of the unusual
circumstances, or sheer relief my grandmother appeared to
have the situation in hand, I couldn't say. Whatever the reason,
I allowed myself to be cleaned up.

"Now, that's better." She handed me the handkerchief,
which was stained with eyeliner and mascara, and patted my
hair down.

"Are we done? May I continue my interview?" Stinky
Pitt's words dripped with sarcasm.

Detective Pitt was a short, fat, balding detective with a
penchant for short, tight polyester clothing and an overabun-
dance of cologne. He'd been labeled "Stinky Pitt" by his boy-
hood classmates. Nana Jo was his third grade teacher and
enjoyed using the old nickname to annoy him whenever she
could. I first encountered Detective Pitt several months ago
when he accused me of murder. Needless to say, we weren't
exactly the best of friends.

Nana Jo and I sat down.

He turned to me. "You were saying your grandmother threatened the deceased?"

Heat rose up my neck and I knew I was blushing. I turned to Nana Jo. "I don't think you should answer any questions without a lawyer." I pulled out my cell phone and pushed my sister's number for what felt like the thousandth time since Nana Jo called. "For some reason it keeps going to voice mail."

"She and Tony are gone on their anniversary cruise. Remember?"

"Ugh. I totally forgot about that." I put my phone down. "You could request a public defender, I suppose."

"Mrs. Thomas has not been arrested." He pounded the table. "We are merely taking her statement." An angry red flame rose up Detective Pitt's neck and a vein bulged on the side of his forehead.

The door swung open and Freddie Williams rushed inside. "Josephine, are you okay? I just heard about Maria." He pulled Nana Jo to her feet and hugged her tightly.

Detective Pitt threw his pen into the air and pounded his notepad onto the desk. He rolled his eyes and shifted in his seat. "Do you mind? I'm trying to conduct an investigation."

Freddie ignored everyone except Nana Jo. He pushed her away from him so he could stare into her eyes. "You know there was never anything between Maria and me. There has never been anyone else in my life once I met you."

Nana Jo's eyes filled with tears and she melted into Freddie's arms. "Oh, Freddie. I've been such a fool. Of course I knew it. I knew it with my heart, but my head wouldn't listen." She pulled away and looked into his eyes. "Can you ever forgive me for doubting you?"

"Darling, there's nothing to forgive." He kissed her soundly. "I remembered you said your granddaughter was going on a cruise, so I took the liberty of calling my friend, Judge Ben Miller. He's in River Bend." He looked at his watch. "It'll be about thirty minutes before he can get here, but he said don't say one word until he does."

Detective Pitt looked as though he would explode. "Judge Miller? What's a judge going to do?" He ground his teeth. "She isn't under arrest. I'm just taking her statement."

"Well, she won't be saying another word without legal counsel present." Freddie kept a protective arm around Nana Jo's shoulders.

Freddie was usually a very gentle, quiet man, but tonight he exuded an authoritative strength that was comforting. He was in his mid-seventies with white hair, which he kept cut short. He was a retired police detective and his son, Mark, was a state trooper. Nana Jo always said she liked the fact Freddie was taller than she was and still had all of his own teeth. The look in her eyes showed she was more serious about Freddie than she had ever admitted.

My grandmother was a strong woman. She was a smart, wise-cracking, sharpshooting, Aikido black belt. I never thought of her as needing protecting, but when she placed her head on Freddie's shoulder, I glimpsed a vulnerability she rarely displayed.

"I just want to ask Mrs. Thomas a few questions," Detective Pitt explained.

The door burst open and in walked Irma, Dorothy, and Ruby Mae.

"You okay? We just heard that crazy woman went and got herself killed," Dorothy said.

"One of my sons is an attorney in Chicago." Ruby Mae held up her cell phone. "I called him on the way downstairs. He's not licensed to practice in Michigan, but he'll be here in two hours if you need him. Just say the word."

Irma coughed. "I used to date an attorney. He's a bit of a

leech, but I'd be willing to take one for the team if you need me to." She coughed.

"Oh, good grief." Detective Pitt stared at the crowd. "How many more people are coming down?" He pushed back his chair and stood in the tiny office. "Mrs. Thomas, I'll need a statement from you. You and your posse can come downtown before noon." He snatched his notepad off the desk, sidled through the crowd, opened the door, and walked out. "I'm done."

Chapter 6

The office was crowded, even after Detective Pitt's exit. So, we went to Nana Jo's villa for coffee. The villas were single family homes painted bright coastal colors with porches that looked out on Lake Michigan. Nana Jo's house was a lemony yellow with white trim. The interior looked like a country farmhouse with sturdy oak furniture, handed down from generation to generation. The distressed wood finishes were created by years of wear and tear, as opposed to artistic techniques.

We sat at the large farmhouse table that filled her dining room. I recalled family meals served on the table and instinctively looked for the initials I'd carved into the table decades earlier.

Nana Jo served coffee and apple pie. Despite my protest that I didn't want pie, I found myself scraping the gooey filling from my plate and licking my fork. The odor of cooked apples and cinnamon combined with the aroma of coffee enveloped me like a warm blanket. Outside, the sun was rising and casting rays of red, orange, and yellow across the still-blue water.

"Does anyone know exactly what happened? How did she die? Who found her?" I asked.

Nana Jo sighed. "Maria . . . or someone, left a note in my mailbox asking me to come see her tonight."

"Where's the note?" I asked.

Nana Jo looked into her coffee. "I gave it to Stinky Pitt."

"Ugh," we growled.

"Well, I wasn't thinking straight. I showed up at her door. I knocked. There was no answer, but the door was open. So, I went in. I called out, but there was no answer. I looked around, but I didn't see her, so I left."

"Did anyone see you? Did you touch anything?" The ex-policeman in Freddie kicked in.

"I don't know. I might have, but I certainly didn't kill the silly twit."

"No one is accusing you of killing her." He tried to soothe her.

"Keep going, Josephine," Dorothy said.

"I came back home and went to bed."

Freddie looked uncomfortable. "Can anyone corroborate this?"

"Corroborate?" Nana Jo's eyes squinted. "You don't think I . . ."

Freddie held up his hands. "Now, calm down. You know I don't believe you killed her. I'm just trying to ask the questions Detective Pitt will ask."

"He's right, Nana Jo."

"I know he's right." She sighed. "If you're wanting to know if I have an alibi, then the answer is no. I don't. I was home alone."

"I tried to call and you never answered. I hoped you were out with Sam or the girls. Weren't you supposed to be at a girls' night?"

"I didn't feel up to going out. So, I stayed home."

He swore under his breath and Nana Jo reached over and patted his hand.

"How did you know she'd been murdered?" Ruby Mae asked.

"The property manager, Denise Bennett, came by and knocked on the door. She said there was an emergency at the main complex and I needed to come over," Nana Jo said.

"How was she killed?" I asked.

Nana Jo shrugged. "Beats me, but when I got to the main building, I saw all those police cars and then Stinky Pitt pulled me into that office and started firing off questions like Perry Mason. That's when I knew he thought I killed her."

"Just because you threatened her doesn't mean you killed her." I realized as soon as the words were out of my mouth, how stupid they sounded. "Sorry. I'm sleep deprived."

Everyone had questions, but Nana Jo wasn't able to answer much more. Apparently one of the neighbors saw her leaving Maria's apartment.

Freddie's son, Mark, called. He would get as much information as he could. He promised to report back as soon as he found out something helpful.

Judge Ben Miller arrived later than the thirty minutes Freddie said initially. He was an older African American man with dark skin, white hair, and a white beard. He had soft, friendly brown eyes and a quick mind. I'd read about his retirement from the bench in the newspaper. He had been one of the first African American judges in River Bend. He was a big advocate for civil rights, dating back to his time marching with Dr. Martin Luther King. He'd retired from the bench but was now the full-time dean of JAMU's law school.

He shook all of our hands and shared a moment of *aren't you related to such and such* with Ruby Mae. Apparently, his wife, now deceased, had been Ruby Mae's third cousin or something like that. Irma flirted. Dorothy asked a few tough questions about Judge Miller's ability to represent Nana Jo, which he answered calmly. He wasn't licensed to practice in

Michigan or Indiana anymore, for that matter. However, he was able to advise and would recommend good counsel to stand in until Jenna returned from her cruise.

Nana Jo and I agreed not to telegram the ship. Jenna and Tony rarely took time off and both deserved to enjoy their anniversary without worry. If Nana Jo was arrested, that would be a different matter. However, for now, we would handle things ourselves.

Judge Miller, Freddie, and Nana Jo went to the living room to talk.

"We certainly have our work cut out for us this time," Ruby Mae said.

"What do you mean?" I asked.

"We're going to have to figure out who wanted Maria dead more than Josephine." Dorothy stared at me.

"And we'll have to be quick about it." Irma was hit by a coughing fit. She poured the contents of her flask into her coffee.

"Why?" I asked.

Dorothy, Ruby Mae, and Irma all stared at me.

Dorothy leaned forward. "Regardless of what happens, the show must go on. We have a performance to do, and Josephine will have to take the lead part. It's the only way we can be ready in time."

I groaned. "Detective Pitt will take that as another motive for Nana Jo to have murdered Maria."

Ruby Mae nodded. "He'd be a fool not to."

"We have to clear Josephine's name," Dorothy said.

Ruby Mae knitted. "That means finding the killer."

"Before the bus leaves for New York." Irma coughed. "I've already paid for my ticket and Horace promised to take me to the top of the Empire State Building and then dinner and drinks." She coughed. "People used to say I looked like Fay Wray." She patted her hair.

Ruby Mae rolled her eyes and Dorothy groaned.

"But the trip to New York is only one week away." I stared at her and then glanced at the girls.

"Then we better get cracking." Dorothy pushed herself up from the table.

Chapter 7

Sundays were typically spent hanging out with my mom. Given the fact that I hadn't slept, my plan was to beg off. After more than thirty years, I should have been prepared to deal with my mom's guilt mojo. All it took was, "I'm so disappointed. I was really looking forward to spending time with you," and I caved in. Nana Jo said I have a guilty conscience and I need to *get over it*. She's right, but Rome wasn't built in a day, and I hadn't managed to grow a backbone overnight, or over the last thirty-five years. Jenna said I needed to stand up for myself and *just say no*. Easy for her to say.

Several cups of coffee and a hot shower and I was wide awake—mostly. I picked up my mom and drove the short distance to her church. The church had undergone a bit of a transformation after the pastor died and a younger pastor was installed. The congregation had grown significantly since Pastor Timmons took over and now had a much younger crowd attending. Some of the older members resisted the changes. From traditional hymns to contemporary music and from sermons of condemnation, fire, and brimstone to messages of love and acceptance, there had been lots of change. Pastor Timmons was a bridge between the two generations and offered a solution which worked for the majority of people, two services. The early service included traditional organ music and hymns while the later service offered contemporary songs. My mom preferred the early service. I expected the organ music and hymns would put me to sleep, but between standing to sing, kneeling for prayer, and my mom's elbow in my side whenever I blinked, I was wide awake for the entire service.

Afterward, we went to brunch at a new restaurant in downtown South Harbor. Riverside Foodworks was a renovated warehouse in an old knitting mill. The restaurant was packed and we were lucky to get a seat without reservations. The food was excellent. I ordered banana bread French toast and it was delicious. One of the restaurant's biggest selling features was one-dollar mimosas.

"Are you sure you should be eating all of that syrup? You've taken off some weight and you don't want to get fat."

I was five feet four and had been described as *pleasantly plump* my entire life. It was only since I hit my thirties that I'd become comfortable with my curves. I could stand to lose about fifteen pounds, but I wasn't fat. Nevertheless, my mom's words made me feel fat and ugly. I downed my mimosa. When the waiter came by and asked if I wanted another, I said yes.

My mom declined. "Are you sure you should? You've already had one and I've always heard alcohol has a lot of calories."

The waiter looked at me to see if I was going to change my mind.

I stared him in the eyes. "On second thought, you better make it a double." This was going to be a long day and without sleep, I needed fortification.

Mom pursed her lips and shook her head. Barely five feet tall and less than one hundred pounds, Mom was a full foot shorter than Nana Jo. The casual observer might not see a resemblance between the two women, but a deeper look would show they had the same nose, mouth, and cheekbones. Pictures of my great grandmother Pearl showed a petite woman who could have passed for my mom's twin sister. Nana Jo was definitely more forceful and independent while my mom was more of a pampered princess.

She squirmed in her seat and took a drink of tea. "I'm glad to see you've been taking a little more care with your appearance lately. Your hair looks nice. You're wearing makeup and your clothes fit your body."

I stared at my mom, waiting for the other shoe to drop. There were a lot of compliments in there, which I refused to analyze for double meanings. I decided to accept when she said, "*your clothes fit your body,*" that she meant it as a compliment on the new clothes I'd purchased as opposed to a backhanded insult on my body size.

"Thank you."

"I wanted to talk about something." She fidgeted with her napkin and avoided looking me directly in the eyes.

This must be serious. I waited.

"Your father has been gone for over ten years now. You know I loved him very much and no one will ever be able to replace him."

The waiter brought my double mimosa.

"But, I'm sure you know how lonely it is for a woman when your husband is gone."

Oh God. I knew where this conversation was going. "Mom are you trying to tell me you've met someone special? If you are, I think that's great."

She smiled. "Thank you. dear, but it's actually a little more than that. Harold and I have been *keeping company.*"

Keeping company sounded so quaint. I smiled. "Mom, I think that's wonderful. I can't wait to meet Harold. You deserve to be happy."

I smiled and took a sip of my drink.

She took a deep breath. "There's no other way to say this, so I'm just going to say it." She took another deep breath. "I'm getting married."

I choked. I wasn't expecting that. When I finally stopped coughing, I stared at my mom. "Married? Sounds like you and Harold are doing more than *keeping company*. When did this happen? Why haven't we ever met this Harold before?"

"I didn't want to upset you. I know you were always really close to your father, and I knew this would be hard for you to accept that someone else might try to fill your dad's shoes."

"Hold on. First, no one will ever be able to fill Dad's shoes—"

"I knew you wouldn't take this well."

"Wait. Let me finish."

Mom sat with her lips pursed and arms folded across her chest.

"No one will be able to take Dad's place in my heart, but that doesn't mean I think you should spend the rest of your life alone. Losing Leon taught me just because I loved him doesn't mean I can never love anyone else."

Mom relaxed and unfolded her arms.

"If you've found someone who makes you happy, I think that's wonderful. I'm just surprised you're talking about marriage to someone you've never introduced to your family. It seems a bit sudden, that's all."

"I've known Harold for almost five years. We met at BINGO at the senior center."

"Five years? Why haven't you ever mentioned him before?"

"I told you, I didn't want to upset you."

I took another sip of my mimosa. "So, you've been dating Harold for five years and now you two are getting married?"

"Yes."

I took another sip of my drink. "When is the wedding?"

"We thought we'd get married on Christmas Eve."

I spewed my drink all over the table, barely avoiding spitting it in my mom's face. Miraculously, most of it landed down the front of my white cashmere sweater.

Mom tsked and patted at her sweater. "Honestly, dear, a woman should always know how to handle her alcohol."

The waiter arrived with our bill but turned and walked away. He returned with a damp towel, a glass of tonic water, and a spot removing pen. He mopped up the table and I tackled my sweater. When we were done, the table was in much better shape than my sweater.

"Christmas Eve as in next month?"

"Yes, dear."

"What's the big hurry?"

"It's not exactly a hurry." Mom avoided eye contact again. "Harold asked me to marry him over a year ago, but . . . well, time just got away from me." Mom fluttered her hands.

"Time got away from you? It's been a year, Mother."

"Well, it never seemed like the right time. I was going to tell you and then Leon died."

"You're joking, right?"

"I thought telling you I was getting married after your husband died was in very poor taste." She looked at me as if surely any imbecile should know that. "Then, that man was murdered and the police thought you did it, and I couldn't tell you then."

The waiter brought me a new drink and I thanked him, ignored the look my mother gave me, and took a sip.

"Then that nice boy, Dawson, was accused of killing that girl and you were all involved in helping him. I didn't think that was the right time." She fluttered her hands again. "Before I knew it, the wedding was nearly here."

"Does Jenna know?"

"No. She and Tony are on a cruise. I was going to wait until she came back so I could tell you both together, but Harold thought I better tell you so you would have time to shop for an outfit."

I took a couple of deep breaths and tried to put everything in perspective. My mom was in her late fifties. She was still active and vibrant and had many good years in front of her. She deserved to be happy, and if Harold made her happy, more power to her. I got up and walked around the table and gave my mom a hug. "Congratulations, Mom."

"Thank you, dear."

I sat down and called the waiter over. "Could you please get my mom a glass of champagne. We're celebrating. My mom is getting married."

He looked at my mom, who beamed. He hurried away and returned with a small bottle of champagne and two fluted glasses. He placed them on our table. "Compliments of the house." He filled our glasses.

We held up our glasses. "Mom, I'm very happy for you and I wish you and Harold many years of happiness and love."

"Thank you, dear." She took a sip. "I'm sure we'll be very happy together but I'm not marrying Harold because I love him." She took another sip of her champagne. "It's physical. I'm marrying him for the sex."

I tried to wrap my head around the idea of my mom as a nymphomaniac, but try as I might, I just couldn't. I left the waiter a large tip, especially after he had to clean up our table the second time. At least when I spewed out the champagne, it hadn't stained as badly as the mimosa.

My mom made a couple of comments about my state of inebriation and questioned my ability to drive. I finally convinced her I wasn't intoxicated by pointing out most of my drinks were splattered down the front of my sweater and across the table. She threatened to take a taxi home, and I almost let her. I wasn't nearly intoxicated enough to fight with her.

Eventually, her majesty deigned to permit me to drive her home, but not without showering down guilt on my head. "If you get in an accident and kill me, just know it'll be all your fault. If you live, you'll have my death on your conscience."

I blamed the toll of the last twenty-four hours and my lack of sleep for eliminating my filter. I backed out of the parking lot. "I can live with that."

Chapter 8

My fingers itched to call my sister. How dare she enjoy a weeklong Caribbean cruise while I was left here to deal with our grandmother's potential arrest and our mother's impending marriage to *Harold Somebody-or-Other*. Someday I'd ask my mom what her intended's last name was, but it was not this day. I paced across my apartment. The image of my sister lying on a white sandy beach holding a fruity drink with an umbrella made me angry. The fact it wasn't her fault and I was being totally unreasonable just made me angrier.

The doorbell rang and the poodles ran downstairs to bark and let the doorbell ringer know that fierce toy poodles lived inside.

Even before I got downstairs, I knew by the scratches on the glass and the whimpering rather than barking, my visitor was someone well-known to the pack. I was pleasantly surprised to see Frank's face smiling at me through the glass door.

I opened the door. "You may not want to come inside. It's been a crazy day and I haven't had sleep."

Frank stepped inside. "I'll take my chances." He looked at me. "You look like you could use a hug." He opened his arms.

I took one step forward and melted into him. It felt good to lay my head on his chest and feel his strong arms wrap around me. I stood there, absorbing the warmth and strength of his body, dissolving my tension and stress. It had been a long time since I'd been held like that and felt like I had someone to shoulder my burden. I was a strong woman and I was accustomed to handling things on my own, but sometimes it was nice when you didn't have to be strong. For the past twenty-something years, Leon and I had shared the good and the bad. He was gone, and I hadn't realized how alone I felt until now.

The tears started slowly but increased. I had no idea how long I cried, but Frank held on until the waterworks finally dried up.

"You okay?"

I hiccupped. "I am now, although I look horrible and your shirt is ruined."

Frank had on a white shirt and my makeup left an imprint of my face on his shirt. He looked down and shrugged. "That's pretty cool. It's almost like a picture."

"I'll get you a stain removal wipe. It'll get the makeup out and . . ."

Frank took my face in his hands and stared into my eyes. "I don't care about the shirt. I want to know what's wrong and how can I help?"

The concern and affection in his eyes made me weepy.

I sniffed and started to cry again. "That's so nice."

He patted my back and would have pulled me close again, but I pushed away. "No. I'm fine. Let's go upstairs." I used the sleeve of my sweater to wipe my eyes. This sweater would never be the same again anyway. "I need a cup of tea."

Moving toward the stairs roused the poodles, who had given up scratching at our legs while I cried and had lain down on the rug.

I turned to Frank. "Would you mind letting the poodles out while I go upstairs and get myself together."

"Come on, guys." Like the Pied Piper, he led the poodles outside to take care of business.

I went upstairs and changed out of my mimosa and champagne soaked sweater into a JAMU sweatshirt the twins gave me for my birthday. One look in the bathroom mirror reinforced that crying was something I needed to only indulge in privately. My eyes were red and puffy. I had mascara and eyeliner rings under each eye that made me look like a raccoon. I washed my face and used a cold compress to reduce the swelling before joining Frank.

He was sitting on the sofa. Snickers was on his lap, flat on her back. Belly exposed, she angled her body and used her paw to manipulate his hand to scratch her in just the right place. Her lips were curled into what appeared to be a smile and her eyes were rolled back in her head in a look of ecstasy. Oreo sat on the opposite side while Frank scratched behind his ear. He had found the exact spot that made Oreo's leg twitch uncontrollably.

I stood for a few moments and watched the peaceful scene. "Do you guys need a moment? I can come back."

Frank smiled. "They're your dogs. If they're spoiled . . ." He stopped scratching the dogs and the barking started immediately.

I picked up Snickers and sat next to Frank. I put my head on his shoulder and Snickers on my lap.

Frank put his arm around me. "Want to tell me what's been going on?"

I took a deep breath and poured out my heart. I told him about Maria's murder and Nana Jo. He asked a few questions but let me finish unloading. When I finished updating him on Nana Jo, I told him about my mom. I suspected he was laughing, but when I tried to turn to look at his face, he was careful to remove any signs of amusement.

"Wow. Your mom's getting married in less than a month. Do you think your grandmother knows?"

I sat up and stared. "Oh my God. There's no way Nana Jo knows about this. She would have told me."

We sat in silence for a few seconds while I mulled over the idea. I felt vibration. I turned and stared and this time he wasn't able to hide his amusement. Frank laughed.

I stared at him for several seconds. "This isn't funny."

"You have got to be kidding." He laughed. "Your grandmother is going to blow a gasket."

I imagined Nana Jo's face and laughed until my sides hurt. "I needed a good laugh." I stood. "I'm going to make a cup of tea. Do you want something?"

Frank had to go back to the restaurant later, so he asked for a cup of coffee.

I used my single serve coffee maker to make both. We sat at the breakfast bar and finished off Dawson's lemon bars while we finished our drinks.

"Have you heard how things went with your grandmother's statement?"

"No. We agreed to meet at your place later for drinks so we can get started on our investigation."

He nodded absentmindedly. "That's good. I don't think your grandmother should stay in her villa."

I looked at him. "You don't think she's in any danger, do you?"

He shrugged. "Probably not, but better safe than sorry. Based on what you said, a lot of people heard her threaten Maria. It's unlikely the murderer killed Maria just to spite your grandmother, but . . ."

"Nana Jo's a pretty tough cookie."

"Oh, I know. There's just something a little fishy about this whole thing." His brow was furled. "Someone had to have been watching your grandmother. They left that note to lure her to Maria's condo."

"Maybe Detective Pitt can get some fingerprints off the note."

Frank shook his head. "I doubt it. You'd have to live under a rock not to know to wear gloves these days." He shook his head again. "I doubt the killer left prints."

"I suppose that would make things a bit too easy, wouldn't it?"

He smiled. "Yep. You're going to have to work a lot harder than that."

I yawned. "I'm sorry. I haven't slept."

He drank the last of his coffee and put the mug down, got up, and kissed me. "You better get some sleep."

I protested but he persisted. "I actually have to get back to the restaurant. The brunch crowd is over, but I have quite a bit of prep work to do before the dinner crowd."

"You work too hard."

He laughed. "If you knew what I did before I got this restaurant, you wouldn't say that."

Frank didn't share a lot of information about his previous life. I knew he retired from the military, but not much else. When asked, all he ever said was, "*It's classified.*" I knew he traveled all over the world and knew how to do a lot of things the average person didn't, like how to fly a helicopter and how to kill silently. This came up when I was talking to him about an idea for my manuscript. I wanted to write a scene where one of my characters came up behind someone and cut his throat. Frank listened quietly and then said if a quiet kill was important, then I needed to stab him in the kidney. The throat contracted and they would die quickly and quietly. He spoke softly and his eyes looked as though he was seeing something he didn't want to remember. Ultimately, I decided against using the scene. Murder might be acceptable in a cozy mystery, but the reader didn't need to read about the gory details. That was one of the times when I suspected his role was a lot more clandestine and dangerous than he admitted.

Frank went back to work, and I went to bed. Often when I was tired, my mind refused to slow down so I could sleep. This wasn't one of those times. I slept like a log, or a pig in slop, as Nana Jo would say. It was only a few hours, but I slept hard and woke up feeling refreshed. Fortunately, I'd set my phone to wake me up or I might have slept well into the night.

I showered and dressed. The swelling had gone down and my eyes no longer looked as if I was wearing goggles. I made an extra effort with my makeup and hair. Frank saw me looking pretty bad earlier, but I was at home. In public, I didn't want to embarrass him or myself.

Despite all of the delicious goodies Dawson prepared, I had lost a little weight. I think it came from running up and down the stairs from my apartment to the bookstore multiple times every day. Combine the stairs with lifting boxes of books, squatting low and reaching high to shelve the books, and I was getting a pretty good workout from my new life activities. My new jeans made my butt look good and my legs longer. I put on a V-neck sweater and stacked-heel boots. I took one last look in the mirror and approved the reflection staring back at me, then headed down the street to my meeting.

The temperature had dropped considerably from earlier in the day. I shivered and hurried down the block. The heat inside the restaurant fogged my glasses, but I made out our table even without my glasses. Frank had pushed several tables together and had a reserve sign on them. Nana Jo, Ruby Mae, and Judge Miller were already seated. Irma, Dorothy, and Freddie were at the bar. I walked over to the table and took a seat across from Nana Jo.

"Hello, Judge. I'm glad you decided to join us."

Judge Miller smiled. "I'm glad to have been asked. Freddie told me a lot about you and the North Harbor Irregulars." He laughed.

Before I opened Market Street Mysteries, I never realized how many mystery book readers lived in North Harbor. I learned there were a lot more mystery, thriller, suspense, and true crime book readers in this area than I previously thought. I was no longer surprised when I ran across references to Sherlock Holmes or Agatha Christie. Judge Miller's reference to the North Harbor Irregulars was obviously meant as an homage to Sherlock Holmes's Baker Street Irregulars, a band of street children Holmes used as intelligence agents in some of his capers.

"Are you a fan of Sherlock Holmes?"

Judge Miller chuckled. "I am indeed. Josephine has been telling me about your wonderful mystery bookstore." He leaned close and whispered, "As well as your sleuthing ability."

A waitress I wasn't familiar with came by the table and smiled as she placed a glass of water with lemon in front of me, along with a glass of Moscato from a local winery. I wasn't a wine drinker. In fact, I wasn't much of a drinker. I preferred sweet, fruity drinks with very little alcohol. Frank was a wine connoisseur and was attempting to indoctrinate me. So far, he'd discovered I liked a classic white Demi-Sec grown at a local winery and a California Moscato.

I turned to the bar and gave him a big smile in thanks.

The restaurant was very busy, but he smiled, raised an eyebrow, and tilted his head in a way that let me know he approved of the way I looked.

Nana Jo banged the table. "Let's get this party started."

I turned around.

Nana Jo took her iPad out of her purse. "Ben, Freddie, and I went to the police station and gave a statement, but you all already know everything anyway."

Dorothy turned to Judge Miller. "Are they going to arrest her?"

Judge Miller took a moment before he answered. "I don't know. I doubt it, but it'll depend on what they find out from the autopsy and the forensic report." He looked around the table, as though he were addressing a jury. "It'll depend on what evidence they find. Unfortunately, Josephine was heard threatening the deceased—"

"Pshaw." Nana Jo scoffed.

Judge Miller shook his head. "Whether you meant to do harm or not, you were heard having a big argument only hours earlier. You don't have an alibi and you were seen in the vicinity around the time of death."

"Isn't that all what they call circumstantial?" I asked tentatively.

He nodded. "Oh, yes, but people have gone to jail on a lot less than that. Josephine had motive, she had opportunity, and she had the means."

I frowned. "So, why haven't they arrested her?"

Judge Miller shrugged. "It's still early and the district attorney will want to make sure all of the i's are dotted and t's crossed."

"So, where do we start?" Dorothy asked.

Freddie cleared his throat. "I talked to my son, Mark. He's going to get as much information as he can." He pulled a notepad from his pocket. "He ran a background on the deceased." He pulled a pair of reading glasses from his pocket and put them on. "Maria Romanov was born Mary Rose Pratt in Goshen, Indiana."

"I knew it." Nana Jo crowed. "I knew she was a liar. A Russian princess my big toe. Ha!" She slapped her hand on the table, rattling the dishes.

Freddie smiled indulgently. "Yes, you were right. She was arrested once for blackmail, but nothing was ever proved and the charges were dropped." He was silent a few minutes. "There was nothing else, about her, but . . ."

We stared.

"But what?" Nana Jo asked.

"He said there was some talk going around that Detective Pitt was not very well liked. In fact, the chief inspector is tired of his incompetence and plans to fire him."

I stared at Freddie. "I don't like him, but I hate for anyone to lose their job."

Nana Jo was less sympathetic. "Serves him right. I think he's got it in for our family. He wanted to arrest you for murder. He did arrest Dawson and he thinks I murdered that pumpkin-haired hussy."

"I know, but I just feel badly about someone losing their job." I sipped my Moscato.

"Humph." Nana Jo folded her arms across her chest. "I don't feel badly for him. You shouldn't either." She uncrossed her arms to point at me. "You've had to do his work for him and solve his last two cases."

I recognized the stubborn look in her eyes and the obstinate set of her chin. Nana Jo had made up her mind and she would not be moved.

Freddie winked at me and took off his glasses. "I'm not usually at these meetings. What happens now?" He looked from Nana Jo to me.

Nana Jo was still angry, but she uncrossed her arms and picked up her iPad. Soon, she looked at me. "Well?"

"I've been thinking about this." I looked around at the girls. "Normally, you all use your connections to get information about the people involved. This time, you know the people involved. You live with them."

The girls nodded.

"I've been thinking about some of the things you've told me about Maria . . . ah, Mary."

Nana Jo looked up from typing on her iPad. "I think we need to agree to continue calling her Maria. It'll be less confusing." She looked around at each of us, and we nodded.

I turned to Irma. "Irma, can you see what you can find out from Horace Evans about why he really gave Maria the lead in the Senior Follies?"

Freddie nodded. "Good idea. Clearly Josephine was far more talented and deserved the lead role."

"Josephine has more talent in her baby finger than that shrieking hyena." Irma coughed.

"How long has Maria been at Shady Acres?"

The seniors looked from one to the other.

"Maybe two months," Dorothy said.

"That's one of the things bothering me." I looked around. "Remember the other night she said she moved to a new apartment and no one would be able to find her medicine."

"Everything is in turmoil." Nana Jo mocked her accent and dramatic gestures.

"Well, if she'd only been at Shady Acres for two months, why did she move again?" I looked around.

Everyone shook their heads.

"You're right, Sam. That move was suspicious. Her new unit was bigger with better views than her other one. Ruby Mae wanted that unit." Dorothy looked angry.

"I sure did want that one. When Esther Gordon had her stroke and moved into a nursing home, Denise said my name was at the top of the wait list. Next thing I knew, she'd given it to Maria."

I looked at Ruby Mae. "Who's Denise?"

"Denise Bennett is the property manager. Want me to take that one? I'd like to find out what's up with that," Ruby Mae said with a firm conviction that left no doubt. Denise Bennett would have to answer for a number of things.

"Great. Now, does anyone know where Maria lived before she came to Shady Acres?" I asked.

Freddie put his glasses on again and looked through his notes. "Mark didn't say, but I can find out for you." He pulled out a pencil and took notes.

"What do you want me to do?" Dorothy asked.

"Someone said they saw Nana Jo leaving Maria's room. I was hoping you could find out who and what else they saw."

Dorothy nodded. "Sure thing. If they saw Josephine, maybe they saw the killer too."

"Or maybe they are the killer and want to throw suspicion on someone else," I said.

"Good point," Dorothy agreed. "I'll be careful."

I looked around at our group. "Actually, I think all of you can *casually* talk to the other residents. Someone is bound to have seen or heard something."

They nodded.

"What do you want me to do?" Nana Jo looked up from her typing.

I had been dreading this moment. I looked down. "I would prefer if you stayed out of it."

Nana Jo frowned. "You have got to be kidding. I'm the one here with the most at stake. There's no way in tarnation I'm going to sit back and do nothing while you all investigate and figure out who murdered that silly woman."

Freddie squeezed her hand. "She's just trying to protect you."

"Well stop it. I'm a grown woman and I can darn well take care of myself."

Freddie was right. I wanted to protect my grandmother, but when I was in her position, I didn't sit still either. So, I sighed. "Okay. I was afraid you'd say that. Actually, there are two things you can help with."

Nana Jo picked up her iPad. "Fire away."

"Are you still friends with the reference librarian from MISU?"

Nana Jo shot a quick glance at Freddie and then nodded. Apparently, Freddie didn't know about one of her old flames, Elliott Lawson.

"I'd like to know more about Maria's background. Does she have any children, siblings? How was she able to pass herself off as a descendant of Russian royalty?"

Nana Jo nodded. "Got it." She typed. "What's the other thing?"

"I want to know if Maria really did have a bad heart. If she did, who else knew about it?"

Nana Jo looked skeptical. "She certainly complained about her heart and her *delicate constitution* enough."

"Did she have any friends?"

Nana Jo and the girls looked at each other.

"She talked to Magnus a lot," Nana Jo added. "I don't know if I'd call them friends, but she certainly spent more time with him than just about anyone else. I'll talk to him."

Ruby Mae looked thoughtful. "Now that you mention it, I remember seeing her talk to the chef, Gaston." With Ruby Mae's southern accent, she pronounced the name like *gas town*. "He didn't look happy about whatever she was saying either. I think I'll have a word with him after I finish talking to Denise Bennett."

"Great." I looked around the table. "Everyone has their assignments."

They all nodded. Judge Miller cleared his throat. "Excuse me, but I don't believe I have an assignment." He smiled sheepishly. "I'd like to help."

"Certainly." I looked at Judge Miller. "Do you think you

could get access to the autopsy and any forensic data the police come up with?"

Judge Miller nodded. "Certainly."

"What will you do?" Nana Jo asked.

"I'm going to have a word with Detective Pitt. I've got a proposition for him."

Chapter 9

We enjoyed a delicious dinner and left the restaurant with our assignments and a plan to meet the next evening for dessert at the River Bend Chocolate Factory. I'd hoped to convince Nana Jo to stay with me, but she said she'd get more done if she were *"closer to the action."* Freddie saw my concern and before he left, he whispered in my ear a promise to keep a close eye on her. I thanked him but knew he wouldn't be able to be with her the entire time. My head knew she was tough and able to take care of herself, but my heart ached.

I said goodbye to Frank, who apologized for not being able to spend more time with me. We made plans to have dinner Monday night.

The wind was brisk, and I was thankful I didn't have far to walk to get home. Inside, I let the poodles out to take care of business and then went upstairs. I washed off my makeup and put on a pair of sweats. I brewed a cup of tea and went to my bedroom. The poodles climbed in their beds and curled into balls. I noticed again how white their muzzles had gotten. In the corner of the room was a large basket full of stuffed toys in various stages of disrepair. I couldn't remember the last time Oreo and I had played a good game of tug-of-war. Snickers had never been particularly fond of the game, preferring a rousing round of fetch instead. I'd been really busy with the bookstore and our excursions to the dog park had been rare lately. I did a little mental calculation and realized that at twelve and fourteen, they were old. I made a mental note to schedule an appointment with their vet for a checkup. I couldn't imagine life without them and got weepy at the thought.

I shook myself. "I've cried enough today." I spoke the words aloud to clear the gloom out of my head and provide something audible and real to drag me out of the sad funk I felt closing in. Between my mom and my grandmother, the last thing I needed was anything else to stress about. I decided to lose myself in 1938 Great Britain.

"I think this is my favorite room in Chartwell House." Lady Elizabeth stared out of one of the seven round-headed windows that overlooked the sloping landscape. The dining room was simple. White walls, green curtains, glazed chintz, a large round seventeenth-century unstained oak table and rush matting created a room that was comfortable and elegantly simple.

"It is a nice room." Clementine Churchill looked around the room. "Winston got architect Phillip Tilden to renovate the house before we moved in. It was a wreck." She looked out the window. "The house was constructed on the side of a steep hill, which created a lot of levels. I think I would have preferred to have the dining room up a level so the view looked over the grounds. Tilden and Winston wanted it on the same level as the garden." Clementine frowned.

"The windows let in a lot of natural light." Lady Elizabeth tilted her head toward one of the windows, which went from the floor to ceiling.

Mrs. Churchill scowled. "It fades the floors awfully."

Lady Elizabeth was about to comment when Randolph Churchill entered the room accompanied by a woman who looked as though she'd stepped off an East London stage.

Lady Elizabeth whispered, "Is that Randolph's fiancée?"

Mrs. Churchill frowned. "I don't know that he's actually engaged, but I suspect that's why he's brought her here. I only hope he doesn't ruin things."

"She certainly looks . . . glamorous." Lady Elizabeth kept her voice neutral, careful not to allow any hint of disapproval to ring through.

Mrs. Churchill sniffed. "If by glamorous you mean common and tarted up, then yes, she is definitely glamorous."

Randolph grabbed a drink from a passing footman and tossed it back as though he was taking medication, placed the empty glass on the tray, and grabbed another within seconds. If his eyes were any indication, he'd already had several drinks before coming down to dinner. He looked up and apparently noticed the look of distaste on his mother's face. He smiled, raised his glass in salute, and then downed that glass as quickly as the first.

Mrs. Churchill huffed. "Obviously, my son is intent on embarrassing me." She looked around for Winston, who was standing in a corner talking to Lord William, Leopold Amery, and Lord William Forbes-Stemphill. "I only hope he doesn't upset Winston."

Lady Elizabeth focused her attention on Randolph's escort. She was almost as tall as Randolph. Her hair was a glossy raven-black shade that nature could never produce. She wore a bright red, strapless mermaid gown that fit her body like a mummy wrap until the bottom, where it flared out into a cascade of ruffles. Her face was very white, with pencil-drawn brows and bright red lipstick. The hair, makeup, and dress were a bit much for dinner at a country house party, but what really took the outfit over the top was the bright red boa she had draped around her shoulders.

Daphne and James stood nearby and the contrast was like night and day. Daphne looked elegant and beautiful in a gold lamé gown purchased from French designer Madeleine Vionnet. The gown had a shimmering gold lamé halter design with a black gossamer overlay with velvet appliqués in the shape of bows. Soft golden waves framed her face, while the rest of her hair was pulled into a chignon. She looked stunning and Lady Elizabeth smiled as she looked at her. Daphne was her niece, but she'd raised her since she was a baby and couldn't help but look upon her and her sister, Penelope, as the children she never had.

Lady Alistair was the last to join the group. She wore an elegant hunter-green velvet gown with matching gloves, shoes, and jewels. Her gown was trimmed in green fur around the neck and cuffs. Her hair and makeup were flawless and she looked stylish and elegant.

James escorted Daphne to his mother's side. He

kissed his mother's cheek and appeared to introduce Daphne to his mother.

A slight pink flush crept into Daphne's face, which looked apologetic and beautiful.

From where Lady Elizabeth stood, Lady Alistair's greeting seemed reserved and cool.

Thompkins announced dinner and the party moved to sit at the round table.

Lady Elizabeth noticed Lady Alistair took James by the arm and pulled him forward to escort her to the table. James glanced around at Daphne, who fell back a few paces. Apparently, all was not forgiven.

The round dining table had several extensions which were all in place to accommodate the large party.

Lady Elizabeth sat between Clementine Churchill and Daphne. Lady Alistair found two seats opposite Daphne. Randolph sat next to his father, which caused Mrs. Churchill to sigh when she noticed.

Lady Elizabeth leaned toward her friend. "Weren't there a couple of others here?"

Mrs. Church nodded. "Guy Burgess and Anthony Blunt. Apparently, they're old friends from Cambridge and begged off dinner tonight." She stared down the table at her son, who had finished his champagne and was getting a refill. "I suspect Mr. Burgess was just demonstrating good manners since he hadn't been invited. I wish my son had learned that lesson about showing up uninvited."

Winston was an intelligent man with a gift for oration. When he wanted to, he had the power to hold a room in the palm of his hand as he told tales of everything from ancient Rome to neighborhood tom-cats. Tonight was not one of those nights. Winston sat quiet and sullen, answering questions when asked directly but not initiating conversation. His mood filled the room like a blanket.

Randolph continued to drink, eventually giving up the pretense of eating and sat drinking a bottle of scotch he had one of the servers bring him. He seemed to be deliberately stoking the flames.

Everyone felt the strain in the air and endeavored to eat as quickly and quietly as possible. A storm was brewing.

Daphne looked as though she would like nothing better than to run upstairs and cry but was putting on a brave face. Then, Lady Elizabeth turned to Mrs. Churchill, whose face waffled between pity when she looked at her husband to disdain and contempt when she looked at her son. Lady Elizabeth hoped for both their sakes the meal would end without a scene, but alas that was not to be.

As the dessert course was served and it appeared the end was in sight, the shoe fell.

Randolph turned to his father. "Papa, you haven't said one word about my lovely guest." He picked up Jessica's hand and kissed it. "Isn't she lovely?"

Winston stared at his son and then inclined his head the slightest bit.

Jessica giggled and pulled her hand away. "Oh, Randolph, you're such a card. You shouldn't put your father on the spot like that."

"Oh, he's accustomed to being 'put on the spot,' as you say. Isn't that right, Papa?"

Winston refused to rise to the bait but sat fuming like a teapot on a flame, ready to blow.

"Randolph, that's enough," Mrs. Churchill practically spat the words, which fanned the flames.

He leaned across the table to address Leopold Amery, upsetting the silverware and knocking over a glass of water in the process. "Mama doesn't like it when anyone upsets the great man, but with the opening of Parliament and no positions of importance being offered, how great is he really?"

That was the last straw. Winston stood up and banged his hand on the table, knocking over glasses. He grabbed a cigar out of his pocket and stuck it in his mouth and then turned and stormed out of the room.

Randolph laughed. "Was it something I said?"

‍

Chapter 10

Monday morning, I got up, dressed, and performed the rest of my morning routine on automatic pilot. My brain was occupied with the plan I'd formulated the previous night. In the shower, while I dressed and ate breakfast, I rehearsed what I would say to Detective Pitt. Before leaving the restaurant the previous night, I had arranged for Nana Jo to cover at the bookstore so I could go to the police station this morning.

Nana Jo arrived early and Snickers and Oreo heard her coming in long before I'd finished my coffee. I was thankful when they ran down to greet her, knowing she'd let them out before coming upstairs.

When she did come up, she looked more like herself than she had in the past three days. Since learning she was passed over for the leading role in the Senior Follies, Nana Jo had aged before my eyes. I stared at her closely and noticed the dark circles under her eyes, which she had skillfully concealed with makeup. Apparently, I stared too long.

"Take a picture. It'll last longer." Nana Jo poured herself a cup of coffee.

"Sorry. You okay?"

She nodded. "I will be as soon as I drink this, but we do need to talk." She sipped her coffee, put the mug on the counter, and turned to face me. "I know you're concerned, but I'm fine."

I started to protest, but she held up a hand to stop me. "I may not be totally back to normal yet, but I'm on my way. I've had a lot of shocks over the past three days, and I'll admit, they threw me for a loop, but I'm making progress. I slept last night and that helped. I just need time." She stared at me. "What I don't need is a lot of people staring at me and treating me like a daft nitwit."

I laughed. "No one would ever take you for a nitwit, but I understand what you're saying."

"Great. Now, what kind of proposition are you planning to make to Stinky Pitt?"

I avoided going into details about my proposition last night because the idea popped into my head while we were sitting there and I needed to wrap my mind around it. However, after a night of writing and sleep, what started out as a glimmer of an idea had now formed into a full-blown plan.

I outlined what I planned to Nana Jo. While I talked, her face changed from one of polite inquiry to surprise.

"Well, hot damn! That takes guts. You definitely take after your Nana Jo. I wish your mother had inherited a fraction of that courage and backbone."

Nana Jo's comments reminded me I hadn't told her about Mom's impending nuptials. My lips twitched.

"What is it? I could use a good laugh."

"Well, you may need a stiff drink more than a laugh." I joked but then told Nana Jo about my lunch with Mom and her upcoming betrothal.

Surprise didn't begin to come close to the emotions that crossed Nana Jo's face. When she was finally able to speak, she asked the one question that had plagued me too. "Well, I'll be jiggered. Who in tarnation is Harold?"

The North Harbor Police Department was in a large complex, which included the courthouse and jail, and sat on a strip of land between two of the drawbridges which allowed passage over the St. Thomas River between North and South Harbor. Prior to last month, I hadn't been to the police station for anything other than paying parking tickets. When Dawson was arrested for murder, I spent more time at the police station than I ever wanted. I couldn't help looking at the video cameras as I approached the metal detectors, which brought up horrible memories of Nana Jo and me on the ground when her iPad set off the metal detectors and the police thought it was a gun. Knowing my grandmother as I did, I was fortunate she hadn't been carrying her *peacemaker* that day. Today's visit was uneventful.

I asked for Detective Pitt at the main desk and waited until he came to get me. Surprise registered on his face as he looked at me. Apparently, I had interrupted his breakfast as he was munching on a breakfast sandwich.

"You here to confess?" he asked with a full mouth.

"I was hoping we could have a talk. Is this a good time?"

Detective Pitt stared at me for a few seconds and then stepped aside and permitted me to pass behind the counter. Either he had several pairs of tight polyester pants or he wore the same ones over and over again. I was almost certain these were the same pants he had on Saturday night or Sunday morning when I saw him. I probably wouldn't have noticed them if they weren't so tight and so short. He wore a large white belt and a vibrant flowered polyester shirt. Few people would forget seeing that outfit.

He escorted me into a small office that wasn't much bigger

than a closet. It didn't have any windows and there was barely room for his desk and a guest chair. He sat and continued to eat his sandwich.

I sat down in the stiff-backed chair and waited for Detective Pitt to finish eating.

"You want something?" he asked in between bites.

"I can wait until you finish eating."

He looked at me and then put down his sandwich, wiped his hands, and turned to face me. "How can I help you?"

I ignored the sarcasm. "Detective Pitt, I know we haven't always seen eye to eye."

He snorted. "That's putting it lightly."

"However, you have to admit my grandmother, her friends, and I have been right about quite a few things."

He mumbled something that sounded like "beginner's luck."

I didn't want to upset him, so I pretended not to hear. "I've read mysteries for as long as I can remember and while I'm not a professional, like you." I thought a little ego stroking would be good. "I have learned how to find clues and put them together. I was hoping that rather than us working against each other, maybe we could work together. Maybe I can help."

Detective Pitt's eyes narrowed. "What do you mean, help? How exactly are you and a couple of old busybodies supposed to help me?"

I took a deep breath, thankful Nana Jo wasn't here to hear. "I've heard a rumor that maybe . . . you might be in a bit of trouble. . . ."

His face turned red and I thought he was going to explode. He got up so suddenly, he pushed his chair into the wall. He reached across and slammed the door.

I wasn't expecting the sudden movement and jumped.

He leaned down, his face just inches from my face. "What have you heard?"

"Well . . . I heard the new chief wanted . . . well, that he wasn't happy with how you . . ." I fidgeted and hemmed and hawed and tried to find the right words. I was nervous and dropped my purse in my agitation. I bent down to pick it up.

Detective Pitt must have had the same idea because he bent down at the same time. Our heads smacked together. The impact made me lurch back and when I sat up, we collided again.

"Ouch."

I was sitting. So, while the collision was painful, the top of my skull took most of the blow. Unfortunately, Detective Pitt wasn't so lucky. The first blow hit the front of his head, but the second connected with the bottom of his jaw.

He muttered a few expletives that would have made Irma feel right at home with her truckers and then flopped into his chair.

I reached over to help.

He leaned away from me. "Don't touch me."

"I'm sorry. It was an accident." I stared at him as he held the bottom of his chin with one hand and his head with the other.

"What do you want?"

I sat back down in my chair. "I'm trying to help you."

"How? By killing me?"

I'd had enough. "Oh, stop being such a baby." I swatted his hand away from his chin.

There was a small cut on the underside of his chin.

"Open up?" I used my best schoolmarm voice, which brooked no opposition.

Detective Pitt obeyed.

I examined his mouth. "You bit your cheek." I turned around and grabbed my purse and pulled out a small first aid kit I'd picked up at the dollar store. Inside, there was a tiny plastic bag with three cotton balls and a gauze pad. I folded the gauze pad around the cotton. "Open up."

His eyes were wide and his brow furrowed, but he opened up. I shoved the pad in his mouth. "Now apply pressure." I opened the door.

"Where're you going?" The cotton and gauze muffled his words so badly I could barely make them out but used my deductive reasoning to guess what he said.

"I'll be right back. Wait here."

I left and closed the door behind me. I walked down the hall. The good thing about all the time I'd spent in the police station was I knew where every vending machine and water fountain was located. I went to the break room and grabbed paper towels. I took the salt shaker and shook quite a bit of salt into the bottom of a Styrofoam cup and then filled it with cold water. I got a bottle of water from a vending machine and two empty cups and filled another with ice water and then returned.

Detective Pitt hadn't moved.

I handed him the empty cup and the cup with salt water. "Rinse your mouth with the salt water and spit it into the empty cup."

He scowled at me for a few seconds but eventually pulled the bloody wad of cotton and gauze out and did what I told him. The first couple of times, the spittle was dark red, and I could tell by the way he winced, the salt burned. But as he continued the process, it became pinker and eventually was practically clear. When he had rinsed with the entire saltwater solution, I handed him the cup with the water.

I picked up my purse and got some ibuprofen and handed him two pills. "Take this." I filled the cup with water.

He took the pills and drank the water. When he was done, I dumped some of the ice into the water bottle and wrapped it in the paper towels. "Now hold this on your jaw."

He looked pretty pathetic sitting at his desk with a bottle of water on his cheek, but he'd be fine once the ibuprofen kicked in.

"Now, just sit and listen and don't interrupt." I sat down.

He mumbled something that sounded like "menace to society."

I ignored him and took a deep breath. "I heard the chief hasn't been happy with you and wants to fire you."

His eyes got big and he looked as though he wanted to speak, but I hurried on. "I think we can help each other."

There was a question on his face, but he remained silent.

"I know you think I'm a rank amateur who's gotten lucky, but that's not true. I've spent most of my life reading mystery novels, and I'm good at figuring out whodunit. Nana Jo and the girls may be old busybodies, but that's what makes them so good at getting information. They've lived a long time and have a lot of connections. If they don't know someone, then they know someone who knows someone. You were wrong when you thought I killed Clayton Parker. You were wrong when you thought Dawson killed Melody Hardwick, and you're wrong if you think Nana Jo killed Maria Romanov or Mary Rose Pratt."

He sat up. "How do you know her real name?"

"One of the old busybodies told me." I huffed. "Look, I know things don't look good and you have every reason to suspect her, but she didn't do it. I know it and just like I figured out who killed Clayton Parker and Melody Hardwick, I am going to figure out who killed Maria Romanov." I stopped. This conversation hadn't gone at all as I'd planned, but I needed to get my proposition across. "I was hoping that rather than working against each other, we could work together."

"How?" He looked leery.

"You share information with us and—"

"If you're so good, what kind of information do you need from me?"

"Forensic information, the coroner's report, any evidence that will help. I'll share anything we learn in the course of our investigation. What's more, when I figure out who killed Maria Romanov, and I will figure it out, I'll come to you and only you. You'll take full credit for catching a murderer. The chief inspector will be happy and you'll get to keep your job."

I could tell by the way his eyes moved around he was considering my proposition. He shook his head. "Nope. Can't do it. Too risky. If the chief found out I was working with civilians, he'd fire me on the spot."

"He won't find out. We can meet at the bookstore. He'll never know."

"I need to make an arrest soon."

I was desperate. "I guarantee you'll have your murderer by Thanksgiving."

"Thanksgiving? That's only ten days away."

I felt sick to my stomach and wanted to pass out. "I know."

Detective Pitt was fully attentive and sitting up straight. "I can probably stall until Thanksgiving, but what if you don't figure it out by then?"

I wracked my brain. "Then you can always arrest Nana Jo."

Chapter 11

"You told him what?" Nana Jo's voice rang loudly throughout the store.

There was a small book club meeting in a reading corner we set up a few months ago. Heads turned, but no one ventured over to see what the disturbance was about.

"Shhh. I'm sorry, but I had to say something." I'd had a terrifying flutter in the pit of my stomach and buzzing in my ears ever since I left the police station. In my head, I knew Detective Pitt could arrest Nana Jo whenever he wanted. I still felt horrible. "I'm so sorry."

Nana Jo stared at me for what felt like an hour. Then she reached out and hugged me close to her. "It's okay. I knew you were going to try and get him to help you. It was just a bit of a shock to hear . . . well, it was a shock."

I pulled away and looked her in the eyes. "Are you sure you're okay?"

"Yes, I'm fine. I know Stinky Pitt could arrest me any time he wants to." She took my face in her hands. "I also know you're going to figure out who killed her. I have faith in you."

I hugged her and prayed her faith would be rewarded.

We worked the rest of the day in peace and harmony, although I was a bit distracted.

Dawson stopped by after class.

"Hey, there. Congrats on the win," I whispered when he hugged me.

Dawson was fine with being the center of attention on the football field but preferred to stay low-key everywhere else.

"Did you see the polls?" Nana Jo was an avid football fan. "MISU's in the top ten."

Dawson smiled. "Yeah, I saw them yesterday, but I'm not going to let myself think about the polls. Next week's game won't be so easy."

"You'll roll right over them like you've rolled over everyone else," Nana Jo said.

He grinned and pointed to a large bag of laundry. "You mind if I—"

"You don't even need to ask. Go on up."

He adjusted his backpack and picked up his laundry bag and headed upstairs.

Dawson's studio over my garage was small, with no washer or dryer, so he did his laundry upstairs while he studied or baked. I'd thought about installing a compact washer/dryer combo, but when I asked, he said he didn't need it. He was more than willing to go to a laundry mat or do his laundry on campus. I enjoyed having him there. I think he enjoyed it too. He was the son Leon and I never had. His mom died when he was a baby, so I was the mom he'd never known. All in all, it was an agreeable situation.

Nana Jo was an avid mystery reader and was great with customers. I told her she was free to go, but she stayed until closing. It was nice having her there with me. Working side by side was like old times. When the last customer left, we cleaned, reshelved books, and took out the trash.

"Thank you so much for all of the help." I hugged her. "You didn't have to stay, but I really appreciated it. I love working with you."

She squeezed me tight. "I enjoyed myself. I like working and helping people find books they love. Plus, it helped take my mind off things."

"Were you able to get in touch with your friend, the research librarian?"

She looked at her watch. "Actually, I'm meeting Elliot for drinks in thirty minutes."

I smiled. "Drinks."

"Oh, knock it off."

"Does Freddie know you're going for drinks with Elliot?" I grinned.

"No, he doesn't, and if you know what's good for you, you won't tell him either."

"Secrets?" I joked. "That's never good in any relationship."

She stopped reshelving books and looked at me. "I know you're having a good laugh, Sam, but I'm not telling Freddie I'm going for drinks with Elliot for two very good reasons." She held up one finger. "Freddie's been overly protective since this whole thing happened. He thinks someone has it in for me and that's why they're trying to frame me for Maria's murder."

I dropped the smile from my face. "I hadn't thought about it like that. He might have a point."

"No, he does not!" Nana Jo said emphatically. "I agree someone is trying to frame me, but I refuse to believe there is a big conspiracy theory where Maria was killed merely to set me up for murder."

"Well, you know the plot in my last book sort of did just that—"

"Sam, I love your books, but they're fiction, not real life. I'm not important enough. Besides, I know I can be irritating, but I doubt I've irritated anyone to that extent."

"I don't know. You can be pretty irritating," I joked.

She swatted my butt.

"Okay. I concede your argument. What's the second reason you aren't telling Freddie about Elliot."

"I don't think of Elliot as anything more than a friend. I don't tell Freddie when I go out to drinks with my girlfriends. Why should I have to specifically mention when I go out for drinks with a guy friend?"

I looked at my grandmother with a new respect and awe. "You're right. If Elliot is truly nothing more than a friend, I agree. His sex shouldn't matter." I squinted at my grandmother. "Except that Elliot used to be more than just a *friend.*"

"That was over a long time ago, long before I met Freddie."

"Be careful."

"Oh, I will. Besides, I've got my peacemaker just in case."

That's what I was afraid of.

Nana Jo left and I headed upstairs. As I reached the top of the stairs, my phone vibrated. I saw my sister's face on the screen.

"Hello—"

My sister, Jenna, had a loud voice. Perhaps it was honed over her years of speaking to jurors in the courtroom. Whatever the reason, her voice was loud. When she was upset, it was even louder. On a cell phone on a Caribbean island where I could hear the rhythmic beat of steel drums and snatches of tourist conversation in the background, she sounded even louder. Combine everything together and I literally had to hold the phone about six inches from my ear to protect my eardrums.

"What happened? I got fourteen messages from you to call. We have poor reception on the ship. This better be good. I'm paying a small fortune in roaming charges for this call." She said everything really quickly so the words all ran together and at a decibel level that made my insides quiver.

"Sorry for all the calls. I forgot you were on the cruise." Nana Jo and I talked about whether we should call Jenna or not. She and her husband, Tony, were celebrating twenty-five years of wedded bliss. There wasn't anything they could do and there was no reason to ruin their anniversary with unnecessary worry. We agreed only to call Jenna if things looked dire and if Nana Jo was arrested. However, with my older sister on the phone, I was tempted to spill my guts about Nana Jo as well as our mother's impending marriage. Misery loved company and I felt resentful my sister was enjoying herself while I had to track down a murderer. Instead, I took a deep breath and lied through my teeth. "Sorry about that. I went out with Nana Jo and the girls and must have had too much to drink. I think I called quite a few people that night."

My sister's end of the conversation went silent.

"Hello? You still there?"

She must have hung up.

I took a deep breath and thanked my lucky stars she bought it. She was angry with me, but she'd get over it. With any luck, by the time she got home next week, we'd have this whole thing wrapped up and maybe we'd all be able to laugh about it.

I had three hours before our meeting. After my meeting with Detective Pitt, he'd left me alone in his office with his notepad from his interviews. I read them quickly and took a few notes of my own. I sat down with a cup of tea and read through my notes. Detective Pitt's writing was horrible. In some cases, I'd had to guess what he meant. My own writing wasn't much better, especially given the fact I was under a time crunch. However, I squinted over my notes and tried to make sense of things.

One of the things Detective Pitt's notes helped with was a timeline. After Freddie helped Maria to her room, she attempted to get him to stay. Detective Pitt scribbled a few words near this that didn't take much to translate. Maria made a pass at Freddie, which he declined. Detective Pitt had several personal comments and reminders beside his notes which made for interesting reading.

6:30—Freddie takes Maria to her apartment—*Verified by neighbors

7:00—Horace Evans entered apartment—*Nosy Neighbor

7:30—Horace left apartment–*NN remembered because favorite Britcom was just coming on, Are you Being Served?— Look up Britcom.

8:00—Gaston Renoir entered apartment with food tray— *Same NN

8:30—Denise Bennett entered—Britcom ended and Keeping Up Appearances came on—*Need to look up timetable for PBS station to verify.

8:45—Denise Bennett left apartment—Seen by security guard in elevator—remembers because he didn't want to be caught watching football game on television and JAMU had just scored touchdown to take fourth quarter lead—*Need to check JAMU scores and times.

9:00—Josephine Thomas. Knocked on door—entered— leaves soon afterward—*No verification.

2:00—NN awoken by strange noise—sounded like fireworks—looks down the hall—sees someone head downstairs—doesn't get a good look at face—didn't have spectacles on—*If no glasses, can neighbor be sure of time?

2:30—Denise Bennett knocked—door locked—phoned police—deceased found.

It took me a few minutes to realize NN stood for Nosy Neighbor. I read through my notes several more times but didn't

gain any additional insight. I pulled out my laptop in the hope
that focusing my mind on something else would help organize
my thoughts.

Winston's abrupt exit made things awkward, especially after Clementine excused herself and went
after him. The guests looked at each other for several
uncomfortable moments. Something needed to be
done.

"Perhaps the ladies would join me in the drawing
room for coffee." Lady Elizabeth stood.

Daphne looked relieved, as did Helen Browning.
Jessica Carlisle looked a bit like a deer caught in the
headlights of a motor car but eventually stood.

In the drawing room, Lady Elizabeth sat in the
same seat she had earlier in the day, near the fireplace. She'd left her knitting bag and pulled the needles and yarn out and knitted. Daphne sat in a chair
directly across from Lady Alistair Browning, who sat
on the sofa next to Lady Elizabeth. Jessica Carlisle
stood by the fireplace.

"Lady Alistair, how are things in Kingsfordshire?
It's ages since we've been in that part of the country." Lady Elizabeth smiled.

Lady Alistair sat very stiff and straight. "The
weather's been abysmal. The caretaker's run ragged.
James spends so much time away lately. It's left a lot
in the poor man's hands."

Lady Elizabeth glanced at Daphne, who blushed
but said nothing.

"Of course I help out as much as I can, but with such a large estate, there's only so much one can do."

Jessica had been pacing in front of the fireplace, but at the mention of a large estate, she perked up and looked at Lady Alistair for the first time. "How awful for you." She sauntered over beside Lady Alistair and sat next to her on the sofa. "Where is your estate?"

Lady Alistair was the center of attention, a state she relished. "Oh, didn't I say, my son, Lord James Browning, is the fifteenth duke of Kingsfordshire."

"A duke? Randolph didn't tell me he was a duke."

Thompkins and a footman entered with a serving trolley. The butler scanned the room and then silently directed the footman to roll the trolley in front of his mistress.

"Thank you, Thompkins." Lady Elizabeth put away her knitting. "Lady Alistair, would you care to serve or would you like me to do it?"

"If you don't mind, Elizabeth. I would love a cup of coffee."

"I don't mind at all." She poured a cup and handed it to Lady Alistair. Lady Elizabeth poured a cup for Daphne and reached out to hand it to her, but Jessica intercepted it.

"Let me get that for you." Jessica grabbed the cup. She spun around and walked it over to Daphne.

"Thank you." Daphne looked puzzled as she accepted the cup.

Lady Elizabeth turned her attention to Jessica. "Would you care for coffee?"

"Isn't there anything stronger?"

"When the gentlemen join us, I'm sure we can get them to pour you something stronger."

Jessica poked her lip out in a pout that probably went a long way with vapid men like Randolph but didn't do much in a room full of women. After several seconds, she returned her lip to its original position and turned her attention back to Lady Alistair. "Lady Alistair, I can only imagine the toll it must place on someone to have the burden of caring for a large estate."

Lady Alistair's face took on an air of one who suffers silently. "Yes, it does. There are so many concerns between the servants and the tenants that it is a constant burden." She sighed. "However, one must do one's duty."

Lady Daphne giggled. "One most certainly must." She drank more of her coffee. "This is very good coffee." She fanned herself. "Is anyone else warm?"

Lady Alistair stared at Daphne.

Jessica's eyes filled with concern and sympathy for the plight of the aristocrat. She leaned toward Lady Alistair and grasped her hand. "I understand completely. One must *always* endeavor to do one's duty."

Lady Alistair practically preened under the sympathy, although her eyes bore a slight moment of British aloofness when Jessica held her hand.

Jessica was oblivious to any discomfort her action caused. Overcome with compassion, Jessica placed Lady Alistair's hand on her heart. "I wish there was something I could do to ease your burden, your ladyship."

Daphne giggled and slurped her coffee. "It's so warm in here." She fanned herself more vigorously.

Lady Alistair squirmed slightly.

Jessica smiled. "I hope we can be friends. May I call you Alistair?"

Daphne had just taken a sip of coffee when the question was posed. The shock caused her to choke and she spewed the coffee out of her mouth.

At that moment, the door to the parlor opened and James Browning entered in time to see his beloved spew out coffee onto his mother.

Chapter 12

River Bend Chocolate Factory started manufacturing and selling chocolates in River Bend, Indiana, in the early '90s. The company had now expanded to several locations in Michigan, including downtown South Harbor and a small satellite on MISU's campus. The South Harbor store was on a corner lot on the main street downtown. Unlike downtown North Harbor, which was attempting to rebuild itself by catering to an eclectic group of artists, small business owners, and restaurateurs, downtown South Harbor was already well established and bustling. Poised atop a bluff overlooking Silver Beach and the Lake Michigan shoreline, South Harbor's downtown was flourishing. Cobblestoned streets running parallel to the shoreline were lined with brick storefronts that sold fudge, custom made candles, gourmet jams and jellies, and lighthouse-inspired trinkets for tourists. Tourists described downtown South Harbor with words like "quaint," "picturesque," and "charming." Those same tourists used words like "economically depressed" and "derelict" to describe South Harbor's twin city of North Harbor. If the two cities were indeed twins, then fraternal twins were the best they could claim. However, dedicated residents hoped to rebuild North Harbor, not into a reflection of South Harbor, but into its own thriving image.

I pulled in front of the store and allowed Irma, Dorothy, and Ruby Mae to get out so they could secure a good seat while I found a parking spot. Thankfully, I spotted someone heading to their car and I followed them and then waited with my turn signal on while they got into their vehicle, loaded children into car seats, and then backed out of their parking space. I pulled into the recently vacated parking space, which was only a few doors away from the chocolate factory.

I took a look at myself in the mirror before getting out of the car and realized I was scowling. I took a few deep breaths and forced my body and my mind to relax. The resentment between North Harbor and South Harbor existed long before the chocolate factory and most of the other shops opened here. Most of these businesses were new and consisted of small business owners, just like myself, who were trying to live their dreams and earn a living. I shook off the black cloud that always descended on my mood whenever I came to downtown South Harbor and hurried inside the store.

Inside, I took a deep breath and inhaled the warm, wonderful aroma of coffee and chocolate. I allowed the sweet smells to envelope my body and settle my mind. I spotted the girls and hurried over to sit down. The shop was busy, but there were several tables pulled together with coats, jackets, and a small reserved sign.

"What do you want?"

I hadn't even noticed Nana Jo in the corner until she spoke.

She had her cell phone out and was texting.

"How about a hot cup of Earl Grey tea and a chocolate croissant."

Nana Jo typed my order.

"She'll need some help bringing everything." I rose to go help.

"No need." She pointed toward a thirty-something-year-old man behind an espresso machine. "That's one of Ruby Mae's grandchildren. He said he'd bring whatever we needed."

I followed Nana Jo's finger and saw a man with smooth dark skin and a large smile heading our way with a large tray of pastries, brownies, and other delightful-smelling baked goods.

"Wow. That can't all be for us?" I leaned forward and took a deep breath. The sweet aroma of chocolate and sugary goodness entered my nostrils and spread throughout my body.

"Hello, ladies." He set the tray on the table and then leaned over and kissed Ruby Mae's cheek.

She smiled. "This is my grandson, Jason. He's Joyce's boy. He owns this store." The pride was obvious in Ruby Mae's voice and in her eyes as she looked at her grandson.

Jason smiled. "These are on the house. I hope you enjoy." He waved and another young man brought over plates and silverware. Jason made sure we had everything we needed and then returned to work.

"I'm impressed." I looked across at Ruby Mae. "He looks young to have his own business."

"Jason has always been a hard worker. He graduated from JAMU with the guy who started the chocolate factory and worked with him in the original store. He got Joyce to invest when they were just starting. Thankfully, the business took off and now"—she waved her hand—"he's able to reap the benefits of that hard work with his own store."

The young man who brought the silverware carried Dorothy's tray to the table, which contained all of our beverages. Freddie and Judge Miller arrived soon after.

We spent a few minutes socializing and munching on the delicious goodies Jason generously provided, but then we got down to business.

Nana Jo took her iPad out of her purse. "Now, who wants to go first?"

Freddie said his report would be short. His son, Mark, found out Maria had lived at the NARC before moving to Shady Acres.

Nana Jo whistled.

Based on the looks on the faces of the girls, I knew NARC couldn't be good. Only the judge and I looked puzzled.

"What's the NARC?" he asked.

"North Harbor Apartments for Senior Citizens," Freddie explained. "That place is a real dump."

"I've heard it called the Roach Motel," Ruby Mae said. "I don't blame her for leaving."

"The question is, how could she afford to leave?" Dorothy asked.

No one knew the answer.

Freddie shrugged. "I guess I have some more work to do."

"Who's next?" Nana Jo asked.

I raised my hand. "I have some information I'd like to share." I told everyone of my proposition to Detective Pitt and the timeline I got from his notes. They had a few questions but mostly just listened. Just as I finished, I looked up and in walked Detective Pitt.

"Well, I'll be . . ." Nana Jo muttered.

He walked over to our table. "Good evening. Fancy meeting you all here."

He stood awkwardly at the edge of the table. The atmosphere from those seated was frosty.

"Why don't you join us," I said.

"I'd like to, but I'm supposed to be meeting someone." He craned his neck and looked around.

Initially, I was so shocked to see him I hadn't noticed the large red carnation pinned to his coat. His hair was slicked down to his head and arranged so it *almost* hid his bald spot.

He wore short polyester pants, white shoes, and a white belt. The lapels on his shirt and jacket were indicative of the seventies and he wore so much cologne, he overpowered the chocolate.

"There aren't very many seats here." He scanned the room again, noticing all of the tables were filled.

Nana Jo and the girls took sips of their coffee. None of them made eye contact.

I stared at my grandmother with a pleading look.

Eventually, she rolled her eyes, plastered on a half smile, and waved her hand. "Why don't you sit with us until your guest arrives?"

Detective Pitt looked relieved. "Well, maybe I will for a few minutes."

The detective's arrival was awkward. Apparently, no one was sure whether he could be trusted with the information we collected or not. Something needed to be done if we didn't want to be here all night.

"So, does anyone else have anything they'd like to share?" I took a sip of my tea, which was now lukewarm.

Everyone shuffled in their seats.

Eventually, Nana Jo picked up her iPad. "Well, I met with a research librarian friend of mine today." She pulled a sheet of paper from her purse. "So, Maria Romanov or Mary Rose Platt was an only child. She was born in Goshen, Indiana. It looks like her family was Mennonite."

"Mennonite? Never heard of them," Detective Pitt said.

"Mennonites are a conservative Christian sect. They believe in adult baptism, nonviolence, and pacifism," Nana Jo read.

"Well, I'm Baptist and we believe in adult baptism too," Ruby Mae said.

"Aren't they like the Amish?" Dorothy asked.

"I believe the two groups have similarities from their origins. Initially, both groups were agriculture based, but that's not unique." She surfed her iPad. "Amish shun technology and I haven't found anything indicating Mennonites do." She scrolled further. "There are several different types of Mennonites. Some are like other conservative religious groups. Others more closely align with the Amish."

Irma coughed. "I used to work with a woman who was a Mennonite. She didn't cut her hair and wore it pulled back in a bun with a doily on top." She coughed. "She talked funny too."

"Like Josephine said, some Mennonites adhere to the *old* ways. They homeschool their children and speak Pennsylvania Dutch," Judge Miller added.

"What's Pennsylvania Dutch?" Detective Pitt asked.

"It's very similar to German," Judge Miller said. "I believe it's a dialect that stemmed from the German immigrants who settled in Pennsylvania."

Nana Jo returned to her iPad. "Looks like Maria Romanov's family were the ultra-conservative Mennonites. She married a man named, Abraham Rosenberg when she was fifteen. He died from a plow accident about six months after they were married."

"That's hard. She was married and widowed before she was sixteen." Ruby Mae pulled some fluffy wool from her knitting bag.

"Not much else is known about her after that." Nana Jo looked up. "However, my friend is going to keep digging."

I noticed she was careful never to indicate the sex of her friend.

"Who's next?" Nana Jo looked down her nose. "Ruby Mae?"

"I talked to Denise Bennett, the facilities manager. She *claimed* Maria's name had been on the wait list for years."

"Bulls—"

"Irma!"

She put her hand over her mouth and then burst into a fit of coughing.

I couldn't help wondering if some of her coughing spells weren't related to having to choke down obscenities. Maybe we should just let her swear and see if her coughing decreased.

"How is that possible when she had only been at Shady Acres a few months?" I asked.

"Exactly. Enquiring minds want to know." Ruby Mae pursed her lips. "I asked the same thing." She finished what appeared to be a complicated stitch involving a cable hook and a lot of muttering under her breath, before continuing. "She said Maria called and had her name placed on the wait list for a large unit before she moved in." She knitted in silence.

"Well, I hope you told her she better prove it," Dorothy said.

"Nope, I had my son, Donald, call her. He's a lawyer in Chicago."

Detective Pitt rolled his eyes. "Yes, I know."

Ruby Mae looked down her nose at Detective Pitt. "Did you say something?"

Detective Pitt tugged at his collar. "No, ma'am."

"I didn't think so." Ruby Mae sniffed. She hadn't been a school teacher, but she definitely had the schoolmarm look down pat. I guess it came from single-handedly raising nine children and running her own cleaning business. "As I was saying, I had Donald call her and low and behold, I'm going to be moving into Maria's apartment by the end of the week." She looked over at Detective Pitt. "As soon as the police release it."

"It's a crime scene," he said apologetically.

"Is that everything?" Nana Jo looked at her friend.

It was obvious Ruby Mae was holding something back.

Whether it was due to our police presence or something else was unclear.

"There's something funny about that woman. I can't put my finger on it, but she's sneaky. I don't believe for one minute Maria had her name on the wait list years earlier."

Dorothy shook her head. "Maria never mentioned it."

"And she would have mentioned that. She talked about everything else." Irma coughed.

"Donald said Denise Bennett was very evasive when he talked to her. He also said he couldn't find any information on her."

Judge Miller sat up and leaned forward. "Now, that is interesting."

"Why? Maybe she's a good law-abiding citizen with no prior criminal record," Detective Pitt added.

Judge Miller shook his head. "Lawyers have access to a lot of systems that track more than just illegal activity."

"What kind of information?" Nana Jo asked.

"Anything public. This is a technological age and a lot of information is in public databases. If you went to public school, got a driver's license, bought a house, or paid taxes. All of that is public and lawyers can access it."

"Well, that's scary," Dorothy said.

Judge Miller chuckled. "The data is there. As a society, we use technology without question. The issue is, who has access to the data and when. If he went into one of those systems and couldn't find anything on this Denise Bennett, that is very suggestive."

"Suggestive of what?" I asked.

"The absence of data is just as important as the data itself."

"You mean her data could have been erased?" Nana Jo asked.

"Maybe," Judge Miller hedged. "It could have been erased,

or she could be one of those people who fear technology and *big brother* and stay *off the grid*."

"How do we find out which one it is?" Freddie asked.

"Maybe I can dig into that?" Judge Miller looked around. "If that's okay?"

We nodded.

"I haven't had a chance to talk to Gaston yet, but I'll get to him first thing tomorrow." Ruby Mae finished her row of knitting and updated the small plastic row counter attached to one of her needles.

A woman walked into the café. She was short and plump. She had on a bright green dress that was a couple sizes too small and had a large red carnation pinned to her breast. She stood at the front of the store and looked around.

Detective Pitt stared as a stream of red spread from his neck up into his face. He got up. "Well, I have to go. It was nice meeting with you." He hurried over to the woman, slicking down his hair as he walked. When he reached her, he held out his hand and they shook.

"Blind date?" Nana Jo mumbled. "Poor woman."

We stared at the couple for several minutes as they found a table on the opposite side of the café.

"Let's get back to work," I said.

Irma had a date with Horace Evans tomorrow night and said she'd have something to report Wednesday.

"I haven't found out much today," Dorothy said. "I had some appointments, but I'll do better tomorrow."

"You're not alone," Judge Miller said. "I had to teach at the law school today and had a faculty meeting that went a lot longer than it needed to. However, I did learn the coroner's report isn't completed yet, although my sources tell me the cause of death was a bullet to the forehead."

No one made direct eye contact with Nana Jo, but there were a lot of side looks. Now we understood what made her such a good suspect. We sat in silence for several seconds. This time when Irma swore, no one stopped her.

The only response came from Nana Jo. "You can say that again."

So, Irma did.

I wrote earlier, so I didn't plan on writing when I returned from our meeting, but I needed to think. A lot of things were running through my head, and I was afraid my emotions would prevent me from thinking logically, and I definitely needed logic right now. Just as I sat down and prepared to write, my cell phone rang. My sister's picture popped up and I contemplated letting it go to voice mail. Guilt and curiosity won out and I answered.

"You don't get drunk."

I stared at the phone. "What?"

"You get sick, but you've only been drunk one day in your life. So, what's wrong and don't say nothing."

She was right. I had only been drunk once in my life. In college, I certainly tried real hard. In fact, whenever people heard I hadn't been drunk, they tended to take it as a challenge to try and get me drunk.

I took a deep breath and told my sister everything about Nana Jo and also about Mom's impending nuptials. It took about ten minutes to say everything, but I felt better after I got everything out. Jenna was silent the entire time I talked. When I finished talking, I waited. There was probably thirty seconds of silence. I knew she was still there because I could still see her picture on my phone, but I asked anyway, "You still there?"

"Yes."

"You were so quiet I wasn't sure if we lost the connection or if you were on mute."

"I'm still here." More silence. "Do we need to come back?"

"No. There's nothing you can do here. She hasn't been arrested and hopefully she won't be. With any luck, we'll have this whole thing solved by the time you and Tony get back."

"Judge Miller is a good man, but he's retired and can't represent Nana Jo. All he can do is advise, but I deeply respect him and know he'll do what he can to help, but I need you to take down this name."

She gave me the name and telephone number of a criminal defense attorney she said was very good. If things took a turn for the worse, I was to call him, and he'd take care of things until she got back.

"Okay. Got it. Try to enjoy yourself and don't worry about Nana Jo. She'll be fine."

Jenna grunted. "I'm sure she will. It's Mom I'm worried about. Who in the heck is Harold?"

I had no idea. We talked for a couple of minutes and she hung up with a few complaints about roaming charges. I made a mental note to ask my mother what Harold's last name was and got down to writing.

⸻

The drawing room was so quiet you could have heard a pin drop. In fact, it seemed as though everything had stopped, frozen in time. For an instant, no one reacted, then the dam was released. Lady Alistair looked outraged.

Daphne stared wide-eyed but then belched. "Terribly sorry."

Jessica's lips twitched as she suppressed a smile. Yet her eyes flashed triumphant and bright. "Oh my goodness, Lady Alistair."

Daphne snickered. "I'm terribly sorry." She stood and was a bit wobbly. She stumbled to the French doors and opened it. She leaned with her back against the doorframe and moved the door back and forth.

A red flush rose up Lady Alistair's neck and into her face. She looked apoplectic as though she would explode. "You . . . you . . . oh." She stood up and turned to stare at Daphne. "You're impossible and completely unsuitable. You may have bewitched James, but I can see you were raised in a barn."

Jessica snickered.

Daphne stuck out her tongue, kicked off her shoes, and stumbled outside.

Lady Elizabeth sat quietly for several seconds and then turned to James. "Would you please check on Daphne? Obviously, she's unwell."

James was already halfway to the door when she spoke. He paused only long enough to nod to Lady Elizabeth before he followed Daphne outside.

Lady Elizabeth rose and stared at Lady Alistair. A flame lit inside Lady Alistair and was evident in her eyes.

"That's quite enough, Helen." Lady Elizabeth's voice was soft, but her tone was as cold as steel. "I won't stand by while you or anyone else insults my niece in that manner."

Lady Alistair stared at Lady Elizabeth. In one instant, the look in Lady Elizabeth's eyes must have quenched the flame in Lady Alistair's.

"Anyone with eyes could see something is wrong with her," Lady Elizabeth said with an edge to her voice that left everyone in the room chilled.

James led a dripping wet Daphne back into the room. He had removed his jacket and she was soaked from head to foot.

Lady Elizabeth walked to her niece. "Are you okay, dear?"

Daphne nodded. Her teeth chattered and she shivered.

"Please help her upstairs," Lady Elizabeth directed.

Daphne took a few steps and then turned to Lady Alistair. "I'm so sorry. I don't know what's wrong with me tonight." Her voice tapered off into a whisper and her eyes filled with tears.

Between Lady Elizabeth's wrath, which was barely contained, James's scowl, and Daphne's tears, a chink seemed to have penetrated Lady Alistair's veneer.

"Well, I'm very sorry, Elizabeth. I didn't mean to insult you in any way." After another glance at Lady Elizabeth's stormy face, she quickly turned to Daphne. "Or to you, Lady Daphne. I hope you are better soon and, of course, no offense was taken."

James helped Daphne out of the room and Lady Elizabeth rang the bell by the fireplace to summon Thompkins.

The butler arrived promptly.

"Thompkins, Lady Daphne is unwell. Can you please have the maid prepare several hot water bottles and a pot of strong tea."

"Yes, m'lady." He bowed and retreated.

Lady Elizabeth sat down. "I don't think any damage has been done to your outfit, but we will, of course, have our butler take a look. Thompkins is a wizard at removing stains."

Lady Alistair breathed a sigh of relief. "I'm sure you're right, Elizabeth. No harm done." She stood awkwardly for several seconds. "But I think I will go and lay down now. It's been a long day with the travel and . . . everything." She fluttered her hands. "I think my nerves are a bit on edge. Will you please excuse me?"

"Of course." Lady Elizabeth spoke politely although there was a stiffness in her spine and a frost in her manners.

Lady Alistair stiffly left the room.

James returned to the room a few minutes later.

The party sat very quietly for several minutes.

Jessica moved next to the duke and sat closer than was necessary. She leaned close to him and put her hand on his leg. "Alistair was just telling us about how hard it is to keep things running on a vast estate like yours. I didn't realize you were a real duke."

James looked uncomfortable and puzzled at the same time.

Jessica didn't seem to notice and leaned closer. "I think Alistair is just splendid."

James stared at Jessica. "I don't know what you're talking about? What does my father have to do with any of this?"

"Your father?" Jessica laughed. "Why, silly, I was talking about your mother, Alistair or Lady Alistair."

"I'm going up to check on Daphne." Lady Elizabeth rose. Just as she reached the door, it opened and Mrs.

Churchill entered. She turned to her friend. "Daphne isn't well. I'm going to check on her."

Mrs. Churchill looked concerned. "Of course, dear." She sat in the seat Lady Elizabeth vacated.

Before Lady Elizabeth went through the doorway, she heard Mrs. Churchill ask, "What did I miss?"

Randolph howled in laughter.

Chapter 13

Nana Jo came Tuesday morning to help in the store. Snickers and Oreo had vet appointments. It was always easier to take them together for grooming, shots, and vet visits. Community Animal Hospital was the only place I trusted to look after my fur babies. It wasn't the newest or the most modern clinic in the area, but I'd pit the kindness of the staff and the compassion of my vet, Dr. Brittain, against any vet anywhere. Oreo had gone to Dr. Brittain since he was eight weeks old and had never known anyone else. Snickers, on the other hand, had lived through my first vet, who I'd chosen because I'd seen him on television. He did a pet segment on the weekend news and I thought if he was on television, he must be pretty good. Silly me. He wasn't a bad vet. However, he suffered from the same disorder that affected many doctors. The *I'm a doctor and therefore I know all, and I don't need to listen to anyone who isn't a doctor* disorder.

When Snickers was a puppy, she had frequent urinary tract infections. In fact, she got them regularly every three to four months. The infections were so common I recognized them without analysis. The only time she urinated in her crate was when she had an infection. So, after a crate incident, I collected a sample and dropped it off on the way to work. I became an expert at collecting urine samples from a skittish toy poodle who was close to the ground. In the evening, I picked up antibiotics on my way home from work. Things went along that way for far too long. I questioned why she got so many and he ran tests. The tests didn't reveal anything wrong. The last time I dropped off a sample, Dr. Know-It-All told me she didn't have an infection. Instead, he told me it was psychosomatic and Snickers had become so accustomed to the UTI process she urinated in her crate and exhibited all the symptoms of an infection without an actual infection.

I might not have graduated from veterinary school, but I knew my dog and recognized hogwash when I saw it. A friend recommended Community Animal Hospital, and I secretly took Snickers to Dr. Brittain for a second opinion. Imagine my surprise when Dr. Brittain called Dr. Know-It-All and asked for the results from the urinalysis. Sure enough, she had an infection. It was slight, but it was there. I was furious and immediately transferred all of her records.

After twelve years, the staff knew my poodles and me well. Snickers always kissed everyone in the clinic and received belly rubs in return. Oreo behaved more like the cowardly lion from *The Wizard of Oz,* lots of barking and then running and hiding behind my legs when anyone approached. Thankfully, Dr. Brittain was used to this and knew how to entice him from under my chair. She entered the room with treats and petted Snickers like she was her long-lost friend, which always drew Oreo out from hiding. He fell for it every time.

Snickers had been coughing quite a bit. Dr. Brittain asked a ton of questions, and I answered, to the best of my ability. She coughed more at night and when she went outside to take care of business. Dr. Brittain listened, her best quality. She examined both dogs but took extra care with Snickers, especially listening to her chest. We discussed the possibility of allergies and she recommended a series of blood tests. Snickers didn't like needles, but she endured. We were about to leave when Dr. Brittain suggested an X-ray, just to be on the safe side and make sure we covered all of our bases. This visit was already pretty pricy, but I decided it was worth it to eliminate all of the possibilities. Oreo and I sat back down and waited while Snickers went in the back. When Dr. Brittain returned, I could tell by the look on her face something was wrong.

"I wasn't expecting this, and honestly, we wouldn't have found it without the X-ray. I'm really glad we decided to do that." Dr. Brittain held up three X-rays and pointed to areas that looked like clouds on a radar.

She pointed and explained Snickers had an enlarged heart, which was pushing up on her trachea when she laid down. "That's what causes the coughing."

"An enlarged heart?"

"She has heart disease. I'm really sorry."

"So, how do you fix it?" I stared at Snickers as she lay at my feet, munching on a biscuit.

"We can't fix it."

I stared at Dr. Brittain. Her lips moved, but, for the life of me, I couldn't tell you what she said. The blood rushed to my head and my heart pounded in my ears. I picked Snickers up from the floor and held her tight.

I don't remember leaving the vet's office, but when I got back to the bookstore, I had a bag with three different bottles of medicine. I went in the back door and upstairs. Snickers and Oreo ran to the counter by the jar where the treats were kept and waited. They stood there looking at me and waited for me to open their treat jar. I opened the jar and grabbed a few dog treats and Oreo made a mad dash for the bedroom. Snickers walked leisurely beside me. In the bedroom, Oreo stood in his crate, tail wagging. Snickers looked at me with her big brown eyes. I picked her up and hugged her tight, just as I had when Leon passed. She let me hug her while I cried, and then she licked my face. She licked my cheeks and then moved so she could lick away my tears. She probably liked their salty flavor. Whatever the reason, she licked my face until I had no more tears. When I was all cried out, I held her up and looked her in the eyes.

"Look, Leon's gone, and I can't take another loss right now. So, you're just going to have to suck it up, little poodle girl."

I don't know if she understood me, but I used the term of endearment Leon always used.

She licked me again.

I believed she understood.

I worked on autopilot the rest of the afternoon. Nana Jo noticed I was distracted but thankfully didn't ask about it. I was sure if I had to think about Snickers and the possibility of losing her, I would have burst into tears. We were just about to close when the door opened and a familiar face came in.

"Hello, Mr. Evans." I tried to keep the chill out of my voice, but, even to my own ears, my greeting sounded less than welcoming.

Horace Evans forced a pained smile and pantomimed brandishing a sword. With dramatic gestures and a serious voice, he said,

> "To be, or not to be: that is the question:
> Whether 'tis nobler in the mind to suffer
> The slings and arrows of outrageous fortune,
> Or to take arms against a sea of troubles,
> And by opposing end them? To die: to sleep;
> No more; and, by a sleep to say we end
> The heartache and the thousand natural shocks
> That flesh is heir to, 'tis a consummation
> Devoutly to be wish'd. To die, to sleep;
> To sleep: perchance to dream: ay, there's the rub."

We applauded.

He bowed. "*Hamlet* act three, scene one."

Horace Evans was short, not more than five feet four. He had a large, bald head and usually wore a beret. His face was bare, except for a pencil thin moustache and a rather artistic goatee. He was always immaculately groomed and stylishly dressed. Today he had on a camel-colored overcoat, brown leather gloves, and a matching beret with a white ascot. On most men an ascot would look ridiculous, but on Horace it seemed appropriate.

He bent down on one knee in front of Nana Jo and took her hand. "I deserve nothing better than to be, in the wonderful words of Ebenezer Scrooge, boiled in my own pudding with a stake of holly through my heart. Can you please forgive me?" He kissed Nana Jo's hand.

She stood very still and stared sternly at Horace.

"Please, Josephine, my knees aren't what they used to be."

Nana Jo smiled. "Get up, you old fool, before we have to call an ambulance."

We helped Horace up from his knees.

"Thank you, dear lady. Does that mean I am forgiven for caving into coercion and you will delight us by resuming your role as Eudora Hooper and rejoin our merry band of players?"

"That depends."

"On what, dear lady? Anything? Whatever you want, I am your servant. A larger dressing room? Your name in lights? Just name your price."

"I want to know why you gave the part to that no-talent hack in the first place."

Horace turned red and hung his head in shame.

"I think you owe me that," Nana Jo added.

Horace nodded. "You're right." He took a deep breath. "I gave her the role because she blackmailed me."

I was expecting Horace to say he caved in to the cravings

of the flesh and gave her the part in exchange for sexual favors. I'd seen how she used sex appeal during the rehearsal.

Nana Jo whistled. "What'd she have on you?"

Horace's face turned deeper red. "Many years ago, I did something foolish." He raised his head. "I paid the price for my folly, but she knew."

Nana Jo and I exchanged looks. I wanted to delve deeper, but the pain in his eyes and the set of his chin told me he wasn't ready to elaborate on what his "folly" entailed. Besides, I was pretty sure I knew a way to find out.

Nana Jo paused. "Okay, I'll do it."

A look of relief washed over his face and he bent low and kissed Nana Jo's hand.

Horace stayed a few minutes and thanked Nana Jo profusely until she kicked him out, promising to show up at rehearsal later that evening.

I locked the door after he left and continued my routine. I reshelved books and cleaned in silence.

"You going to tell me what's wrong?" Nana Jo asked as we cleaned.

I shook my head. "Nothing's wrong. I'm fine."

"Baloney. I can tell by your face you're not fine. Now, put that book down and tell me what's wrong."

I started talking, but then the waterworks started. In between blubbering and incoherent babbling, Nana Jo got the gist of the problem. She wrapped her arms around me and, for the second day in a row, I laid my head on someone's shoulder and cried like a baby.

Nana Jo allowed me to cry myself out. She soothed and listened while I blathered on. When I'd cried myself out, I lifted my head and saw tears in her eyes, which started my tears again. We cried together for a while until the back door opened and Dawson came into the store.

He stood for a few seconds and stared at us, his eyes wide, and a look of fear and concern crossed his face. "What's wrong?"

We looked at his face and burst into laughter.

Dawson looked even more concerned when we went from tears to laughter in less than sixty seconds.

Nana Jo recovered first. "I expect the emotions of the past few days have finally caught up with us."

Dawson looked skeptical but was smart enough to nod and let it go. He went upstairs.

Nana Jo left for rehearsal and I went upstairs. I had a date. Dorothy's granddaughter, Jillian, was dancing the lead role in a production of *West Side Story* at MISU. Frank and I were going to meet up with a bunch of people at the college to show our support and then have dinner. Dawson started spending a lot of time with Jillian after she and her friend, Emma, helped clear him from murder. Last I heard, my nephew Zaq was dating Emma. I stayed out of my nephews' love lives. The relationships never lasted long enough for me to get attached. In fact, I stopped trying to remember their names. However, I couldn't help hoping things worked out between him and Emma. She was a nice girl.

The musical was wonderful. Jillian's portrayal of Maria was brilliant. I'd seen her dance before, but this was the first time I'd heard her sing. She had a strong, clear voice which was perfect for this role. The actress who played Anita, Maria's friend, had a classically trained voice. While she was a very talented singer, her voice didn't go with the mood of the musical. Jillian received a standing ovation.

We went backstage after the performance and congratulated all of the actors. Jillian was, of course, the center of attention. While she was gracious, she was also humble. I noticed Dawson hung back in the shadows, practically disappearing while Jillian was lauded with praise.

Dorothy was a proud grandmother and took tons of pictures. Zaq and Emma mingled with the other students and seemed to be enjoying themselves. Even Frank ran into someone he knew and got into a long conversation about fishing. My mind wandered while they discussed rods and flies. I noticed Dawson in a corner, contemplating a large piece of contemporary art hung from the ceiling of the Hechtman-Ayers Performing Arts Center.

I strolled over to him. "What's bothering you?"

He shrugged. "I'm just not good at this."

"Not good at what?"

"Small talk. Mingling. Mixing with complete strangers."

"Okay. However, there are tons of people here you do know like me, Dorothy, Frank, Emma, Zaq, and, let's not forget, Jillian. Yet you aren't talking to any of us."

He shrugged again. "I guess I'm not feeling very talkative tonight."

I glanced around and found a bench in a quiet corner and guided Dawson to the bench. "What's really bothering you?"

He looked down and sat with his hands together. When I refused to break the silence, he leaned back. "I don't know. I guess I'm just feeling out of place. I don't belong here."

"That's because this isn't your world. It's Jillian's. Singing, dancing, performing is what she loves to do, and she's good at it."

"I know. That's what I'm afraid—"

"Ah . . . now I see said the blind man."

"No. I mean, I . . . don't belong here. I don't fit in here. I'm just a dumb jock from the wrong side of the tracks. I don't know the first thing about ballets or musicals or any of the things she likes." He waved his hands around. "This artsy stuff is . . . it's not me."

"And you're afraid she'll figure out you don't know anything about her world and then she won't like you anymore," I said softly.

He nodded.

"Dawson, I have a revelation for you. I'm pretty sure Jillian knows you don't know anything about ballet or musicals or art and she likes you anyway."

"But for how long? She's good. She's really good. She's not going to want to hang around here forever. She's going to go to a big city and go on the stage and she'll meet people. She'll meet someone who knows about all this stuff and shares her same interests."

"Have you talked to Jillian about this?"

He shook his head.

I prayed for the right words to help settle his mind. "It's certainly possible Jillian will want to move away and pursue her dream. She may even meet someone else."

"So, we should probably just end it now before things get too serious."

"You could do that. Or, you could ride the wave and see where it leads."

He stared at me with a puzzled expression. My metaphors were a bit mixed up, so I took a deep breath and tried to figure out what I wanted to tell him. "You know that sign I have in my living room— *'If you always do what you've always done, you will always get what you've always got'?*"

He nodded.

"Do you know what that means?"

He nodded slowly. "I guess so."

"It means you have to take chances in life. If you want your life to be different, you can't be afraid. You have to take chances and do something different. You didn't want to be like your father. You wanted something different for yourself. That's why you went to college, right?"

He nodded.

"Well, the same thing applies to life and love. There are no guarantees. Things may not work out between you and Jillian, but what if they do? You can't just give up because you're afraid one day she might decide she wants more than you're able to give her. You can't let fear hold you back."

We sat quietly for several moments.

"There's one thing I can tell you. When you really care about someone, you can show that by at least trying to spend time doing the things that are important to them. I'm guessing Jillian isn't the world's biggest football fan," I said.

He smiled. "She doesn't know the first thing about football."

"Yet, she goes to your football games. She watches football with you."

He grinned. "Yeah, she does."

"She does that because she cares about you, not because she loves football. You can show her you care about her by attending her performances and at least trying to mingle with her friends and support her."

"You're right." He heaved a sigh and stood. "I'm going to mingle." He grinned. "You coming?"

I shook my head. "I'm going to rest my feet a bit longer."

He turned to walk away but hesitated. Then he bent down and gave me a hug and whispered, "Thank you."

I hugged him back and tried not to get weepy.

Frank walked up as Dawson was leaving. "Is this a private party or can anyone join?"

I patted the bench.

He dropped down next to me. "You okay?"

"I'm great."

"Sorry about that."

I raised an eyebrow.

"You know, the fly-fishing thing. I wasn't trying to exclude you. I was—"

I held up a hand. "No problem. I didn't leave because I felt excluded." I leaned close and whispered, "I have a confession to make."

He raised an eyebrow and waited.

"I can't resist a good sale. My three favorite words are "take an additional . . ." In fact, I can spot a sign like that traveling seventy miles an hour on I-94. When it comes to shoes, my feet will actually shrink while I'm in the store to fit whatever sizes they have."

He laughed.

"I'm serious." I held up my leg to show I had removed my right shoe. "I swear these shoes fit perfectly in the store. They were half-priced and there was a purple sticker on the box which meant an additional 75 percent off. They practically paid me to take the shoes. I couldn't leave them in the store and allow someone else to get the deal."

He shook with laughter. "I can't believe you bought shoes that were too small because they were on sale?"

"I'm telling you, they fit in the store. Unfortunately, my feet always return to their normal size once I get out of the store." I reached down and massaged my foot. "They were so cute. Maybe they'll stretch, but right now they are rubbing a blister on the ball of my foot and pinching my pinky toe."

He laughed and reached down and took my foot and massaged the ball of my foot. We sat there for several moments. I might have moaned, I didn't really know. My eyes were closed. I opened them when I heard laughter.

"Are you going to be able to walk to the car or do you need me to carry you?" he joked.

"I can walk, but I'm not going to be able to wear these shoes now that my foot is back to regular size." I kicked off the other one and put them in my purse.

He stood and pulled me to my feet. "Now I know why you carry such a big purse."

I patted my supersized purse. "Just like the boy scouts. I'm prepared for any emergency; although, if I'd been thinking, I'd have slipped a pair of flats in here too."

I waited in the lobby while Frank went to get the car.

"Are you leaving already?" Jillian met me in the lobby.

"I am. I'm not as young as I used to be, and my feet are killing me, but you were wonderful tonight. I really enjoyed the musical."

She smiled and then looked around. "Would it be okay if I came by your store tomorrow afternoon? I was hoping I could talk to you about something." Her eyes darted around quickly.

"Of course. You're always welcome."

She gave me a quick hug and then hurried away.

Frank pulled up to the building and I hurried outside and into the car. We decided to forego dinner, since even the most casual dining establishments had standards that required patrons to wear shoes. Instead, we picked up Chinese takeout and went back to my place for fine dining while we curled up on the sofa in my living room and watched *Murder, She Wrote* reruns.

I'm not sure what time Frank left. I woke up around midnight with a drool-soaked pillow under my head and a warm blanket covering my body. Snickers was curled up in a ball in the crook of my knees and Oreo was keeping my feet warm. When I stretched, Oreo hopped up and walked up my body, pausing only long enough to make a couple of turns on Snicker's neck, which generated growls from her. Then he walked up my body and stood on my chest. Both dogs tended to confuse my body with a runway and pranced up and down whenever they wanted. The only difference was Snickers liked to stand facing me so she could lick my face. Oreo liked to stand facing my feet and used his tail like a fan. He paused on my chest and fanned my face.

I disentangled myself from the blanket and the poodles. Frank had left a note. Apparently, he took the poodles out before he left. I looked around and saw he had also disposed of the leftovers. He wrote a few nice words that brought a silly grin to my face and warmth to my cheeks. I was wide-awake now. I needed something to focus on, something other than Frank Patterson, so I went to my laptop.

Randolph laughed so hard tears rolled down his face.

Jessica looked around the drawing room. No one made eye contact. Her facial expression changed from confusion to anger. She paced in front of the fireplace. She walked hard; so hard the two Paris vases filled with flowers vibrated with each step. Arms crossed, she scowled at Randolph. "I don't see what's so bloody funny."

Randolph staggered over to her. "Of course you don't. You're a bit too common to realize the social gaffe you just made." Randolph stroked her cheek.

She swatted his hand away. "Why don't you tell me, if you're so smart."

Randolph picked up the large volume of *Burke's Peerage* Lady Daphne had left on the table. "You probably should have read this, but then reading isn't your thing is it?" He flopped down on the sofa, crossed his legs, and took a sip from his glass. "Let's see, where to begin." He paused to take another drink, then settled back. "It's a matter of protocol when addressing the peerage. There are five grades of peers: duke, marquess, earl, viscount, and baron." He waved his hand toward Lord William. "Lord William Marsh was the eldest son of the seventh duke of Hunsford." Randolph tipped his head back and mused. "It will take far too much time to go into the British rules of entailment, so let's just say upon his father's death, Lord William inherited the entire lot. He inherited the title, the land, the money." In a quietly sarcastic tone he continued, "If there is any, he got the lot. He became the eighth duke of Hunsford." Randolph made a dramatic bow in Lord William's direction, sloshing his drink on the sofa.

Lord William fidgeted in his seat as he filled his pipe. His face looked red and his gaze darted around the room.

"Lady Elizabeth was the daughter of a duke and she married a duke and is therefore a 'lady,' referred to as Lady Elizabeth or Her Grace." He drained his glass, walked over to the bar, took a bottle of scotch, and refilled his glass. He then walked back to the sofa and sat down. "Now, where was I?" He took another sip. "Ah, yes. Now, that's all great if you're the eldest son. However, younger sons get royally gypped when it comes to titles and inheritance. They get nothing, not even the honor of being called by a lofty title."

"Titles aren't everything. It's the man that's important," Lord William blustered.

Randolph applauded. "Said every man fortunate enough to have a title."

Mrs. Churchill frowned. "Randolph, do be quiet."

Randolph smiled. "But, Mother, I'm just getting to the crux of the matter." He sipped his drink. "James FitzAndrew Browning, fifteenth duke of Kingsfordshire's father, was *not* the eldest son. His brother, Albert, was the lucky duck who inherited. Unfortunately for Albert, he never married and had no children, so when he kicked the bucket, his nephew, James, inherited."

Jessica stopped pacing and stared at Randolph.

Randolph smirked. "Since Helen Browning was married to a younger son and not the heir, she is referred to by her husband's name, Lady Alistair. Therefore, my dear, Alistair was her husband's name, not her name.

Jessica blushed. "Bugger."

Randolph laughed.

Jessica glared at Randolph. "You bloody idiot. You could have told me before I made a fool of myself."

Randolph smiled. "Sorry, dear. I haven't known you long enough to prevent that. We would've had to have met in the nursery. How was I supposed to know you'd make a fool of yourself by throwing yourself at the first titled trousers you ran into?"

Jessica fumed. She snatched the glass from Randolph's hand and flung the liquid in his face. She turned and stomped out of the room, dragging her boa behind her.

Randolph wiped his face with a handkerchief. He stood. "This concludes your evening entertainment. I hope you enjoyed the show." He picked up the bottle of scotch. He bowed, swayed slightly, and walked out of the room.

Chapter 14

"Sam, are you asleep?" Nana Jo tapped lightly on my bedroom door.

If I had been asleep, I wasn't now. "No. Come in." I glanced at the clock on my nightstand and pushed myself into a sitting position as I reached over and flipped on the lamp by my bedside.

Nana Jo came in wearing flannel pajama pants and a nightshirt with Maxine, the feisty Hallmark greeting card lady, that stated, "I'm a real morning person . . . after about 11:30."

I smiled every time I read that shirt. There were a number of similarities between Maxine and my grandmother. Both were spirited, cynical, and outspoken.

"I'm sorry to bother you, but I just got a frantic call from Irma. She's on the verge of hysterics and begged me to come."

"Did she say what was wrong?" I looked for my house shoes as I got out of bed.

"No. Would you mind driving me—"

"Of course not." I pulled on a pair of blue jeans and tucked my nightshirt into my pants and pulled a sweatshirt over my head. "Just let me take the poodles outside."

"Thank you, honey." Nana Jo turned and hurried to her room to get dressed.

Neither Nana Jo's entrance nor conversation and the lights had roused Snickers from her bed. She was close to fifteen now and few things roused her anymore, except opening the refrigerator door or unwrapping a slice of cheese. Oreo went on alert and sat up in his crate but hadn't bothered to bark. When I opened his crate, he bounded out and pounced on my legs as he ran in circles. I had to pick Snickers up and carry her. A low growl indicated she wasn't pleased.

My only regret in my loft was the walk downstairs to let the dogs out. As the poodles aged, I found them less inclined to run up and down the stairs too. Since they were toy poodles and weighed less than ten pounds each, I counted carrying them as weight lifting.

It was mid-November and the early morning air was chilly with a strong breeze off Lake Michigan. Oreo didn't take nearly as long as usual to find a blade of grass worthy to sprinkle. Snickers wasn't particular. She squatted where I placed her over the threshold. From inside, I could see steam rising from the grass where Oreo took care of his business and from his nostrils as he posed with his leg hiked in the air. Both were done and back inside quickly.

Nana Jo and I were off to the retirement village within minutes.

There wasn't much traffic during daylight hours and virtually none at three in the morning. In fact, most of the traffic lights stopped working after ten in North Harbor and just flashed yellow to allow the few people out and about after dark to keep moving as quickly as possible. The main road followed Lake Michigan, but the fog rolling across the lake hid it from view. We didn't talk during the fifteen-minute ride, but the silence was companionable.

At the retirement village, the night security recognized

Nana Jo and waved as we walked down the hall toward the elevator.

Right before we got to the elevator, I heard a sound.

"Psst."

We turned and saw Irma hiding by the wall. She motioned for us to come.

"Irma, you better be dying to drag us out of bed in the middle of the night," Nana Jo said.

"Shoosh. Follow me." Irma hurried down the corridor, looking over her shoulder like a scared rat. She led us to an apartment which I knew wasn't hers. Without hesitation, she twisted the knob, opened the door, and entered.

Nana Jo and I followed her inside, through the living room, and into a bedroom. She stood back and pointed.

On the bed was a man.

Nana Jo scowled but walked up to the man and stared down.

"Is he dead?" I whispered the question, but in the dead of night, the words reverberated around the nearly empty walls and sounded like a shout.

"Yep." Nana Jo looked at Irma. "Did you kill him?"

"Of course not." Irma's pride was insulted and she straightened her back, pushed her shoulders back, and held her head high. Unfortunately, her actions had the result of opening the baby doll negligee she'd been clutching at her throat and setting her off on a coughing fit that wracked her body and echoed around the room like a canon. The negligee was barely covering her assets. It was sheer and left nothing to the imagination. With six-inch red hooker heels and a tiara on top of her jet-black beehive, Irma Starczewski might have been attractive if it weren't for the eighty years of wrinkles and sagging skin that covered her one-hundred-twenty-pound frame.

"Who is he?" I asked.

"Magnus von Braun. He hasn't been here long. In fact, I

think he moved in a couple of weeks ago." Nana Jo looked at Irma. "You work pretty fast, don't you?"

"Don't start with me, Josephine. What are we going to do?" Irma asked.

"We?" Nana Jo stared. "I'm not sure where you're getting *we* from. Sam and I just got here."

Nana Jo was a little harsh, but Irma had a tendency to whine. Years of heavy smoking left her voice raspy and deep, and I knew Nana Jo had no patience with whiners under the best of circumstances, and this was definitely not the best circumstance.

Irma fidgeted with the tie of her negligee and repeated her question. "What are we going to do?"

"Go down the hall to Freddie's room and ask him to join us." Irma didn't budge.

"Well?" Nana Jo stared at her.

Irma dithered. "What if he's still out there?"

"Who?" Nana Jo asked.

"The killer," Irma said as if she were talking to a dim-witted child.

"Then you'd better run." Nana Jo turned to take in the scene of the crime.

After a moment of hesitation, Irma stomped down the hall. She stomped as well as any woman could in six-inch heels.

Nana Jo turned to me. "She needed a job. She was working on my nerves."

"You're sure he's dead?" I already knew the answer but asked from a need to hear a living voice.

Nana Jo placed her hand on the dead man's wrist. I suspected that was just to kill time. "Oh, yeah. He's dead. You don't live seventy plus years without recognizing death when you see it."

When I looked closely at his face, I could see in his eyes the thing that gave him life was already gone.

"Come here." Nana Jo leaned down close to his face. "Take a whiff."

As I leaned over Magnus's body, the faint odor of bitter almonds was barely perceptible over the overwhelming scent of whiskey. "Almonds."

Nana Jo nodded.

I quickly looked around the room, careful not to touch anything. Considering Magnus von Braun had just moved to Shady Acres, there wasn't much to look at. His apartment was larger than some of the others I'd seen. He had a living room area with a sectional, coffee table, end tables, and lamps. The bedroom was sparsely furnished with a bed, dresser, and folding chair. There were several boxes in a corner of the room and a couple of paintings on the wall. I wasn't an art critic, but the pictures appeared to be really good quality. On his dresser was a small open wooden box with medals and commendations from the war. On top of the dresser were a few framed pictures and two glasses of whiskey. Despite the elapsed time frame, Magnus von Braun was recognizable due to a distinctive birthmark on the left side of his face. The photo was of a young Magnus from the Second World War.

Nana Jo leaned down and looked closely at the photos. "Unless my cataracts are acting up, that's Magnus shaking hands with Hitler."

I leaned in and stared at the photos. She was right.

We heard Freddie and Irma coming into the room.

He took in the situation in a split second. "Did you touch anything?" Even though he whispered, Freddie's voice carried.

"Of course not. I'm not stupid," Nana Jo said with dignity but ruined the effect by sticking out her tongue.

Hiding a grin, Freddie turned to Irma and told her to go down the hall and notify the administrator.

"Freddie. I just don't know how I could go that far all

alone," Irma whined and looked coquettishly at Freddie. Even in the dark room, I could tell she was batting her eyelashes.

"Irma Starczewski, you stop this nonsense at once. Pull yourself together and march down that hall this minute, or, so help me God, I'll wrap that negligee around your neck and strangle you." Nana Jo delivered the threat and followed it up with a look that showed she meant business.

With a humph, Irma turned and left.

"Now, what's this all about, Josephine?"

"I have no idea. I was sound asleep when Irma called and begged me to come. Sam and I got in the car and rushed over here."

"Did she kill him?" Freddie asked.

I shrugged and looked at Nana Jo.

She was silent for a minute. "She says she didn't."

"You believe her?"

Nana Jo nodded. "Irma may be a sex-starved ex-beauty pageant drama queen, but she's honest. She says she didn't, and I believe her."

Freddie grunted and looked around the room, much as I had done, being careful not to touch anything.

"We should probably wait outside." He reached into the pocket of his bathrobe, pulled out a cell, and dialed the police.

"A man's been murdered at Shady Acres Retirement Village. Send word to Detective Pitt. It may be related to an ongoing murder investigation."

Freddie answered a few questions and then hung up. He held out an arm, directing us to leave the room. Nana Jo was first. She headed for the door but veered off and pulled out her cell phone. She quickly snapped several pictures of the dresser and the room. Then she turned and snapped a few pictures of Magnus. When she was done, she hurried from the room.

I followed behind. When I got to the door, Freddie

grabbed my arm and whispered, "Is she involved in this?" He inclined his head in Nana Jo's direction.

It was only then I noticed the muscle twitching at the side of his forehead, the thin line of his lips, and the rigidity of his shoulders and back. In his eyes was concern.

"No." I shook my head and watched as he slowly allowed his body to relax.

When we got out of the room, Freddie closed the door and stood guard outside. "You better go wait in the lobby. The police'll be here soon."

Nana Jo faced Freddie. "I'm not involved with Magnus von Braun."

Freddie hid a smirk. "You heard that?"

Nana Jo smiled. "Just because I'm old doesn't mean I've lost my faculties," she joked but then said in a serious tone, "I'm only dating one man at the moment, and that's you. I have no idea what happened to Magnus von Braun, but it has absolutely nothing to do with me."

Freddie nodded and pulled her close and gave her a kiss and a hug.

Nana Jo smiled broadly. "But I did notice Irma looking at you like some love-sick kid."

"Well, you're the one that sent her to my room in the middle of the night," Freddie joked. "I nearly had a heart attack when she grabbed me."

Something in Freddie's eyes made me ask, "Where exactly did she grab you?"

Freddie grinned. "Let's just say a see-through negligee and tiara aren't the only way Irma grabs a man's attention."

The police arrived in mass and herded us like cattle into the dining room, where we were asked to wait until we could be questioned. Thankfully, it was now time for breakfast and Gaston had prepared a very lavish meal which helped to distract us.

"That smells awesome." Detective Pitt drooled.

"Hmm. It is delicious," Nana Jo said between mouthfuls.

Freddie was also enjoying a large three-egg omelet, fresh croissants with butter and strawberry preserves, coffee, and fresh fruit.

Ruby Mae and Dorothy were there, and they ate heartily too. Irma stared into a cup of coffee which had long ago gotten cold.

Nana Jo walked to the kitchen. After several moments, she returned with a plate heaped full of bacon, sausage, eggs, and toast and placed the plate in front of Detective Pitt.

He nodded a thank-you and then shoveled the food into his mouth as though he hadn't eaten in days. "Been on a diet. I haven't had real eggs in days."

Gaston Renoir was a resident at Shady Acres and a retired chef from one of the best restaurants in Paris. He moved to Michigan to be closer to his grandchildren. When the administration learned of Gaston's culinary skills, they made a deal allowing him to stay for a reduced rate in exchange for cooking for the residents and administrators; it turned out to be a win for everyone.

"What happened?" I asked

Detective Pitt slowed down eating. He looked around the dining room. "You were right. The coroner is almost certain he died from cyanide poisoning. If you hadn't caught that, his death might have been written off as natural causes. He had a bad heart and a host of other medical problems. Turns out he was suffering liver cancer and probably would have been dead in six months."

Freddie nodded and took another drink of his coffee.

"What about his family?" I asked.

"He had a brother." Detective Pitt flipped through a notepad. "A Wernher von Braun. He's dead. The brother had children. Magnus didn't. Early days yet."

I gasped.

"Wernher von Braun?" Freddie asked.

Detective Pitt looked up and noted the looks we exchanged. "What?"

"You've never heard of Wernher von Braun, the famous rocket scientist?" Nana Jo added. "Didn't you pay attention in any of your classes?"

Detective Pitt scowled. "Perhaps you'd care to enlighten me."

"Wernher von Braun was a famous German scientist. He developed the German V-2 missile," I said.

"He was a Nazi." Freddie frowned. "The V-2 missile increased the Nazis' ability to launch bombs that could make their way to England and her allies," he said with a bitter edge in his voice.

Detective Pitt shrugged. "That's the brother. What's that got to do with our dead guy?"

Irma looked up. "Magnus was a scientist too. He worked with his brother. They were very close," she said softly.

Detective Pitt looked puzzled. "Okay, so how'd he get here in the United States?"

Freddie looked angry. "The United States made a pact with the devil in order to defeat the Germans."

"He means the Soviet Union," Nana Jo explained.

"We won the war, but the government was afraid of the Soviets. They were afraid they'd get the technology the Nazis developed and become stronger and more powerful." Freddie looked into his cup as though he saw the past. "So, we made our own pact with the devil. We allowed Nazi and Nazi collaborators to enter our country to gain control over the technology."

Nana Jo clasped Freddie's hand.

"Operation Paperclip, that's what they called it," Irma whispered. "Magnus and his brother were brought here and put to work at NASA. They helped develop the Saturn V rocket that allowed us to beat the Soviets to the moon." She coughed.

We stared at Irma.

She looked up. "He told me."

Obviously, Irma and Magnus had gotten close in many ways during the short period of time he was at Shady Acres.

"Sounds like you knew this Magnus guy pretty well." Detective Pitt stared suspiciously at Irma. "Plus, you're the one that found the body. I'm going to need your statement."

Irma nodded.

I looked at Detective Pitt. "Do you think the two murders are connected?"

"What makes you think it's murder?" he asked.

Nana Jo tilted her head. "You've got to be kidding. Two people die a few days apart? Plus, one was killed by cyanide. We told you that."

He shrugged. "It might be murder and might not be."

Nana Jo snorted.

Detective Pitt's face reddened. "He was old and sick. Not just sick. He was dying. The end was in sight. Maybe he took the poison himself."

Dorothy chimed in for the first time. "Suicide? You think he committed suicide?"

Detective Pitt would have had to have been deaf not to have noticed the cynicism in her voice. He colored further. "That's the problem with amateurs. You jump to conclusions."

Nana Jo bristled at the insult. "He didn't leave a note. If he was going to commit suicide, he would have left a note."

Detective Pitt gave her the "you poor deluded fool" look before adding, "Not all suicides leave notes."

That rankled my feathers. "True. But why wait until you move into a new apartment to kill yourself. He could have done that before he came."

That wiped the smug look off the detective's face.

"And another thing, did you notice the smell of whiskey on his breath?" Nana Jo asked.

Detective Pitt shrugged. "So, what? The man obviously had a drink."

Freddie asked. "Where's the bottle? There was no bottle in his room, at least not that I saw."

"Me either. The murderer made a mistake by removing the bottle," I added.

Irma's face went pale and her hand shook.

It was clear Detective Pitt hadn't noticed, but he wasn't going to let that stop him. "We'll find the bottle." Detective Pitt used his fork to scrape the last morsels from his plate, wiped his mouth, and took a long swig of coffee. He burped and patted his stomach. "Thanks for the grub. You guys eat pretty well around here. Lobster Thermidor and pâté are outside of my sphere." He looked around. "What's a place out here cost, anyway?"

Nana Jo and the others frowned. Finally, Nana Jo said, "It depends on where you live. I bought my house when they were just building, so I got a great deal."

Ruby Mae frowned. "Again, it also depends on where you live. They have single family detached homes like Josephine's. But, there are also town houses, which are less expensive, condos, and apartments."

Detective Pitt looked around. "Nice place. I bet even the apartments are more than a North Harbor cop can afford."

I frowned, not only at the impropriety of talking about money, but something else was bothering me. "Wait. What do you mean Lobster Thermidor and pâté?"

"That's what that Maria woman had for her last meal." He pulled his notepad out and flipped the pages. "Pâté." He looked up. "That's duck liver." He scowled. "Supposed to be some kind of delicacy." He looked at his notepad. "Creamed spinach soup, Lobster Thermidor, grilled asparagus, rice, and pears poached in champagne." He flipped his notepad closed. "Too rich for my blood."

Everyone looked at each other.

He rose and looked at Irma. "Now, I need your statement."

She looked pale but got up and followed Detective Pitt out of the room.

The rest of us sat quietly for several seconds.

"Lobster Thermidor?" I asked. "Gaston is a good chef, but I didn't realize he was serving such fancy food."

"He isn't. At least not to the likes of us," Nana Jo said.

"I'm absolutely going to be talking to Gaston today," Ruby Mae said with a hardened look in her eyes.

I felt a twinge of pity for Gaston, but it passed quickly.

You think we need to call the judge?" Ruby Mae inclined her head in the direction Detective Pitt and Irma just went.

"It wouldn't hurt," Nana Jo said.

Freddie smiled. "I already did. He'll be here soon."

"Something's bothering you, Sam." Nana Jo could always read me like a book.

"It's just something you said." I turned to her. "You said Magnus moved here to be close to his grandchildren."

She nodded. "That's what we were told." She turned to Dorothy and Ruby Mae.

They all nodded.

"But Detective Pitt said he never married and didn't have any children." I looked around.

"You think he was lying about why he was here?" Freddie asked.

I shrugged. "It sure looks that way, but I can't figure out

why. Why not just say, I wanted to be closer to Lake Michigan? I like the town? Heck, he could have said he pulled the name out of a hat. No one would have cared."

Dorothy nodded. "Good point."

"Maybe Irma will know," Ruby Mae added. "Looks like she and Magnus were pretty cozy."

Nana Jo shook her head. "Irma gets cozy with a lot of men."

"Maybe, but she looked upset," I said. "I think Ruby Mae's right."

"So, we're all on the same page in thinking both people were murdered?" Dorothy asked.

I looked around the table. Everyone nodded.

"Then we need to find out all we can about Magnus and any connections between him and Maria."

"Did you notice those paintings in his room?" I looked at Nana Jo.

She nodded.

"I'm no art specialist, but they looked expensive." I sipped my coffee. "Not too many people can afford expensive art."

"Dorothy, does your sister still own that art gallery?" Nana Jo asked.

Dorothy nodded. "Yes, but how—"

Nana Jo pulled out her cell phone. "I took some pictures of the art. I'm sending them to you now." She made a few swipes. "In fact, I'm sending them to all of you. Never know who may need it."

We nodded.

"Freddie, can you and the judge work on finding out as much as you can about Magnus von Braun?" I must have looked nervous.

He smiled. "Don't worry, Sam. I can be objective. I know how to keep my personal feelings about Nazis under control."

Nana Jo patted his hand.

"Nana Jo, I need you to get your reference librarian working on that photo of von Braun with Hitler."

"Sure, but what am I looking for? That photo was taken a long time ago."

"True, but the feelings and emotions from World War II run deep." I tried not to look at Freddie. "Maybe there's someone here who saw the picture on his dresser and wanted revenge?"

She nodded. "Okay. I'll see what Elli . . . ah, my friend can come up with."

"Can we stop dancing around this and just call Elliot by his name?" Freddie looked at Nana Jo. "I've known Elliot Lawson for years. He's a blooming idiot." He sipped his coffee. "Glad your taste in suitors has improved."

Nana Jo swatted his arm playfully. "You've known all this time and never said anything?"

Freddie grinned. "Maybe I was waiting on you to say something."

I looked at the two of them and smiled. They would be okay.

I turned to Ruby Mae. "When you're talking to Denise Bennett, see what she knows about Magnus von Braun."

Ruby Mae nodded. "I'm good friends with the lady who lives across the hall from Magnus. I'll see what she can tell me."

I nodded. "I'm going to invite Detective Pitt to tea."

They looked at me as though they were waiting for the punch line in a joke.

"I want to see his notes and get what information he has about the causes of death for Magnus and Maria."

"I'm pretty good friends with one of the security guards, Larry Barlow," Freddie said. "Larry used to be a cop in New Buffalo. He owes me a favor. If I can get to him before Detective Pitt, I'm sure he'll make a copy of the footage from the security cameras."

I nodded. "Great."

Freddie got up and walked out of the dining room to get to his friend before he gave away the security footage. He returned quickly. "He'll have our copies in less than twenty minutes."

"Everyone has their assignments." I looked around.

They nodded, but there was a feeling of sadness and gloom over the crowd.

"Don't worry. We'll figure this out." I tried to sound encouraging, but the glumness had started to reach toward me. "What's wrong?"

"I guess the reality of this mess has finally settled on us," Nana Jo said. "I've been so busy thinking about myself and clearing my name, I hadn't thought about what Maria's murder and now Magnus's murder really mean."

"What do you mean?" I asked.

"This is a murder investigation. Two people we all knew are dead." Ruby Mae shivered. "We may not have liked them, but we knew them."

"The main gates and the doors at Shady Acres are locked after nine. Whoever murdered Maria and Magnus had to be in the building before nine," Freddie explained.

"That makes the pool of murderers a lot smaller," I said.

Freddie looked grim and got very silent.

Nana Jo squeezed his hand. "Unfortunately, it means the murderer is also someone we know."

The reality finally hit me. They were worried about not only the two people who were murdered, but the murderer. Whoever killed Maria and Magnus was part of their community. Shady Acres wasn't just a sterile retirement community. It was their home, and the people who lived and worked there were family. This wasn't going to be easy.

We talked a bit longer, but I didn't stay long. I still needed to shower and get ready to open the store. Before I left, I tracked down Detective Pitt and invited him to come by the store around four. I promised him tea and one of the cranberry orange scones Dawson whipped up yesterday. I could tell by the look on his face he wasn't thrilled, but I knew the scone would entice him. I suspected, while Detective Pitt might need our help, he wasn't thrilled about not being 100 percent in control. Next time, I'd make sure he felt like it was his idea.

Nana Jo and I drove home and hurried to get ready for the first customers. As a new business owner, I had a lot to learn. Customer service, marketing, sales, advertising, and legal concerns were big components of running a business. I'd read tons of books and attended workshops galore. However, forecasting sales was still a challenge. I didn't know how many customers to expect the week before or the day after a holiday. For some reason, I expected low volume before the holiday. I supposed I thought people would be getting ready to cook or travel home for the holidays. When I was a teacher, the week before Thanksgiving was spent wrapping things up and getting ready for break. The volume of customers in the store today was larger than I expected and Nana Jo and I were busy.

Jillian arrived a little after noon. I barely had time to acknowledge her presence before another wave of customers arrived. When I pulled my head out of the shelves long enough to think, Jillian was running the cash register.

"I hope you don't mind, but you were helping a customer and Mrs. Thomas was busy taking care of the delivery truck, and there was a line," Jillian explained as she deftly checked out customers.

"Of course not. Thank you so much."

She smiled. "My pleasure."

We worked nonstop for the next two hours. Jillian read mysteries, but she wasn't as knowledgeable as Nana Jo and I. However, she excelled at customer service and was a very hard worker.

"You're amazing. Thank you so much for helping out. I don't know what we would have done without you," I said.

Jillian smiled. "I had fun. My first job was working at Robertson's Department Store during the Christmas season."

Robertson's was a family-owned department store.

"Plus, I waitress during breaks."

"I intend to pay you for today."

She protested, but I was adamant.

"Maybe we could come up with a trade." She wiped the counter and avoided eye contact.

"What kind of trade?"

"Can we talk?" she asked softly.

"Of course."

We made our way to the back of the store and sat down at a table in a corner. Once we were seated, Jillian looked at everything except my face.

I reached out and touched her hand. "Is anything wrong?"

She took a deep breath. "Not wrong. Not exactly. It's just, well . . . Emma and I and a few of the kids from school have started reading mysteries and we thought it would be nice if we could maybe meet and have a book club, like the Sleuthing Seniors."

The Sleuthing Seniors was the mystery book club Nana Jo and the girls started earlier this year.

"Certainly. Just tell me what day and time you want to meet," I said. "But, I don't think that's what you really wanted to talk about. Is it?"

Jillian paused. "I saw you and Dawson last night and well, I was wondering if you knew what was wrong? I mean some-times he can be such a . . . such a . . . guy. He keeps everything

bottled inside and he won't talk to me." She paused. "Some-
times I'm not even sure he likes me. He won't talk."

I thought quickly. What should I say? What could I say?
The last thing I wanted was to get in the middle of their relationship. I cared about Dawson and I liked Jillian a lot too.

"I think you and Dawson need to talk to each other. I don't
think it would be right for me to share things he's told me."

She colored and shook her head. "Of course not. I shouldn't
have asked. I'm sorry." She hurried to stand up.

I grabbed her hand. "What I can say is this. Dawson's been
through a lot. He hasn't grown up in the same nurturing environment as you. He's had to hide his feelings from his dad to
protect himself. You may have to prod and poke to get him to
open up. Only you can determine if it's worth the extra work
or not. But, if you do, I think you may find a real gem inside."

She sighed. "I like him a lot."

"Then talk to him."

She nodded and then looked up and smiled. "Thank you. I
will."

I hugged her.

"Thanks, Mrs. Washington. I appreciate you letting our
book club meet here and if you ever need help in the store,
just let me know. I'd love to help out sometime."

I gave her another tight squeeze. I wasn't sure when she'd
have time to work in the store, but I appreciated the offer.

Detective Pitt arrived just as we finished talking. Things
were still pretty quiet in the store. He took Jillian's seat, she
went to the office Jillian went to get the treats I'd set aside, and
I got mugs from behind the counter. "Tea or coffee?"

"Coffee," he said.

Jillian returned from the office and brought a plate with
two cranberry orange scones and placed them in front of us.

I put an individual coffee pod into a single-cup brewing machine and smelled the deliciously strong aroma of Columbian coffee beans. The scent was wonderful and my stomach growled. My head knew if I drank coffee this late in the day, I'd be up all night. However, I allowed my stomach to overrule my head and made myself a cup too.

I placed the mugs on the table and sat down. Detective Pitt had already devoured one of the scones and was starting in on the second one. Apparently, he was under the impression both were intended for him.

"Hmmm. This is delicious." He mumbled around a mouthful of ooey gooey deliciousness.

"Thanks. Dawson's been experimenting with a variety of scone recipes. These aren't the traditional ones you'd get in the UK, but they've been very popular." I sipped my coffee and tried not to feel too bitter about missing out on the last of the scones.

"Whadaya want?" Detective Pitt wet his finger and used his saliva like glue to pick up the crumbs from the plate.

"I would like to see your notes from Magnus von Braun's murder investigation. I would also like to see the cause of death and forensic information."

He halted with his finger halfway to his mouth and stared. "Is that all? How about payroll records for the entire North Harbor police force or the government's sealed reports from Area 51?" he asked sarcastically.

"Look, we both know it's highly unlikely these two cases aren't linked."

Detective Pitt rolled his eyes. "You amateurs are always jumping to conclusions. I've got an old man with a mountain of crud wrong and a death sentence hanging over his head. *IF* he died from cyanide poisoning, there's nothing that says he didn't take it himself. Faced with all of his medical worries, many people would have done themselves in. Myself included."

My blood pressure rose as I got angry. I took several deep breaths to settle my nerves and stalled for time by taking a few sips of coffee. I plastered a smile on my face, which I hoped didn't look as fake as it felt. "Detective Pitt, I know you don't believe that. You're just pulling my leg."

He frowned and stared blankly.

"Besides, we have a deal." I sipped my coffee. "I'm sure if you could get the credit for solving two murders and not just one, the chief will be even more impressed with you. Who knows, you might even be able to get a raise or a promotion. Or both." I took another sip. Surely, he couldn't be naïve enough to believe this nonsense.

"You think so?" Detective Pitt sat straighter and taller in his chair.

"Definitely." Apparently, he did believe it.

He pulled out his notepad and I used my cell phone to snap pictures. I could review them later.

When I finished, Detective Pitt stood. "Maybe I'll come by tomorrow for more of those scone things. Those were pretty good." He raised one eyebrow and nodded knowingly.

I took the look to mean he'd bring the reports I asked for tomorrow.

The rest of the afternoon was uneventful. Dawson arrived right before closing. He and Jillian went to his apartment to study. Those two had a lot of talking to do.

When I got a chance to relax, I went upstairs. I ate the leftover Chinese food Frank put in the fridge and reviewed Detective Pitt's notes. Nothing stood out. Irma had a rendezvous planned with Magnus. They ate oysters and drank whiskey. Irma was afraid she'd be accused of murdering him and dumped the oyster shells and whiskey bottle in the hall trash. The crime lab was testing the shells and the bottle for cyanide. Detective Pitt didn't believe they'd find it, based on the comments in his notes. He tracked Magnus's movements, which included a visit to his oncologist and the pharmacy, lunch in the dining room, and plenty of rest. Detective Pitt questioned whether he was resting from his chemo treatment or resting to prepare for a night of carnal pleasure with Irma. A flash of Irma in her baby doll negligee passed my mind and I blinked rapidly and shook my head to get rid of the image. No one Detective Pitt interviewed saw anyone enter or leave Magnus's apartment. If he'd been killed, Irma was the most likely suspect. I was thankful he wasn't accusing Nana Jo of murder, but I'd grown quite fond of Irma and the girls and the alternative didn't bring me peace either.

I read and reread the notes, but no matter how many times I read them, I couldn't find a solution that pointed to anyone other than Irma. Her behavior in getting rid of the oysters and the bottle of whiskey was suspicious. However, I could believe Irma to be a fool a lot easier than I could believe her to be a cold-blooded murderer.

∾

Lady Elizabeth, James, and Daphne were the only members of the household who came down to the dining room for breakfast. Mrs. Churchill always ate breakfast in her room, and Lady Alistair had requested a tray as well, according to Thompkins. The gentlemen, Winston, Lord William, William Forbes-Stemphill, and Leopold Amery, ate in the wee small hours of the morning and went shooting in the weald. Guy Burgess and Anthony Blunt cried off shooting and were, according to Thompkins, still in bed. The household staff refused to enter Randolph's room before they were summoned, and Jessica hadn't responded to the maid's knock and her door was locked from the inside.

Lady Elizabeth ate a light breakfast of dry toast and strong tea. She always enjoyed the quiet of the morning. James was enjoying a hearty traditional English breakfast of fried back bacon, sausage, poached eggs, grilled tomatoes, fried bread, bubble and squeak, and black pudding. She looked across at her niece and frowned at Daphne's poor table manners. Elbows on the table, body slouched, with her head in her hands, Daphne's eyes were red and she had dark circles underneath.

Daphne sat slumped over a cup of strong tea.

Lady Elizabeth's frown turned to one of concern. "Are you sure you're feeling okay, dear? You look as though you're coming down with something."

Daphne shook her head and winced at the pain the effort caused.

Fork midway to his mouth, James halted. He looked at Daphne. "She's right. You really don't look well."

Daphne slowly turned her head toward James. She glanced at the eggs on his plate and swallowed several times. After several seconds, she whispered, "I'll be fine."

Thompkins entered the room and walked to Lady Elizabeth's chair. "M'lady, Mrs. Churchill is request-ing your assistance."

"Certainly." Lady Elizabeth rose from her chair.

Thompkins took two steps and then stopped and turned back. He coughed discretely. "Perhaps Your Grace should come too."

James rose. "Of course."

Thompkins led the way upstairs to one of the

bedrooms. Outside of the door was a footman, a maid, and Mrs. Churchill.

The maid stood at the back of the hall. She looked like a frightened and timid mouse. The footman was a young, fresh-faced youth, who looked as though he couldn't have been more than sixteen. He was tall and lanky and his uniform had obviously once belonged to someone larger and shorter.

"Elizabeth, thank goodness." Mrs. Churchill turned to James. "I see you brought James. Good thinking."

"Actually, bringing James was Thompkins's idea." Lady Elizabeth looked around at each of those present. "I'm afraid I don't really understand what's going on."

Mrs. Churchill looked at Thompkins.

He coughed. "I thought perhaps you might want to explain the situation."

Mrs. Churchill nodded. "Quite right. Ethel knocked on the door to deliver breakfast, but she hasn't been able to get a response." She glanced at the frightened maid, who flushed and nodded. "The door is locked from the inside and no amount of pounding has been able to wake the girl."

James and Lady Elizabeth exchanged glances. James moved to the door and pounded while twisting the knob.

"Do you have another key?" Lady Elizabeth asked.

Mrs. Churchill shook her head. "Unfortunately, we haven't seen the spare key for years. Inches had a master key, but he's in Scotland with a broken ankle."

James pounded on the door and rattled the knob.

Mrs. Churchill turned to the footman. "Get Randolph."

His eyes got wide and a flash of terror crossed his face. To his credit, he hesitated only a second, bowed, and hurried to Randolph's door. He knocked timidly at first, then louder when there was no answer. He turned and looked back at Mrs. Churchill, who merely stared impatiently, tapping her foot. Thompkins, who stood behind Mrs. Churchill, nodded slightly and the footman turned back to the door, turned the knob, and entered the room. After several moments, they heard Randolph swearing at the young footman and a crash as a glass was flung at the wall and shattered.

The footman hurried out of the room into the hall.

Mrs. Churchill yelled, "Randolph, come here at once."

After several moments, a bleary-eyed Randolph stumbled into the hall. His face was flushed and he frowned. "What the bloody hell is going on out here?"

"Randolph, watch your language," Mrs. Churchill said. "We're concerned your friend may be ill. We've tried to rouse her. Perhaps you can get her to open the door."

Randolph stared at his mother for several seconds, then walked to the door. He grabbed the knob and twisted. He pounded on the door and winced from the effort. "Jessica, open the bloody door." He waited. "Jessica," he yelled.

After a few moments, he stepped back. "Do you have Inches's keys?" He looked from his mother to Thompkins.

Thompkins shook his head. "No, sir."

"You know we haven't seen the spares for ages," Mrs. Churchill replied.

Randolph threw his hands up. "Then I guess you'll have to break the door down if you want to get her out." He stepped aside. "Have at it." He looked at James.

James moved to the door and rammed it with his shoulder several times. However, the solid oak door was sturdy and barely wobbled under the effort. After several more attempts, he stopped. "Is there another way in?"

"There's no connecting door into that room. The only way in will be from the outside," Mrs. Churchill responded.

James looked at the footman. "Get a ladder and meet me outside."

The young footman nodded and hurried down the back stairs. James followed him.

Lady Elizabeth turned to Thompkins. "I think you'd better call a doctor."

Mrs. Churchill said, "You'll find Dr. Wilson's number on a notepad down by the telephone." She turned to the maid. "Ethel, please help Thompkins."

The maid curtsied and hurried toward the back stairs.

Thompkins bowed and followed the maid.

Randolph stood with the two ladies in the hall for a few seconds after everyone else left. "I'm going back to bed." He pulled his robe closed, walked to his room, and closed the door.

Mrs. Churchill looked after her son and then shook her head. "I knew he'd bring nothing but trouble. I wish he'd stayed away."

"I don't know if you can blame Randolph for this, Clemmie."

"Of course I can. He brought her here."

Mrs. Churchill frowned. She paced back and forth in front of Jessica's door. She walked hard, but there was more than anger reflected in her face. Her gaze darted around as she paced. She wrung her hands and her posture, normally very erect and straight, was slouched.

"What's wrong, Clemmie? What are you afraid of?"

She stopped pacing and looked down at the ground. She took a deep breath. "I don't know. I just have a horrible feeling."

Lady Elizabeth took a step toward her friend but stopped as she heard movement behind the closed door. They stood and listened intently for several seconds. They heard a click and watched as the knob turned and the door opened.

James stood in the doorway, blocking the two ladies from entering.

Lady Elizabeth could tell from the look in James's eyes something was terribly wrong. "What is it, James? Is she ill?"

James shook his head. "She's dead."

"Dead?" both ladies whispered.

Lady Elizabeth recovered first. "How?"

"Murdered. We have to call the police."

"Murdered? Are you sure?" Mrs. Churchill asked. "Could it have been an accident?"

James shook his head. "No accident. She was shot."

Mrs. Churchill clutched at the collar of her gown. "Could she have done it herself?" she whispered.

James shook his head slowly. "Whoever did it took the gun. She was murdered."

Lady Elizabeth stared at James. "But the door was locked."

He nodded.

Mrs. Churchill looked from James to Lady Elizabeth to James. "The window?"

"It was locked too. I had to break the glass to get in."

"Then how?" Mrs. Churchill whispered.

He shrugged. "That's what the police will have to tell us."

Chapter 15

"Well, that's going to be a challenge," I said out loud. "A locked room murder? No idea how I'm going to get out of that."

Snickers and Oreo were apparently accustomed to hearing me talk to myself. They didn't move until I stood. Then they both stretched as though they'd just worked a twelve-hour shift.

I put on a simple mid-length black dress I'd ordered online. It was a sheath style with three-quarter-length sleeves. The bust had a crossover detail that created a sweetheart neckline. It was made of rayon, nylon, and spandex and clung to my curves in all the right places. Best of all, the dress was machine washable. It was simple, and basic. Every woman needed a basic black dress, so my sister told me. I liked the fact the dress wasn't covered in lace, tulle, chiffon, or anything super fancy. However, it could be dressed up with the right jewelry and accessories. It was cold, so I pulled on a pair of warm tights rather than panty hose and a pair of ballet flats rather than pumps.

The retirement village had planned a memorial service for Maria and we were going to snoop around for clues. Magnus's death earlier today had thrown a bit of a monkey wrench into the plans and left the staff scrambling. However, Dorothy called earlier to say they were including Magnus in the memorial. Two birds with one stone, or something like that.

I surveyed myself in the mirror and grabbed my purse. Dawson and Jillian were sitting at the kitchen table. Textbooks and papers were strewn over the surface. The apartment smelled of peanut butter and cinnamon. There was a plate of peanut butter cookies and snickerdoodles on the table, along with two large glasses of milk.

Dawson whistled.

"You look really nice, Mrs. Washington." Jillian spoke around a large mouthful of cookie. She quickly swallowed and washed it down with milk. "Sorry about that."

"Thank you. You two are great for my ego." I grabbed a snickerdoodle. "These are delicious."

Dawson smiled. "I found the recipe in an old cookbook I bought at the antique store across the street." He shoved a snickerdoodle in his mouth. "I love old recipes."

I grabbed a glass from the cabinet in the kitchen and poured some milk, then returned to the table.

"Me too." I took a peanut butter cookie this time. It was warm and soft and fine crystals of sugar glistened on top of the traditional crossed fork pattern. I bit into the cookie. It was not only beautiful to look at but delicious as well. "I think this is one of my favorites."

"Mine too," Jillian said.

I noticed the two were seated side by side. Their faces shone with a brilliance that spoke volumes. Without being told, I knew they had talked and everything was good between them. I smiled as they returned to their studies. I wasn't sure where the relationship was going, but, for now, they were happy and that was good enough for me.

I couldn't coax the poodles away from the table. The possibility of cookie crumbs was too great a temptation to miss. I left with assurances from Dawson and Jillian that they would take them out after I left.

Nana Jo was to meet me at Shady Acres, so I drove off alone to the memorial service.

At Shady Acres, pictures of both Maria and Magnus were enlarged and placed on easels in the front lobby. One of the larger reception rooms was filled with people and I headed in that direction.

The room was spacious and included a large fireplace, a bar, and tons of seating. Residents could reserve the space for parties. I'd attended a couple of tailgate parties here a few years ago when JAMU played in the Cotton Bowl. Today, people mingled and spoke quietly while chamber music played over the sound system.

I scanned the room for familiar faces. Ruby Mae was seated on the sofa, with her knitting bag next to her. She had a glass of wine and a plate of hors d'oeuvres on the coffee table in front of her. A large woman with long, curly gray hair sat next to her. She wore a brightly colored loose-fitting dress with a lot of gaudy jewels. She had rings on every finger and bracelets on both arms and even around her ankles. She had a plate of food on her lap and held a glass of wine. If the flush in her face was any indication, this wasn't her first or second glass. She leaned close to Ruby Mae and whispered intently. Her eyes darted around the room as she spoke.

Judge Miller and Freddie stood nearby. They were talking to a man who looked familiar, but I couldn't place him. It wasn't until he looked up at someone who entered the door and waved that I recalled where I'd seen that gesture before. He was the security guard I'd seen a hundred times sitting behind the desk. In casual clothes and without his uniform, he blended in with everyone else.

Irma stood near the bar. In un-Irma-like fashion, she was

alone and not flirting with any of the men. Not only was she not flirting, but something else seemed wrong. Again, it took a bit of staring until I realized what it was.

I jumped when Nana Jo whispered in my ear. "Looks weird to see Irma when she isn't tarted up like a five-dollar hooker, doesn't it?"

I was so intent on figuring out what was different with Irma, I hadn't seen Nana Jo's approach. "Now that you mention it, I'd have to say yes."

Irma was dressed conservatively in dark slacks, loafers, and a pullover.

"I don't think I've ever seen her when she wasn't wearing six-inch heels." I accepted the glass of wine Nana Jo gave me and took a sip.

"That's probably the only pair of flat-heeled shoes she owns." Nana Jo shook her head. "On anyone else, it would be okay, but somehow, on her, it just seems . . . odd."

"I know. I was thinking the same thing. What's wrong with her?"

She shrugged. "Been that way ever since she came back from talking to Stinky Pitt."

"Maybe he scared her."

Nana Jo laughed. "It'd take more than Stinky Pitt to scare Irma Starczewski. She's made of sterner stuff."

"Something's definitely different about her." I looked at Nana Jo. "Maybe you could talk to her and find out what's wrong."

She nodded. "I'll talk to her as soon as this shindig is over."

"Who's Dorothy talking to?"

Nana Jo glanced casually around the room until her eyes rested on Dorothy. "That's Denise Bennett."

Denise Bennett was a tall, slender woman. She was probably in her mid-forties, although her hair was completely white and she wore it cut short.

"Oh, I remember her now. What do you know about her?"

"Not much. She doesn't talk about herself. She's hard-working and efficient. Runs this place like a drill sergeant."

We were so engrossed in our conversation neither of us had noticed Freddie and Judge Miller had joined us until Freddie spoke. "I had drill sergeants in the Marines with more compassion than that woman."

"A bit of a martinet when it comes to following the rules. The restrictive covenant for Shady Acres states you can't shake your rugs outside. Can you believe that?" Nana Jo looked at each of us.

I smiled. "Did she catch you shaking your rug outside?"

Nana Jo nodded. "Apparently one of my nosy neighbors reported me. She told me if I got caught doing it again, I'd get a fine." Nana Jo's eyes flashed. "Well, I showed her."

Freddie pulled out a handkerchief and wiped his face, but he wasn't able to hide a smirk or the twinkle in his eyes.

"What did you do?" I asked.

"The next time I needed to shake my rugs, I brought all of them here into the lobby and shook them out right there."

Judge Miller nearly choked on his drink. Freddie and I laughed.

"She never questioned me about shaking my rugs outside again." She grinned.

We chatted for a few minutes and then split up to mingle.

Memorial services weren't my favorite places, but Nana Jo and the girls had taught me a lot could be learned. I sauntered around the room looking for a familiar or friendly face. In a quiet corner of the room, I saw an old gentleman sitting alone in a chair. He wore a yarmulke. He looked angry, which was probably why he was alone. I couldn't have said what drew me to him, but I sat down in the chair opposite him and smiled.

He looked up but didn't return my smile.

The force that drew me to this angry man vanished as soon

as I sat down. I tried to compel myself to speak, but no words came. I sat there in the hostile silence, unable to speak. After what felt like an hour, but was more like a few minutes, I noticed tears stream from his eyes. I reached in my purse and pulled out a packet of tissues and silently shoved several into his wrinkled, gnarled hands.

I half expected he would fling the tissues back at me. Instead, he used them to dab at his eyes and blew his nose. When he recovered, he looked up and thanked me.

I reached out and squeezed his hand.

"You must think I'm a foolish old man," he said with a heavy Eastern European accent.

I shook my head. "No, of course not. There's nothing foolish about grief." I squeezed his hand again. "Did you know Maria or Magnus well?"

His eyes widened and he stared at me. Then he shook my hand away. "Grief? You think I shed tears of grief for that . . . that animal?" He spat on the floor. "No. These are tears of thanks. I thank God that I have lived to see my enemy vanquished. God has smote my enemy at last and I rejoice."

The violence of his words left me staring with my mouth opened. "What did she do to you?"

He tilted his head, puzzled. "She? I barely knew that silly woman. No, I speak of him." He inclined his head toward the picture of Magnus on an easel. "Magnus von Braun."

It took a few seconds for me to recover. "You knew Magnus von Braun?"

He smirked. "Not personally, but I was a scholar. I studied. There is a verse in your Christian Bible, 'You will know them by their fruits.' Yes? I knew Magnus von Braun by his fruit. He and his brother built bombs that destroyed millions. They used men, women, and children as slaves to build their weapons." He pulled up his sleeve and showed his arm. Five numbers were tattooed on his inner arm.

"I'm sorry."

He stared into the distance. "I was fourteen when they took my parents away. I hid with my brother in the woods for months, surviving on berries, squirrels, and other vermin. I learned of a couple in Lisbon who helped children escape to England. We walked miles, hiding during the day and traveling only by night. By the time we arrived, we were nothing more than savages." He paused. "I was too old. Martha Sharp was her name. She was an angel. She tried to get papers to take us both, but I knew the guards would not be fooled. I sent my brother, Aaron, with her on the train. He didn't want to leave me, but I made him go. I told him I would join him one day." He paused.

I waited for him to collect himself. Then I prodded. "Did he make it?"

He had a faraway look in his eyes and a smile crossed his face. "Yes. He made it. Aaron made it to England." He pulled out a wallet and took out a picture and handed it to me. "That's my brother, Aaron, and his wife, Mildred, and their children. Now they have grandchildren and great-grandchildren."

I looked at the picture. It was creased and tattered with dog-eared corners. It was fragile and I handled it accordingly. "He looks happy."

He nodded. "Yes. He was lucky."

I handed the picture back. "But you weren't so lucky?"

He shrugged. "Luck . . . what is luck? I survived a few weeks after Aaron left before they found me. I was sent on a train to Belzec."

I knew from my research Belzec was a death camp in Poland. "Not many people survived Belzec."

He shook his head. "No. I was *lucky*. I survived. But, I cannot forget the things I saw there. I can't forget the stench of it. I close my eyes and I see the horrors." He shook his head. "But as you say, I was lucky. I escaped but was captured and taken to

Dora—Mittelbau in the Harz Mountains." He wiped his face and returned his wallet to his pocket. "From there, I was taken to work the caverns. Magnus von Braun was a monster. I don't forget. I don't forgive. I am thankful God allowed me to live to see him get what he deserved."

I sat quietly, unsure of what to say or do next. This man had a strong motive for wanting to kill Magnus von Braun, but had he killed him? My brain was spinning. Without a thought to the consequences, I blurted out, "Did you kill him?"

He stared for what felt like a minute and then laughed for what felt like ten. "I wish I could take credit for that service to humanity, but unfortunately, I did not. I didn't even know he was here. I was away visiting my grandson in Holland, Michigan." He hoisted himself up out of his chair. "However, if you find out who did, please let me know. I would like to buy them a drink."

I watched as he ambled out of the room. It wasn't until he was completely out of sight I realized I didn't even know his name.

Denise Bennett tapped her glass with a pen to get everyone's attention. She stood in front of the fireplace and waited for silence.

"On behalf of the Shady Acres Retirement Village management and staff, I want to express our condolences to the friends and family of Maria Romanov and Magnus von Braun. We are, of course, extremely saddened when any of our Shady Acres family are taken from us. However, we must recall the good times we spent together. Please join me in raising a glass in salute to our departed friends." She lifted her glass. "To Maria and Magnus. May their memories live on in the hearts of those who loved and cared for them." She drank.

Everyone lifted their glasses and drank. I couldn't help wondering what memories would live on after Maria and Magnus. I'd just learned Magnus was a cruel Nazi responsible for atrocities in building the V-2 missiles, which were responsible for death not only through the exploded bombs, but to the innocent people who were enslaved and forced to work in the mines. My research had given me a very grim picture of conditions for anyone not reflective of Aryan beliefs. Then there was Maria. She was a liar who apparently concocted stories about not only her own life but others to get what she wanted.

Later, I described my encounter with my Jewish friend to Nana Jo. She recognized him immediately. His name was Isaac Horwitz.

The rest of the memorial was uneventful. I stayed about twenty minutes after Miss Bennett's toasts. Everyone mulled around for a bit and then disbursed. On the drive home, I reflected on the evening. Apart from Isaac Horwitz, nothing else memorable happened, at least not to me. I hoped the others would have more to report when we met tomorrow at the bookstore.

I tried not to think about how quickly the days were speeding by and how far away from a resolution I was. Tomorrow was Thursday and exactly one week before Thanksgiving. That meant I had less than one week to clear Nana Jo's name or Detective Pitt would arrest her for Maria's murder. The pressure of that knowledge made my heart race and my breathing was labored. Despite the cold temperatures, I rolled down the windows and let the cold air hit my face.

When I got home, Snickers and Oreo met me at the bottom of the stairs. I let them out before heading upstairs for the night. Dawson and Jillian were gone and the kitchen table was devoid of papers, crumbs, and all evidence of the earlier disarray. There was a plate of cookies on the counter and several dozen in containers for the store. I grabbed two cookies and a glass of milk and headed to my bedroom. I needed to think. Writing and cookies would help expedite the process.

⌒﹏

The local police were called. A short, plump young man with a baby face and dark, curly hair arrived twenty minutes later. From an upstairs window, Lady Elizabeth watched as he cycled up the long, winding driveway and then fell trying to dismount his bicycle when his pant leg got caught in the chain. He looked around to see if he was observed and then wrested his pants from the chain and tossed his bike to the ground. He took a few seconds to straighten his uniform and adjust his cap before he rang the bell.

She heard the footsteps as the constable followed Thompkins upstairs. There was a discrete knock and Thompkins entered.

"Sergeant Turnbull," Thompkins announced and stepped aside for the sergeant to enter the room.

The young man timidly entered the parlor. He started to speak and then appeared to remember his manners and promptly removed his hat and held out his hand. His face was flushed and he looked from Mrs. Churchill to Lady Elizabeth, unsure of which lady protocol dictated he should address first.

Lady Elizabeth stood, extended her hand, and walked toward the young man. "Sergeant Turnbull, I'm Lady Elizabeth Marsh and this is Mrs. Churchill."

He bowed to Mrs. Churchill and dropped his hat.

Lady Elizabeth and Mrs. Churchill exchanged glances.

"I suppose you'll want to see . . . the body . . . uh . . . Miss Carlisle," Lady Elizabeth said.

The sergeant looked puzzled. "Excuse me, m'lady?"

"The young woman who was shot . . ." Lady Elizabeth walked toward the door.

"Yes. Of course." He followed Lady Elizabeth out of the room and down the hall to a bedroom. The footman Lady Elizabeth met earlier and now knew as Albert had been placed on guard duty in front of the door.

"It's just in here." She smiled at Albert.

He smiled, relieved at seeing a familiar face. "Hullo, Duck, am I glad to see you."

Sergeant Turnbull looked anything but glad to see Albert. He blushed and dropped his hat again. "Sergeant Turnbull," he said firmly as he picked up the hat.

"Sorry Duc—ah . . . I mean Sergeant Turnbull."

Lady Elizabeth hid a smile as she unlocked the door and stepped aside so the sergeant could precede her into the room.

Sergeant Turnbull took a few steps into the room and stopped abruptly. He looked at the bed where Jessica lay with a bullet through the center of her forehead. The sergeant turned very pale and then clapped a hand over his mouth and ran from the room, dropping his hat in his haste to leave.

Lady Elizabeth looked around the room while she waited for the constable to return. She noted the window. There was glass on the floor beneath the window James had broken to get inside. She carefully avoided stepping on the glass or disturbing any of the evidence. She glanced around the room. Jessica had clothes strewn all over. She was still wearing the dress she'd worn the night before, but the boa was on the floor, along with other items she had discarded from her suitcase. It appeared Jessica had tried on several outfits before landing on the one she'd chosen. At least, that was the impression Lady Elizabeth got from the disarray. She felt confident the young maid Ethel would have unpacked Jessica's suitcase when she arrived, just as she, or someone, had unpacked hers.

James entered the room. "Thompkins said the police were here." He looked around.

"I believe he was taken ill." Lady Elizabeth turned to face James. "He's young and I doubt if he's ever investigated more than a brawl at the local pub."

"Probably not much more than that happens in sleepy country villages like Westerham." James frowned.

"Agreed, but when a prominent member of the British Parliament has a murder at his country estate, it could mean trouble." She looked around to make sure they weren't overheard.

"I see what you mean."

"Add in a BBC producer and this could ruin Winston."

"Where is Burgess, anyway? I'd expect him to be all over this."

"I believe he and Anthony Blunt drank a lot more than they should. They're still in bed, as far as I know."

James looked at his watch. "It's almost noon."

"Let's be thankful for small favors. We need this resolved quickly and efficiently. We need an expert."

Recognition dawned on the duke's face. "Detective Inspector Covington?"

Lady Elizabeth nodded. "See if you can reach him and I'll check on Sergeant Turnbull."

They left the room. Lady Elizabeth locked the door behind her. She looked at Albert. "Where's . . . ?"

"He's in the loo. Barely made it." His lips twitched as he tried to hide a smile.

"When he's done, can you please send him down to the parlor?"

Albert nodded.

Lady Elizabeth hurried downstairs. Just as she got to the door of the parlor, she saw Thompkins.

"Telephone, m'lady." In response to the question in her eyes, he added, "Lady Penelope Carlston."

Lady Elizabeth hurried to the telephone. "Penelope dear, are you and Victor at the station? I'd completely forgotten you were coming today. Do you need us to send a car?"

"I'm sorry, Aunt Elizabeth, but it doesn't look as though we'll be able to come after all. Victor's great-aunt Prudence arrived unexpectedly."

"Oh dear. I'm so sorry. We were . . . well, we were looking forward to seeing you both."

"Is anything wrong?"

Lady Elizabeth hesitated a half second and then hurriedly responded. "What could possibly be wrong? I know Clemmie and Winston were looking forward to seeing you both. That's all."

"Are you sure? I can gladly pack Aunt Prudence off to one of her other relatives if you need me."

"Don't be silly, dear. Please send Prudence my love and don't worry about a thing. All is well here."

Lady Elizabeth hung up the telephone. She turned and nearly collided with Daphne.

Daphne looked at her aunt. "You better be careful. You know what happened in that book you read to us as children about the little boy who told false-hoods?" She smiled.

Lady Elizabeth patted her nose, took Daphne by the arm, and led her into the parlor. "Let's hope not, dear. I may have to tell a good many more falsehoods before this day is over."

Chapter 16

I loved hosting new mystery book clubs. It felt good to see people who were new to the genre discover a new book or author. Their enthusiasm and excitement were infectious and always reminded me why I did this. Jillian's group was no exception.

Jillian and Emma were the first to arrive. Five other young ladies arrived shortly afterward. All were students at MISU.

I set them up in a quiet space in the back and set out a large plate of Dawson's cookies. I didn't want to interfere, so I made sure they knew where the bathroom was and made a speedy retreat to the main area of the store. Traffic was a bit slow, so I had plenty of time to get caught up on the endless paperwork. I sat on a stool behind the register and propped my laptop on the counter. I had an office in the back of the store but since I was working alone today, I needed to be visible in case customers needed help.

I'd just figured out where I left off when I looked up and saw Jillian standing at the counter. "Is everything okay?"

She fidgeted with the scarf around her neck. "I hate to bother you, but we seem to be . . . stuck. None of us really knows what to do or where to start. I was hoping maybe you could help us get started."

"Certainly." I would take any excuse to get away from paperwork, but, thankfully, this was something I enjoyed. Deep down I knew I should hire an accountant, but I thought it would be too expensive. However, the more I stared at income sheets and tax forms, the more stressed I became. I made a mental note to contact an accountant before the year ended.

I followed Jillian to the back room. The girls were munching on cookies but not saying much.

So, I said, "I have several book clubs that meet here regularly. Most read mysteries or suspense but a couple are just general book clubs. What kind of books do you like?"

A big-boned Amazon of a girl with purple hair raised her hand. "I've seen a few mysteries on television and I enjoyed them, but I don't know a lot about what kinds of mysteries there are."

I nodded. "Well, there are lots of books that fall in the mystery classification. Mysteries fall within a category of Crime Fiction. There are cozy mysteries, police procedurals, historic mysteries, suspense, thriller, and true crime. Within each classification, there are subgenres. So, you can have British historical cozy mysteries or contemporary cozies."

"What's a cozy?" the Amazon asked.

I got in teacher mode. "It's hard to come up with a hard set of rules for any book these days, but cozy mysteries are typically set in a smaller, contained area (think country village or manor house) and they have an amateur sleuth who has to figure out whodunit. Rarely is there violence, gratuitous sex, or bad language."

"Sounds boring," a petite girl with red hair and a brown sweater chimed in.

"They don't have to be boring. The focus of a cozy mystery is on the clues and figuring out whodunit. Agatha Christie was the queen of the cozy mystery. You read a story and the author drops clues in along the way. Does it mean something that the butler had mud on his shoes or the maid lied about being in the pool house earlier? It's a puzzle and you, as the reader, need to put the pieces together to figure it out, hopefully at the same time as the detective."

"I like books that make my heart race and keep me up all night." The red-haired girl added, "I don't mind blood and violence."

"Not all mysteries are cozies. Traditional mysteries can be quite violent."

One young lady dressed completely in black, with black fingernails, black lipstick, and a tattoo of Tigger from *Winnie-the-Pooh* on her neck raised her hand. "I like mysteries, but I also like vampires. Are there any vampire mysteries?"

A couple of girls rolled their eyes.

"There are all kinds of paranormal mysteries. To be completely honest, when you think about it, most books have some type of mystery elements. Charlaine Harris's Sookie Stackhouse books could be considered mysteries."

The Goth vampire lover smiled. "Really? I love the True Blood series. I didn't know it was a mystery."

"Well, the classification is questionable, but if you think about the first book, *Dead Until Dark*, there's a murder that has to be solved. I actually used it when I was teaching high school."

A girl dressed in black leggings with a short plaid skirt and turtleneck, who looked like a beatnik with long hair pulled back into a ponytail, laughed. "There's a lot of sex in those books. I'll bet the students loved it, but I can't imagine the parents were thrilled."

"Actually, my principal was concerned too, so we required

a permission slip from the parents. Most were just happy their kids were reading, and they signed." I looked around the room.

Emma raised her hand. "I don't know about anyone else, but I do *not* want to read about vampires."

A few others nodded.

"There's a couple of different directions you can go with this." I walked around so I could see all of their faces at the same time. "You could all read the same book, which might be a bit challenging if your tastes vary. Or, you could all read different books and share your thoughts."

They looked at each other and nodded.

"I have an idea." I quickly went out to the bookstore and came back with several books and laid them on the table. "These are all books by Charlaine Harris." I held up the Sookie Stackhouse book, which I handed to the Goth girl. I learned later her name was Taylor. I picked up another book. "She also writes an Aurora Teagarden true crime mystery series. This is a traditional cozy mystery about a group of people who study true crimes. It features an amateur sleuth, Aurora Teagarden, who is a librarian in a small town in Georgia." I handed the book to Emma and picked up another one. "This is her Lily Bard series. It's set in a town called Shakespeare, but it can be sort of dark." I picked up another book. "This is the Cemetery Girl Trilogy, which is a graphic novel. This is the Harper Connelly series, which features a woman with a power that allows her to find dead people and share their final moments. The Midnight Texas Trilogy is similar to the Sookie Stackhouse series, but darker."

The girls sorted through the books on the table.

"Is it common to have so many different types of books by the same author?" Jillian asked.

"Not really. Most authors tend to write one particular type of book. Few authors are as diverse and prolific as Charlaine Harris."

The girls each found a book they wanted to read. I suggested they set a deadline for when they wanted to have the book finished, allowing time for schoolwork and time with family during the upcoming Thanksgiving holiday before they reconvened.

They agreed and stayed to finish off Dawson's cookies. Most spent time browsing through the bookshelves. A few asked my opinion. Based on what they told me they liked to read, I steered them toward authors I knew wouldn't disappoint. Almost all of them bought other books. Emma and Jillian were the last to leave.

Jillian kissed my cheek and gave me a hug. "Thank you so much. You were amazing. Have you ever thought of teaching at MISU? You'd be fantastic."

"Thank you. I considered adjunct teaching, but between the bookstore and writing and . . . well, other things, I haven't had much time."

Emma gave me a hug too. "Zaq said you really knew your stuff. I was afraid we'd all be stuck reading about vampires or gruesome serial killer books, but you saved me."

I laughed. "Thankfully, there are so many different types of mysteries, I know there's something to suit just about every taste."

"You should charge for things like this. You spent a lot of time with us." Jillian looked concerned.

"Thank you, but things were slow today, so it wasn't a problem. Besides, I sold quite a few books, thanks to you."

The rest of the day went quickly and before I knew it, Nana Jo and the girls arrived for our meeting. We agreed to meet at the bookstore today.

I waited until everyone arrived before I put the closed sign out and locked the door. I grabbed another plate of cookies from the back and brought them out. Nana Jo made a pot of coffee and everyone sat around the same table the younger crowd had vacated earlier.

Judge Miller picked up a copy of *Secret Rage,* one of the stand-alone books by Charlaine Harris that featured a former model in a small town in Tennessee who got caught up in a string of brutal crimes. "This looks interesting. I might have to read this."

"Consider it a gift."

He smiled. "Then I know I'll be back. You've found my kryptonite."

"Books?" I laughed.

"Not just any books," he joked. "I love grisly mysteries. It's what led me to become a lawyer and later a judge."

Nana Jo pulled her iPad out of her purse. "If it's okay, I'd like to go first."

No one objected.

"First, Elliot researched Magnus and also looked into the photo with Hitler. Magnus was the youngest of three brothers. Sigismund was the oldest. Wernher and then Magnus. The two older boys were not really indoctrinated into the Nazi culture, but Magnus, who was eight years younger, apparently was. He was thirteen when Hitler became chancellor and was part of the Hitler Youth and other fascist organizations." She frowned and pursed her lips as though she'd eaten a lemon. "Magnus was a chemical engineer and pilot in the Luftwaffe. In 1943, his brother Wernher arranged for him to join him in working on the V-2."

"Probably wanted to make sure his baby brother didn't get shot out of the sky by the allies," Freddie added.

Nana Jo nodded. "Probably. Anyway, he found a lot of information about their capture. Apparently the von Brauns didn't want the Soviets to get the missile technology they'd been working on and Wernher tried to make sure all of the reports, as well as his team of scientists, were captured by the Americans. Magnus rode his bike to an American anti-tank division and announced the inventor of the V-2 rocket wanted to surrender to them. The Americans were suspicious but investigated anyway and found out he was telling the truth."

"About this anyway," Freddie said.

"Magnus, Wernher, and the scientist closest to the V-2 surrendered to the Americans and we got all of their documents and files."

"Small consolation for all the people killed by it," Freddie griped.

"True, but at least it didn't end up in the hands of the Soviets or the cold war might have gone differently." She flipped through her iPad. "He came to the United States in November 1945 through that Operation Paperclip Irma told us about. In 1955, he started working at Chrysler. I guess that's when he moved to Michigan. Later, he moved to the UK and worked in London and Coventry. He retired from Chrysler in 1975. Lived in Coventry for a while and then moved back to the States."

Freddie snorted. "That takes nerve, moving to Coventry. That city was destroyed by the Luftwaffe. Have you seen pictures of the bombing? It was—"

"Freddie, stop it. I know you have a lot of passion around World War II, but this isn't helping. Magnus is dead." Nana Jo squeezed his hand.

He nodded. "I know. I'm sorry." He took a deep breath and looked around at the rest of us. "I lost my brother in the war."

We expressed our condolences. Irma sat quietly with her head bowed.

Nana Jo went back to her iPad. "Elliot's still working on finding out what he can about the photo, but he thought it looked authentic. He also looked into Maria's family tree. As

we suspected, there's nothing connecting her to Russian royalty. He couldn't find anything about her medical health, but
then HIPPA laws are pretty strict."

"I might be able to help," Judge Miller said. "I got a look at
the forensic team's report. The police found some medicine
bottles in her room." He pulled out a notepad. "The coroner
says the meds were basically sugar pills."

"You mean she didn't have a bad heart?" I asked.

"Nope." The judge shook his head.

"Why that lying little b—"

"Irma!"

"I agree with Irma," Nana Jo said.

Judge Miller held up his hands. "Hold on. I happen to
know the doctor who prescribed the pills. He wouldn't give
me specifics about Maria. He made it clear he couldn't talk
about her but was only talking in general terms. He gave me a
report on hypochondriacs. Apparently, it can be a debilitating
psychological condition. For some people, their mental belief
in a medical condition is so strong they can make themselves
physically ill."

"Even though there is nothing medically wrong?" I asked.

He nodded. "He told me a story about a man who got
trapped in a refrigerated train car who died of hyperthermia
even though the refrigerator wasn't turned on."

"You mean he froze to death?" Dorothy asked.

Judge Miller nodded. "He believed the refrigeration was
turned on and his body responded accordingly. The mind is
very powerful."

"So, Maria believed she had a heart problem, so she gave
herself a heart problem?" Nana Jo asked.

"Again, my friend wouldn't specifically say he was talking
about Maria Romanov, but what he said was if someone believed they had a heart problem, their body could respond

with the symptoms of a heart problem. However, giving medicine, like say, Digitalis, to someone who doesn't have heart
disease could prove fatal."

"Mystery writers use Digitalis a lot," I mused. "Agatha
Christie and Dorothy Sayers both used it as a lethal poison."

"Isn't Digitalis used to help heart disease?" Ruby Mae looked
up from her knitting. "I had an uncle who used to take it."

Judge Miller smiled. "Yes. That's why it was such a good
way to poison people who had bad hearts. It used to be prescribed a lot more, but it's tricky. Too much can kill someone
who is already taking it for heart disease. Doctors expected to
find the Digitalis in the blood, so it might not raise any flags
unless the dosage was exceptionally high." He shook his head.
"Fascinating stuff."

"But how does this help?" Nana Jo asked.

"Sorry, I got distracted." He grinned. "Someone who believed they had a bad heart might be prescribed something
harmless to help alleviate the symptom their mind might produce."

"So, if Maria believed she had a heart problem and he did
nothing, then her body could replicate the symptoms," I said.
"A doctor couldn't ignore it, and he couldn't prescribe the real
pills because they would be deadly because there wasn't actually anything wrong."

He nodded.

"So, he prescribed a harmless sugar pill," Nana Jo said.

"That's the scenario I put forth and he agreed that a physi-
cian might do something like that, especially if the patient had
been to a number of doctors and wouldn't accept there was
nothing wrong with them."

"For all intents and purposes then, Maria did have a heart
condition." Nana Jo typed.

"That's about the size of it." Judge Miller sat back. "There wasn't really anything else in the forensic information I looked through that raised any flags."

Dorothy leaned forward. "Well, I talked to my sister, Gertie, and showed her the pictures from Magnus's room and boy, was she excited."

"Why?" Nana Jo asked. "Are they valuable?"

Dorothy nodded. "She said she would have to examine them in person to be sure, but if they're the pieces she thinks they are, they're not just valuable, they're priceless."

Her comments had the desired effect of generating awe and Dorothy didn't let her moment pass. "She said this one"— Dorothy pulled out a paper copy of the picture Nana Jo sent— "might be *View of a Dutch Square* by Dutch artist Jan van der Heyden, painted in the seventeenth century. Apparently before the war, the painting was owned by a family named Krauss." She read through her notes. "Yes, Gotlieb and Matilde Krauss. They were Jews who fled Vienna before the war, but the Gestapo confiscated their art."

We stared at the small painting with a new look of awe.

"The ballet dancers look like a missing painting by Degas." Dorothy read through her notes and then looked up. "Of course, they could just be imitations. Only an art expert could tell for certain."

"Suppose these paintings are the real deal. What does that mean?" I asked.

Dorothy leaned back. "She said they would have to be authenticated. The tricky thing is proving ownership. Apparently, some of the art was stolen. Others may have been forcibly sold."

"What's that?" Ruby Mae asked.

"The original owners may have been forced to sell against their will. The new owners may have all of the right paperwork to show they paid for the art. All of the original parties are most likely dead now, so it could prove hard to show ownership." Dorothy passed around the other papers she'd printed from her sister. "She suggested we contact this organization with the details."

They looked at the papers and then handed them to me. I looked up.

"You should pass that along to Stinky Pitt," Nana Jo said.

I folded the papers and nodded.

Dorothy didn't have anything else, so I went next. I recapped the information I'd learned about Magnus from Isaac Horwitz.

Irma was exceptionally quiet. She eventually looked up. "I didn't know all of that about Magnus. If I had, I would never have . . ."

We all looked at each other, unsure of how to proceed.

Nana Jo looked at Irma. "Irma, you need to tell us what you do know about Magnus and what really happened that night." She stared hard at Irma. "I mean all of it." Her tone was kinder than her words.

Irma took a deep breath. "He told me he'd been a German pilot during the war. He also told me how he worked as his brother's personal assistant." She looked around at each of us. "But he never mentioned a word about hurting people. He said he wouldn't have been allowed in the country if he had been guilty of war crimes." She looked down. "I guess he only told me what he wanted me to know. I didn't look at the art in his bedroom. I'd only been in there once before and I wasn't exactly looking at his artwork."

Irma seemed so despondent, no one made comments.

She then told about bringing oysters and whiskey to his room the night he was murdered. She swore they both ate and drank the same things, so the cyanide couldn't have been in the food.

"I panicked and tossed the shells and the whiskey before

the police came. That detective made me show him where. He got it out. Said it was evidence." She coughed.

"I'm really confused," I said. "If you two both ate and drank the same things, how *did* Magnus get cyanide poisoning?"

Irma shrugged.

"Sam's right. He had to have eaten or drank something you didn't. Now think," Nana Jo ordered.

Irma paused for a few minutes but then shook her head. "Well, let me see." She recapped each moment from the time she knocked on his door. "We ate the oysters and then moved into the bedroom." She recalled. "He . . . that's right. He went to the bathroom. Said he had to take his medicine."

"Did you tell the police?" I asked.

Irma shook her head. "I forgot. Do you think that's when it happened?"

"Depends. What happened when he came out?"

"He came back to the bed and we were . . . well, you know, but then he started choking and clutching his chest and shaking." She shivered. "I thought he was having a heart attack." She coughed and took a drink from her flask. "Then he died."

"That has to be when it happened," Freddie added.

I thought for several seconds.

"What's wrong, Sam?" Nana Jo asked.

"I was just wondering how the poison got in the medicine. Detective Pitt didn't mention it, but I'll ask him tomorrow if he checked the medicine for cyanide."

We discussed cyanide further and Nana Jo pulled up an article on her iPad and read it to us. Depending on the dosage, it could have done the trick.

"I guess cyanide capsules might have been given to important German officers," Freddie spoke softly. "In case they were captured. That's how Himmler died."

"What did they do with the pills after the war?" Nana Jo asked.

No one knew the answer.

Freddie went next. "I watched the copy of the security footage. There wasn't anything memorable on it. I'm going to go back and look through some of the other footage from the day Maria died. Maybe I'll find something helpful."

Ruby Mae finished the row she was knitting. "Well, I got some information I think you all are going to find very interesting." She looked up. "I talked to Gaston Renoir."

Judge Miller looked puzzled.

"He's the chef at Shady Acres. Remember Sam told us someone saw him bringing a tray to Maria's room the night she was killed?" She looked around and we nodded.

"Plus, Detective Pitt mentioned the contents of her stomach, Lobster Thermidor, asparagus, pears poached in champagne." She sniffed. "Well, I asked him about that. He didn't want to say anything, but I could tell he was terrified. Turns out Maria was blackmailing him."

We gasped. "Blackmail?"

Ruby Mae nodded. "She found out he'd been arrested and tried for murder."

She looked at all of the stunned faces and paused to pick up her knitting before she continued. "He was a prestigious chef at Le Cordon Bleu and left to open a five-diamond restaurant in New York. He was very successful until he got embroiled in scandal."

"What kind of scandal?" Irma leaned forward. "This sounds juicy."

"His lover's husband was poisoned."

"Poisoned?"

She nodded.

"Was it cyanide?" I asked.

She paused and then shook her head. "No. He said the

man was allergic to shellfish. The police believed he knew and deliberately put something in the food to cause him to go into some kind of shock."

"Anaphylactic shock," Judge Miller added. "I had a case like that once when I was a public defender."

"So, our chef is a convicted felon?" Nana Jo looked incredulous. "That Miss Bennett must be out of her mind. If the residents knew about this, there's no way she'd be able to charge what they charge for the place."

"He was never convicted." Ruby Mae stared at Nana Jo. "He was in prison in upstate New York during the trial but got released on a technicality."

"Doesn't matter. He shouldn't be allowed to cook. What's happening to this place." Nana Jo pounded the table. "This needs to go before the board of directors."

Ruby Mae looked sad. "I suppose, but I don't believe he killed Maria."

"Why not? He had motive. He had opportunity and he had the means." Nana Jo wasn't going to be distracted.

"But you're forgetting something. Maria wasn't poisoned," I said.

"He could have shot her." Nana Jo didn't look as though even she believed that. She shook her head. "I guess you're right."

"I could be wrong," Ruby Mae said, "but he sounded sincere. He cried when he talked about how his greatest regret was not having had an opportunity to clear his name." She looked around the room. "I gathered he must have had it pretty rough after that. He struggled to get work in New York for years. No one would hire him. Later he moved to Michigan."

"What happened to the woman?" Irma asked. "The one whose husband got poisoned?"

Ruby Mae shrugged. "I didn't ask him. I don't think they got married, though. He didn't get married until he got to

Michigan. He lived a quiet life until his wife died. He sounded like he was pretty lonely. I guess that's why he came to Shady Acres. He didn't have a lot of money and was renting a small apartment. The old manager, the guy who was here before Denise Bennett, knew about his past and must have felt sorry for him. So, he offered to let him stay in exchange for cooking. He's lived in fear of his secret coming to light."

"So, how did it come to light?" Nana asked. "How did Maria find out?"

She shrugged. "He didn't know, but she demanded special treatment to keep his secret."

"Well, that dirty, b——"

"Irma!"

She put her hand over her mouth as she broke into a coughing fit.

We talked for several minutes, but no one had any useful ideas. We decided to call it a day. We would dig deeper and reconvene tomorrow. Hopefully, the new day would bring new answers.

Nana Jo had been staying in her villa at the retirement village a lot, but tonight she stayed with me. We went upstairs and found a batch of cookies in the freezer. We heated them in the microwave for a few seconds until they were warm and soft and gooey. I poured milk, but Nana Jo made a cup of coffee to drink with hers.

We sat on the barstools and ate our treats.

"Something on your mind, Sam? Want to talk about it?"

I munched my cookie and tried to put the questions floating through my mind into some type of logical order. "How did Maria find out about Gaston? It sounds like the incident happened years earlier in New York. So far, we haven't found anything to indicate she knew him."

"Maybe someone told her?"

"Maybe, but who?"

She shook her head. "No idea."

"And another thing, didn't Detective Pitt say Maria's door was locked?"

She nodded. "Denise Bennett opened it and found her."

"Then how did the murderer get in?" I stared at her. "I hadn't thought much about it, but you know how when I write, it tends to parallel things going on in my real life, well, I wrote a locked room murder."

"Who'd you kill?"

"Jessica Carlisle. She was dating Randolph Churchill, Winston Churchill's son, but planned to toss him over for James."

"I thought Daphne and James were a couple?"

I nodded. "They are, but that's just how things went. I made Jessica into a real tart and I guess her nature just came out. Someone like that would try to go after a duke."

Nana Jo stared at me. "Interesting."

Something in Nana Jo's eyes made me suspicious. "What?"

"It's just like you said, your writing imitates what's going on in real life."

"I know."

"Well, Jessica is a tart in the book. Maria was a tart in real life. Jessica is killed in a locked room murder. Maria is killed in a locked room murder. Maybe your subconscious can figure out how the real murder was done if you can figure out how the murder in your book happens?"

We stared at each other for several seconds. "I don't see how. It's not like I know what's going to happen. I'm not a plotter. I don't write out my entire plot ahead of time. I just create the characters and let them do what they do." I shrugged.

"Your subconscious follows the personalities of the charac-ters. Your characters share characteristics of real people. So, if you write, maybe your subconscious can help figure out who killed Maria while you're figuring out who killed Jessica."

I smiled. "Well, then, I guess I better write more."

"Write more and write faster."

We talked a little longer and then went to bed. I let the dogs out and processed what Nana Jo said. I wasn't sure her logic was sound, but there was a tiny . . . germ of something that rang true. I knew my writing helped clear my thoughts, but the idea that it could help me solve this murder seemed farfetched. However, time was running out and desperate times called for desperate measures. So, I pulled out my laptop.

James, Lord William, and Mrs. Churchill were already in the parlor when Daphne and Lady Elizabeth entered. Lady Elizabeth took a quick look around and then rang the buzzer she knew would summon Thompkins.

James was seated on the sofa and moved over to make room for Daphne, but she sat in one of the chairs near the window. A look of disappointment flashed across his face briefly but was quickly concealed.

Thompkins opened the door to the parlor, stepped in, and coughed discretely. "M'lady?"

Lady Elizabeth hurried to her seat on the sofa. "Thompkins, come in and close the door. We may not have much time."

The butler obeyed and stood quietly near the fireplace.

"What's this all about, Elizabeth?" Mrs. Churchill asked.

"We've got to get some things arranged before that young sergeant's return." She turned to James. "Did you ring Scotland Yard and arrange for Detective Inspector Covington to come out?"

James nodded.

She turned to Mrs. Churchill. "I hope that's okay, Clemmie. We've worked with him before and I trust him."

Mrs. Churchill looked dazed. "Yes, of course. Whatever you think best."

James nodded. "I have a small job I need to tend to in London, so I'll pick him up and bring him down."

"Perfect."

"Thompkins, we're going to need your help on this one."

"Of course, m'lady."

"You know the servants better than any of us, except perhaps Clemmie." She smiled at Mrs. Churchill. "No offense, dear, but you've not investigated a murder before and it might be faster and easier if Thompkins does it."

Mrs. Churchill's eyes got larger, but she nodded.

"Thompkins, find out if anyone heard or saw anything that might help figure out who killed that girl."

He bowed. "Yes, m'lady."

"James, I'll need you to work on Randolph. He'll be one of the top suspects, and I think you may be better suited to his . . . disposition than any of us."

"Of course."

"Find out how long he's known her. Where did they meet? Any background information you can get will help."

James nodded.

"Randolph isn't the only person the police will suspect." Daphne's face was flushed as she picked at an invisible piece of lint on her tweed skirt.

Everyone reassured her, but she held up a hand. "You don't have to sugarcoat it. Randolph and I will be top suspects for the police."

"You're probably right, dear," Lady Elizabeth spoke quietly but with confidence. "That's another reason why we need to work quickly to find the *real* killer."

Daphne appeared to take courage from Lady Elizabeth's words and sat straighter and nodded.

"Now, Daphne, do you think you could talk to Mr. Blunt and Mr. Burgess? Find out what they were doing last night and early this morning?"

Daphne nodded. "I'll do my best."

"William, I'm going to need you to distract Winston and Leo. The last thing I need is Winston putting in his oar. He may be a brilliant man, but subtle he is not. I think Leo Amery may be useful in keeping Winston distracted but also find out if he had any contact with the girl. I know it's a long shot, but he has a son who . . . well, hasn't been a credit to him and there's always a chance he might know something."

"Certainly. Diversionary tactics and reconnaissance." He filled his pipe. "Leave it to me."

"Perfect." Lady Elizabeth nodded. "I really wish Penny and Victor were coming, but I guess we'll manage."

"Aren't they coming?" Daphne asked.

"Unfortunately not. That's who I was talking to on the phone. Victor's great-aunt Prudence arrived unannounced and they have to stay and entertain her. We're going to have to double up on this one."

She looked around. "Now, who's left? I shall tackle Lord Stemphill. I have a feeling there's more to him than meets the eye."

Mrs. Churchill looked expectantly at her friend. "I want to help. What can I do?"

Lady Elizabeth smiled. "I have three very important jobs for you. First, we're going to need some time to work. Mr. Burgess works for the BBC and he's going to smell a story. I need you to have Winston talk to him. Get him to promise not to go public with anything for a week. I doubt he'll agree, but maybe he'll give us the weekend." She stared at her friend. "Do you think you can do that?"

Mrs. Churchill nodded. "I'm sure Winston will agree. The last thing he needs right now is more negative publicity."

"Winston can be very persuasive when he wants to be."

"What's the second thing?"

Lady Elizabeth smiled. "I need you to distract Lady Alistair." She looked shyly at James. "If I know Helen, she'll be ready to pack her bags as soon as she learns about this. Obviously, she didn't know the girl . . . Alistair, indeed?" Lady Elizabeth shook her head. "However, she may have seen or heard something. Do you think you can manage?"

Mrs. Churchill smiled. "I've managed ladies like Lady Alistair my entire life."

"Wonderful." Lady Elizabeth released a heavy sigh. "Good. I think that's everyone. Now, we are going to need to come up with something to say to this sergeant. The poor man has never seen a dead body before and is clearly out of his depth—"

"You said there were three things you wanted me to work on. You only mentioned two of them. What's the third?" Mrs. Churchill asked.

"The third thing may be the most important thing of all. We need to find out how the killer got in that room."

Chapter 17

Friday at the bookstore felt like old times. I hadn't realized how much I missed Nana Jo until she wasn't there every day. We worked like a well-oiled machine and time passed quickly. We weren't running around like headless chickens, but there was a steady flow of customers that kept us busy.

The biggest surprise for me came when Taylor, the MISU Goth student, returned.

"Back already? I hope it's not to return the book?"

She smiled. "Oh, no. I loved the book so much I read it in one night. It isn't exactly like the television series, but it was cool."

"Wonderful. I'm glad you enjoyed it. What brings you back so soon?"

"I want more. I'm going to get the rest of the books in the series, plus anything else you recommend."

I laughed. "As long as the reading for pleasure doesn't interfere with your schoolwork."

"Well, actually I've been thinking . . ." She shuffled her feet. "I'm a sophomore and I've been taking all kinds of classes, trying to figure out what I want to do. My dad wants me to take math and science. He says scientists always get jobs."

"It's good advice, but let me guess, your dad's a scientist?"

She nodded. "Exactly. I'm good at it, especially computers and technology but . . ."

"But it's not what you want to do with the rest of your life," I finished.

Her eyes got large and she beamed. "Right."

"What do *you* want to do?"

She glanced around. "What I really want . . ." She looked sheepish and shy. "Is to write." She paused and then her face lit up. "I love reading. I read all the time. I write too, poetry, short stories, fantasy, and even mysteries. I've always loved writing. My mom said I wrote my first book when I was in second grade. She still has it." Her words tumbled out rapidly. "I want to make people laugh and cry. And get scared and angry." She scrunched her shoulders up to her ears. "I daydream about alternative universes where all sorts of weird creatures live and love and fly and use magic." She stopped abruptly, almost giddy. Then she looked timidly at me. "Sounds crazy, doesn't it?"

I smiled. "Not at all. I know exactly how you feel."

"You do?"

"I guess Jillian didn't mention I'm an aspiring writer too," I said softly.

Her eyes flashed and her face lit up. "You are? That's wonderful. What have you written. I can't wait to read it."

I held up my hands. "Whoa. Slow down." I laughed. "I said aspiring. I've written a book. Actually, I've written two mysteries, but I'm not published yet." I considered whether I should share more but decided she needed a bit of encouragement. "I did get an agent," I whispered.

"OMG. That is so amazing."

"It is amazing, and scary too."

"Oh, I know what you mean. I mean, I think I do. It's

something you want so badly and then you move forward and you're afraid to tell people and hear their comments, right?"

I nodded. "I never even told my family I wanted to write until recently."

"How did they take it?"

"They were all supportive and encouraging," I said tentatively. "But, I'm older and in a different place in my life than you. It sounds like you don't think your dad will support you becoming a writer."

She shrugged. "I don't know. He says he wants me to be happy, but I need to grow up and get a *real* job. Reading books and playing video games won't put food on the table or pay the rent."

"I'm sure he wants to make sure you're able to support yourself. Life as a writer isn't easy. Most new writers don't make huge salaries."

Her shoulders drooped.

"What does your mom think?"

"My mom wants me to get married and have babies." She held up a hand. "In that order." She chuckled. "I think she'd be fine with whatever. It's my dad that'll be the challenge."

"Have you talked to your guidance counselor?"

"Not really. I've been too scared to tell anyone what I really want." She looked up in surprise. "Except you. You're the first person, outside of my best friend, I've told."

"I feel honored." I smiled. "I recommend you talk to your counselor. He or she might be able to recommend a program that will make both you and your dad happy."

"Really? Is there fantasy writing for scientists?"

"I was thinking more about writing for video and role play games. I don't know much about it, but it seems like they would need creative people to work with programmers to design all those fantasy worlds."

Her eyes got big and she looked like she was going to hyperventilate. She spoke rapidly, "OMG. OMG. OMG." She took a deep breath and forced herself to speak slowly. "Oh my god, that would be so freakin' amazing. It would combine my two favorite things in the entire world."

I held up a hand. "I don't know for sure that it's a real thing, but maybe your guidance counselor could help you find out."

She hugged me. "You just made me super happy. I'm going to talk to my counselor as soon as I get back on campus." She looked at her watch.

"Have you ever read the Dresden Files? They're by Jim Butcher. Harry Dresden is a private detective who also happens to be a wizard."

She looked like her eyes would pop out of her head. "OMG. That sounds perfect." She nodded vigorously.

I helped her buy the next two books in the Sookie Stackhouse series and the first three Dresden Files books. Normally, I encouraged readers to a new series to start with the first one in case they didn't like it. However, I felt confident Taylor would like the Dresden Files.

She hugged me before she left.

I stood in the middle of the store staring after her with a large smile.

"You seem very pleased with yourself," Nana Jo said.

Her words snapped me back to the present. "It's days like today that remind me why I wanted to open a bookstore."

I told Nana Jo about Taylor and how excited she was to discover new books, especially when they combined worlds she loved like fantasy and mystery.

Nana Jo smiled and patted me on the back. "You've done well here." She looked around.

I hugged her. "Thank you."

She looked at me in surprise. "Why are you thanking me? You're the one that had the guts to quit your job, buy a building, and start a bookstore. According to the news, no one reads books anymore. They're all into electronic books and book-stores are all going the way of the dinosaurs." She took my face in her hands. "That took courage and that was all you."

"I couldn't have done it without my family's support, especially yours." I hugged her. "I've missed working with you every day."

"I've missed being here." She looked serious. "I enjoy working. It keeps me young to have something useful to do." She looked around. "I love books and I enjoy working with you every day."

There was a lull in the bookstore and the few people who were there were so engrossed in their books they weren't paying us any attention. "I just don't want you to feel like you *have* to stay with me or work here. I know you have a life and—"

"I know, and I don't want to invade in your space. I came for a few days after that guy was killed in the backyard. You were still grieving for Leon and you'd just quit your job and were trying to get this place open and I wanted to help. I only intended to stay for a few days, but then the days turned into weeks and then months. Now you're finally allowing yourself to date again and well . . . I don't want to cramp your style."

"Is that why you went back to your house?"

"Partly." She nodded.

"You aren't cramping my style. I really like you being here. I like working with you. I just didn't want to make you feel obligated to be here."

We stared at each other for several seconds and then laughed.

"What do you think we should do about this?" I asked.

"I have an idea. I need to talk it over with Freddie, but I think he'll go for it." She thought for a few minutes. "Let's get a cup of tea."

We went to the back of the store, got some tea, and sat down at one of the bistro tables. I waited for Nana Jo to start.

"Freddie's been talking about moving out of Shady Acres. Rent is pretty outrageous and he spent most of his savings in medical costs before his wife died. He's too proud to take anything from me." She rolled her eyes. "But, I was thinking maybe he could move in."

"Okay," I said slowly.

"My house is paid for, thanks to your grandfather." She smiled. "He may have been a tightwad, but he left me in good shape financially. Plus, I got in on the ground floor when Shady Acres was nothing but a big mound of dirt and dreams, so I got my place for a reasonable price. Villas now are running almost double what I paid." She shook her head. "Freddie'll want to pay rent, but we can work that out." She sipped her tea. "What do you think?"

I forced a smile. "I think it's great if you and Freddie want to move in together."

She looked up. "Oh, hold on there. I was thinking I would spend most of my time here with you. I like Freddie. I like him a lot, but I can only take a couple of days with him. The man was in the military. He gets up at four thirty every day, even on Saturday. He's like a drill sergeant when it comes to cleanliness. 'A place for everything and everything in its place.'" She saluted. "The man even folds his dirty laundry. Can you believe that? I can only stand three or four days of it and then I'm ready to strangle him. I'm too old to learn to compromise. I made compromises when I married your grandfather." She grinned. "He made them too, but we were young and pliable." She shook her head. "Now I don't want to compromise. I like my life. I like who I am and I like the way I live. I don't want to change. I'm too old to change."

"You're not old."

"Oh, yes I am and I'm good with that. I'm old, but I'm not decrepit, and I'm not dead. It's not that you can't teach an old dog new tricks. You can, but the dog has to want to learn the tricks, and I don't. I can tolerate about three or four days with *Captain Clean* and then I'm ready to throttle the man. So, I'm thinking I'd stay with you during the week and spend the weekends with Freddie. What do you think?"

I hopped up and gave her a huge hug. "I think that's a great idea. I'd love for you to move back."

She patted my arm. "That's good. I can continue to help here and continue tutoring Dawson and solving crimes." She laughed and then looked sober. "Now, sit back down. I have something I want to say."

I sat down and wondered what could be so serious. Instantly my mind went to disease, but I quickly pushed the thought away and focused.

"I need you to promise me you'll be honest and tell me when you need your own space. You and Frank are . . . well, you're dating now and I know you may not feel comfortable with me around all the time."

I tried to interject, but she held up a hand and hurried on.

"Let me finish. I need you to promise you'll tell me when you want to be alone. I'm a pretty sound sleeper, so as long as you aren't swinging from the ceiling or anything . . . too adventurous . . . I'll give you your own space—"

I spit my tea out and laughed so hard it started to come out of my nose. It took several attempts before I stopped laughing. "Frank and I are good friends."

She started to speak, but I held up a hand.

"I can't say things won't progress to more, but for now, that's where we are. However, I appreciate what you're saying and I give you my word we will talk about privacy should the need arise."

She patted my hand. "Well, that's good. I'm glad we talked."

The bell chimed, indicating someone had entered the store. We looked up and saw Detective Pitt.

"I sure hope Stinky Pitt hasn't reneged on his word and

come to throw me in the hoosegow just when we've figured out all of our housing dilemmas. We haven't even started on world peace."

Detective Pitt made his way to the back of the store and stood in front of our table.

Nana Jo rose from her seat. "Hey, Stinky Pitt. You here for Sam or me?"

He turned red but forced a smile. "I'm here to see Mrs. Washington, but I do wish you would remember not to call me that." He looked around. "Especially in public."

Nana Jo feigned surprise. "I'm sorry. It just slipped out before I thought." She turned away from Detective Pitt and winked at me.

"How can I help you, Detective?" I waved a hand for him to sit in the seat Nana Jo vacated.

One of our customers moved toward the register, and Nana Jo motioned for me to say seated. "I've got this. You talk to"—she spoke slowly and deliberately—"Detective Pitt."

He smiled. "See, that wasn't so hard."

Nana Jo mumbled, "Harder than you know, Stinky," as she moved to the front of the store.

Thankfully, Detective Pitt's cell phone rang and he was engaged and not paying attention. When he was done talking, he looked around as though he was afraid of being seen. He reached inside his coat and pulled out a file and placed it on the table. "If my chief finds out I'm showing this to you, I won't even be able to get a job as a meter maid." He took a napkin from the table and wiped his brow.

I opened the folder. It contained information from the coroner's report, the crime scene investigators, and forensics. The file was hefty and it took quite a while for me to sift through all of the information.

Detective Pitt watched nervously, alternating between wiping beads of sweat from his brow and looking over his shoulder.

"You're making me nervous. Why don't you get up and make yourself a cup of coffee or tea." I pointed to the single-cup brewer on the counter. "Or Nana Jo made a pot of coffee if you'd prefer."

He didn't look as though he was going to move so I upped the ante.

"Plus, if you look behind the counter there's a plate of cookies."

That did the trick. "Any more of those scone things?"

I shook my head.

He got up and went for the cookies.

I had hoped to save those for our meeting tonight. Between the MISU book club, our meetings to talk about the murders, and store patrons who'd come to love Dawson's baked goods, the supply hadn't lasted as long as I hoped. I sighed. I could always make more tonight.

I returned to the file. It took over thirty minutes for me to get through everything, partly because I didn't understand the abbreviations and acronyms. I made notes and focused on the things I thought would be most critical. I didn't bother to think or ponder. I was under a time crunch.

Detective Pitt ate at least a dozen cookies, dropping a trail of crumbs my dogs would be able to follow like bloodhounds. He paced. He scanned shelves. He took books out and then couldn't remember where they belonged and left them on tables.

I tried to concentrate on what I was reading and ignore him, but it was a challenge. Finally, I got through the file and replaced all of the papers.

Detective Pitt paced behind my chair. When he saw me close the folder, he quickly snatched it up and returned it to his inside pocket.

I thought about the depth of those pockets that could hold

an entire file but shook my head to clear my thoughts. "Can I ask you a couple of questions?"

He was about to take off but stopped and looked back. "What?"

"The coroner didn't find Nana Jo's fingerprints anywhere near the bedroom. They were only on the door to the apartment."

"Doesn't mean anything. She could have worn gloves when she shot her. Or she could have wiped off anything she touched in the bedroom."

"But if she was going to wear gloves, she would have put them on before she entered the room, and if she took the time to wipe her fingerprints off the bedroom, why not the doorknob?"

He shrugged. "Doesn't matter. She had motive. She had opportunity and means. She's still our number one suspect." He headed away.

"Did you know Maria was blackmailing Horace Evans?"

That stopped him in his tracks. "What?"

"And Gaston Renoir."

He turned. He looked puzzled.

"The chef?"

I nodded.

"How did you find that out?"

"We have our ways." I grinned. "I take it from the look on your face you didn't know."

He shook his head. "What kind of blackmail? What did she have on them?"

I explained to Detective Pitt what we'd found out about Gaston. Maria found out something about Horace Evans. We didn't know what yet, but whatever it was, she threatened to get him fired if he didn't give her the lead in the Senior Follies.

He looked shock. "She blackmailed him to get a lead role in some senior citizen play?"

I nodded. "Apparently, but don't belittle it. The production is very good. They've been invited to walk in the Macy's Day parade and perform on Broadway with the Rockettes."

He shook his head. "What did this Gaston guy do?"

I explained about the poisoning and that was why Maria had eaten such elaborate meals like Lobster Thermidor. "She was blackmailing him to get special accommodations."

He took notes but continued to shake his head as he wrote. "That's crazy. She risked her life to get a part in a musical and special food." He finished his notes and looked at me. "Anything else?"

I told him about the lost art and pondered whether I should tell him about Isaac. Isaac Horwitz might have had a reason to kill Magnus von Braun, but he didn't have one for killing Maria. Besides, he was out of town and couldn't possibly have killed either one, but I didn't want to withhold information. So, I told him.

The cynical gleam was gone when he asked, "Anything else?"

"No. That's all for now."

He nodded and walked out of the store without a backward glance.

Nana Jo and I worked companionably until the store closed. We then set up for our meeting.

Judge Miller was the first to arrive. He spent time perusing the shelves while Nana Jo and I continued to set up. He came into the back room for the meeting with a gleam in his eyes and a book by *NY Times* best-selling author Stephen L. Carter with the intriguing title *The Impeachment of Abraham Lincoln*. He showed me the book. "Have you read this?"

"No. I've heard good things about the author and the concept is pretty creative."

"Fascinating. An alternative history where Abraham Lincoln survives the attack at Ford's Theatre but goes through an impeachment trial for violating his constitutional authority during the Civil War . . . it sounds absolutely fascinating."

He looked so excited, like a kid at Christmas. Today was definitely one of the days when I loved my job.

When everyone arrived, we started the meeting.

Nana Jo pulled out her iPad and started to type. "Who's first?"

I raised my hand since I wanted to share the information I got from Detective Pitt. I pulled out my notes and read the items I thought were pertinent. Thankfully, Judge Miller was able to decipher some of the confusing acronyms.

"So, Maria ate her dinner and then about two hours later someone shot her. Her door wasn't locked when Josephine arrived, but it was locked when the police arrived," Dorothy asked.

"That's about the size of it," I said.

"Well, that doesn't make any sense. If the room was unlocked when Josephine stopped by at nine, then how was it locked at twelve thirty, unless Maria locked it?" Ruby Mae said.

"Maybe she did." I shrugged.

"Then who locked it after they shot her?" Irma asked before breaking into a coughing fit.

"Maybe the killer locked the door." Ruby Mae pulled her knitting out of the bag and started to knit.

"Neat killer. He or she shoots Maria and then locks the door from the inside?" Freddie shook his head. "The dead bolt was engaged. The only way that could happen would be if Maria did it herself."

"Then there must be another way for the killer to have escaped." Judge Miller looked around. "What about a window?"

We all shook our heads.

"Nope. That apartment is on the fourth floor," Freddie explained.

"Well, it's definitely a puzzle." Judge Miller looked around.

"That's all I have." I folded up my notes. "Who wants to go next?"

Irma raised her hand. "I never reported on what I found out from Horace." She took a sip from her flask. "He wouldn't talk about why he was being blackmailed. In fact, he got quite angry when I asked. It took quite a while for me to smooth things over." She had a sly smile that indicated she had quite enjoyed smoothing his feathers. "So, I wasn't able to find out anything about that, but I did find out who the nosy neighbor was." She took another nip. "Sara Jane Howard."

There were groans and eye rolls from all those who lived at Shady Acres. Judge Miller and I stared in confusion.

Finally, I asked, "Who's Sara Jane Howard?"

Irma was still drinking from her flask.

So, Nana Jo explained, "Sara Jane Howard is the nosiest woman I have ever met. Frankly, I don't think her elevator goes all the way to the top." She made the universal signal for crazy with her hand.

"Okay, so what's wrong with her?" I asked.

"She sits at her window and looks out with binoculars every day. She watches everything and everybody that comes and goes."

"If you ask her about it, she'll say she's bird watching." Ruby Mae frowned.

"Bird watching my a—"

"Irma!"

"She's not afraid to ask anybody anything," Dorothy said. "When I moved in, she had the audacity to ask me how much I paid for my unit."

"She asked me why my husband and I had nine children," Ruby Mae added. "Then she asked how much I made with my cleaning business."

"Close your mouth, Sam," Nana Jo said.

I was so shocked I hadn't realized it was open. "Those are pretty personal questions. Why did she want to know?"

Ruby Mae shrugged. "I have no idea, but I told her flat out it was none of her business."

"She asked me what my intentions were to Josephine." Freddie looked shyly at Nana Jo.

"Why that little . . ." Nana Jo seemed to hunt for the right word, "busybody."

"What do you suppose she did with all this information?" I asked.

"I can't imagine anyone actually answering her," Ruby Mae said.

"Oh, I'm sure there are people stupid enough to answer her questions," Nana Jo muttered.

When the general outcry died down, Irma continued, "I should have guessed, but she doesn't live on the same floor with Maria. Or, at least she didn't. Apparently, she was supposed to be watering Agnes Littlefield's plants."

"I forgot Agnes went out of town to visit her sister in Florida. Agnes is 'bout the only friend Sarah's got." Ruby Mae frowned.

"The only one willing to put up with the woman," Freddie said.

"She talked about the comings and goings that took place at Maria's apartment." Irma smiled. "Glad she can't see the comings and goings in my apartment."

"That'd probably give her a right good shock," Nana Jo quipped.

"You got that right." Irma laughed and then coughed. "That's about it."

"Well, I decided to take Denise Bennett's art class today," Dorothy said. "She isn't very good, but I thought it might give me a chance to talk to her. She doesn't talk much, that one. Trying to get something useful out of her is like getting gold from Fort Knox." Dorothy looked disgusted. "I asked her if she'd heard about Gaston Renoir having been on trial for murder and she merely looked at me. She wouldn't say one word."

"Maybe she's trying to protect the property," Judge Miller said. "Perhaps she doesn't want to admit she knew anything in case there's ever a lawsuit. She won't be able to claim ignorance." He shook his head. "Not that ignorance is an acceptable defense in court, but you'd be surprised how many people think it is."

"The only thing she said was Maria's body would be buried in accordance with her faith," Dorothy said.

I wondered how she knew what Maria's faith was, but then I wasn't familiar with Maria. She might have told her. I would have to ask someone.

Judge Miller raised his hand. "I found out something." He pulled a paper from his pocket and put on his reading glasses. "You asked if I could find out about Horace Evans's background." He looked at me. "He went to prison for embezzlement."

I gasped. "Isn't he the bookkeeper for Shady Acres?"

Everyone nodded.

"He sure is," Nana Jo said.

"I wonder if Denise Bennett is aware of that?" Ruby Mae asked.

"Looks like Shady Acres is a halfway house for ex-cons," Freddie said.

Judge Miller held up a hand. "Now, hold on folks. The embezzlement was over forty years ago. Best I can tell, his biggest issue was sloppy work and trusting the wrong person. Money was withdrawn from the production company and he was the producer. There was no proof that he took the money, but it happened on his watch. So, he was held responsible." He read on. "He served his debt to society. Two years in a minimum security prison in upstate New York. He was released on good behavior."

"Well, I'll be." Nana Jo typed. "Elliot wasn't able to find out a lot about Maria, but he did find out she spent some time in upstate New York too. Apparently, she worked at a prison in upstate New York."

"I wonder if she knew Horace," I said. "Did he say if it was a men's or women's prison?"

Nana Jo looked through her e-mails. "He didn't say, but I'll send an e-mail and ask him to find out." She typed for several seconds and then looked up. "That's about all I have."

Irma smiled. "I had no idea Horace was an ex-con. I can't imagine him in prison. It's rather sexy." She coughed.

I pulled out my notes and looked at Detective Pitt's timeline. "Both Horace and Gaston visited Maria the night she was murdered."

"So, either one could have done it," Dorothy said.

"I don't know about that, but at least they were in the general vicinity." I didn't want to sound too discouraging, but I couldn't see how they could have killed her and locked the door from the inside and escaped before the police arrived.

Freddie volunteered to go next. "I finally got a chance to watch the security footage from the night Magnus died and the night Maria died." He shook his head. "I didn't see anything unusual or anyone suspicious." He pulled out a small notebook. "We already knew Magnus had treatment the day he died. He also had a prescription delivered. But, unless the North Harbor Pharmacy had a reason to put cyanide in his pills, I can't see any reason the prescription would be poisoned—"

"Oh, I remember one more thing." I looked at Freddie. "I'm sorry. I didn't mean to interrupt."

"No worries." He shook his head. "I was done."

"Well, Detective Pitt had the pathology report from Magnus. Cause of death was cyanide poisoning, but nothing else they found in his apartment had cyanide." I looked at Irma. "Nor was cyanide found in the oysters, whiskey, or medicine bottles."

She brightened up like a lightbulb. "Really?"

I nodded.

Irma looked as though a heavy weight had been removed from her shoulders. She sat taller and straighter.

Ruby Mae said she didn't have anything to contribute but promised to get something for tomorrow.

We talked for a while, but nothing significant was decided.

It was Friday night and we were all tired. Nana Jo and the girls decided to go out to unwind. Normally, I was the designated driver on these excursions, but tonight I had a date. Nana Jo promised she'd make sure everyone stayed safe. I'd have to accept that promise and not worry. At least I tried not to worry.

I hurried upstairs to change. I avoided the torture shoes from the other night and put on a brown wool skirt and burgundy cashmere sweater with tights and flats. The local Chamber of Commerce was having a wine and food tasting at the college. Frank was one of the judges and was going to be sampling some of the local cuisine.

"You look lovely," he said when he picked me up.

"Thanks. You look very nice yourself."

Frank was wearing a pair of brown corduroy pants and a turtleneck. He looked scholarly and confident, but I knew he was nervous. This was his first time judging at a local event and he wasn't sure about the local politics.

I gave his hand a squeeze. He'd be fine.

At the college, the Hechtman-Ayres reception room was crowded. There were tables set up around the perimeter. We walked to the registration table. There was a large packet with Frank's name tag and one for his guest, me. We had a few minutes to stroll around before he was pulled away to start the judging.

I stood around and tried to look supportive. However, once the tasting started, Frank was in his element and he didn't need any support or encouragement from me. I stayed and watched for a while but then wandered around and looked at the various booths.

I was surprised to see Shady Acres had a booth. Businesses from North and South Harbor and surrounding villages participated and not all of these businesses were traditional restaurants or bars, but still it was unexpected to see the retirement village had a booth.

Denise Bennett and Gaston Renoir were the representatives. I was glad to see familiar faces and approached the table with a big smile. "Mrs. Bennett, I don't think we've ever been formally introduced. I'm Samantha Washington. My grandmother, Josephine Thomas, lives at Shady Acres."

The smile froze on her face. "It's *Miss* Bennett, and yes, I remember you."

The frost from her greeting was palatable, and I shivered, although it might have had something to do with the fact someone had just opened a nearby door and a cold breeze had just blown through the building.

"I didn't know Shady Acres participated in things like this." I tried to maintain a jovial demeanor, even though I wanted to tell her maybe she should try to be friendlier to one of the judges' girlfriend or girl-something/date/friend. Or whatever.

"This is our first year competing. When the board learned of Gaston's credentials, they were anxious to capitalize on it from a marketing perspective." She looked at me as though I couldn't possibly know what marketing meant.

I smiled broadly. "Interesting. I'm rather surprised the board would want to flaunt the fact their chef was arrested for poisoning. Most places would try to hide something like that."

If looks could kill, I'd be dead where I stood with a frozen dagger through my eye socket. Miss Bennett's face turned purple and she looked as though she might have a stroke. "How dare you." She looked around to ensure no one important was nearby to hear and then leaned close and whispered, "If you breathe one word of those lies, I'll sue you for libel."

"Considering I haven't written anything, I think the word you want is slander. However, that will only work if what I've said is proven to be false."

Miss Bennett took a step forward. For a brief moment, it looked as though she would strangle me. Fortunately for me, the judges made their way to the Shady Acres table and she had to force a smile. Her eyes were cold whenever she looked in my direction, but she was forced to cut short any further threats until after the judging.

Frank glanced in my direction and smiled big. He sidled up to me and put an arm around my waste and whispered, "You okay?"

I nodded. "I'm fine."

He looked carefully and then tasted the offerings Gaston and Miss Bennett provided for his judging pleasure.

I stole a glance at Miss Bennett and noticed, although she pretended she wasn't noticing, she was definitely keeping a close eye on Frank and me. Maybe she thought I was whispering about Gaston's past.

Gaston was fully decked out in his chef whites. He had a white double-breasted jacket, hound's-tooth-patterned black-and-white pants and tall toque blanche, the traditional chef's hat. Around his neck were two medals. One was a combination star on top of a square. The other was a large gold circle. I didn't know what they were, but they looked impressive.

Gaston beamed. His face glowed. There was a twinkle in his eyes and a smile on his face. I would never consider saying or doing anything to destroy that look of pure joy on his face.

I let Denise Bennett provoke me and I felt ashamed to think I'd been so petty. When Gaston provided Frank his sample, he noticed me and smiled big. It was obvious cooking gave him great joy. I prayed he wasn't Maria or Magnus's killer.

Frank tasted the sample. His eyes rolled back in his head and a low primal groan followed.

Once the judges had tasted the items provided, they moved on to the next table.

More time alone with Denise Bennett would be bad for my mental, emotional, and possibly physical health, so I followed the judges to the next table. One backward glance told me she would hold me personally responsible if Shady Acres didn't win.

Fortunately, Gaston and Shady Acres won two medals. I was pretty confident Miss Bennett wouldn't or couldn't prevent me from coming on the grounds, although, I was less confident about the future of my tires. Tomorrow I needed to confirm my insurance included towing services, just as a precaution.

The event was a success and Frank was happily in his element. He talked about the great food and wines the entire drive home. We sat in the car in the parking lot next to my building. "I'm sorry. I've been going on and on and ignoring you." He turned in his seat and faced me.

"It's fine. I'm glad you're excited and you had a great time." I tried to sound reassuring.

"So, what's bothering you?"

I thought for a minute. "Nothing—"

He looked as though he was going to interrupt and I held up a hand. "Seriously, nothing's wrong. I've just been thinking." I told him about my altercation with Denise Bennett.

He looked concerned. "Do you think she would have harmed you?"

I pondered the question. "I don't think so, but the incident reminded me we still don't know much about her." I told him how we couldn't find any information about her in any of the police or legal databases.

He frowned. "That's odd."

I nodded and stared at him. "I was wondering if you could use your contacts to help us find out about her and another small thing." I grinned.

He raised an eyebrow.

"Maria blackmailed Horace Evans to get the lead role in the Senior Follies. She blackmailed Gaston Renoir to get special food and, while we don't know that she blackmailed Denise Bennett, it seems awfully suspicious that she jumped to the top of the wait list for a bigger apartment."

"You think she was blackmailing Denise Bennett?"

I nodded. "So, I was hoping you could see if there was any link between Maria and Denise Bennett. I mean, how was Maria able to just come in and find out all this stuff?"

He smiled. "Anything else, Sherlock?"

I shook my head.

He looked at me intensely. "I'll see what I can find out, but . . . what's in it for me?" He grinned.

My face warmed, and I was grateful we were in the dark car. "Well, I could . . . get Dawson to bake you some cookies."

He shook his head. "I was thinking of something a little more personal." He leaned closer and I smelled his aftershave.

"Your next spy thriller is on the house?" I teased.

He leaned closer and his breath brushed my cheek. "Closer, but still not what I was thinking of."

I smiled and turned my head and we kissed. It started off pretty light but quickly grew in intensity. After a few seconds, or days, he pulled away. "Okay, that's enough of that." He pulled back and unbuckled his seat belt.

I felt cold and confused for a second.

He opened his door. "Any more of that and you'll have me divulging national secrets."

I smiled.

He got out of the car and walked around to open my door and help me out. He was always such a gentleman.

We walked hand in hand to the door.

"You coming up for a coffee?" I asked.

He shook his head. "I better not." He kissed me again. This time slowly and gently before he pulled away. "I need to keep my wits about me."

I smiled all the way upstairs. I smiled as I let the poodles out to do their business and I was still smiling when I got undressed and climbed into bed. My thoughts drifted in a direction that caused a lot more smiles and plenty of giggles. Thankfully, Snickers and Oreo ignored my schoolgirl antics. I tried to sleep, but that didn't work. I tried to focus my breathing and my thoughts, but try as I might, my thoughts continued to drift in a different direction. I needed a diversion, so I got up, made a cup of tea, and pulled out my laptop.

The kitchen at Chartwell House was a beehive of activity, not unlike kitchens in other stately British homes. Maids, footmen, housekeepers, and butlers rushed in and out lugging, carrying, and doing whatever it took to tend to the needs of the family and their guests. The cook ruled the roost, and Chartwell was no different. Mrs. Churchill often employed family friend Georgina Landemare to help cook for house parties, and this week was no exception.

Georgina was a large, plain, good-natured woman, renowned for her culinary ability, despite the fact that as a coachman's daughter, she had no formal training. Thompkins noted the other servants liked and respected her. She entered service as a scullery maid at the age of fourteen and the servants viewed her as *one of them*. She was highly sought after by the aristocracy and cooked at events like the races at Newmarket, debutante balls, and weekends at Cowes.

Thompkins respected Georgina and the two worked well together. His many years working with Mrs. Anderson, the Marsh family cook, had taught him how to step softly in the minefield of the kitchen. He knew the other servants were younger and more easily intimidated by his stiff demeanor and rigid adherence to order. The group had worked well together, but he wasn't sure if they would feel comfortable opening up to him. However, he had been given a task and he would accomplish it if it was the last thing he did.

The butler hesitated a moment and then entered the kitchen. The other servants were sitting at the table enjoying a cup of tea. They started to rise, as a courtesy to his rank in the age-old tradition of the British servant hierarchy, but Thompkins waved his hand, indicating they could forego the courtesy and remain seated.

"It's been a very busy day. A hot cup of tea would be wonderful right now," he said.

Mrs. Newton, the housekeeper, poured a cup of tea and passed it down to the butler.

The conversation stalled after Thompkins joined the group. He sipped his tea silently.

Albert, the young footman, looked flushed. He sat next to Sergeant Turnbull, who looked pale as he stared into his cup.

"Are you okay?" Thompkins asked kindly.

The sergeant looked up at the butler. "Yes, sir." He paused. "It's just I've never seen a dead body before." He spoke quietly. "Not one like that, least ways. You know, just me gram and she didn't 'ave no 'ole in 'er 'ead." He looked around at the women. "Sorry."

"Is that what she 'ad?" the maid, Ethel, asked with a slight bit of excitement in her voice. "Was she shot?"

The sergeant nodded and then rose. "I best be getting back to the station. I'll need to file a report or something."

Thompkins rose to show the young man out, but he shook his head.

"No need to show me out, sir. I'll just nip out this back door." He rushed from the room and out the back door.

"He seems like a nice lad." Thompkins took a sip of his tea. "I hope he's up to dealing with something like this."

"He's a local boy. Known him his whole life," Mrs. Newton said as though that should be enough to vouch for his character.

"He's alright. His brother is one of my mates," Albert added.

"I didn't mean any disrespect," the butler added. "I'm sure he comes from a very fine family. It's just that murder isn't very common in quiet villages like this."

They accepted the butler's explanation in silence.

Eventually, Mrs. Newton nodded. "Well, you're right about that. We've certainly never had any murders for at least a hundred years. None as far back as I can remember, least ways. Only one bad seed too." She pursed her lips.

"Bad seed?" Thompkins asked.

"Lord Amery's son used to get into quite a bit of trouble before he up and left." She nodded. "And good riddance to bad rubbish." She sipped her tea. "Apart from him, this is a right quiet place with hard-working, respectable people."

"Poachings and drunk and disorderly is mostly all we have in these parts," Albert said. "Imagine someone around these parts getting murdered."

"I wonder who done 'er in?" Ethel said. "You think it was 'em?"

Mrs. Newton looked crossed. "You bite your tongue, girl." She glanced sideways at Thompkins. "You got no 'count to be accusing Mr. Randolph." In front of strangers was left unsaid, but the words hung in her silence nonetheless.

Ethel glanced at Thompkins. "I didn't say as 'e done it, but everyone 'eard the two of 'em arguing."

"Did they argue?" Mrs. Landemare asked.

Ethel glanced sideways at Mrs. Newton. "Almost the entire time she were 'ere. Nothing was right. She wanted more sunlight in 'er room or more 'ot water in 'er bath."

"Well, good Lord, what was she arguing with him about that for?" Mrs. Landemare asked.

Ethel shrugged. "I guess she expected 'im to lift a finger to do something to fix it for 'er." She laughed. "But she soon found out, Mr. Randolph don't take kindly to orders from anyone, least of all the likes of 'er."

"Hush," Mrs. Newton ordered. "You can't know that." She looked at the cook and the butler.

"Well, that's what 'e told 'er."

A look of shock crossed Mrs. Newton's face. "Even so, that don't give you any right to accuse him of murder." Having reprimanded the maid, she took a sip of her tea. "Besides, there were plenty others that didn't get along with her."

"Oh my." The cook leaned forward. "Don't tell me she fought with other people too?"

"Well, I don't like to speak out of turn." The house-keeper glanced at the butler. "I heard her arguing on the telephone with someone and it couldn't have been Mr. Randolph because I had just passed him in the parlor."

"Really? I don't suppose you 'eard what she was arguing about?" the cook asked.

The housekeeper bristled. "I'm not one to listen to conversations that don't concern me."

Thompkins coughed. "No one would ever accuse you of such a thing. However, sometimes it is almost impossible to avoid hearing things." The butler sized up the housekeeper and gave a meaningful look. "Especially when dealing with people of a certain class and breeding are concerned."

Mrs. Newton nodded. "You're so right, Mr. Thompkins, sir. That's exactly what I says to me sister, Lillith. Common. That's what she was." Her eyes gleamed and her face flushed. She was the center of attention. "Well, Lillith, I says, I've never heard such foul language in my entire life as that little piece of baggage used. 'I've got a chance to bag something a lot bigger than some stuffy old journalist, and I'll not have you coming up here and pulling the rug out from under me.'"

There were looks of surprise on everyone's faces.

"Then she swears and says, 'Don't you dare try and stop me. I'm going to get rid of Miss Goody Two-Shoes, and then I'll be set for life right here in good ole England.'"

Ethel gaped at the housekeeper. "What else did she say?"

Mrs. Newton waited a moment. "She said, 'You can go off to the Siberian arctic and freeze your . . . I won't say what she said, but you know what I mean, 'off if you want to, but I'm staying right here.' Then she slammed the receiver down."

There was silence as everyone stared at the housekeeper.

"Lawd," Ethel said.

"I wonder who she was talking to," Mrs. Landemare said.

Mrs. Newton shrugged. "I have no idea."

Albert leaned forward. "I'll bet that's who I saw in the garden the other night."

Thompkins stared at the footman. "You saw some-one in the garden?"

"I went out to . . . get some air." Albert flushed as he avoided eye contact with the butler.

Thompkins knew the footman had left the house after dinner. He'd gone looking for the young man when he came down to ask the maid for water bot-tles for Lady Daphne. He'd guessed the young man had a girl in the village.

"When I was outside, I thought I saw the light from a torch in the back garden, but I figured it was

Mr. Randolph. I didn't want anyone to see me, so I just hurried into the house."

"Couldn't you see anyone?" Thompkins asked.

"No, but it sounded like two people were having a row, but I couldn't make out what they was saying." He looked down and sighed. "But it was a man and a woman."

"Did you tell anyone about this?" the butler asked.

Albert shook his head. "I forgot about it until Newton said what she heard." He looked at the butler. "Do you think it's important?"

Thompkins thought for a few seconds. "I don't know, but I think we should tell Lady Elizabeth and Mrs. Churchill." He rose from the table. "It might prove vitally important."

Chapter 18

Saturday at the bookstore was busy. I wasn't sure if the increased foot traffic was because it was the last Saturday before the Thanksgiving holiday or because it was a MISU football weekend. It wasn't just any football game. Today was MISU's last game of the season. The team was undefeated and there was an electricity that had the locals abuzz with the possibility of a bowl game and maybe a championship. I wasn't sure how the selection of a champion collegiate team worked anymore. It used to be the team with the best record was selected as national champions, but the collegiate football playoffs changed that. Now, the top four teams were selected to participate in a mini-playoff which would determine the champion. I didn't understand the selection process, but then I never understood the old system either.

I'd become accustomed to crowds on game days. People enjoyed coming into the bookstore and listening to the game on the radio. I knew Frank would be busy too, and every television in his restaurant would be tuned into the game. I expected crowds, but today surpassed them all. Dawson sent a text at five in the morning reminding me to take the extra dough out of the freezer. I was thankful for the reminder. All I had to do was slice and bake the cookies. He'd thought of everything. I said a silent prayer as I carried another batch of cookies downstairs. I wasn't sure if God intervened in the outcome of football games, but if so, I hoped He would favor MISU. In our MISU sweatshirts, Nana Jo and I consulted, advised, recommended, sold books, baked cookies, and restocked when needed; we also cheered whenever MISU scored.

Jillian and Emma stopped by in the afternoon while I was explaining the difference between a thriller and a suspense to a nerdy young man. When he finally chose a book and was ready to checkout, Jillian was behind the counter, checking customers out.

I mouthed, *Where's Nana Jo?*

She pointed to the back room.

I thanked her and was immediately accosted to help a customer locate a Rex Stout novel. I sold new books. Many mystery readers fell in love with authors, like Stout, who were out of print. Finding an old Rex Stout or Patricia Wentworth could be a challenge. Leon and I used to bemoan the fact older books were so hard to find. So, I was ecstatic when I learned of the Espresso electronic book machine, basically a huge beast of a printer that allowed me to print books. When I first investigated the Espresso machine, the price was twice what we'd paid for our first house. As technology advanced, more books were available online and the price for the Espresso machines dropped. When a university's bookstore in Chicago closed, I was able to buy their machine for a fraction of the original price. Not being the most technologically savvy person on the planet, I'd moved the machine to the back and allowed it to collect dust. Thankfully, my nephews were around to help me out. Zaq figured out how to get the machine working and printed instructions for me. Christopher, my marketing wizard nephew, created signs and advertisements, which drew in mystery readers from three states to see if they could get older, hard to find books. These one-off situations certainly didn't make the machine cost effective. However, Christopher's other ideas, like print-on-demand for indie authors, or offering writing workshops which could end with printed books, made the machine an attractive option.

I copied down the name of the book and went to the back to tackle the Espresso beast. Despite the detailed instructions, I wasn't confident in using the machine. I passed Emma on my way to the back and must have grumbled.

She laughed. "Based on the look on your face, I'd say you were heading back to the Espresso machine."

I nodded. "Sorry."

"Would you like me to print the book for you?"

"Seriously?"

"I don't mind."

I handed her the paper. "Bless you."

She went to the back.

I noticed the cookie plate was empty and grabbed it and went upstairs to bake a couple dozen more cookies.

The rest of the day went by in a blur. I was grateful for Emma's and Jillian's help. When the last customer left, we locked the door and flopped down onto chairs.

"I'm worn out," Nana Jo said. "This had to be the busiest day ever."

I groaned. "I don't know what we would have done without you two. I can't believe you both stayed all day." I looked at both of them. "I want to thank you and I definitely intend to pay you for all of your hard work." I started to rise, but they waved me back down.

"Please, don't get up. We both enjoyed it," Jillian said.

"I totally enjoyed it. I wish I wasn't going home for Thanksgiving break. I'd stay and help out," Emma said.

"Well, this is home for me, so I'm staying and I'm helping," Jillian said.

"You have to let me pay you. It's only fair."

"You let us have our book club here. You helped us get started and you gave everybody a 25 percent discount on the books." Jillian ticked off each item on her fingers.

"Plus, you gave us cookies," Emma added.

"I do that for everyone. Well, not the discounts, but you're college students."

"Why don't you let us buy you dinner?" Nana Jo said.

The girls looked at their watches and nodded.

"That sounds good. We never turn down free food," Emma said.

"Where are we meeting tonight?" I asked Nana Jo.

She pulled out her cell phone. "I'm texting everyone to meet at Frank's place."

I pulled out my cell to make sure he would be able to accommodate us. His response was immediate and made me smile.

"What are you grinning like a Cheshire cat for over there?" Nana Jo asked.

"Frank said give him five minutes to throw the mayor out and he'd have seating for us."

We hoisted ourselves up and prepared to leave. The worse part about sitting down when you were really tired was getting up again. However, we made it. I looked at the stairs I'd climbed at least a dozen times today and balked. I considered asking one of the younger girls if they'd run up and let the dogs out but changed my mind when I remembered where I was going. Instead, I climbed the stairs, got the dogs, and let them out, then freshened up and fixed my hair and makeup. Dating was a pain in the butt. Since I was in the bathroom, I took a couple of ibuprofen and then headed downstairs.

North Harbor Café was bustling too. In fact, there was a

line at the door when we arrived. However, the hostess recognized me and immediately directed us to the back of the restaurant and upstairs. Unlike my building, the upstairs of North Harbor Café had not been converted into living space. Instead, it was set up for additional seating. Frank hadn't opened the upstairs yet but apparently was making an exception for us.

There was another bar upstairs. Several tables had been pulled together and there were tablecloths, silverware, and glasses set up. One of the waitresses waited at the top of the stairs and took drink orders. After we were seated, Frank popped up to check on us.

He brought two large carafes of lemon water and placed them on the table. He stopped behind my chair and whispered in my ear, "Is this okay?"

"Perfect. Thank you." I smiled. "I think I owe you one."

He smiled. "I'll add it to your tab." He looked serious for a moment. "I haven't had time to fill your previous request, but I should have something by Monday. Is that okay?"

I nodded. I knew he was busy and I was grateful.

The rest of the crew arrived, and we enjoyed a few drinks and let the waitress take our orders. We toasted the victorious MISU Tigers in their undefeated season and spent some time speculating about bowl games. When Nana Jo pulled her iPad out, it was time to get down to business.

Emma and Jillian hadn't been involved in this investigation, so we took a few minutes to fill them in on Maria's and Magnus's murders. Both girls had helped come up with useful evidence when Dawson was accused of murder and hopefully a new perspective might be just what we needed.

When we finished explanations, Nana Jo looked around. "Who wants to go first?"

Since I had so little information to share, I volunteered. I told the group about my encounter with Gaston and Denise. It probably wasn't significant to the murders, but it was all I had.

"I've asked one of my sources to look into Denise Bennett's background and any connections to Maria."

Irma raised her hand to go next. "I had a heart to heart with Horace last night and he still wouldn't talk about his time in prison." She coughed. "When I told him I already knew, he got upset at first. He claimed he was completely innocent."

"That's what they all say," Freddie and Judge Miller said together.

"Well, he claimed he was an innocent pawn in the entire thing." She coughed and took a long drink and requested another from the waitress. "He said one of the backers had some underworld connections."

"Underworld? Sounds like he made a deal with the devil," Ruby Mae said.

"He said one of his shows fell on hard times. He needed backing and allowed himself to get taken in by some hooligan with a lot of money and"—she used air quotes—" 'underworld' connections."

"Did he give you a name?" I asked.

She rummaged in her purse and pulled out an envelope. "Borrelli." She coughed and then took a drink from the glass the waitress placed in front of her.

"Anything else?" Nana Jo looked up from her iPad.

Irma shook her head. "Not really. He basically confirmed what the judge already told us. He went to a low security prison in upstate New York and when he got out, he moved here."

Nana Jo stared off into space and tapped her fingers on the desk.

"What're you thinking, Josephine?" Freddie asked.

She looked around. "Well, I asked Elliot to look up everyone: Denise Bennett, Horace, Gaston, and Magnus."

Freddie snorted when she mentioned Elliot, but she ignored him.

"He couldn't find anything on Denise Bennett, but Horace was Jewish." She paused dramatically.

I waited. Everyone looked as confused as I felt.

Nana Jo continued, "Don't you get it? They were Polish." She read through her notes. "His mother and grandparents died in Auschwitz. His father was in the French resistance but was killed by the Luftwaffe."

"How old was he?" I asked, even though I wasn't sure it mattered.

"Less than one," she said. "Don't you get it? He might have felt some animosity toward Magnus if he knew who he was."

Freddie sat up in his seat. "He was on the tape."

"What?" we asked.

"The surveillance tape I watched with Larry, the security guard. Horace was at the front desk the day Magnus's prescriptions were delivered. He was standing there talking to Denise Bennett."

"If he knew Magnus had a prescription delivered, he could have decided that would be a good opportunity to get his revenge," Judge Miller chimed in.

"Sam, do you still have that timeline you got from Stinky Pitt?" Nana Jo asked.

I looked through my purse and pulled out the timeline. "He was seen by the Nosy Neighbor entering the apartment at seven."

Freddie held up a hand. "But wait, Horace didn't just stand there when the prescription was delivered." He was silent a moment. "Denise Bennett signed for the prescription and took it into her office. Then Horace went into the office and talked to her. Later, he came out and if I'm not mistaken, he was carrying the prescription."

"What?" I asked.

"I'm almost sure of it. I'll need to look over the tape again to be sure, but I'm almost certain he left with the prescription."

"So he could have put the cyanide pill in the medicine bottle before he took it to Magnus's room," Judge Miller said.

"Motive, opportunity, and means." Freddie nodded.

"But why would he kill Maria?" I asked.

"Because she was blackmailing him." Nana Jo looked at me as though I was a bit daft.

"I know, but all she wanted was the lead in the Senior Follies and he gave it to her." I tried to wrap my brain around the idea of Horace as a killer.

"Blackmailers never stop," Judge Miller said.

Freddie nodded. "Especially after the first success. She did it once and it worked. What's to stop her from trying again and again and again?" He shook his head. "They never learn. That's how we catch 'em. They get greedy. If they stopped after the first time, they'd probably get away scot free. But, if it worked once, they keep going back until they get caught."

"Or dead," Nana Jo added.

We talked about Horace and the longer we talked, the more the evidence seemed to fit.

The waitress brought our food and we paused long enough to enjoy our meals. When we finished eating, we ordered coffee and continued our discussions.

Ruby Mae pulled out her knitting while she talked. "I spent the afternoon trapped with Sara Jane Howard." She frowned. "That woman is the biggest gossip I've ever met. If someone at Shady Acres sneezes, she can tell you the time, date, and type of tissue they used to clean their nose." She looked at the stitches on the section she just knitted and muttered under her breath. "She watches everyone that comes and goes on her floor and out through the window. She did say she thought Horace and Maria were more than friendly. In fact, she said Maria was more than friendly with a number of men."

Irma crossed her arms. "Well, that dirty little—"

"Irma!"

She coughed and then pulled her flask from her purse and took a swig.

Dorothy had endured another torturous day in Miss Bennett's art class as they worked on the set for the Follies. Her only contribution was to comment that a reporter from the *North Harbor Gazette* had stopped by during their class. He wanted to do an article on Shady Acres and their award-winning chef. When the photographer took a picture, she came unglued and started screeching like a banshee. She threatened to sue the paper if they printed any pictures without her consent.

"I wonder why?" I asked. "The way she talked last night, the board was excited for the marketing."

Jillian timidly raised a hand when no one commented. "Maybe she didn't want them to dig too deep into Gaston's past."

"It sure wouldn't look good if someone recognized him from prison," Emma said.

No one else had any contributions, so we discussed next steps. Tomorrow was Sunday, so we decided even God rested on the Sabbath, and we would too. However, we would meet on Monday and hopefully have something to present to Detective Pitt.

The Senior Follies' opening night was coming up. Nana Jo had rehearsal tomorrow and I was spending time with my mom. Hopefully, Frank would be able to get in touch with his contact soon. Thanksgiving was fast approaching and, unless I tied up the loose ends and presented a killer to Detective Pitt in the next couple of days, he might arrest my grandmother. The pressure of finding the killer weighed on my mind. I barely heard a word anyone said the rest of the evening as I sifted through all of the information we'd discovered. I didn't want to believe Horace Evans was the killer. I liked Horace.

We walked back to the store and I offered to drive Jillian and Emma back to campus. They'd taken the bus earlier and I didn't feel good about them taking the bus at night. The drive gave me an opportunity to think. I used to drive whenever I was upset, confused, or just needed to think. US-31 went from Holland, Michigan, to Indianapolis, Indiana. In River Bend there was a bypass that went around the city. The speed limit was seventy and I could get on in North Harbor and drive south for as long as it took to clear my head. Usually, that happened before I reached the Indiana border, but for exceptionally tough problems, I had been known to drive to the south side of River Bend before turning around and driving back.

Tonight's drive didn't take me quite that far, but I enjoyed the solitude. I'd recently bought a new car. Well, new to me anyway, and I still enjoyed having a car that was quiet and where I didn't feel every bump in the road.

Nana Jo promised to make sure Snickers's and Oreo's needs were met. Thankfully, that didn't involve much more than food, water, and access to the outside. When I got home, the lights were out and they were in bed. Oreo barked when I approached the bedroom door, but Snickers barely moved.

I got ready for bed, but my mind still wouldn't settle. During the drive, I came to a conclusion. I accepted the fact Horace was the killer. He had motive, means, and opportunity. I think I knew how he'd killed Magnus, but Maria's murder was still a puzzle. I needed to figure out how he'd killed her. Once I knew that, I could go to Detective Pitt with my conclusions. Like *Jeopardy*, the drive gave me the question, but I still needed the answer. I hoped Nana Jo was right about my subconscious mind figuring things out through my writing. I opened my laptop and tried to settle my conscious mind to give my subconscious a chance to work.

By the time James returned with Detective Inspector Covington, Sergeant Turnbull had also returned with his boss, Inspector Simon Woodson. When Inspector Woodson discovered Scotland Yard on the scene, he turned red and looked as though he would explode.

"This here's my patch and no ruddy Scotland Yard whippersnapper, still wet behind the ears, is gonna come down and tell me how to do my job." Inspector Woodson was short, fat, and bald and when he yelled, his voice went up a couple of octaves and his face turned red.

Detective Inspector Peter Covington was young, tall, lean, and gangly, with a head full of curly brown hair. He looked like a fresh-faced kid in comparison to the inspector. However, the mild-mannered detective had a boiling point and Inspector Woodson had found it.

Detective Inspector Covington pulled himself up to his full height, which made him appear to be two feet taller than Inspector Woodson. He removed his hat and got in the inspector's face. "I've investigated and solved more than fifty murders. How many have you solved?"

Woodson sputtered. His face turned from red to purple. "You . . . You . . . I'll have your badge. I'll—"

"If you use your head for more than just a hat rack, you'll sit down and listen." Winston's voice bounced around the rafters of the vaulted ceiling and the wooden floors. He entered the large room and marched over to his desk and sat down.

Rufus and Tango followed. Rufus sat on the rug under the desk. Tango hopped up into the windowsill and groomed himself.

Inspector Woodson removed his hat and smoothed down the few strands of hair that remained. "I'm very sorry for losing my temper like that, Mr. Churchill, sir." He glared at the Scotland Yard detective and gripped his hat so tightly he crushed the brim.

"Sit down," Winston ordered.

Inspector Woodson nodded and quickly plopped down on the edge of the nearest chair. Unfortunately, the chair nearest to him was not close to Winston. He looked around, unsure of whether he should scoot his chair closer or remain where he was.

"You too." Winston glared at Detective Inspector Covington.

Covington took a few moments to find a comfortable chair closer to Winston and a seat of power. He sat down and waited.

Lord William had followed Winston into the study and was seated on a sofa near the bookshelf. He filled his pipe and sat quietly.

James leaned against a bookshelf. He watched the drama through a smoke-filled haze.

Winston turned to look at Detective Inspector Covington. "You must be the Scotland Yard detective Lord William was telling me about."

Detective Inspector Covington nodded. "Yes, sir."

Winston nodded. "Thank you for coming so quickly. I'm sure"—he turned and stared at Inspector Woodson—"our local police, while a fine group of men, recognize this is a very sensitive matter. I have no doubt that, when given a moment to reflect, they will appreciate the offer of assistance."

Inspector Woodson choked and sputtered and looked at everything except Mr. Churchill. Eventually, he sighed and nodded.

"Thank you, Inspector. I'm glad you were able to see the importance of utilizing all resources at your disposal to ensure victory by *asking* Scotland Yard for assistance." He smiled. "After all, things like murder don't happen in Westerham. You run a very well-regulated ship down here." He chuckled. "It takes keen insight to recognize this murder is probably going to be a London affair." Like the Pied Piper led children with his pipe, Winston led men with his words. He wove words together into a beautifully lyrical cadence which lulled the strongest men into relaxed positions of comfort where they were most vulnerable. He used that gift to convince the unwitting Kent policeman not only that he wanted Scotland Yard to investigate the murder but that contacting Scotland Yard had been his idea the entire time.

As Winston spoke, Inspector Woodson's face underwent a series of rapid changes. From an initial look of contained rage, it softened to one of humility and pride. Woodson leaned back and smiled. "Well, of course, you're right. The girl came from London and, while I don't like to brag, we've certainly never had any murders in this neck of the weald." He laughed at his play on words, using the old English term to describe the Kent countryside. "You're right, sir, this is most likely a London matter and the killer will most certainly be a Londoner." He smiled.

"Would you care for a drink?" Winston rang for Thompkins, who arrived so quickly he must have been outside the door.

"Well, I don't mind if I do."

"Scotch," Winston ordered.

Thompkins returned carrying a tray with a bottle of Johnny Walker Red Label Scotch and glasses already filled.

Inspector Woodson took a glass and sipped the amber liquid.

Detective Inspector Covington and James declined.

Lord William pulled out his pocket watch. "A bit early for me, Thompkins."

Inspector Woodson and Winston drank.

"Perhaps we should let the younger set get about clearing this mess up while we catch up," Winston suggested.

Lord William, Detective Inspector Covington, and James left while Inspector Woodson and Winston started a conversation about horses and the races.

Outside the room, Detective Inspector Covington whistled. "He's good. I thought for sure they'd send me packing on the next train back to London."

Lord William smiled. "We're all just soldiers following orders."

Detective Inspector Covington raised a brow in surprise.

"Are you married?" Lord William asked.

"No." He shook his head.

Lord William smiled. "Well, one day I think you'll understand." He returned to the study.

James led the detective upstairs to the room where Jessica Carlisle had been murdered. Albert, the footman, had been replaced by Sergeant Turnbull on guard duty. The lad was still a bit pale but looked better than he had hours earlier.

Detective Inspector Covington showed his warrant card to the sergeant, who moved aside and allowed the men to enter.

Inside, a body lay on the bed, covered in a sheet. Lady Elizabeth and Mrs. Churchill examined the walls as though they were looking for something.

"James," Lady Elizabeth said. "I'm so glad you're back and you brought Detective Inspector Covington." She introduced the detective to Mrs. Churchill.

Detective Inspector Covington went to the bed and examined the body. He looked around the room, under the bed, in drawers, and checked the window, noting the glass where James had broken in. The others stood by silently until he finished his examination of the crime scene. He called for Sergeant Turnbull. "What's been done?"

Sergeant Turnbull sputtered. "Well . . . I . . . I mean inspector . . . nothing, sir."

Detective Inspector Covington ordered the man to call for the coroner. The small Kent Police lacked the same resources as Scotland Yard, so he told him to telephone the Yard to send down a team to aid in the investigation.

When the sergeant left to carry out his orders, Lady Elizabeth asked, "Detective, I hope James explained the delicacy of the situation."

He nodded.

"Good. So, you understand we need to keep this as quiet as possible. The last thing we need is to have a member of Parliament involved in a murder investigation."

"I understand you don't want a lot of publicity, but I have a murder to investigate. The duke said there's a BBC producer here too. I don't know how you plan to keep him out of this."

"Just leave that to us." Lady Elizabeth and Mrs. Churchill exchanged glances.

"May I ask what you two were doing when I came in?" Detective Inspector Covington asked.

Lady Elizabeth went to one of the walls of the bedroom that had a large fireplace and built-in bookshelves. "We were looking for a way the killer could have gotten into the house. The door was bolted from the inside and James had to break the window to get in from outside."

Detective Inspector Covington looked at Mrs. Churchill. "Wouldn't you know if there was a secret entrance?"

Mrs. Churchill shrugged. "Not necessarily. To be completely honest, I never really liked the house and didn't pay a great deal of attention to the details. This was Winston's baby." She looked around. "It was a wreck when he bought it. It looked like a huge money pit to me." She sighed. "He worked with an architect, Philip Tilden, to make it habitable."

Detective Inspector Covington looked as though he wanted to speak but a glance at Lady Elizabeth changed his mind.

"You should talk to Winston or one of the children." She paced. "Randolph might know."

Detective Inspector Covington asked questions until the coroner arrived.

Dr. Wilson returned to Chartwell House for the second time that day. He didn't look pleased at being summoned again but summarized his initial findings and gave an estimated time of death to Detective

Inspector Covington and the Scotland Yard detectives who arrived soon after he did.

The house was abuzz with all of the activity of Scotland Yard. The detectives photographed the room and the grounds from virtually every angle imaginable. The staff and guests were questioned and requestioned and when they thought they'd answered every question possible, they were questioned again. At long last, the ambulance arrived and removed the body and the flurry of activity died down to a flutter.

Lunch consisted of a cold buffet. Winston didn't look thrilled. However, Mrs. Churchill said it showed respect. Detective Inspector Covington was invited to stay at Chartwell, so he joined the house party for lunch.

James was mindful of his assignment and stayed close to Randolph. He tried to engage him in conversation but was unsuccessful. Randolph was red-eyed and drank rather than ate his lunch. He barely spoke during the entire meal, except to ask for more wine to go with his scotch.

Conversation was somewhat constrained during the meal. Winston announced he would grant Guy Burgess an interview on the Mediterranean and talked about the importance of the Mediterranean to the commonwealth and the role of Indian independence.

Leopold Amery listened and intervened only to soften any of Winston's comments which might be damaging to the conservative party.

James noted Lord Stemphill was particularly attentive to Lady Alistair, who fidgeted and stammered.

Daphne listened attentively while Anthony Blunt delivered a monologue about the great works of art and their importance to the British realm and the world.

Lunch was soon over. Lord William, Winston, and Guy Burgess moved to the study to continue the interview. It took both James and Anthony Blunt to get Randolph to his room. He was too drunk to walk.

Lady Alistair claimed she had a headache and retired to her room.

Lord Stemphill held the door as James and Anthony Blunt dragged Randolph from the room. James couldn't help but notice a sinister smile on his face as he passed through.

Lady Elizabeth was the first to arrive in the drawing room and sat knitting. She was joined by Mrs. Churchill, Daphne, James, Lord William, and Detective Inspector Covington. When everyone was seated, Mrs. Churchill rang for tea. Thompkins rolled the tea service to Mrs. Churchill, who sat by the fire. Normally, the butler would have left after tea was delivered. Instead, Thompkins stood near the back wall, tall, straight, and proper.

"Now, we may not have much time before anyone else joins us, so we'd better be quick," Lady Elizabeth said.

Thompkins coughed discretely and stepped forward. He told the group what he learned from the servants. He'd already told Lady Elizabeth, who had taken a few minutes to talk to Albert and the housekeeper. The butler would have preferred for Lady Elizabeth to deliver the information, but she had insisted Thompkins do the honors in case the others had questions.

Mrs. Churchill listened attentively and then sighed. "That means there's someone else who might have killed her?" She looked at Lady Elizabeth. "Someone other than Randolph might have done it?" She spoke softly.

Lady Elizabeth reached over and squeezed her friend's hand. "Yes, dear."

Mrs. Churchill gave a quick hysterical laugh and then pulled out a handkerchief and cried softly.

The others remained silent for a few seconds and then proceeded on.

"Winston was successful in getting Burgess to hold off on reporting the murder, but only through the weekend." Lord William filled his pipe and smoked.

"Wonderful, dear. Were you able to talk to Leo?" Lady Elizabeth asked.

"Only had a few minutes. Chap claimed he'd never laid eyes on the girl before he came here. Hasn't seen his son in months. Doubt there could be anything there." He huffed.

"Son?" Detective Inspector Covington asked. "There was some trouble with his son, wasn't there?"

Lord William frowned. "Bad seed that one. Joined the fascist. Been trying to recruit British soldiers to join Hitler."

Detective Inspector Covington slapped his knee. "I remember now. He was one of those Bolsheviks. Got himself arrested, but they let him go. Moved to the continent." He looked around. "Is he involved in this?"

Lady Elizabeth shook her head. "I don't know. He's the right age and I was just wondering." She turned to Mrs. Churchill. "Didn't you say John Amery introduced Randolph to Jessica?"

Mrs. Churchill looked as though her mind was far away. "Did I? Yes, I'm sure Randolph mentioned Amery." She stared at Lady Elizabeth. "Do you think it's important?"

"I don't know. At this point, I'm just collecting information." Lady Elizabeth knitted in silence for several seconds and then turned to her niece. "Daphne?"

"I talked to both Anthony Blunt and Guy Burgess. They claimed they ate dinner at the George and Dragon. After dinner, they played darts and didn't get back until nearly two."

Detective Inspector Covington took notes. "That'll be easy enough for my men to check."

"They said they ran into Lord Stemphill when they returned and stayed up drinking and talking for a couple of hours," Daphne said.

"That's awfully late to be up talking," Lady Elizabeth said.

Daphne smiled. "They said they were discussing the George and Dragon's famous unsolved murder."

Lady Elizabeth nodded.

"What unsolved murder? Maybe it has a bearing on this case." Detective Inspector Covington sat on the edge of his seat.

Lady Elizabeth knitted. "I very much doubt it. Mr. Humphrey was killed over a hundred years ago."

Detective Inspector Covington sat back. "Never mind."

James stood near the fireplace. He made several glances in Daphne's direction, but she didn't look up.

"I didn't get much out of Randolph. He's been on a bender all day." He stared at Mrs. Churchill and apologized.

She waved away his apology.

"I did learn Jessica Carlisle used to work for the Royal Aeronautical Society. John Amery introduced her to Randolph at a party in London." James smoked.

"Didn't Stemphill work for them too?" Lady Elizabeth asked.

James nodded. "He did."

"That's interesting. The victim worked with Stemphill and she knew John Amery, son of Leopold Amery. Amery introduced her to Randolph." Detective Inspector Covington scribbled in his notebook.

Lady Elizabeth sighed. "I agree it seems odd, but it's a small world. That's how people meet. They're introduced by someone they both know." She put down her knitting and sat for a few moments. Then she shook herself and picked up her needles and continued. "I wasn't able to talk to Lord Stemphill, but I'll get with him tonight after dinner."

"He seemed particularly interested in my mother." James frowned.

"I noticed that too." Lady Elizabeth took a sip of tea. "Clemmie, did you talk to Lady Alistair?"

Mrs. Churchill pulled herself up tall and dabbed at her eyes. "I did. She isn't going to leave."

Lady Elizabeth stole a glance in Daphne's direction. "Thank you. Perhaps you could—"

"I'd like to talk to Lady Alistair." Daphne blushed. "If that's okay?"

Lady Elizabeth stared at her niece but then smiled. "Of course, dear." She looked around. "Is that everyone?"

"I didn't figure out how to get into the room yet," Mrs. Churchill said softly.

Lady Elizabeth knitted. "Actually, I've been thinking about it and I have an idea."

"Well, I wish you'd share your idea with me," Detective Inspector Covington said. "I'm clean out of ideas on how the killer got into and out of that room."

Lady Elizabeth smiled. "I need to test my theory first."

Chapter 19

The last thing I wanted to do on a snowy, cold Sunday morning in November was get out of bed, especially when I had stayed up half the night writing. I contemplated calling my mom and telling her I wasn't going to make it to church. The various scenarios of that conversation floated around in my head, and the muscles in my stomach tightened. Resistance was futile. It was easier to comply, so I forced myself out of bed.

Snickers didn't budge until I turned on the lights. Then she stood, turned around in a circle, and laid back down with her back to me. The look on her face before she buried her muzzle under a blanket spoke volumes about what she thought about being roused from her bed before noon. Even Oreo, normally bouncing off the sides of his crate whenever I rolled over, just stared at me as if to say, *Really? Didn't we just go to sleep?*

I liked to keep the house cool at night but had purchased a programmable thermostat, which kicked in around six on weekdays and eight on weekends. So, the floors were still cold and it took longer for my shower to get hot. Needless to say, I hurried to get showered and dressed. My body had acclimated by the time I was dressed, but when I looked out the back window and saw the ground covered in snow, I cringed at the idea of heading out in what the app on my phone told me were single-digit temperatures. I hunted through a drawer and found a set of sweaters for the dogs and then coaxed them into the garments. Snickers looked bored and humiliated, as if wearing a sweater was an affront to her dignity.

I looked her in the eyes. "You'll thank me for this when you get outside. Now, suck it up and give me your paw."

She yawned, but I was bigger and more experienced. Oreo wagged his tail and bounced around. However, he too was soon dressed. When the deed was done, he rolled on his back and generated static electricity, which caused the hair on his ears to stand straight out. He was such a goofball.

We went downstairs and I opened the door to let them out. Snickers took one look at the snow, turned, and looked at me. I gave her a nudge over the threshold and quickly closed the door. Oreo went bounding out into the snow with a zeal that always put a smile on my face. He stuck his nose into it and then barked and ran in circles until he was covered in snow. I loved watching him play in the snow. His zest and total abandon was refreshing. However, experience told me I needed to watch because he invariably forgot why he was there until his under belly and legs were cold. Then he wanted to come back inside, without taking care of business. He needed to be watched. He made his way to the door and stood barking. I hardened my heart and refused to open the door. Eventually, he went to the fence and did what needed to be done. Then, and only then, did I let them back in. He shook himself, leaving a pile of wet snow on the floor. I wiped the pilled snow from their legs and feet. Nothing like stepping in melted snow in wet feet to teach dog owners the importance of wiping your pet's feet in the winter.

I opened the garage door and turned on the remote start

for my car so it would be nice and warm when I left. Automatic lights, remote start, and heated seats were the best things man ever invented, apart from the brilliant soul who discovered ground coffee beans and hot water made the elixir of life.

A quick cup of coffee and dog biscuits for the pack and I was out. I drove to my mom's house and picked her up. I headed for her church and was surprised when she suggested we skip church and go to breakfast instead. I had to stop and do a double take to make sure the woman in my car was actually the woman who raised me.

"Sure. I'm fine with that. Where do you want to go?"

She fidgeted and avoided eye contact, which was the second clue that made me think I should check the back of this alien imposter's neck for signs of a pod. "I would like to go to Tippecanoe Place. I hear they have a wonderful Sunday brunch."

It was a good thing I was at a stop light because I sat and stared at her for several seconds until the car behind me honked its horn. I drove down the street for a couple of blocks and then pulled into a nearby parking lot. "Okay. Who are you and what have you done with my mother?"

She looked wide-eyed and innocent. "I don't know what you mean?"

I held up my hand and began to tick each item off. "First, you don't want to go to church. My mother always goes to church. In fact, she thinks I'm going to hell if I miss one Sunday. Second, you want me to drive to the Studebaker Mansion over thirty miles away when it's snowing, which means I will need to drive on the interstate. My mother cringes when I drive in the city when the roads are completely dry." I stared. "Who are you?"

My mother shook her head. "Stop being melodramatic. I just thought it would be nice to go to Tippecanoe Place today." She paused.

I folded my arms across my chest and waited.

"Oh, alright. Harold says it's about time he met you and Jenna. He suggested Tippecanoe Place."

I was surprised. "I think that's a really good idea, but Jenna's not here. She and Tony are on a cruise."

"They got back late last night. I called and told her you'd pick her up on the way."

I stared for several seconds. However, the idea that my mother had called and ordered my sister to get up and get dressed early on Sunday morning made me giddy. Jenna was not a morning person. If she had only arrived home a few hours ago, she'd be even less enthusiastic about this excursion. It was a real effort to keep the smile off my face.

I pulled into the first Starbucks I crossed.

"Why are we stopping for coffee if we're going to breakfast?" Mother asked.

"Trust me. You aren't going to want to see Jenna without caffeine."

When I pulled up in front of my sister's North Harbor Victorian, my mother got in the back seat. For some reason, she never liked riding in the front when I was driving on the interstate. It made me feel like I was driving Miss Daisy when it was just the two of us.

I honked the horn and Jenna came out bundled up like the abominable snowman. She got in and glared at me.

I handed her a large hot tea and smiled.

She held it close to her face and let the steam warm her hands and face before she took a sip. "Thanks."

"How was your trip?" I pulled onto the street.

"Warm." She took another sip of her tea.

I suspected one-word responses were the best I would get for a while, so I stopped trying to make conversation and focused on the roads, which were wet and slick.

There were basically two types of snow in southwestern Michigan on the shores of Lake Michigan. We had system snow and lake effect snow. Meteorologists can tell the difference between the two in technical terms. For most of us Michiganders, we notice system snow was heavier and wetter than lake effect snow. Lake effect snow was light and fluffy and blew in the wind and didn't pack well for snowballs or snowmen. However, it was the pretty stuff that made for great pictures. System snow was what I was driving through, and I needed to keep my wits about me to keep from skidding. Thankfully, the snowplows had been through and plowed and salted the interstate, but passing semis still splashed the wet muck onto my windshield and heavy gusts shook my SUV and kept me gripping the steering wheel.

The amazing thing about snow in southwestern Michigan was that thirty miles could make a world of difference. By the time I got to River Bend, there was barely any snow on the ground and the roads were dry. I released my grip on the steering wheel. I looked in the rearview mirror. My mom still had one hand on the grab assist handle and the other on the middle seat rest.

Tippecanoe Place was a first-class restaurant and the name of the former home of the Studebaker family. The stone mansion was huge with more than 24,000 sq. ft. of space on four levels. Forty rooms, twenty fireplaces, and ornately carved woodwork made the mansion a showplace, almost one hundred fifty years after it was first constructed. The mansion was a museum, complete with furniture, pictures, and Studebaker family memorabilia.

I pulled up to the driveway and let Mom and Jenna out at the door. Fortunately, I found a parking space close by, which didn't involve a long trek through the parking lot since my boots were more for beauty than inclement weather and a few steps was all it took before my feet were cold and wet. Not all boots were created equal and these were definitely not intended for Michigan winters.

Inside, I hung up my coat and prepared to wait with the others crowded into the lobby. The house was decorated for Christmas and looked festive. There was a small trio dressed in formalwear playing Christmas music near the grand staircase. Sundays were a big time for Tippecanoe Place, especially after JAMU home football weekends. There were stations set up around the main dining area offering omelets, Belgian waffles, and hand-carved ham and roasts.

Harold must have made reservations because we were shown to our table immediately. The drawing room was a large rectangular space with an alcove. The alcove had a wall of windows, a large fireplace, and French doors that allowed the space to be closed off from the rest of the room. At the table, I was pleasantly surprised to see my nephews, Christopher and Zaq. I looked at my sister and raised an eyebrow. She merely shrugged and hugged her sons, whom she hadn't seen for over a week. The twins were students at JAMU, so going across town to Tippecanoe Place wasn't nearly the journey we'd endured driving from Michigan.

"You must be Harold." I held out a hand but was totally taken off guard when I was grabbed and pulled into a large bear hug.

Harold was tall with white hair, a white mustache and beard, and a happy, jovial face that reminded me of Santa Claus.

He hugged Jenna too, who wasn't a hugger, but something about Harold's friendly nature made her smile. "Where's your husband, Tony?"

"He couldn't make it. He has to be in court tomorrow and has a ton of paperwork to do," Jenna apologized.

"I hope this is okay with all of you." He held the chair for my mom to sit before sitting himself. "But, I thought it was about time we all got acquainted."

My mother giggled like a schoolgirl and looked at Harold as though she would melt.

I glanced at my sister, who just stared.

A waiter poured champagne for everyone. The champagne was included in the brunch, another great reason for having brunch at Tippecanoe Place. My nephews had just turned twenty-one and had to show their driver's licenses before they were served. Once we were served, Harold announced we would all be enjoying the buffet on him, but first, he wanted to make a toast.

He stood. "To Grace." He stared at my mom. "The most wonderful woman who has finally agreed to make me the happiest man on the planet."

We raised our glasses and drank.

The meal was delicious, and I found Harold to be open, friendly, and surprisingly likeable. He catered to my mom's every whim. When she shivered, he had the waiter add another log to the fire and a throw was brought to cover her lap. When her beef was a little too rare, he had the waiter bring her another slice. When this new offering was cooked enough but too dry, he had yet another slice provided with au jus. When she praised the lemon tart, he purchased an entire pie for her to take home. No request was too small. When Mom choked on a piece of meat and Harold took her knife and fork and cut her meat into smaller pieces, I thought Jenna was going to puke. The twins snickered. I couldn't help staring.

Jenna stood. "I need to go to the ladies' room."

I hopped up. "Me too." I hurried after her. Just as the door closed to the restroom, we burst out laughing. I laughed so hard my sides hurt. There were two other women in the restroom with us, and when they saw how much we laughed, they laughed too. When we tried to explain why or stopped for a few seconds, we started right up again. We finally pulled ourselves together.

"I can't believe he cut her meat," Jenna said and that started us off again.

I wiped the tears from my eyes. "I don't know where she found him, but he's perfect for her."

Jenna nodded. She reached in her purse and pulled out some papers and handed them to me.

"What's this?" I asked.

"Well, I sent a message to one of the investigators in my office when you told me Mom was getting married. I asked him to find out what he could about this guy."

I read through the report. "I can't believe you found out this much information while you were on a cruise. We didn't even know his last name."

"Robertson. His name is Harold Robertson."

"Robertson? You mean as in *the* Robertsons like, in Robertson's Department Store?"

Jenna nodded. "Yep. Harold's family owned Robertson's Department Store."

Robertson's was the premiere department store in the area when we were children. They had a huge store in downtown River Bend and smaller stores in North Harbor and Elkhart, Indiana.

"You have got to be joking." I read through more. "He's a rocket scientist?"

She nodded. "He didn't follow in the family business. He went to school to be an Aerospace Engineer. He worked for NASA for forty years but decided to move back after he retired."

"Married for thirty years until his wife died two years ago." I read more. "She died of cancer."

That sobered us both up. "He cared for her until she died."

"I like him," I said.

She nodded. "I like him too, but more importantly, I think he'll make her happy."

"I can't believe Mom is getting married again."

Jenna got up and we prepared to leave. "Well, I guess it's a good thing, since she apparently is enjoying the sex so much."

We all chatted for a bit but then decided to call it a day. Mom rode back with Harold, so it was just Jenna and me on the return trip. Thankfully, the sun was out and the roads were much less slippery than they were earlier. I filled Jenna in on what was going on with Nana Jo and the investigation. When I dropped her off at home, she was fully updated.

The rest of the afternoon was uneventful. I cleaned, but the house wasn't really messy so that didn't take long. After a half hour of putzing around, I decided to write a bit before my date with Frank.

James walked into the drawing room but stopped at the sight of Daphne staring out of the window. She stood with her back to the door, facing the weald. A beam of sunlight landed on her hair, casting a hazy halo-like glow over her golden hair. It was a sunny day, despite the brisk wind. James stared for several seconds and remained perfectly still. Tango snuck in beside him and brushed his leg, causing the floor to creak.

Daphne turned at the sound and the spell was broken. "James, I didn't hear you come in."

"I just got here." He crossed the room and opened his arms to embrace her.

Arms folded across her chest, she stepped out of reach. "There's no easy way to do this, so I'm just going to say it." She turned back to face him. "I can't marry you."

He stood there and stared. "What?"

"I can't marry you. I thought I could, but I can't."

"You can't be serious?"

"I'm very serious."

"This is about my mother, isn't it?" He paused, but when she didn't respond, he hurried on. "She'll come around. This has been a crazy time, but once she gets to know you like I do, I know she'll love you."

Daphne shook her head. "This isn't about your mother."

He looked surprised. "Don't say you don't care. I don't believe that."

"I do care. That's why I can't marry you."

"Can we talk about this?"

She shook her head. "Talking won't change anything."

James started to interrupt, but she stopped him.

"Look, there's no point talking about it. I've made up my mind. I won't marry you. You deserve someone who will be a credit to you." She stared. "I'm just not that person." She released a heavy sigh. "I'm sorry." She turned and walked out of the room.

James stood glued to the spot for several minutes after she left. The door to the drawing room opened and Thompkins entered. "Telephone, Your Grace."

James nodded and walked out of the room.

Daphne knocked on the bedroom of Lady Alistair. "Come in."

She took a deep breath and entered the room.

Lady Alistair sat in a chair near the window. The lights were out and the curtains were drawn, which made the room very dark.

"Lady Alistair." Daphne walked forward.

Lady Alistair stood and turned so her back was to Daphne.

Daphne stopped and took a deep breath. "Lady Alistair, I am really very sorry for the way I've behaved the past few days. I have no excuses to offer. I could say this isn't normal, but . . . then, I don't think that really matters. I just want you to know, I care very deeply for James, which is why I told him I can't marry him."

Lady Alistair turned to look at Daphne. She spoke softly. "You what?"

"I don't want to hurt him in any way. I have no explanation. He deserves someone who will be a credit to him. Someone who won't embarrass him." She looked down. "Someone who isn't involved in scandal." She took a deep breath. "I know Mrs. Churchill would like you to stay and I hope you will." She paused. "That's all I wanted to say. Thank you." She turned to leave but stopped when she heard a sob. She turned to face Lady Alistair.

Lady Alistair's shoulders shook and tears streamed down her face.

Daphne walked to the woman. She stood, unsure of what to do. However, another glance at the sobbing woman and she embraced her. For a moment, Lady Alistair stood stiffly but soon relaxed and lay her head on Daphne's shoulder and sobbed. After several moments, the crying subsided and Daphne helped the woman into a seat. She opened the window and sat next to her.

"I'm so sorry. I can't believe I did that." Lady Alistair dabbed at her eyes with a handkerchief.

"Can I help you?" Daphne asked.

Lady Alistair stared at Daphne. She reached in her pocket and pulled out a crumpled letter. She handed it to Daphne.

Daphne unfolded the letter and read. She frowned as she read. When she finished reading, she looked at Lady Alistair's face. "That's blackmail. This would ruin James."

Lady Alistair nodded. "I know. I was such a fool, but it was a long time ago. Long before I met James's father. I was . . . involved with a man, with a married man." She sniffed. "I was young and foolish. It didn't last long. My family managed to hush things up, and I thought that was the end of it. Then I met Alistair and got married. Now this."

Daphne picked up the letter and reread it. "He says unless you do what he wants, he'll expose everything. Your past will be plastered all over the newspapers."

Lady Alistair choked. "I know. This is horrible."

"Who sent it?" She looked down. "It's signed, *A Friend.*"

Lady Alistair shook her head. "I have no idea. I thought it was that Jessica person, but now she's dead."

"Well, if she's dead, that would be an end to it."

"It can't be her. I only received the note today."

Both ladies looked at each other.

Daphne's brow furrowed and she stared off into space, as though she was trying to remember something. Finally, she stood. "May I keep this?" She held up the letter.

Lady Alistair looked up with fear in her eyes. "What are you going to do?"

"I'm going to put a stop to this. I'm not going to stand by while anyone hurts James." Daphne stood straight, pushed her shoulders back, and set her chin.

Lady Alistair nodded and Daphne turned and marched out of the room.

Chapter 20

"Still no idea how someone got in that room and killed Jessica. Plus, now I've got another plot twist. What was I thinking?" I looked at Snickers, who was using my foot as a pillow. She didn't like when I moved and gave me a look that let me know I had better make sure all of my papers and shoes were out of her reach the next time I left the house.

I looked at my watch. Frank would be by soon. We were going to dinner. I took a good look at myself and contemplated changing into something a little . . . less academic school teacher and more single woman who was open to dating. A quick look outside showed there was about a foot of snow on the ground. The streets looked wet and slushy. I looked at my closet and shivered at the idea of removing my tights for panty hose. I compromised by exchanging my turtleneck sweater for a V-neck that was fitted and showed off my waist and other endowments. And chose a pair of thigh-high black boots that I'd purchased years ago for a Halloween costume at the high school for a '70's celebration. The boots were cute, with high chunky heels that were back in fashion. Frank arrived early and, based on the look he gave me, I'd say my outfit met with his approval.

We were supposed to eat at one of the local wineries, which had a great restaurant and wines to please both a wine-challenged newbie like me and a wine connoisseur like Frank. Unfortunately, the location involved traveling a lot of back country roads. These roads were beautiful the other three seasons of the year. However, in the winter, the narrow, winding roads were last on the list to be plowed. There were vast open fields on each side of the roads with nothing to block the winds and experienced tremendous snowdrifts, which made them virtually impassable by anything except a snowmobile or four-legged beasts. Getting stuck in a snowdrift was not my idea of a good time. Thankfully, Frank was willing to forego the winery for a new restaurant in downtown South Harbor.

The worse part of downtown South Harbor had to be finding parking. Thankfully, The Lighthouse Bar and Grille offered valet parking. We pulled up to the front. During good weather valet parking wouldn't be needed. However, on days like today, it was wonderful. The restaurant was in a two-story building on quaint State Street. In warmer weather, diners took advantage of rooftop dining, which provided views of Lake Michigan. There was a decent crowd and I wondered if we wouldn't be better off grabbing a pizza and going back to my place. However, when Frank approached the hostess, she hurried away. Within minutes, a well-dressed man with a huge smile came up and hugged Frank as though he were a long-lost relative. The man spoke in another language, which sounded a lot like German. Surprisingly enough, Frank not only seemed to understand him but responded.

When they finished their greeting, Frank introduced us. "Sam, I'd like you to meet Gunther Muller." He turned to the man, "Gunther, this is Samantha Washington."

I reached out my hand to shake, but Gunther wasn't having it. He pulled me toward him and gave me a hug and then kissed me on each cheek. "Any friend of Frank Patterson is a friend of mine."

Gunther said a few words to the hostess and then promptly escorted us to a table by a large fireplace. The lighting was low and candles at each table provided a romantic atmosphere. Even in the dim lighting, I could tell the restaurant was excellently furnished with heavyweight white tablecloths, silver that was hefty, and crystal stemware.

Gunther and Frank spoke briefly before he hurried off.

"I'm sure the people who reserved this table are going to be very upset." I smiled. "You really know how to impress a girl."

Frank grinned. "If I'd known bringing the girl to a fancy restaurant was all it took to impress her, I'd have brought her long ago."

I was thankful for the dim lighting as heat rushed to my face. I took a sip of water to give myself a minute to recover. "This is very nice, but I didn't know you spoke German."

"There's a lot you don't know about me." He grinned and reached across and took my hand. "But, I'd like to change that."

We sat there for several seconds until a waiter came by and brought a bottle of wine. Frank raised an eyebrow but was told Gunther had insisted. The waiter uncorked the bottle and offered Frank the cork to sniff. He then poured a small amount in a glass and offered that. Frank twirled the wine in his glass, sniffed it, and then sipped it. He nodded his approval. Only then was the wine poured into our glasses.

I took a sip. I'd never been a big wine drinker. I tried to hide the pucker that came to my face, but I knew I'd failed when Frank laughed.

"It's a bit dry, but it's actually a very good wine. Gunther's family owned a winery in Switzerland and this is part of his private stock," he explained.

"I'm sure it's very nice."

"We're going to have to work on your palate."

I looked at the menu. There weren't a lot of choices and many of them appeared to be in another language, probably German. Most restaurants served chicken. It was always a safe bet. I never took German in school and was contemplating pulling out my cell phone and asking Siri for the German word for chicken when the waiter returned.

Frank reached across and pulled my menu down. "Do you trust me?" He held my gaze.

I raised an eyebrow but put down the menu and nodded.

Frank ordered and, although he spoke English, I had no idea what he'd ordered.

The waiter bowed, clicked his heels, and left.

"This should be interesting," I said.

He smiled. "Food should always be interesting, if nothing else." He sipped his wine. "Although, I think you'll like it. Gunther's a world-class chef. I was surprised when I found out he was here."

"Have you known each other long?"

He sipped his wine. "Twenty years." He got the faraway look in his eyes he always got when he thought about his life before North Harbor.

I waited, but I knew he wouldn't, or couldn't say more. So, I changed the subject. "I met Harold today."

The waiter brought our first course. It was a soup. I had no idea what it was, but it tasted good and I ate every drop while I told him about our brunch with Harold. There were three more courses, all delicious. Again, I decided to throw caution to the wind and simply eat and enjoy them without asking questions. Frank knew there were only a few foods I absolutely detested, like tomatoes, beets, and Brussels sprouts. If any of the

dishes I ate contained them, they were completely camou-
flaged.

The final course was a dessert that was so light and fluffy I
might have closed my eyes and moaned when I tasted it. Frank
laughed and I opened my eyes.

"Now, that is the perfect response," he said.

"I'm sorry, did you say something?"

He shook his head. "Not at all." He stared while I scraped
every last morsel from the dish. Then he slid his across to me.

Pride should have stopped me from eating it, but where
this chocolate delight was concerned, I had no pride. I ate his
dessert too. "I'm going to regret that tomorrow, but tonight it
was delicious."

"No regrets. I love to watch people enjoy food. I think
that's why I wanted to own my own restaurant."

"That was the most amazing thing I've ever tasted in my
life. I'm so glad it snowed."

He looked surprised.

"If it hadn't snowed, we wouldn't be eating here. We
would have gone to the winery. Thanks to the snow, I got to
try something new."

He raised his glass. "To the snow." He took a sip and looked
around. "I have some information for you." He reached in his
pocket and pulled out a small notepad. "My friend finally got
back to me about Maria and Denise Bennett." He looked
around again and then leaned closer. "I think he found the
connection you were looking for. After her husband died,
Maria Romanov moved to upstate New York for a few years.
Apparently, her husband had family there. She got a job as a
matron at a minimum security prison."

I stared. "The same one Horace Evans was in?"

He nodded. "Not just Horace, but Gaston Renoir as well."

"I thought Gaston was tried in France?"

Frank shook his head. "Nope. New York City."

"Well, I'll be. I assumed everything happened in France. So that's how Maria knew about Gaston and Horace to blackmail them."

"That's not all." Frank looked serious. "Apparently, Denise Bennett has a connection to that prison too."

"No way. Was she in prison too?" I was starting to agree with Nana Jo that Shady Acres employed an excess of ex-cons.

He shook his head. "Denise Bennett isn't her real name."

I stared and waited for an explanation.

"Denise Bennett was born Dorothy Smith. She married Antonio Borrelli."

I whistled. "*The* Antonio Borrelli, the mobster?"

He nodded. "The Feds have been trying to convict him for everything from drug trafficking to organized crime. They've never been able to get anything to stick. Whenever they thought they had a case against him, the person either went missing or died. Finally, six years ago they got him on tax evasion. Dorothy helped put him away and entered the witness protection program."

"So where does Maria come into it?"

"Antonio Borrelli was at the same prison. I guess there must have been a lot of media coverage around the time. Anyway, Maria must have recognized her."

"Wow." I sat there flabbergasted and stared. "Wow."

"No one is supposed to know this," he stressed.

I nodded. "Denise Bennett is living her new life in sleepy little North Harbor, Michigan, far away from her mob boss husband and along comes Maria Romanov, threatening to expose her." I frowned.

"What's wrong?"

"Maria was blackmailing Gaston, Horace, and, most likely, Denise Bennett. They all had reasons to want her dead, but not all of them had a reason to want Magnus von Braun dead."

"Good point. So, who did it?"

I shook my head. "No idea. I feel like if I can figure out how it was done, I might be able to figure out whodunit."

We talked about the suspects and their motives. When the waiter came at last, we were no closer to figuring out who killed either Maria or Magnus.

When Frank asked for the check, he was informed that Gunther refused to accept his money. He was, the waiter explained, indebted to Frank. I could tell Frank was uncomfortable about the debt Gunther felt he owed him but eventually he graciously accepted and left a large tip for the waiter and we left.

Frank drove me home and we sat in the car and talked for a while, which was a really pleasant experience since Frank drove one of the nicest, most luxurious German SUVs I'd ever seen, a Porsche Cayenne. I wasn't an automobile enthusiast, but even I knew Porsches were special. I didn't know they made SUVs, so the first time he picked me up, I asked what kind of car it was. It was tacky to ask what something cost, but I admit to googling this baby. Fully loaded, with all the bells and whistles, and he had them all, this car cost more than twice what my husband and I paid for our first home. However, when you rode in it, you felt like you were floating on air. Sitting in heated leather seats that engulfed you like a warm blanket while the moon and stars shined down through the panoramic moonroof was a treat. We steamed up the windows for a while, but it was late and we both had work tomorrow.

Frank got out and opened the door for me and walked me to my door. We kissed good-night, and he left. I stood inside and watched him drive away, with a smile on my face.

Snickers and Oreo brought me back down to earth with their demands to be let out. So, I obliged. It was still cold, so they didn't dally and we were upstairs quickly.

Frank's information about Denise Bennett and Maria Romanov tied up some of the loose ends still floating around in my head. Maria knew Gaston and Horace from the prison in upstate New York. She would know all about Horace's past. If she was blackmailing him, he could have killed her. He had a good motive. Denise Bennett might have even been in on it. She had access to files on all of the employees. Horace had a motive for killing Magnus too. Plus, he was seen talking to Denise Bennett when Magnus's medicine was delivered and he took the medicine to Magnus. That meant he had the means and the opportunity. The only thing that still had me puzzled was how Horace got into Maria's room—a locked room. No matter how hard I thought, I couldn't come up with anything. I pulled out my laptop and prayed inspiration would come from writing. Tomorrow was Monday. That meant I only had a few more days to figure this out.

Lady Elizabeth entered the bedroom where Jessica Carlisle was murdered. She looked around the room and shook her head at the condition Scotland Yard left the room. She walked around the perimeter and examined books on the bookshelf and the fireplace.

James entered. "What's wrong?"

Lady Elizabeth stood in the center of the room and shook her head. "I don't know. Something seems off somehow, but I can't place my finger on it." She looked up at James. "Is something wrong?"

He paused. "Daphne's thrown me over. She refuses to marry me."

Lady Elizabeth walked forward. "I'm so sorry. I knew something was up earlier when she wanted to talk to your mother, but I had no idea."

James paced. "I have no intention of taking this lying down, but . . . I have to go to London on business. I'll be back later." He paused. "Do you think . . . you don't think she'll leave?"

She thought for a few minutes. "No. I don't think she'll leave. At least not until this murder is solved."

He laughed. "Can you do me a favor and not solve this one? At least not until I get back." He looked pleadingly at Lady Elizabeth.

"The way things are going, I don't think that will be a problem."

James nodded and then turned. As he got to the door, he seemed startled when Daphne entered.

She was clutching *Burke's Peerage* to her chest. "I'm glad I caught you before you left. I was hoping you would give me a lift," she said.

James raised an eyebrow. "Of course. I'll be happy to take you anywhere you need to go. I have something I have to do, but after that—"

"That won't be necessary. I just need a lift to London. I can take a cab after that and catch the train back."

James opened his mouth to speak, but one look in her normally warm blue eyes, which were cold and distant, and the determined set of her shoulders must have told him it would be best to remain silent. He nodded. "May I ask where you'd like to go?"

Daphne paused for a second before responding. "Somerset House."

James started. Obviously, that wasn't the response he'd expected. However, he recovered quickly. "I'm going to Thames House, just across the river. It's less than ten minutes away."

"Thank you. I'll get my jacket." Daphne turned and left.

James looked at Lady Elizabeth and then turned to leave.

"James, wait." Lady Elizabeth hurried to catch him. She pulled a small envelope from her pocket and handed it to him. "I wonder if you could have this analyzed."

He looked at the envelope. "What is it?"

"I suspect it's some type of drug. I found it in Jessica's handbag."

His eyes narrowed and he raised an eyebrow. "You removed evidence?"

"Only a small amount. I hope it's enough to test." She looked at James. "I suspect it's whatever Jessica slipped into Daphne's tea that made her act so . . . out of character."

James stared at Lady Elizabeth. After a moment, he nodded, placed the envelope into his pocket, turned, and left.

Lady Elizabeth watched him go and stood quietly for several moments. She eventually shook herself and returned to her examination of the room. She muttered silently to herself as she examined every crack, crevice, and cranny. She looked behind pictures, lifted statues and vases, and knocked on various wall panels. "Something just seems off about this room." She twirled around and tried to place her finger on the problem. She noticed there were two sconces on either side of the large four-poster bed and they were not aligned with the sconces on the opposite wall. The room's symmetry was off. "Is it just the symmetry that's bothering me?" she muttered aloud. She paced off the length of the room, then did the same thing for the depth. "That's odd. It's almost as though . . ." She looked at the bookcase that flanked either side of the fireplace. She whispered, "As Sherlock Holmes would say, 'when you've eliminated the impossible, what remains, no matter how improbable, must be the truth.'" She scanned the bookshelf and then pulled all of the books off the shelves and onto the floor. She cleared two shelves before she noticed a small lever behind one of the books. She examined the lever and then pulled it forward. The bookshelf squeaked and then slid back, exposing a dark corridor. She looked inside the corridor and started to take a step forward but stopped. "Alexander Pope was right, 'Fools rush in where angels fear to tread.' I'm not an angel or a fool." She turned and walked out of the room.

Lady Elizabeth, Mrs. Churchill, and Thompkins returned, along with Detective Inspector Covington and Sergeant Turnbull. The opening in the bookshelf was still ajar.

"I had no idea that was there." Mrs. Churchill stared at the opening.

"I think you should wait here," Detective Inspector Covington said to the ladies. "Sergeant Turnbull and I will go in and see how far the tunnel goes. Thompkins, you stay with the women."

"Oh, no you don't." Lady Elizabeth rose to her full height. "There's no way you're leaving us behind while you go exploring. I found the tunnel and I'm not missing out on seeing where it leads."

"I'm coming too." Mrs. Churchill didn't look enthusiastic, but she looked determined. "Besides, it's my house."

Lady Elizabeth gave her friend's arm a supportive squeeze and then turned to the butler. "Thompkins, we're going to need more torches."

"Yes, m'lady." He left.

"I really think you ladies should remain here. There's no telling what's in this tunnel." He stared at both ladies, but Lady Elizabeth merely shook her head. "There could be rats or snakes."

Mrs. Churchill shivered. "Good point."

Detective Inspector Covington released a sigh.

Thompkins returned with the torches. Lady Elizabeth held out her hands and he handed over the torches.

Mrs. Churchill turned to the butler. "Detective Inspector Covington just pointed out there might be creatures inside the passage." She reached down and picked up a fireplace poker. "Could you bring a couple more pokers and Rufus?"

Detective Inspector Covington shook his head in frustration.

Thompkins hurried from the room and quickly returned with the poodle, Rufus. Tango followed of his own free will.

Lady Elizabeth looked around. "Are we all ready?"

Everyone nodded.

She turned to the detective. "Lead the way."

The detective shook his head but moved forward and led the way inside the tunnel. He was followed by Lady Elizabeth, Rufus, Mrs. Churchill, Thompkins, Tango, and Sergeant Turnbull, who brought up the rear.

The passage was dark and there were spiderwebs and the click-clack of scurrying creatures along the way. The tunnel sloped downward and turned twice.

The unusual party walked for a few minutes and eventually came to a wall.

"Looks like we're at the end of the road." Detective Inspector Covington waved his torch around the dark stone passage.

"It can't be," Lady Elizabeth said. "Why would anyone build a tunnel that ends at a brick wall?"

"Maybe it was closed off," Mrs. Churchill said. "I never got a chance to ask Winston, but the architect did quite a lot of work on the house before we moved in. I suppose they could have discovered it and simply closed it off."

Lady Elizabeth continued to shine her torch around the wall. She stopped at an area of the wall that was about three feet from the ground. One of the bricks protruded out farther than the others. "Shine your torch this way, Detective."

Detective Inspector Covington obliged.

She pushed the brick and heard a click. There was a gust of wind and a portion of the wall slid open.

"Well, I'll be." Detective Inspector Covington examined the opening. "Sergeant, give me a hand."

Detective Inspector Covington moved forward and he and the detective pushed the wall. A narrow opening about two feet wide and five feet tall swung back as if on hinges. "Please wait here." The detective and Tango the cat moved forward through the opening. The sergeant followed. Rufus stayed behind in an attitude of alert.

A cold breeze blew in from the opening. After a few minutes the detective returned. "We're outside. I'd say we're in the woods across from the north side of the house near the garden wall. There's a brass ring here that operates the door from the outside."

"I never knew this passage was here." Mrs. Churchill looked a bit dazed. "This means someone else could have come into the house. Someone else could have murdered that girl."

Detective Inspector Covington looked skeptically at Mrs. Churchill. "Who would know this passage existed? It would have to be someone very familiar with the house."

Mrs. Churchill turned pale.

Lady Elizabeth squeezed her friend's hand. "This house has been here a lot longer than the Churchills. People from the village might know about it. Or, as Clementine said, it could have been discovered during the renovations." She turned to Mrs. Churchill. "Didn't you say Leopold Amery was involved with the renovations?"

Mrs. Churchill nodded. "Yes. Leo and his son spent a lot of time helping out. I think Philip Tilden, the architect, hired several lads from the village to help with some of the heavy lifting."

"John Amery was here during the renovations?" Lady Elizabeth asked.

Mrs. Churchill nodded. "Yes, he was here quite a lot back then. He used to be good friends with Randolph and he had a bit of a crush on one of the girls. I think it was Sarah. He was a couple years older than her. Girls always like older boys . . . bad boys."

Lady Elizabeth stared off into space. "Interesting."

"What's so interesting about a young girl's crush?" Detective Inspector Covington asked.

"Perhaps we should go back inside. It's rather cold and I could use a nice cup of tea." She turned to the butler. "Thompkins, could you please see to tea in the parlor." She turned to Mrs. Churchill. "Oh, I'm sorry, Clemmie, if that's okay with you, of course."

Detective Inspector Covington and Sergeant Turnbull made certain the door was secured.

Mrs. Churchill nodded. "Of course. Tea would be perfect. Then you can explain what John Amery's crush on Sarah has to do with any of this."

"I'd appreciate hearing that myself," Detective Inspector Covington said.

"Of course." Lady Elizabeth walked with her friend back toward the warmth of the house.

Chapter 21

I didn't sleep much Sunday night, so when I woke up Monday morning, I was more than a little grumpy. Sometime between two and three in the morning, the reality that there were only a few days left before Nana Jo could get arrested, if I didn't figure out how Horace Evans got into Maria's room at Shady Acres and killed her, hit me. There was no way I could leave for New York with my grandmother in jail. She wouldn't get an opportunity to perform in New York and I'd miss meeting my agent. What a mess.

She was already downstairs when I got the courage to come out of my room.

"You look like death warmed over." Nana Jo stared at me. "You realize you've got your shirt inside out and you're wearing one blue shoe and one black shoe, right?"

I looked at my feet and sighed. It would have been an easy mistake if the shoes were the same type or if the heels were even the same height. I remembered trying them on to decide between the blue flats and the black heels. "I got distracted." I ran upstairs and put on the two blue shoes and turned my shirt to the right side.

When I got back down to the bookstore, Nana Jo was sitting at a table with two mugs of coffee. I sat down in the seat across from her and took a long drink.

"Now, what's wrong?"

It would be best to lie. I could tell her I was thinking about Leon. I hated the idea of lying to my grandmother and especially using my dead husband as an excuse, but I didn't want to worry her with the truth. I took a sip of coffee and opened my mouth and the next thing I knew, I was bawling like a baby. Nana Jo slid her chair around next to mine and put her arms around me. I sat and cried until I had no tears left.

When I was done, she handed me a handerkerchief. "Do you feel better?"

I shrugged.

"Now, tell me what's wrong."

I told her how sorry I was for letting her down because I had no clue how Horace killed Maria. I should never have bargained with Detective Pitt for her freedom. I begged for forgiveness. I cried again.

Nana Jo listened patiently. "Sam, stop it. This isn't your fault. All you did was buy me some time. I was the prime suspect in Maria's murder. If you hadn't made your deal with Stinky Pitt, I would already be behind bars." She patted my hand. "Now, stop crying and worrying yourself. We're not defeated yet. Besides, I have faith you'll figure this out. Now, pull yourself together. Customers will be coming soon and we're going to have to open those doors." She gave me a big hug. "You've been trying too hard. Stop thinking about it. We'll talk things out later. Now, let's sell some books."

Business was brisk, more brisk than most Mondays. I would have to take note. The Monday before Thanksgiving was a busy time. Next year, I'd plan better.

Jillian and Dawson arrived before lunch.

"What're you two doing here? Shouldn't you be in class?" I asked.

Jillian smiled. "I'm done. I had a test earlier and a paper I turned in about an hour ago. So, I'm officially on Thanksgiving break."

Dawson smiled. "I've got a paper due tonight and a test tomorrow, but I want to study here, if that's okay." He shuffled his feet. "I'd rather not be on campus. Too many reporters."

"Of course it's okay." I hugged him. "Congratulations. Does this mean MISU will go to a bowl?"

He nodded. "We should get an invite to a bowl game. I just hope it's a good one."

I didn't realize there were bad bowls. I'd ask Nana Jo later. For now, there was a line of folks waiting to be rung up.

Dawson had cookies baked and on the counter in record time.

We were so busy we didn't have time to stop for lunch. Frank stopped in, but I didn't have time to chat, so he just waved and left. I was disappointed until he came back an hour later with soup and sandwiches. He left the food in the back, waved, and walked out again. I smiled and realized my debt to him was getting longer and longer. My face heated when I thought of repaying him. Thankfully, things were too busy for me to dwell on those thoughts for very long.

We took turns running to the back to eat. The day went by in a blur. When the last customer left, we were exhausted.

Jillian and Dawson went upstairs to study.

Nana Jo and I sat and caught our breath.

"You ready for our meeting?" She got up.

I'd totally forgotten we had a sleuthing meeting tonight. My lack of sleep and the hard physical labor of the day combined with my emotional meltdown from the morning had pretty much sucked all of the life out of me.

Nana Jo pulled me to my feet. "Come on, Sherlock. We've got to get ready."

Something flashed in my head for about two seconds and then quickly flitted away.

"What?"

I shook my head. "I don't know. It's gone now."

Nana Jo smiled. "Good. It'll come back." She gave me a gentle shove. "Now, get moving."

Everyone arrived and we went into the back room. Dawson had placed a plate of sugar cookies in the center of the table, along with napkins and plates. I would have to do something extra special for that kid. He was amazing.

Nana Jo pulled out her iPad. "Who's going first?"

I raised my hand and shared the information I'd gotten from Frank about Denise Bennett and Maria.

Irma seemed unusually quiet.

"What's wrong with you?" Nana Jo asked.

She coughed. "I was just thinking about Magnus. He seemed like such a nice man." She pulled a cell phone from her purse and swiped the screen until she got to her pictures. "We took this the first night we . . . well, you know." She coughed. "We ate dinner and then came back to his apartment for . . . dessert."

I looked at the picture. It was the weird angle that indicated Irma had taken the picture herself. It showed a smiling Irma and Magnus standing near a wall in his apartment. There were two large pictures on the wall behind them.

"Irma, we don't have time for any treks down memory lane." Nana Jo typed. "Who's next?"

I tapped the photo, enlarged it, and readjusted so the focus was slightly behind their heads. "Wait. Something's wrong." I looked around. "This picture on the wall." I pointed to the picture and everyone crowded in to see. "It's gone."

I stared at Irma and Nana Jo. "Do either of you remember seeing it in the room?"

They shook their heads.

We all looked at Freddie. He stared at the phone and then shook his head. "I'm positive that picture was not there the night Magnus was killed."

"Irma, when was the last time you remember seeing that picture?" Nana Jo asked.

She looked up as she thought. "It was there the night before. I'm positive."

"Think back to the night of the murder. Do you remember if anything else was missing?" I asked.

We all stared at her.

She shook her head. "I don't think so."

Nana Jo pulled out her phone and handed it to her. "Here, look at these pictures from the night of the murder."

Irma looked through the pictures. She paused when she got to the one of the small ballet dancers. "Wait. I think there was another one." She tapped her hand on the desk. "It was one of those blotchy pictures where you had to squint to tell what it was." She coughed.

"Impressionist?" Dorothy asked.

"Yeah, it was a street somewhere in Europe. It was yellowish and there were buildings and the people were on horses and buggies."

Dorothy pulled a book from her purse and flipped through the pages. "After I talked to my sister, I picked up this book about missing art from World War II." She flipped to a page and pushed the book across the table to Irma. "Was it like this?"

Irma's face lit up in recognition. "That's it. That's the picture."

I leaned over and looked at the picture. "Pissarro, *The Boule-*

vard Montmartre, Twilight." I read further. "It says the painting was looted by the Nazis and sold. It's shown up since the war, but the current location is unknown."

We talked about art for several minutes.

"You'd better tell Detective Pitt," Nana Jo said.

"So, you think Horace killed him for the paintings?" Freddie asked.

I shrugged. "It looks that way."

Judge Miller had been very quiet. "I think Pitt has enough to get a search warrant."

Something nagged at the back of my mind, but I ignored it and pulled out my phone. I dialed Detective Pitt's number. The phone rang four times and then I heard a recording telling me to leave a detailed message. I left my name and number and asked him to call me when he had a chance.

The mood in the room lifted from gloom to elation. Everyone talked at once. Despite all of the noise, I zoned out. It wasn't until Nana Jo shook me that I came out of my fog.

"Earth to Sam."

"I'm sorry." I yawned. "I'm really tired and I think everything is just catching up to me."

No one else had anything to report, so we ended the meeting and promised to get together tomorrow. By then, I would have talked to Detective Pitt and hopefully he would have made an arrest.

I went upstairs. Dawson and Jillian were studying at the dining room table. Snickers was curled up in Jillian's lap and Oreo was under Dawson's chair. I went to my room and flopped down on the bed, not even bothering to get undressed. I was out before I knew it.

I slept hard and fast. I woke up at two and thought it was time for work. One look outside showed me it was still dark.

Dawson and Jillian were gone and they must have taken the poodles with them, because the house was quiet.

I changed into my pajamas and tried to go back to sleep, but my brain wouldn't cooperate. I was wide-awake now. I pulled out a notepad from my nightstand. I tried to organize my thoughts. I wrote down everything that popped into my head. I wrote words like "Degas," "Pissarro," "New York," "prison," "painting," "mob," "cyanide," "locked room," "nosy neighbor," and "Sherlock." I read the words aloud, and I knew I was onto something, but, like smoke on the wind, the thought was clear one second and evaporated the next. I was close. I pulled out my laptop and tried to focus on something else.

⸎

Thompkins pushed the tea cart into the drawing room. Mrs. Churchill stood with her back to the room, staring out of the window. He pushed the cart to Lady Elizabeth, bowed, and walked to the door.

Lady Elizabeth stopped him. "Thompkins, I think it would be better if you stayed."

"Yes, m'lady." The butler bowed and stood near the door.

Lady Elizabeth sat on the sofa near the fireplace and poured the tea. She handed the cup to the butler. "Would you take that to Mrs. Churchill, please."

Thompkins took the tea and stood for a few seconds. However, Mrs. Churchill was lost in her own world. He coughed discretely. "Ma'am."

Mrs. Churchill turned and looked at the tea as if it was her first time seeing such a thing. After a second, she shook herself and accepted the cup. "Thank you, Thompkins."

Lady Elizabeth poured tea for Detective Inspector Covington, Sergeant Turnbull, Lord William, Anthony Blunt, and Guy Burgess. Leopold Amery arrived soon after. Lady Elizabeth poured out.

Mrs. Churchill looked around. "Where's Winston?"

Daphne entered. "He and James are in the studio."

"When did you get back?" Lady Elizabeth smiled at her niece.

"We only just arrived."

Guy Burgess and Anthony Blunt stood near the fireplace. They were engaged in an animated discussion of the Mediterranean and didn't seem to notice the tension that permeated the room.

Lord Stemphill arrived. "Tea in the drawing room. Wonderful." He accepted a cup from Lady Elizabeth and looked around the room. A brief flash of disappointment crossed his face, but he received a smile from Daphne and sauntered over to the chair where she sat.

Detective Inspector Covington raised a brow to Lady Elizabeth.

Lady Elizabeth took a sip of tea. "You'll never guess what we found today." She spoke to no one in particular.

"I couldn't hazard a guess," Leopold Amery said.

"We were in the bedroom where that poor woman died and we found a secret tunnel."

Detective Inspector Covington stared at the faces in the room.

"How fascinating." Amery turned to Mrs. Churchill. "Surely you knew of this tunnel?"

Mrs. Churchill shook her head. "Actually, no. I was as surprised as everyone else."

Guy Burgess finally turned and looked from Mrs. Churchill to Lady Elizabeth. "How fascinating. Where does the tunnel go?"

"We followed it out into the weald," Lady Elizabeth added.

Lord William huffed on his pipe. "You don't say? Extraordinary. I suppose it's to be expected in an old house like this."

"Oh, yes, secret passages and priest holes were quite common in old country estates like this one." Anthony Blunt sipped his tea. "I'd be surprised if there wasn't one."

Guy Burgess's face lit up. "Say, you don't think that's how the killer got in to do the deed, do you?" He pulled a notepad from his pocket and looked at Detective Inspector Covington. "What does Scotland Yard have to say about it?"

Detective Inspector Covington looked as though he had a lot he'd like to say to Burgess but swallowed the words. "Scotland Yard has no comment for the press at this time."

"Oh, I'm sorry, Detective. Perhaps you'd have preferred for the tunnel to remain a secret." Lady Elizabeth fluttered her hands and gave the detective a wide-eyed look that belied her intelligence.

"Does this mean the Yard believes the murderer was someone outside of the family?" Burgess pressed.

Detective Inspector Covington pursed his lips into a straight line. "No comment."

"I suppose this eases your mind, Mrs. Churchill."

Burgess turned to Lady Elizabeth. "And yours." He glanced significantly at Lady Daphne.

Lady Daphne's face flushed, but she smiled coldly at the BBC producer.

Mrs. Churchill went pale and swayed. For a second, it looked as though she would fall. However, she recovered herself, pushed her shoulders back, and raised her head tall. "I don't know what you're implying, Mr. Burgess, but I don't like it, and I won't stand for it in my house."

"What's this?" Winston Churchill boomed from the doorway.

Everyone had been so focused on Mrs. Churchill, they hadn't noticed James and Winston entering the room. James carried a large satchel, which he conspicuously kept by his side.

"I won't have you upsetting my wife, Mr. Burgess."

Guy Burgess hung his head. "I'm very sorry, Mrs. Churchill. I didn't mean to insult . . . I'm sorry."

Mrs. Churchill gave a subtle nod in acceptance of Burgess's apology.

Winston walked over to his wife. "Are you okay, Clemmie?"

She nodded. "Yes, dear. I'm fine." She looked at her husband. "Tea?"

He sat down on the sofa and Rufus curled up at his feet.

Lady Elizabeth handed Winston a cup of tea. "We were just talking about the tunnel that leads from one of the guest bedrooms out to the weald."

Winston chomped on his cigar and balanced his tea on his lap. "Tunnel?"

"Didn't you know about it either, dear?" Mrs. Churchill asked.

He was silent a moment. "I recall Tilden mentioning something about an old passage when we were renovating the place back in '22. Told him to close it up. Last thing a man with four . . . ah, three daughters needs is a secret passage into the house."

Clementine Churchill gasped but quickly recovered. She sat down on the sofa next to Lady Elizabeth, who gave her hand a squeeze.

Lady Elizabeth knew Winston's gaffe about the number of daughters he had was not due to poor memory but was an indication that even after twenty years, Marigold, the daughter the Churchills lost at the age of two, was never far from his thoughts.

Detective Inspector Covington moved to the edge of his seat. "Who else would know of the tunnel?"

Winston thought. "Tilden, the architect, and probably some of the workers who helped close it up."

"What about the children?" Detective Inspector Covington asked hesitantly.

Winston blanched. "You'd have to ask them."

"Why would someone inside the house need to use the secret passage?" Daphne asked.

Everyone turned to stare. "I mean, if Randolph knew about the tunnel, he wouldn't have had to use it to get into Jessica's room. He could have knocked."

"Or used the key." Randolph stood in the doorway. His face was red and flushed. He looked as though each breath caused him pain and he stumbled forward into the room. "If I'd wanted to get into Jessica's bedroom, I could have simply used the key."

He fumbled in his pocket and pulled out a set of keys and tossed them on the table.

"We've been looking all over the house for those keys. Where'd you find them?" Mrs. Churchill whispered.

"Where they've always been, on the hook in the larder." He stumbled across the floor and flopped down into a chair. "Gawd, I feel bloody awful."

"Randolph. Watch your language. There are ladies present," Winston said.

Randolph stumbled to his feet and bent over in a bow. When he stood up, he swayed and lurched. He nearly tumbled over, but James hurried to catch him.

James tried to steady him but had trouble balancing Randolph and his satchel and was clumsy.

Between the sudden movements and the beatings with the satchel, Randolph didn't look well. The color drained from his face and he clasped his mouth.

James turned Randolph toward the door and Thompkins hurried to help. Each man took one arm and dragged Randolph from the room. Just as they got to the door, it swung open and Lady Alistair stood in the middle of the doorway, blocking the way.

Randolph pitched forward and vomited, just missing Lady Alistair.

No one wanted to remain in the drawing room afterward and filed out of the room. When Lord Stemphill stood up, Daphne approached him. She was still carrying the copy of *Burke's Peerage,* which had become her constant companion.

"Do you have a minute? I'd like to have a word."

Lord Stemphill smiled. "Of course, Lady Daphne."

She turned to Lady Alistair. "Would you stay too, please?"

Lady Alistair nodded, went to a chair by the window, and sat very stiff and still.

When the last person left, Lord Stemphill walked to the window where Daphne stood. "What can I do for you?"

Daphne turned and faced him. "You can stop bothering Lady Alistair. I know you were the one trying to blackmail her, so you can just forget it. I won't permit you or anyone else to hurt James."

Lady Alistair gasped. "Lord Stemphill?"

Daphne nodded.

Lord Stemphill stood with a look of shocked disbelief for several seconds and then laughed heartily. "Oh my, Lady Daphne, I do believe you've gotten me confused with someone else. I have no idea what you're talking about."

Daphne folded her arms. "Don't bother lying. I know it was you." She held out the letter. "When Lady Alistair told me about the blackmail letter, it reminded me of what you did before when you needed money. You betrayed your country and then blackmailed the person who was helping you. Leopards don't change their spots. If you tried blackmail once, you'd try it again. So, I had the handwriting verified by an expert."

Lord Stemphill's face changed from one of shocked innocence to casual acceptance with a slight glimmer of respect in his eyes. "Alright, suppose it was me. How do you intend to stop me? Tell your precious James about his mother's dirty little secret?"

Lady Alistair sat still, her hand to her throat.

Daphne stared. "No. You're going to go away and keep any information you have to yourself."

Lord Stemphill laughed. "I don't think I will. I think I'll go upstairs and tell Mr. Guy Burgess of the BBC an interesting tale."

The color drained from Lady Alistair's face, but she remained quiet.

Daphne's eyes narrowed. "No. You won't. You're going to pack up your bags and you're going to go away tonight, and you're never to bother James or Lady Alistair again."

"Or what? You'll tell the police? Sue me for libel or is it slander? I get those two mixed up."

"Today, I made a trip to Somerset House."

Lord Stemphill raised an eyebrow. Some of his bravado decreased, but he continued his nonchalant attitude. "Really?"

"Yes. I checked the public records of births and marriages. I also looked up the details of your baronetcy. You inherited from your uncle, the eighteenth Lord Stemphill." She held up the copy of *Burke's Peerage*.

Lady Alistair's eyes grew wide as she stared from Lady Daphne to Lord Stemphill.

Lord Stemphill's smile froze and his forehead creased with a frown. He shrugged. "You didn't need to go all the way to Somerset House for that. It's public knowledge." His hand shook slightly as he lit a cigarette.

"Something about the dates of your baronetcy bothered me." Daphne continued, "Based on the documents I reviewed, you couldn't possibly be the legitimate heir to the baronetcy. The dates just don't mesh. Your cousin, Fergus, is the rightful heir to Craigevar Castle and the true nineteenth Lord Stemphill."

"Fergus is a fool." Lord Stemphill frowned and spat the words out with venom. "He's locked up in an asylum, where he spends his days drooling in a corner."

Daphne shrugged. "Maybe he is, but that doesn't change the facts. Besides, he wouldn't be the first mentally ill peer." She walked to within inches of Lord Stemphill. "The important point is you aren't entitled to the peerage, the inheritance, or anything."

He snorted. "Inheritance? A title with no money is hardly an inheritance."

"The title allows you entrée into homes you wouldn't have otherwise." She waved her arms to indicate Chartwell House. "It also provides the connections to the royal family, the same connections which prevented you from hanging for treason when you betrayed your country and leaked secrets to the Japanese in the '20's."

Stemphill's eyes narrowed. "You're very well informed."

"Yes, I am."

He stared at Daphne as though sizing her up. "That sounds very messy. I can't imagine a lady like yourself would sully herself with such matters."

Daphne inched closer to Stemphill and stared in his eyes. "There is nothing I wouldn't do to protect the people I love."

Lady Alistair stared at Daphne and shivered.

The two adversaries stood toe-to-toe for several seconds. Then Lord Stemphill cocked his head to the side and made a sweeping bow. "I concede." He turned and walked toward the door. Just as he grabbed the doorknob, he turned to Daphne. "You are an amazing woman, Lady Daphne Marsh. Lord Browning is a lucky man, a very lucky man, but you haven't seen the last of me." He opened the door and walked out.

Chapter 22

When I finished, I picked up the list I'd made earlier and read through it several times. Like tumblers in a lock, the pieces clicked together. *"When you eliminate the impossible, what remains, no matter how improbable must be the truth."*

I put on clothes and hurried to Nana Jo's room. "We've got to get to Shady Acres. I know who did it and I know how the murders were done."

Nana Jo was groggy, but she nodded. "Give me two minutes to get dressed."

I hurried to put my clothes on and glanced at the clock. It wasn't five yet. I grabbed my cell phone and keys and hurried down to the garage. I explained my theory to Nana Jo on the drive to Shady Acres. She listened quietly but pulled out her phone and starting typing.

I pulled up to the front and hopped out of the car. When we got to the lobby, Irma, Ruby Mae, and Dorothy were already waiting. Freddie arrived moments later.

The security guard, Larry Barlow, looked confused by five half-dressed women in the lobby demanding to see the property manager, Denise Bennett.

"Miss Bennett isn't up yet. She'll have my guts for garters if I wake her up now."

"That's nothing compared to what I'll do to you if you don't take us to her room right this minute," Nana Jo said.

"You better do it, Larry," Freddie said.

He nodded and pushed the buzzer that allowed us to get behind the desk so we could get to the property manager's apartment.

"I've tried to reach Detective Pitt several times, but I haven't been able to get him. Maybe you could see if your son knows how we can reach him," I said.

Freddie nodded and pulled out his phone.

I knocked on Denise Bennett's apartment door. A light shined from under the door and I knew she was awake.

"Come in."

I reached for the handle, but Freddie stepped forward. He waited a moment and then turned the knob and pushed the door open.

There was a loud bang and a flash and Freddie was on the floor.

Nana Jo's face drained of color as she saw Freddie lying on the floor. Then she looked as though she could rip apart telephone books and barged forward.

There was another blast. Nana Jo stopped.

"That was a warning. The next one will be aimed at your heart," Denise Bennett said in a cold, calculating voice. "Now get in here."

We walked into the room.

"Slowly, and close the door."

We bent down and helped Freddie move to the sofa.

"Keep your hands where I can see them."

We held up our hands.

Two large suitcases were on the floor, along with a flat container.

"Is that where you've got the paintings?" I asked more to have something to say.

"What's it to you?" She grabbed the container and clutched it to her chest. "These are mine. I recognized the paintings the first time I saw them. They didn't belong to that Nazi. He stole them." She laughed. "I just stole them from him."

"No, you didn't just steal them. You killed him, you dirty b—"

"Irma!"

Old habits died hard, but curtailing Irma's habit to swear was only part of the reason we stopped her. Provoking a crazy woman with a gun who'd already killed two people and just shot another was a major factor.

She laughed. "Of course I killed him. I did him a favor. He was dying anyway."

"How did you get Horace to put the cyanide in his pill bottle?" I asked.

Denise laughed again. "Horace? That fool didn't do anything. I put the cyanide in the bottle."

"We saw him taking a bottle of pills up to Magnus's room the day he died."

I must have looked skeptical because she moved closer so she could sneer in my face. "I put the cyanide in the bottle right after he arrived." She smiled smugly. "One pill, that was all it took. He would take the cyanide sooner or later. He'd die eventually. I just needed to be ready."

"Maria knew who you were, didn't she, Dorothy?" I took a chance by using her real name.

"How'd you find out my real name?" She stared. When I didn't respond, she shrugged. "No matter. You won't live long enough to tell anyone." She grabbed a purse and her passport from the table. "I'm tired of people threatening me. First, it was my husband, Antonio. Always threatening. 'You tell anything and I'll kill you,'" she said with a thick accent like

Robert De Niro in *The Godfather.* "Well, I showed him. I turned him in and went into the witness protection program. They promised me a new name and a new identity." She shook her head. "Then Maria showed up with her threats. Give her a bigger apartment or she'd tell Antonio where I was." She paced.

"So, you used your master key to get into her room and killed her. Then you locked the door with your key so when the police arrived, they would think the door was locked."

She laughed. "That was my best plan yet. We're not supposed to have master keys, but when she demanded the larger apartment, I had an extra key made for myself."

She walked over to us and stared. "Now, here you all are. Threatening to tell the police about me."

I expected Nana Jo to try and whip out her pistol or Dorothy to drop into an aikido stance and flip Denise Bennett like a bag of potatoes. Instead, Nana Jo simply started to hum. I wasn't the only one who looked confused.

Denise Bennett frowned. "What're you doing, old lady?"

Nana Jo ignored her and continued to hum the tune from the Senior Follies' final number.

Ruby Mae, Irma, and Dorothy all locked arms.

"Stop it." Denise Bennett raised an arm and pointed the gun directly at Nana Jo.

Nana Jo stared her down. "One, two, now!"

In perfect unison, Nana Jo and the girls all lifted their legs and performed a Rockettes kick, dislodging the gun from Denise Bennett's hand.

I pounced on the gun and Dorothy kicked off her shoes and crouched into a low aikido stance. But before she could flip Denise Bennett, Nana Jo hauled back and punched her with a sharp right cross.

Denise Bennett dropped to the ground like a bag of sand.

"Quick! Get something to tie her up with," Ruby Mae ordered.

Irma rumbled through the drawers in the kitchen. Just as she came back with a roll of twine, Detective Pitt bust through the door.

"Glad you could make it," Nana Jo said.

Detective Pitt handcuffed Denise as she lay on the floor. She was conscious but still groggy. We waited for an ambulance, although Freddie swore it was only a flesh wound. Nana Jo was giving the orders and he was ordered to lay still and be quiet.

I explained to Detective Pitt what happened.

"You mean she killed two people over some paintings?"

I opened the container and gently pulled out the artwork. "These are not just any paintings. These are rare works of art missing since World War II." I held up the paintings and put them on the dining room table.

Dorothy came over to the table. "My sister said they're worth billions."

Detective Pitt whistled. "Billions with a *B* billions?"

We nodded.

He gently took the paintings, holding them by the corners as though they were contaminated.

"Perhaps you should wait until an expert can be found who knows how to properly handle them," I said

He nodded.

Freddie really did have a flesh wound, which the doctors were able to patch up quickly. Nana Jo, on the other hand, broke two bones in her hand when she punched Denise. She left with a cast.

I was thankful Dawson, Jillian, and the twins were willing and able to swing by the store and open up. By the time I made it home, the place was buzzing with activity.

My adrenaline levels were drained and I went upstairs and crashed for several hours until Snickers woke me with a lick on the nose.

I got up and took a nice, long shower. Once I was dressed and ate, I pulled out my laptop.

———

Lady Elizabeth tried not to stare at the damp stain on the dining room carpet, which was all that remained of the unfortunate incident with Randolph.

"Lady Alistair must think we're savages. I don't think anything can coax her to stay now," Mrs. Churchill said. "She's taking dinner in her room."

"I'm not sure there's a reason for her to stay now." Lady Elizabeth stared at her niece. She looked around. "Did Lord Stemphill give a reason for his sudden departure?"

Mrs. Churchill shook her head. "No, he just said something came up." Mrs. Churchill sighed. "I can't say I'm sorry. I never cared for the man. I only invited him because his mother was such a dear, sweet woman."

Detective Inspector Covington looked uncomfortable in one of Randolph's suits and pulled at the collar.

"Who are the additional guests Winston mentioned?" Lady Elizabeth asked.

"American missionaries of some kind, is all I know. He sprung their visit on me at the last minute. Thankfully, Mrs. Landemare is a genius at making a meal stretch." She looked around. "Even though, he wasn't sure they'd make it in time for dinner." She looked at her watch. "It's very late and I think we need to eat or everything will be ruined." She made a slight move with her head to Thompkins.

"Dinner is served," he announced.

As the guests went to their seats, a loud crash came from the hall and the door was flung open. A young man stood in the doorway with a gun pointed at the group.

Mrs. Churchill gasped. "John?"

Leopold Amery's face turned beet red. He rushed to his feet, knocking over his chair in his haste.

The sudden movement startled John, who fired a shot, which shattered a glass, spilling wine on the tablecloth. "Hello, Father. Don't get any bright ideas that I won't shoot you. You don't have a son anymore, remember?" He leered.

He was young with dark hair and a lean, angular face. His eyes were wild and his glance went from one side of the room to the other, constantly making note of movements. "Sit," he ordered.

Detective Inspector Covington slowly prepared to sit.

"Not you, Copper. I think I want to see you." He used his gun to point. "Over there. Move and keep your hands where I can see them."

Detective Inspector Covington raised his hands so they were visible and moved so he stood in front of the window, open and exposed. "Now, there's no need to get excited. You haven't done anything serious yet."

John laughed. "Serious? You don't call murder serious?"

"Murder?" Leopold Amery asked. "It was you? You killed that girl?"

John's laugh sounded hysterical. "Got greedy. We had a plan. Get invited to the house. Then she was

supposed to let me in so I could get those paintings."
He waved his gun toward James.

Daphne's face grew pale. "Paintings?" Daphne
whispered.

"Come on, Your Grace," he said with a snide smirk
on his face. "Hand them over."

James hesitated and John pointed the gun in
Daphne's direction. James reached down and got the
satchel, which hadn't left his side since he arrived. He
picked it up.

John laughed. "Good. Now, slide it over here."

James slid the bag across the floor.

John picked it up and opened it. He started to
look inside.

"Why are you doing this?" Winston asked.

John looked up. "There's a new order coming, a
new Reich. Hitler's taking over Europe one country at
a time. He's raised up an army that'll march its way
across the channel and topple Britain's aristocracy
with its dukes and lords." He snarled at Lord William
and James. "You'll be replaced with enterprising
young men who're loyal to the führer. Men with the
vision and the gumption to do what it takes to suc-
ceed."

"That's treason." Leopold Amery looked as though
he would have a stroke. "My own son, a traitor *and* a
murderer. You're a disgrace."

John's face turned red and his eyes narrowed. His
hand shook with anger. "You shut up."

"You may be right. War with Germany will come
to these shores, but you and Herr Hitler have under-
estimated the British resolve. We will fight and keep
on fighting. We will not stop until we are victorious."
Winston's voice rang with fervor and strength. "Now

go. You've got what you came for." Winston pointed toward the door.

John Amery stood for a few seconds but then closed the satchel and ran out the doorway.

Detective Inspector Covington hurried to pursue him but was halted in his tracks when Winston reached out and grabbed him by the arm.

"He's getting away," the detective yelled.

Winston inclined his head in the direction of Leopold Amery, who sat stunned with his head in his hands. "Which is worse, Detective, that a guilty man go free or that an innocent man should pay for a crime he did not commit?"

Detective Inspector Covington shook his head. "I don't know, but I'm sworn to uphold the law and that's what I intend to do." He wrenched his arm free and hurried from the room.

The house was in chaos as police came and went. Randolph went to his room with a bottle of scotch. Everyone else waited in the drawing room. Leopold Amery looked as white as a sheet. Winston ordered him to drink a brandy. His hand shook as he put the glass to his lips.

The only time he spoke was to mutter, "My son . . . my own son."

After nearly an hour, Detective Inspector Covington came into the drawing room. He walked in front of Leo Amery and stopped. He removed his hat and looked down. "I'm very sorry to have to tell you the body of your son was found at the pond at the crossroads at Four Elms by the junction of Pootings Road."

Leopold stared at the detective and then muttered, "Thank God." And burst into tears.

Sergeant Turnbull and Thompkins helped him out of the room.

"So, you shot him?" Winston asked.

Detective Inspector Covington shook his head. "No, sir. It wasn't us. At least, it doesn't appear to be the police that shot him."

"Then who?" James asked.

Detective Inspector Covington shrugged. "We're still investigating. However, he was found with a black mask laying next to him."

Winston choked on his drink.

Mrs. Churchill dropped her teacup and the china cup shattered.

"A black mask?" Winston asked. "Interesting."

"What's this about a mask?" Lord William asked.

Winston poured a brandy and his hand shook slightly. He took a drink. "There's a tale of the murder of Mr. John Humphrey back in 1908. Mr. Humphrey was a rich farmer. He and his two companions stopped for a drink at the George and Dragon after spending the day at the market. The three men left together, but Mr. Key ran into an acquaintance and stopped to talk. Mr. Holmden and Mr. Humphrey walked on alone. They came to Mr. Holmden's farm first and he bid his friend a good-night." He sipped more brandy. "Mr. Humphrey walked on alone to his farm at Hever Castle. Around ten, Mr. Holmden heard a shot coming from the Four Elms. Mr. Key claimed to have heard the same thing. At the cross-roads for the Four Elms, Mr. Key ran to the spot, where he found Mr. Humphrey, shot and beaten. He raised the alarm and got help. They took Mr. Humphrey to a nearby pub, but his wounds were too grave. He died the next day." Winston paused. "Before he passed, he claimed he was robbed at the Four Elms. The villain shot him and then bludgeoned him with the butt of his gun. He was found with a black mask lying nearby."

The group was silent for several seconds.

Daphne shuddered. "Did they ever find the man?"

Winston shook his head.

Detective Inspector Covington snorted. "Got away or else it was one of those so-called friends, if you ask me. Mr. Key, indeed."

Detective Inspector Covington stood up as though he were about to leave, but Winston held up a hand.

Before he could speak, Thompkins entered and announced, "Reverend Waitstill and Martha Sharp."

A tall, slim, haggard couple entered. They looked to be in their early thirties.

Winston stepped forward and extended his hand. "Reverend Waitstill." He shook the minister's hand. "Mrs. Sharp. I am so glad you could make it." He shook the hand she extended.

Winston introduced them around the room. He took the most care when introducing the couple to Detective Inspector Covington. The pair looked dazed when all of the introductions were completed. They declined a drink.

"You must be very tired after your long trip from America. So, we will not keep you longer than is necessary." Winston looked at James, who left the room briefly and returned with a small bag. He handed the bag to the couple, who thanked him profusely.

The couple clutched the bag and rose. "Please excuse us. We still have a long way to go."

"Of course, but perhaps you would like to stay overnight and leave in the morning?"

The couple declined. They were boarding a ship scheduled to cross the channel very early the next day. After several more expressions of gratitude, the couple left.

"What was that all about?" Mrs. Churchill asked.

Winston turned to Detective Inspector Covington. "That was the reason why John Amery may be many things, but a thief he is not."

Detective Inspector Covington's eyes got wide and he opened his mouth, but Winston held up a hand.

"James, perhaps you would care to explain."

James stood up. "Reverend Waitstill and Martha Sharp are missionaries from the Unitarian church. They have agreed to travel to Czechoslovakia to help with the paperwork so Jews can leave the country and travel to the United States and other countries open to immigration. Mrs. Sharp is a social worker. A donation was made to help them with their work, a donation of art. It should be easy enough to sell when they get abroad and less conspicuous than British currency."

"Less conspicuous and harder to connect to the British government?" Lady Elizabeth asked.

Winston smiled. "You're a shrewd woman."

"That's why you're here." Lady Elizabeth turned to Anthony Blunt, who bowed his head.

"Mr. Churchill asked if I would value the art," Mr. Blunt said.

"But if that's the art, then what did John Amery take?" Lord William asked.

"I thought someone was following me when I came back from London with the paintings. So, I made a little switch." James smiled.

"James came to me and we exchanged the valuable paintings he had with several of my own." Winston smiled. "I wonder what Herr Hitler would have thought of those."

Detective Inspector Covington said, "You mean Amery committed murder and risked hanging for a few worthless paintings?"

Winston chomped on his cigar. "I consider the paintings a gift. With any luck, it'll be as close as Herr Hitler ever gets to this British countryside."

The next day, Randolph, Guy Burgess, and Anthony Blunt left early. Winston and Lord William were enjoying a game of Bezique at a table near the window. Lady Elizabeth sat on the sofa knitting. Mrs. Churchill sat near Lady Elizabeth and chatted. Daphne sat on a chair near the window with a book and Tango curled up on her lap. Lady Alistair and James entered the room.

James walked to Daphne and dropped to one knee.

His intentions were obvious, and Daphne was so startled, she dislodged Tango and dropped her book.

James picked up the book and tossed it aside. He clasped Daphne's hands. "Darling, I love you with all of my heart. Will you please do me the honor of accepting my hand in marriage?"

Daphne gasped. She tried to remove her hands, but James held them.

"I should tell you I don't intend to take no for an answer."

"James, I—"

"Oh, and just so you know, I got the report on the powder Jessica slipped in your tea the night you behaved so . . . oddly."

"What?"

"Your aunt found it in her handbag and I had it analyzed. It was a drug called Pervitin." He stared at Daphne. "That's why you acted so strange that night. There's nothing wrong with you, except you were drugged." He scowled. "If Amery hadn't killed her, I might have strangled her myself."

Lady Alistair walked up behind James and smiled. "I want to add that I have already given James my blessing. I would be honored to have you as a member of our family."

Daphne stared from one to the other. She looked at her aunt, who smiled, then turned to her uncle, who tried to hide the twitching at his lips.

"I gave my blessing last month when he asked for your hand," Lord William said.

"Well?" James searched Daphne's face.

Tears rolled down her cheeks, and she whispered, "Yes."

James stood, took Daphne into his arms, and kissed her.

When the two parted, Winston clapped James on the back. "It's about bloody time."

He bent down and kissed Daphne on the cheek, and then he walked over and rang for the butler. Within seconds, Thompkins entered.

"Bring a couple bottles of Pol Roger, Thompkins. We're celebrating."

Thompkins nodded. The butler returned quickly with two bottles of champagne and several glasses. He popped the cork, poured the champagne, and distributed the glasses.

When everyone had a glass, Winston held up a glass. "A toast. Long life and many blessings. May your lives together be full of love, mystery, and adventure."

Chapter 23

When I finished writing, I took another nap. When I woke up, it was dark outside. There was a knock on the door.

"Sam," Nana Jo said.

I got up and opened the door.

She looked around. "Where's your suitcase?"

"I haven't packed yet."

Nana Jo looked shocked. "Not packed? Why not? Our bus leaves in a few hours."

"But, it's only Monday. We don't leave until Wednesday. I have a whole day."

She looked at me as if my elevator didn't go to the top floor. "You slept through Monday. It's now Tuesday morning. I have a performance in a few hours and then our bus leaves immediately afterward. I have to be in New York on Wednesday for rehearsal and you're meeting with your agent on Wednesday for lunch."

My days were mixed up. I hurried to find my suitcase and tossed clothes in as fast as I could. Nana Jo helped and, in less than thirty minutes, I had a suitcase and a carry-on packed. I wasn't sure if I had all of the essentials, but Nana Jo reassured me whatever I forgot we could pick up in New York.

Dawson and the twins were already downstairs when we lugged our suitcase down and helped to get everything in the car. I hugged everyone and gave the poodles an extra cuddle. As we walked out the door, I turned and took one last look around my bookstore. Christopher and Zaq were helping customers while Dawson made sure the baked goods were out and then pulled a box of books from the back room and began stocking the shelves. When I looked at my helpers and the new friends the bookstore had brought into my life, I smiled. I couldn't believe it had been less than a year since I walked around the empty store, wondering if I was making a mistake by quitting my job to open a mystery bookstore. Now, I couldn't imagine my life without it. I said a quick prayer and whispered a thank-you to Leon for the push. I thought about how empty my life was after Leon's death. I looked around at all of the people that now filled the empty spaces of my life and added excitement to my days. Life wasn't easy, but it was, indeed, an adventure worth taking. A quote from Winston Churchill popped in my head.

> *Every day you may make progress. Every step may be fruitful. Yet there will stretch before you an ever-lengthening, ever-ascending, ever-improving path. You know you will never get to the end of the journey. But this, so far from discouraging, only adds to the joy and the glory of the climb.*

—Sir Winston Churchill

Please turn the page for an exciting sneak peek of
the next Mystery Bookshop Mystery

WED, READ & DEAD

coming soon wherever print and e-books are sold!

Chapter 1

"If you don't get your fanny out of that dressing room in the next thirty seconds, I'll come in and drag you out."

I recognized the tone in my grandmother's voice well enough to realize she meant business. Three hours of trying on every bubble-gum-pink bridesmaid dress in South Harbor's one and only wedding shop had left all of us in a foul mood. I took one last look at my reflection in the mirror and resigned myself to my fate. The hoopskirt under my ballroom gown was so large I had to turn sideways and wiggle to get through the dressing room door, but given this was the seventh or eighth dress I'd tried on, I had mastered the technique fairly well.

In the main viewing area at the back of the large store, I walked up the two stairs and stood atop the platform designed to look like a wedding cake to showcase the dresses to loved ones. I stood atop the platform of shame and waited for the laughter I knew was inevitable.

My timing was impeccable. Three other brides and their guests had just walked to the back of the store, so my audience had tripled since my last humiliation. I heard snickers and one guffaw from the store personnel. Initially, the sales consultants had contained their reaction much the same as the Queen's guard outside of Buckingham Palace, not showing one iota of a smile. However, three dresses ago that all changed. Now, they smiled and snickered openly.

My grandmother, Nana Jo, and my mother, the impending bride and source of my current embarrassment, sat on a comfy sofa sipping champagne. Nana Jo had just taken a sip when she looked up and saw my latest ensemble.

Nana Jo snorted and champagne squirted from her nose. "You look like a giant pink piñata."

I turned and stomped down the stairs and headed back to my dressing room.

In between the laughter, my mom said in a confused voice, "I don't understand it. It looked so cute on the hanger."

I squeezed back into the dressing room, caring little if this satin and tulle monstrosity got snagged or not. My sales consultant helped me get out of the dress while she avoided making eye contact. I suspected a few of the chuckles I'd heard had come from her, although I couldn't be sure.

"Your mom has a very distinct taste." She picked the pink piñata off the floor and made sure it was returned to its protective plastic.

"You can say that again." I took a drink from the glass of champagne she'd snagged for me after I'd walked out in a hot pink version of the velvet draperies Scarlett O'Hara had fashioned into a ball gown in *Gone with the Wind*. "How many more?"

I should have been suspicious when she didn't respond and quickly turned away, but I was too busy texting my missing sister, Jenna, who'd managed to back out of today's humiliation by declaring she had an important legal brief to write. Her day would come and revenge would be sweet. When I turned around and saw the next fluffy pink concoction, I nearly spit *my* champagne. Instead, I grabbed the champagne bottle and took a long swig.

The eighth, *or was it ninth,* dress was a tight-fitting mermaid-style gown with a super tight sequined gold bodice layered to look like scales that went down my hips to my knees and then the fluffy tulle skirt expanded in waves into a long train of pink, which puddled at my feet. I didn't even bother looking in the mirror. One look at the sales consultant's face told me everything I needed to know. From her raised eyebrows to the twitching lips, I knew I looked absolutely ridiculous. I contemplated taking it off and refusing to wear it out of the dressing room, but it was the last one. I might as well get it over with.

Mermaid dresses looked great on tall women, but I was only about five feet three, so the tight part of the dress fell lower on me. The sequined upper part of the gown was so tight I couldn't open my legs to walk and had to shuffle out of the dressing room. Climbing the stairs to get atop the platform required the help of two sales consultants and a great deal of tilting on my part.

Nana Jo laughed so hard and so long, she started gasping for breath and tears rolled from her face. My mom just stared at me as though I truly had just crawled out of the sea.

"Look, we've been at this for over three hours. I'm tired and hungry and my patience has waned," I announced to anyone listening.

I was about to turn and shuffle back to the dressing room when I looked up and saw my mom's fiancé, Harold Robertson, and my friend-who-is-more-than-a-friend, Frank Patterson, gawking at me from behind my mom's chair.

"You're just hungry, dear. I'm sure you'll feel better after you eat something. That's why I invited Harold and Frank to meet us for lunch." Mom smiled.

I stared openmouthed into Frank's eyes and saw the look

of shock and mirth he tried to hide reflected back at me. I'd endured ridicule and degradation from my family and complete strangers, however, Frank Patterson was different. It had taken quite a while after my husband Leon's death before I was even ready to entertain the idea of a male friend, let alone a romantic relationship. So, I wasn't quite ready for Frank to see me in all of my mermaid glory.

I took a step backward in my haste to find a place to hide and tumbled off the back of the platform. My only consolation was if I'd still been wearing a ball gown with a *Gone with the Wind* hoopskirt, when I fell on my rear, my dress would have lifted like the rear hatch of my SUV. Instead, the long flowing train got wrapped around my feet and I lay trapped on my back like a mummy.

I didn't believe Nana Jo could have laughed harder, but she managed. After my first few seconds of stunned embarrassment, where I flopped and wiggled around on the floor like a fish out of water, Frank's arms went around my waist as he lifted me to my feet.

Once I was upright, I made the mistake of trying to walk and realized my legs were still trapped and nearly toppled over again. Thankfully, Frank was still there and grabbed me before I fell again. His soft brown eyes sparkled and his lips twitched as though a laugh was just seconds away.

"Laugh and you're a dead man," I whispered and gave him a look that had once brought a two-hundred-pound football player to tears when I taught in the public high schools.

The look worked, and Frank wiped the mirth off his face and helped the sales consultants untangle the fabric binding my feet. Once I was free, I turned and stomped, well shuffled, back to the dressing room with as much dignity as I could muster. Oh, yes, my sister, Jenna, would pay dearly for leaving me to suffer alone.

Dressed, and in my own clothes, I marched out of the

dressing room to find my audience had dwindled down to a party of one, Frank Patterson.

"Where'd they go?" I looked around.

Frank opened his arms and engulfed me in a warm hug. "You look like you could use a hug."

I sighed and snuggled closely. I took a deep breath and released the tension that had built up in the past few hours. Frank owned a restaurant a few doors down from my North Harbor bookstore and he always smelled of coffee, bacon, herbal Irish soap, and red wine. I took a large sniff and felt the ripple of laughter rise up inside him.

"Let me guess, I smell like bacon and coffee?"

I took a big whiff. "Don't forget the Irish soap and red wine."

He laughed. "It's a good thing I don't serve liver."

My stomach growled. "I'm so hungry I'd probably eat it if you did. Where'd they go?"

He pulled away. "I told them we'd meet them at The Avenue."

I raised an eyebrow. "Let me guess, that was Harold's idea?"

"Actually, I think Grace suggested it. Your mom wants you to taste some pastries or cake or something."

I sighed. "I thought when they said they wanted a small wedding, it would be simple."

We walked to the front of the store and Frank held the door. "Small doesn't necessarily mean simple."

I should have known my mother well enough to know better. She'd always had *grand* taste. Nana Jo blamed my grandfather. He'd always referred to my mom as his little princess and she'd spent her entire life living up to it. My father had been equally guilty of perpetuating the princess mindset. He'd done everything for her. When he died, she couldn't write a check or pump her own gas and she had never paid a single bill. Jenna and I spent quite a bit of time arranging her finances so her rent and utilities were automatically withdrawn. Jenna took away her credit cards and arranged for Mom to have a weekly allowance, which was the only way she seemed to grasp the concept of budgeting. Now, she'd met and fallen for Harold Robertson, one of the wealthiest families in Southwestern Michigan. Harold was a widower who seemed content to continue the princess legacy.

Frank drove us the short distance to The Avenue hotel, one of the finest hotels in South Harbor. The Avenue was an older building that sat atop the bluffs and looked out over the Lake Michigan shoreline. From a distance, the hotel looked grand and imposing. Up close and personal, the wear and tear of chipped paint, cracked marble floor tiles, and wallpaper that had once been white but was now yellow showed. The bones were there, but the building needed an update. Despite these shortfalls, the grand staircase that greeted guests at the entry was still quite impressive.

Guests entering the building from the semicircular driveway found themselves on the landing and could ascend to the lobby or descend to the dining area. We spotted Mom and Nana Jo and followed the downward path to the restaurant. Waiters hovered around in red livery with gold braids and black pants. Frankly, it seemed a bit much for lunch, in my opinion, but my mom loved it and smiled brightly at the young freckle-faced youth who brought her iced tea.

"Are you sure you're warm enough, Grace?" Harold took my mother's hand and stared into her eyes.

Mom shivered and looked into Harold's eyes like a lost fawn in a vast forest. "It is rather chilly, but I don't like to be a bother."

Harold hopped up and removed his jacket. With a flourish, he draped his suit coat around her shoulders. Then he turned and got the attention of a passing waiter. "Can you please see the heat is turned up?"

The waiter practically snapped to attention and hurried off to see the heat was increased.

Before Harold was settled back into his seat, the manager came to the table, apologized for the inconvenience, and offered a complementary hotel blanket to go over her lap, and another log was added to a nearby fireplace.

I felt drenched just watching all of the activity.

Nana Jo picked up a menu and fanned herself. "Grace it's an oven in here. Your hormones must be out of whack. You need the patch."

Mom ignored her mother, a skill she'd honed over the decades, and I removed my cardigan and drank a half glass of ice water to help lower my core temperature.

Ignoring Nana Jo wasn't an easy task. She was tall, loud, and very opinionated. Few people would recognize Grace Hamilton as a relative, let alone the only child of Josephine Thomas. Nana Jo was tall, while my mom was petite, barely five feet tall. Nana Jo was about a hundred fifty pounds heavier than Mom, who weighed an even one hundred pounds. However, the two women were alike in their ability to annoy and aggravate their children.

Lunch itself was uneventful, apart from seeing the attention the hotel and restaurant waitstaff dedicated to Harold and consequently to Harold's guests. Harold Robertson was a tall, white-haired, bearded man who was one of the only people I had ever met I would describe as *jolly*. He had been a successful aeronautical engineer with NASA for over forty years. However, his brain power wasn't the reason the waitstaff were falling over themselves to ensure his every wish was fulfilled. Harold's claim to fame in Southwestern Michigan was that he had the good sense to be born into one of the wealthiest families in either North or South Harbor. Robertson's Department Store had been the premiere store in this area for over one hundred years. The store catered to the lakeshore elite.

As a child, I remembered the grand building with its high ceilings, crystal chandeliers, and marble columns. Even though we couldn't afford to shop on the upper floors, I remembered the red-coated doormen and elevator operators. My excursions to Robertson's were limited to the bargain basement. The store had weathered the economic downturn of North Harbor better than most and had only closed its doors completely about ten years ago. In fact, I went to the liquidation sale, expecting to finally buy things like furs and jeweled evening gowns like the ones I'd dreamt about as a child. Unfortunately, the old building had lost its charm. I was underwhelmed and depressed by the yellowed, peeling wallpaper, the threadbare carpets, and the smell of mothballs that assaulted my senses when I stepped through the door. The world had changed, but Robertson's had failed to adapt. The old cage-styled elevators were a fallback to a time that no longer existed.

Harold inherited the store and the family fortune, but he had pursued his dreams by becoming an engineer with NASA. He'd only returned after his wife became ill and he wanted to be close to family. He nursed her until she took her last breath. He now seemed dedicated to caring for my mom in much the same way.

I couldn't help but smile as I watched the way he catered to her every whim. No detail was too small.

Nana Jo leaned close and whispered in my ear, "I wonder how she manages to find men who fall over themselves to make her happy."

I shrugged. "Luck, I guess."

Nana Jo snorted. "Luck, my big toe. More like a curse, if you ask me." She shuddered. "Who wants that kind of attention?"

I agreed with Nana Jo. Harold's constant attention, no matter how well-meaning, would drive me batty. However, my mother was a different breed.

"I prefer a man with more spunk, someone you can argue with." She laughed. "You should have seen some of the fights your grandpa and I had." She gazed off into the distance. "Makes a marriage stronger." She tsked. "Of course, then you get the fun of making up." She guffawed.

"Nana Jo, I don't want that image in my brain." I shook my head as if trying to erase an Etch A Sketch.

She laughed.

Lunch was tasty. Good food and a glass of wine restored my humor. After lunch, we ate cake. In fact, cake was the main reason Mom wanted us to eat at The Avenue. The pastry chef presented us with samples from three different cakes as possible choices for the reception.

The pastry chef was a tiny little woman with electric blue hair. She presented the first sample. "This is a chocolate almond cake with raspberry mousse filling topped with chocolate ganache." She watched our faces as we tasted.

"This is delicious. Chocolate cake is my favorite." Harold's eyes sparkled, but then he turned to my mother. "What do you think, Grace?"

Mom took a small bite and then washed it down with a long drink of water. "It's very good, and I know a lot of people like chocolate, but . . . well, I was hoping for something a little more . . . well, unique."

Harold promptly nodded in agreement. "Of course, you're right. It's delicious, but you can eat chocolate cake anywhere. A wedding is a special occasion." He gazed at my mother as though she was the first person to entertain the idea the earth was round.

For the second tasting, we were presented with a white cake. "This is a traditional white cake with vanilla mousse filling and white fondant topping."

I'd never quite understood if you're supposed to eat fondant. It made the cake look nice and smooth, but it wasn't the tastiest topping I'd ever had. This one was no exception.

Based on the look on my mom's face, she wasn't a fan of this one either. "White is definitely traditional, but not very unique, is it?"

I agreed with her on that one.

The third tasting was presented. "This is a pink champagne cake with a filling of rum-infused custard and whipped cream frosting."

"Hmm. That's good stuff." Nana Jo licked her fork.

Harold turned to see my mom's reaction so he could know what his opinion should be.

Mom took a bite and smiled. "I really like the pink, don't you, Harold? It will go with the color scheme."

The cake wasn't the bubble gum color my mom seemed to like best, but it was definitely pink. Regardless of the cake's color, it was by far the tastiest of the selections. The chef explained she used champagne in place of water for the cake. I struggled to think of anything that wouldn't taste good if it was doused in champagne.

Cake choice made, we moved on to the ballroom, which was massive. The crystal chandeliers and marble columns, with views of Lake Michigan from nearly every window, would be an ideal space for a large wedding.

"Grace, I thought you wanted a small wedding? You could hog-tie cattle in this room," Nana Jo said.

Mom fluttered her hands around. "Well, we want to make sure the guests have room to dance, but maybe you're right."

"Our library can accommodate up to thirty-six guests comfortably and the patio could be used for cocktails," the manager continued his sales pitch.

"Well, this room isn't big enough to cuss a cat," Nana Jo said.

Frank whispered in my ear, "How much space does it take to cuss a cat?"

I shrugged. "Beats me. None of us have one."

"What do you think, Sam?" Mom asked.

"I agree with Nana Jo."

The manager looked as though he was about to provide all of the sales features for the library, but I'd beat him to the punch.

"The ballroom is too big. The library is too small. The—"

"If you say, there's a room that's just right, I'll gag." Nana Jo stuck her finger in her mouth but thankfully didn't actually gag.

"Actually, I was going to say the library is too small for the reception, but it might make a nice place for a family breakfast."

"Oh, what a wonderful idea," Mom said with such amazement the compliment made me question when was the last time I'd had a wonderful idea.

I mumbled, "I do get good ideas every decade or so."

Frank chuckled until he saw the look my mom shot my way and then coughed to cover up his laughter.

We reserved the library for a family breakfast and avoided the manager's sales pressure to reserve the ballroom to ensure it would be available. His, *I'm only looking out for your best interest* suggestion would require a nonrefundable thousand-dollar deposit, which Harold was glad to pay, but Nana Jo's Midwestern frugal nature refused to concede.

"I have to get back to work," I said.

"I'd better go with you." Nana Jo grabbed her purse.

"Well, if you must go." Mom fluttered and looked around in the "I'm so helpless" way she had.

However, Nana Jo and I were immune.

"Yep, we gotta go. See you tonight at Frank's place for the family dinner. We'll talk then." Nana Jo gave Mom a kiss on the cheek and hurried out of the door mumbling, "Once I've had a glass of whiskey to steady my nerves."

"Don't be late to dinner tonight," my mom yelled at our retreating backs as we made a quick exit out the door.

Despite my frustration with shopping for bridesmaid dresses, I wouldn't have missed tonight's *family* dinner for all of the fish in Lake Michigan. Tonight, my mom and Harold were introducing the two families. I didn't know a lot of truly rich people. This would be my chance to see how the other half lived. Plus, it would allow me to be nosy and learn what I could about my mom's intended.

Frank drove us back to my car, and I drove the short distance over the bridge from South Harbor to North Harbor. All of the one-way streets in downtown South Harbor made the drive about two miles total. However, the differences between North Harbor and South Harbor felt like the twin cities were separated by more than a bridge. The two cities shared the same Lake Michigan shoreline but were light-years apart. South Harbor was affluent and thriving, with cobblestone streets, a bustling downtown, and beachfront property both on the beach and on the bluffs above the Lake. In contrast, North Harbor had abandoned and burned-out buildings and boarded-up houses and downtown offered very little foot traffic. There was a small area of renovated buildings, bakeries, art galleries, and cafés, which were trying to revitalize the economy and bring people back downtown. My bookstore, Market Street Mysteries was one of those. The brick brownstone stood on a corner lot with a parking lot shared with a church. There was an alley that ran behind the buildings, and I was fortunate to have a garage. The previous owner built a fence to connect the garage to the building, probably in an attempt to keep the homeless and late-night bar hoppers from trespassing. However, the result was it created a nice courtyard area where my dogs, Snickers and Oreo, loved to play. The garage had an upstairs studio apartment my assistant, Dawson Alexander, called home.

Nana Jo and I entered the store through the back. There was a glass door that led up a flight of stairs to the right. Snickers and Oreo must have heard us coming because they were waiting at the bottom of the stairs. The two chocolate toy poodles pounced and barked their greeting. I hurried to let them out to keep the noise down while Nana Jo went through to help Dawson take care of the Christmas crowds. This was my first Christmas season, and I'd been pleasantly surprised by the traffic we'd received so far.

December in Southwest Michigan was cold and snowy. Christmas was only a few weeks away, and the wind off Lake Michigan was harsh and bitterly cold. Snickers, the older of the two poodles, true to her nature, stepped over the threshold, squatted and took care of business quickly, and hurried back inside to heat and warmth. Despite the red and green Christmas sweater she wore, she didn't like the cold and would just as soon have taken care of her bio needs inside as out. Oreo, on the other hand, had a more carefree, frolicking nature. He leapt into the air and tried to catch snowflakes. He was halfway across the yard before he realized his paws and his underbelly were cold. He then hurried to the back door, expecting to be let back inside. After ten years of Michigan winters, you would expect him to have caught on that snow was cold. Unfortunately, he was a slow learner. Snickers and I coldheartedly stood our ground and watched him through the glass until he hurried to the corner of the fence, hiked his leg, and heeded the call of nature. Snickers looked up at me as though to say, *Remind me again why you wanted a second dog?* I shrugged and opened the door to admit him as he bounded inside. He shook, scattering wet snow around the room, and then pounced, getting my jeans wet. I pulled the towel I kept at the back door off its hook and cleaned as much snow from his underside and legs as I could before letting him down. The static from the towel made the hair on his ear flaps stand out, and I smiled. Oreo might not be the brightest member of our pack, but his zeal and energy always put a smile on my face.

I went upstairs to the area I'd converted into a loft where I now lived. I grabbed a couple of dog biscuits from the jar I kept on the counter and tossed them into the dogs' beds and then hurried downstairs to help.

Each time I went into my bookstore, I was overcome with joy. Owning my own mystery bookstore had been a dream my husband and I shared. After his untimely death just over a year ago, I fulfilled my promise to him to sell our house and take the insurance money and live out our dream. Death of a loved one helped to put things into perspective. For me, Leon's death reminded me life was too short not to be happy. So, I quit my job as an English teacher at the local high school, sold the house Leon and I had lived in, and bought the brownstone we'd walked by and dreamed of one day owning. It was bittersweet to live the dream without him by my side, but, over the past year, I'd found a host of friends and family who helped to fill the void.

The store was bustling and Nana Jo was running the cash register. My assistant, Dawson Alexander, was stocking a shelf. Dawson was the quarterback for the Michigan Southwest University Tigers—or, MISS YOU, as the locals called it. He was tall and slender, the MISU trainers asked him to "bulk up." So, he'd gained over twenty pounds of pure muscle, which was helpful on the football field and also came in very handy for hoisting boxes of books. The fact Dawson loved to bake, and was exceptionally good at it, provided the conduit for some of the weight gain. Unfortunately, I suspected I too had gained a good ten pounds since he started working here and baking all sorts of sweet delicious items.

Market Street Mysteries wasn't on the same level as big-box stores, but business was steady and that was enough to keep the lights on. My staff consisted of my grandmother, Nana Jo, who refused to accept a salary; Dawson, who rented the studio apartment above my garage and received a small salary, which he more than earned by providing baked goods; and my twin nephews, Christopher and Zaq, when they were on break from college, which thankfully, would be in a few days.

Dawson, Nana Jo, and I worked steadily for the remainder of the afternoon. When my older sister, Jenna, walked in, I looked at the time and realized we'd been working nonstop for four hours. It was time to close shop and it wasn't until I sat down that I realized how tired I was.

"You owe me big-time." I glared at my sister, who stared innocently and fluttered her eyelashes.

"I have no idea what you mean."

I pulled out my cell phone and swiped until I came to the selfies I'd snapped before I gave up and delegated the task to my sales consultant.

Jenna looked at the pictures and tried to keep from laughing but failed and eventually gave up and laughed long and hard.

Nana Jo and Dawson looked over her shoulder. Nana Jo had seen the originals but still laughed at the shots as much as Dawson and Jenna.

"Great. Laugh, but I won't be alone in those pink concoctions. Just remember that." I pointed at my sister.

"*Your mother* is crazy if she thinks I'm wearing any of these clown dresses." Jenna handed back my cell phone. It was always *your mother* when Mom was being demanding or irritating.

"I don't understand how she thinks she's going to plan a wedding in three weeks." I hoisted myself out of the chair and went to the back and got the broom. After sitting for just a few minutes, my joints felt tired. I knew if I continued sitting, I'd never get the store cleaned and ready for tomorrow.

Christmas was just three weeks away, and my mother was getting married on Christmas Eve. I tried not to stress out about all of the things that needed to happen in the next three weeks. Bubble-gum-pink-piñata-gone-with-the-wind-mermaid dresses were just the tip of the iceberg. Unlike most brides, who spent over a year planning the perfect wedding, my mother told us just two weeks ago she was getting married on Christmas Eve. Thinking about everything that needed to happen made me want to scream. I must have looked like a crazy woman.

"Don't worry about cleaning, Mrs. W. We'll take care of that." Dawson took the broom from my hands and held out a chair.

I stared. "Who's we?"

The bell that chimed whenever someone entered the store jingled and Jillian Clark and Emma Lee entered the store.

"Hello, Mrs. Washington," both girls said.

Emma Lee gave Jenna a hug. "We knew you'd be tired after wedding shopping." She took off her coat and placed it over the bar at the back of the store.

Emma was a petite southern belle with long, dark hair and almond-shaped eyes that showcased her Asian heritage. Emma was a student at MISU and was dating my nephew Zaq. At about five feet and one hundred pounds, Emma was often dwarfed by my nephew's six-feet frame. When the two were together, he towered over her, but the two didn't seem to notice or care.

"We would have been here earlier, but I had a rehearsal." Jillian placed her coat on the bar next to Emma's and went to the back to get a duster.

Dawson followed her and I couldn't help but smile. He and Jillian were a couple, and he followed her so they could have a few moments alone.

Jillian was the granddaughter of one of Nana Jo's friends, Dorothy Clark. She had a tall, slender body and walked with the grace that only a ballerina possessed. She had dark eyes and dark, frizzy hair, which she'd tried to tame by braiding and pinning to her head tonight. However, several curly tendrils refused to be contained and created lovely curls on the sides of her head.

When Jillian and Dawson returned, she was wearing an apron and proceeded to dust. "Now, you better go upstairs and get dressed or you'll be late for the party."

I looked at my watch. "You're right."

"Shake a leg." Nana Jo hurried to the steps. For a woman in her seventies, who was a couple inches under six feet and well over two hundred fifty pounds, my grandmother was still pretty spry. It probably had something to do with her yoga and aikido classes. She was a brown belt.

I followed at a slower pace. This was the first opportunity any of us, my mother included, had had to meet Harold's family. I knew she was nervous and, despite the humiliation she planned for me in a pink bridesmaid gown, I wanted to make a good impression.

I showered and dressed in a vintage print A-line-high-waist dress. The top was navy with three-quarter-length sleeves and a scoop neck, while the skirt had a bold navy and white floral imprint. Since I'd started writing historic British cozy mysteries, I'd found myself drawn to clothes from the late 1930s and early 1940s, the period I wrote about. The dress had a vintage feel, without being too kitschy. I had a pair of navy heels that matched the outfit perfectly. The dinner was only a few blocks away, which was the only reason I dared wear the shoes in the middle of winter in Michigan. Plus, Frank promised to make sure the sidewalk from my store to his restaurant was not only free of ice and snow but was well salted.

When I came out to the main living space, Jenna and her husband, Tony, were sitting at the large dining room table with their sons, Christopher and Zaq. The twins were dressed in dark jeans with white shirts and jackets. Despite the fact that the twins were dressed in similar items of clothing, their personal style showed through, distinguishing each boy. Christopher was serious with a preppy style, while Zaq was the techie and tended to be nerdier in the way he dressed. Tonight, that was obvious from the tweed jacket and bow tie Zaq wore. Christopher looked dapper with a solid-color suit jacket and tie. Only when I got close enough to hug him and took a good look at the tie, did I realize what I had initially mistaken for a paisley print was actually a skull and crossbones.

I hugged my nephew. "Nice tie."

"Thanks, Aunt Sammy." Christopher bent down to hug me.

"Don't encourage him," Jenna said.

Tony shook his head. He was a man of few words.

I looked around. "Where's Dawson?"

Jenna tore a page from a catalog.

"What are you doing?" I walked over and picked up the page.

"You'll thank me." She smiled and ripped another page from the catalog I'd just recognized was one of my favorite stores.

"Not likely. I just got that catalog today and I haven't even had a chance to look at it." I picked up the other pages she'd ripped out and scattered across the table. "What are these?"

"Potential bridesmaid dresses." She smiled. "I'm not wearing that pink crap you tried on today." She cocked her head to the side and looked at another picture but must have decided against it and flipped to the next page. "Besides, we don't have time to get any of those dresses altered and delivered in three weeks. We're going to order nice dresses or suits that we won't be ashamed to be seen in public with and can wear for more than a few hours."

I picked up the pages again. "I'm sold, but how are you going to convince *your* mother?"

"Simple. I'll just tell her I saw it in a fancy magazine and it's the latest thing for the twenty-first century." She folded the pulled pages and put them in her purse. "The boys will need interview suits, so they'll be fine." She looked at her sons.

Nana Jo came out of her bedroom dressed in a royal-blue pantsuit with rhinestones around the neck and cuffs. Her statuesque build and auburn hair looked stunning.

The boys whistled. "Looking good, Nana Jo."

"Thank you. Thank you." She twirled. "Now, let's go so we can get this party started before your mother has a cow. She's texted me at least four times, reminding me not to be late."

I realized I'd left my cell phone in the bedroom and hurried to get it. Sure enough, I had several messages from Mom too.

We bundled up for the short walk down the street. Dawson looked as though he'd rather have a root canal but helped Jillian with her coat.

"Dawson, can I talk to you for a minute?" I stood back to allow the others to pass. "You all go on ahead. We'll catch up."

Jillian smiled and hurried downstairs with the others. Dawson lingered back, head down.

"Is anything bothering you?" I asked.

He shook his head but avoided looking at me.

I waited. Years as an English teacher in public schools taught me the power of silence and it didn't fail me this time either.

"I just feel awkward. I mean, this is a family dinner and I'm not family. You've all been really kind to me, but I was thinking your mom might not want me there."

I suspected this was the problem. Leon and I had never been blessed with children, but, in the months since Dawson moved into the garage loft, I'd come to view him as the son I'd never had. He'd never known his mother and his father was, last I heard, in prison. When Alex Alexander wasn't in jail, he was an abusive alcoholic. I prayed for the right words to say. I looked at Snickers and Oreo, who'd been fed, let out to take care of business, and were waiting for me to leave and drop their dog treats on the floor, a ritual whenever I left. "Family is about more than blood and shared DNA." I picked up Snickers. "I've had this dog since she was six weeks old. She's fourteen and has a bad heart, but she's still my baby. If anyone tried to hurt her, I'd . . ." I swallowed the lump that rose in my throat. "I don't know what I'd do, but she's my baby." I looked up. "I may not have given birth to you, but I've come to look at you like a son. I care about you just as much as I care about Christopher and Zaq." I looked at Dawson and saw his eyes fill with tears. "We consider you a part of our family. Families aren't finite. When Jenna married Tony, he became a part of our family. When my mother marries Harold, our family will expand again, and each time someone special enters one of our lives, we expand and make room in our hearts. My mom invited you because she looks upon you as family. I can't force you to come, but you are welcome."

Tears streamed down his face, and I reached up and hugged him. We stood that way for several minutes until Snickers squirmed her way up and started to lick away Dawson's tears. He made the mistake of laughing. When he opened his mouth, she stuck her tongue in.

"Eww, plagh, ick. She got me." He tried to wipe the dog kiss out of his mouth.

I put Snickers down and reached in my purse for the bottle of Listerine spray I kept for just such situations as this.

He sprayed his tongue and Snickers made a deliberate maneuver to sit with her back to Dawson. He laughed. "I think I hurt her feelings." He picked her up and gave her a hug, careful to keep his mouth well out of reach of her tongue.

For several seconds, she turned her head and refused his friendly overtures. Eventually, he found the right spot on her stomach and scratched while she closed her eyes and leaned back against his chest.

"Do you two need a moment alone?" Jillian joked from the top of the stairs.

Dawson put Snickers down and gave Oreo, who had been waiting patiently by the biscuit jar, a pat. He then reached into the jar and pulled out a couple of dog biscuits and tossed them down for the poodles. I picked up the remote and turned on the jazz station so they would have something to listen to while we were out, and we all made our exits while they were distracted with treats.

North Harbor Café was just down the street from my bookstore and the cold December night meant we wouldn't linger to look in store windows along the way. Frank's restaurant had a reputation for good food and drinks and business had been doing very well since he'd opened. The crowds standing and waiting for seats was a testament to its popularity with the locals.

We waved at the hostess as we passed on our way to the back of the restaurant and walked up the stairs. I glanced back at the looks we received from some of those waiting. While the upstairs of my building had long ago been converted into a loft apartment, Frank's restaurant was not. One day, he planned to open the upstairs up for dining, but for now, it was closed off and only opened for private parties.

The rumble from a multitude of conversations and televisions mingled with laughter and the clang of plates and glasses followed us through the restaurant and wafted up the stairs. As we climbed, the noise from below grew fainter. The first-floor ceiling was high, so we had to climb quite a few steps to make it to the second floor. I'd accounted for the walk in heels from my store but had neglected to account for the trek up Mount Everest. In tennis shoes or flats, I could have made the climb like a pro. In three-inch heels it was an adventure. At the top of the stairs, I stopped to get my breath. I expected to be assaulted by the same noise level I'd encountered on the first floor. However, the silence hit me like a ton of bricks. The contrast between the noisy lower level and the funerary silence upstairs was jarring, and I felt disoriented. I looked around to get my bearings and reorient myself.

There were less than twenty people milling around. After less than a minute, it was clear there were two distinct camps. The Robertsons huddled on one side of the room. The Hamilton clan was on the other.

Dawson leaned close and whispered a quote from *The Lord of the Rings: The Two Towers,* one of my favorite movies, in my ear, "You'll find more cheer in a graveyard."

Frank Patterson walked up to me and handed me a glass of champagne and kissed me on the cheek. "I think you're going to need this."

I made eye contact with Jenna and looked the question, *What's going on?* She shrugged and inclined her head toward Nana Jo.

I walked over to my grandmother. Nana Jo was certainly no wallflower and could talk to anyone about anything. I was shocked she hadn't extended an olive branch and crossed the chasm that separated the two families. "What's going on?"

She sipped her champagne. "I used to believe I could talk to anyone, but those tight-lipped, hoity-toity aristocratic wannabes can kiss my grits." She tossed back the champagne and sauntered over to the drink table and picked up another glass.

I was so shocked I didn't hear Emma's approach until she spoke. "Boy, you guys missed the sparks. I thought Nana Jo was going to drop-kick Harold's sister in-law." She inclined her head slightly, and we glanced in that direction.

A middle-aged woman with dark eyes and dark hair in a black suit, with a matching fur coat and more jewelry than I'd

seen on one person, stood near the window. She looked as
though she was afraid to touch anything. Next to her stood a
short, bald man with glasses. He was one of those nondescript
men who blended in with their environment so well people
never noticed them.

"I don't think I've ever seen that much jewelry before,"
Dawson said.

"Check out the fur coat," Jillian whispered.

"Full-length sable." Emma nodded knowingly. "My great-
aunt Vivian Anne has one. Although if I didn't know better,
I'd say this one is fake."

"She probably needs it to cover up that stick up her—"

"Nana Jo!" I turned and stared at my grandmother, who
merely shrugged. "What on earth happened?"

There was silence for several minutes and then Nana Jo re-
luctantly explained. "I waltzed over to the Ice-Princess over
there and held out my hand and introduced myself." She took
a sip of her champagne.

I waited for the rest.

"Frosty looks down her nose, sniffs, and refuses to shake
my hand."

"Really?" I asked.

Emma and Nana Jo both nodded.

I stared openmouthed. "Maybe she . . ."

"Maybe she's deaf, dumb, blind and was raised in a barn?"
Nana Jo added.

I shook my head. "I can't think of any good reason for bad
manners."

"There are no excuses for bad manners." Nana Jo finished
her champagne and exchanged her empty glass for mine and
took a sip. "She looked down at me like Mr. Darcy looked at
Mr. Collins in that movie you like to watch."

"*Pride and Prejudice,*" Emma, Jillian, and I all said together.

"Whatever." Nana Jo sipped my champagne. "I was madder than a wet hen and about to give that stuck-up ninny a piece of my mind when Harold and Grace strolled over. Harold was so excited and wanted to introduce Grace to his sister-in-law, Margaret." She stared daggers at Margaret across the room. "That uppity witch had the nerve to sneer at Grace as though she'd just pooped on her best shoes."

I was shocked by bad manners and poor breeding until I learned she'd snubbed my mom. "Really?" I could feel my eye start to twitch.

Jenna and the others had joined the group while Nana Jo was talking.

Jenna nodded. "That's not all. So, Harold introduces Mom and Margaret stares down and says, 'I thought you worked here,' as though Mom was a servant or something."

I raised an eyebrow, cocked my head to the side, and stared openly at the enemy. It was one thing for Jenna and me to mock our mother. We were entitled, but how dare this pretentious upstart think she was going to do anything to ruin my mother's happiness.

"Who's the man?" I asked.

"What man?" Nana Jo didn't even bother to look. "The marshmallow is Harold's brother, Oscar."

I turned to Frank. "Would you get me another glass of champagne, please."

He looked warily at me.

My brother-in-law, Tony, patted him on the back. "I've seen that look before. When a Hamilton woman gives you the look Sam just gave you, it's best to walk away. Do not pass Go. Do not collect two hundred dollars. Just walk away."

Frank started to speak, but Tony shook his head. "It's best not to know. Plausible deniability."

Frank nodded knowingly. Christopher and Zaq nodded and the four men walked away.

I glanced at my mom, who was standing near the center of the room. She looked as though she would burst into tears at any moment. Harold too looked as though he would weep. He petted and attended to my mother.

Jenna leaned close. "Okay, what's the plan?"

I looked at my sister. "What do you mean?"

"Don't give me that. I know my sister. When you start enunciating each and every syllable and you get that look in your eye, I know something's up and you have a plan. Now, spill it."

I shrugged. "No plan. Not yet anyway." I sighed. "Let's just provide as much support to Mom as we possibly can and get through this."

Everyone nodded and we walked over to where my mom and Harold were to provide a wall of love and support.

Jenna held back and whispered in my ear, "So, we wait until it's over and then we slash her tires, right?"

I shook my head. "Nope. We wait until it's over and then we let Nana Jo shoot her. She can claim she thought it was a bear."

I walked over to the Ice Princess and introduced myself. "Hello, I understand you're Harold's sister-*in-law*." I emphasized the in law. She looked as though she didn't appreciate the reminder she wasn't a direct descendent of the wealthy Robertson family. Score one for our side.

She stared down her nose at me, but I stood tall and straight and stared back. "Since we're going to be related, albeit by marriage, I wanted to introduce myself. My name is Samantha Washington. Grace Hamilton is my mother." I turned to my sister. "This is my sister, Jenna Rutherford."

Frank, Tony, and the twins walked over. Frank handed me a glass of champagne.

I took a sip. "And this is her husband, Tony. They're both

attorneys." I didn't bother to wait for her to acknowledge them but continued on with my introductions. "These are Jenna and Tony's sons, Christopher and Zaq."

The boys bowed.

"We're so proud of them. They're both on the dean's list at Jesus and Mary University."

JAMU was to the Midwest what Harvard and Yale were to the East Coast. In fact, in some polls, JAMU actually ranked higher than the two prestigious Ivy League schools.

I turned to Dawson. "This is Dawson Alexander, he's the quarterback for the MISU football team and like a son to me."

Dawson bowed respectfully.

"Frank Patterson is the owner of this establishment and a very good friend." I noticed, with each introduction, my words became more clipped and my tone dropped. Unlike most people, when I was angry, I tended to get very quiet and enunciated more.

Frank inclined his head. "My pleasure."

"I think you've already met my grandmother, Josephine Thomas."

Nana Jo glared.

"Nana Jo recently returned from a performance in New York." I leaned forward and whispered conspiratorially, "She's a bit of a local celebrity."

Margaret's expression became shocked as she nodded to Nana Jo.

I looked around. "I can't forget our dear friends, Jillian Clark and Emma Lee. Jillian is a student at MISU. She sings, dances, and was just offered an internship with the Bolshoi Ballet for the summer."

Jillian blushed but stood tall and straight.

"And Emma Lee is a brilliant premed student at MISU. She comes from a long line of doctors." I turned to Emma.

Did you say there's been a doctor in every generation of your family for two hundred years or three hundred?"

Emma smiled. "Actually, it's four hundred."

"Of course, she can trace her family lineage back to the Mayflower." I looked around. "I think that's everyone." I stared at Oscar. "It's obvious you're Harold's brother. I can see the family resemblance."

He smiled and nodded but didn't say anything.

I turned to Margaret. "And you are?"

She hesitated and a flush rose up Margaret's neck and left her skin blotchy.

"I've heard so much about southern charm. You are from the South, aren't you?" I added.

She gave a false nasally laugh. "Well, yes. Yes, I am. I'm from a small town in Virginia. I doubt you've heard of it. Few people have."

"Try me," I said.

She hesitated a few seconds.

"Sam used to be a teacher before she retired to start her own business," Jenna said.

Margaret plastered on a fake smile. "Lexington. I'm from Lexington."

"Lexington is where Washington and Lee University is. My uncle's the president of the university," Emma said with enthusiasm.

I smiled. "Emma *Lee,* you know, descendant of General Robert E. Lee . . . Washington and *Lee.*"

Emma laughed. "Well, we don't talk about that much, other than to mention how grateful we are he wasn't successful."

Harold walked over to our group. "Aren't you a relative of General Robert E. Lee too?"

Margaret laughed deprecatingly and fanned herself. "A distant relative . . . a very distant relative."

Harold muttered, "I could have sworn you said you were a descendant." He waited for an explanation, but none came.

Eventually, dinner arrived and we sat down to eat. Margaret barely said a word throughout the entire meal. However, we kept up a steady stream of conversation and ignored her. Mom no longer looked as though she would burst into tears at any moment, and we were on cruise mode. Engagement cake and coffee and we could get out of here. I breathed a sigh of relief too soon.

Margaret looked at her watch and leaned across the table. "What plans have you made for the wedding?"

Mom fluttered her hands. "Well, we haven't nailed down our exact plans yet."

Margaret gasped. "Not nailed down your plans? But, I thought I understood you are getting married on Christmas Eve."

"We are getting married on Christmas Eve." Harold patted Mom's hand. "There are a lot of decisions to be made, but we've picked the cake and are close to picking the venue."

"Dear me." Margaret tsked. "I was afraid of this. The longer you wait, the less likely you are to get the *best* venues." She glanced around the room as though to say this was clearly not the best, and I had reached my fill when it came to swallowing my words.

"Are you implying there's something wrong with North Harbor Café?" I folded my napkin and stared at her. "Because if you are, I'm about two seconds from—"

No one got to hear what I was two seconds away from doing because, at that moment, a whirlwind came up the stairs wearing three-inch heels and a white suit with a white mink coat and matching hat. When she reached the top step, she stood for dramatic effect, shrugged out of her coat, tossed it over the railing, and announced, "No fear, Lydia Lighthouse is here."

We stared at the figure, but before we could figure out what on earth a Lydia Lighthouse was, Margaret hopped up from her seat. "Lydia, darling." She hurried over to the woman and the two air-kissed. Then Margaret turned to face the group. "When I heard my brother-in-law was planning to get married in a few weeks, I knew I'd find the perfect wedding present." She turned to the white clad figure. "Lydia Lighthouse is the wedding planner for the elite. She's traveled all over the world and will be able to insure all of the *right* people are invited and the wedding will be in the society pages and best magazines." She paused as though waiting for applause. None came.

Lydia Lighthouse was my mom's height, slightly over five feet, but not by much. She was as thin as a rail and looked to be in her early fifties.

Nana Jo leaned close to me. "She's got on more makeup than a five-dollar hooker."

Lydia Lighthouse definitely wore a great deal of makeup and her false eyelashes were so long, it looked as though she had caterpillars on her eyelids. She had blue eyes, fair, pale skin, and her hair was bright red; she wore it pulled back under her mink cap. Lydia Lighthouse waltzed across the room, placed a white clutch handbag on the table, and pulled out a long cigarette holder and gold lighter.

"Is that a real cigarette?" I was stunned. It had been such a long time since I'd been around anyone who smoked a real cigarette, let alone inside a restaurant.

"Sure is." Nana Jo grinned.

Frank walked over to Lydia Lighthouse. He discretely whispered, but he might as well have saved his breath.

Lydia stared at him as though he'd just landed from an alien spaceship. "What do you mean I can't smoke inside? What kind of establishment is this?"

Frank gritted his teeth. "It's actually illegal to smoke inside restaurants in this state."

Lydia made an elaborate motion of flinging her lighter down. She huffed and then collected herself and plastered on a smile. "Oh, well, when in Rome." She smiled. "Would you please get me a glass of champagne," she ordered rather than asked.

Frank hesitated for a moment but smiled and gestured to one of the waitstaff, who promptly brought the whirlwind a drink.

Unlit cigarette dangling from one hand and glass of champagne in the other, the whirlwind stood at the head of the table. "A toast."

Everyone stood and raised their glasses.

"To the happy couple, may they enjoy many years of wedded bliss." Lydia raised her glass.

We all raised our glasses and toasted Mom and Harold.

Lydia sipped her champagne.

"Who the hell are you?" Nana Jo asked the question that was dancing around inside all of our heads.

Lydia looked up in surprise. "I thought I'd introduced myself." She smiled and spoke loud and very slowly as though Nana Jo was hard of hearing and losing her faculties. "I'm Lydia Lighthouse."

Nana Jo narrowed her eyes and stared. "I heard you the first time you gave that ridiculous name. What I mean is *why* are you here? This is a private party. Who invited you?"

Lydia's smile froze and her icy blue eyes grew as cold as Lake Michigan right before a storm.

Margaret must have noticed the temperature drop and a

quick headcount had to tell her she was drastically outnumbered
if a brawl started. She hurried to intervene. "I was just explaining that Lydia Lighthouse is the premiere wedding planner in
the country and she's agreed to help plan Grace and Harold's
wedding."

You could have heard a cricket chirp in the silence that
followed.

"Now, who is the bride?" Lydia looked around the room.
Her gaze rested on Emma and Zaq and her brow furrowed. "I always tell my couples how important breeding and pedigree are."

Emma colored and Zaq started to stand, but Emma re-
strained him. His eyes were stormy and he looked ready to explode.

I could see Jenna bristling. However, Lydia continued,
oblivious to how closely she was to being tossed out on her
ear. "I breed Yorkies. You have to be really careful of the bitch
because you never know what you'll get in the end." She
laughed.

Nana Jo stood. "What in the name of God are you talking
about, and you'd best be careful because you're pretty close to
getting stabbed." Nana Jo fingered her knife.

Lydia looked at Nana Jo, puzzled. "I was talking about the
importance of breeding. Weddings are a union. What you put
into this union will determine what you get out of it." She
stared at Margaret, who looked embarrassed and blushed. "For
example, my entire family is full of blue-eyed redheads with a
fiery temper. Me, my brother, my husband, my parents, my
grandparents—nothing but redheads. So, you always know
what you're getting." She laughed, but when no one joined in,
she sighed. "However, when you combine a loving, generous
man and a sweet, caring woman, you will have a union that
overflows with love and is able to survive anything."

Nana Jo sat down and muttered something that sounded like "crazy witch."

"Who's the bride?" Lydia looked around.

Mom raised a tentative hand. "I am."

Lydia waltzed over to my mother. "You just leave everything to Lydia. I'll make sure your wedding is the event North Harbor, Michigan, will never forget."

Connect with 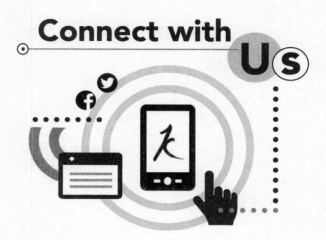Us

Visit us online at
KensingtonBooks.com
to read more from your favorite authors, see books
by series, view reading group guides, and more.

Join us on social media

for sneak peeks, chances to win books and prize packs,
and to share your thoughts with other readers.

facebook.com/kensingtonpublishing
twitter.com/kensingtonbooks

Tell us what you think!

To share your thoughts, submit a review,
or sign up for our eNewsletters, please visit:
KensingtonBooks.com/TellUs.